Praise for Sarah Price

"As soon as I neared the end of this book I intentionally started reading very slowly. I wanted to stay with the characters for as long as I could. Their love story is beautiful, emotional, and raw. *Plain Change* is the most romantic Amish fiction book that I have ever read, hands down. I fell in love with these unique characters in *Plain Fame*, only to fall deeper down the rabbit hole with this book. Why can't I stop thinking about Amanda and Alejandro? Things are heating up between our unlikely lovebirds, and that's all I am going to say! Sarah Price has written a book that will consume your every thought and literally sweep you up into the most endearing love story. I read *Plain Change* last weekend, and I already want to read it again just to make sure that I didn't miss something! Usually I don't reread books until months or even years later. Not so with this one. I will immerse myself back into a truly charming and delightful book in the not-so-distant future. The bar has been set with this book, and let me tell you, it is high. *Plain Change* is not to be taken lightly, so prepare yourself and hold on tight for the journey of Amanda and Alejandro has only just begun . . ." —Sue Laitinen, book reviewer for DestinationAmish.com

"Sarah Price delivers another great story in *Plain Change*, the second book of the Plain Fame series. As Alejandro and Amanda's relationship unfolds, it all continually centers around this quote from the story: one thing is all that matters above all others—God. The story has surprises throughout, with an ending that you 'didn't see coming,' but that prepares the way for book number three." —Dali, review from Amazon.com

"After reading *Plain Fame*, I could not wait to get my hands on *Plain Change* and see what happened next in the lives of Amanda Beiler and Alejandro 'Viper' Diaz. I was not disappointed. This book lets the reader see the . . . world through the eyes of an innocent Amish woman, who just happens to be in love with a famous singer. We see all of the vulnerability in Amanda as she tries to adjust to the world that Alejandro lives in. Sometimes she adjusts, and sometimes trying to adjust triggers memories of something from her past. Will she finally adjust or will Viper's world be too much for her? That and a few surprises are what make this book a wonderful read. I cannot wait for the [next] book in the series to find out how it all ends. I can tell you one thing: I will miss these characters. Ms. Price has done a wonderful job of helping the reader get to know the characters. I highly recommend this book!" —Lynne Young, review from Amazon.com

"*Plain Change* by Sarah Price deserves more than five stars, but since that is all I can give it, I give it five stars. Once again, Sarah Price leaves me wanting to read any book that she has written that I haven't read yet!" —Book review from *Debbie's Dusty Deliberations*

Plain Change

ALSO BY SARAH PRICE

An Empty Cup

An Amish Buggy Ride

The Plain Fame Series

Plain Fame

Plain Change

Plain Again

Plain Return

Plain Choice

The Amish of Lancaster Series

Fields of Corn

Hills of Wheat

Pastures of Faith

Valley of Hope

The Amish of Ephrata Series

The Tomato Patch

The Quilting Bee

The Hope Chest

The Clothes Line

The Amish Classic Series

First Impressions (Realms)
The Matchmaker (Realms)
Second Chances (Realms)

For a complete listing of books, please visit the author's website at www.sarahpriceauthor.com.

Plain Change

Book Two of the Plain Fame Series

Sarah Price

This is a work of fiction. Names, characters, organizations, places, events, and incidents are either products of the author's imagination or are used fictitiously.

Published by Waterfall Press, Grand Haven, MI

www.brilliancepublishing.com

ISBN-13: 9781503945388

ISBN-10: 1503945383

Cover design by Kerri Resnick

Printed in the United States of America

In Plain Fame, *I dedicated the book to the singers, performers, artists, authors, and entertainers who give so much of themselves for our own enjoyment. As for this book, it is dedicated to all of the people who adore them. Having fans is a great responsibility as well as a humbling honor. Without fans, fame would not be possible. We must never forget that.*

Behold, I shew you a mystery; we shall not all sleep, but we shall all be changed.

1 Corinthians 15:51 (KJV)

About the Vocabulary

The Amish speak Pennsylvania Dutch (also called Amish German or Amish Dutch). This is a verbal language with variations in spelling among communities throughout the United States. For example, in some regions, a grandfather is *grossdaadi*, while in other regions he is known as *grossdawdi*. Some dialects refer to the mother as *mamm* or *maem*, and others simply as *mother* or *mammi*.

In addition, there are words and expressions, such as *mayhaps*, or the use of the word *then* at the end of sentences, and, my favorite, *for sure and certain*, that are not necessarily from the Pennsylvania Dutch language/dialect but are unique to the Amish.

The use of these words comes from my own experience living among the Amish in Lancaster County, Pennsylvania.

Chapter One

The sunlight shone through the sheer curtains covering the long windows in the bedroom. It cast a soft and golden glow throughout, painting the thick white comforter on the bed in dancing shades of sunrise. Small specks of dust floated, imprisoned in the sunbeams penetrating the room. But no one saw them. Not yet. The radiance of that particular early-morning phenomenon went unnoticed in the bedroom where Amanda lay, for she wasn't yet awake.

Outside the window, a car horn blasted from the street below. Noise. A fluttering of eyelids. A bit of light. Slowly, Amanda rolled over in bed, lifting her arm to cover her eyes, shielding herself from the morning sunbeams, even if only for a few more seconds. The previous day had been long, and she'd had an even longer night. Sleep had not come easily, and what little she had was fitful.

Everything seemed strange to her as she began to wake up and take in her surroundings. Different indeed. From the brightness of the room to the high, vaulted ceilings with thick white moldings and fancy paintings on the walls, she knew that she was not at home this morning, and all of the memories from the previous day started to flood her heart with emotion.

***

The drive from her parents' farm to Philadelphia seemed to never end. She sat in silence in the back of the SUV, staring thoughtfully out the window, too aware that Alejandro was watching her. His eyes on the back of her neck caused the color to rise in her cheeks, so she kept her head turned away, not wanting him to see the effect he had on her or the tears that were gathering at the corners of her eyes.

As the farmland rolled away and the small meandering roads had turned into a highway, she sighed.

"Princesa?"

She wanted to turn to look at him, but she was afraid.

He reached out and touched her hand. For a moment, she froze. His touch was soft and gentle, reassuring her that he was going to take care of her. When his fingers finally entwined with hers, the warmth of his skin touching hers pushed her over the edge.

The tears fell.

"Princesa," he whispered again and reached out to force her to look at him. He wiped the tears from her eyes, staring deeply into her face. "It's going to be all right, *sí?* I came for you, and you will be fine."

She nodded.

"You believe me, no?"

Again, the simple nod.

He smiled. "You have no words? That is unusual."

She swallowed, wanting to say something, but the feeling of weightlessness hung over her. She felt as if she were floating above herself, watching the two people in the back of the SUV, being driven by a chauffeur who headed toward the big city whose skyscrapers were already visible on the horizon. It was surreal. Certainly this woman who sat here, with a white prayer *kapp* on her head, holding hands with a Cuban singing legend, was not her. Not Amanda Beiler.

"I have left everything I know," she finally whispered.

"You have the future ahead of you," he replied, trying to reassure her. "And there would be no future for you now at home, not with the paparazzi following your every move."

She knew that he spoke wisely. She had known those words to be true. That was why she had finally sent the message to him. Her life was over in the Amish community. No one would ever believe that she had not been romantically involved with Alejandro. No man would want to court the most famous Amish woman in the world. And no community would welcome her to live among them, not with cameras gathering wherever she went.

"What will happen now?" she asked.

"You will change," he said with a shrug of his shoulder as though it was the most natural thing to do. "And you will live."

She tossed back the covers of the bed and sat up. Looking around the strange surroundings, she caught her breath as she took in the opulence of the hotel room. The high ceilings with thick, ornate moldings painted in high-gloss white with gold layered in between the carvings. There was a brass chandelier hanging from the center of the ceiling with crystal beads dangling from each arm. When the sunlight hit them, rainbow colors danced around the room. It was beautiful and mesmerizing, unlike anything she had seen before . . . dancing colors of red, purple, blue, and gold.

Amanda was wearing her white nightgown, her hair hanging down to her waist. Her small suitcase was on top of a dresser, where she had put it the previous night. It was open, and she could see where she had folded her dress and left it when she had changed. Her black shoes were on the floor, beside the dresser, exactly where she had left them.

Standing in the middle of the room, she turned around, inhaling the foreign ambience. Once again, she felt that floating feeling, as if she were watching someone else's life. It was surreal, dreamlike, and certainly not happening to her.

The room was magnificent with a large vase of fresh flowers, mostly white roses and lilies, set upon a circular table near the door. There were white roses and lilies. She walked to the flowers and leaned over, breathing deeply. The sweet scent took her back to her parents' farm. She had always loved gardening, spending long spring mornings tending to the vegetables but also to the flowers that Mamm had planted around the porch. Amanda loved to prune back the roses and clip the thorns. Sometimes her mother had even let her keep one or two roses in her own room. Always out of sight of visitors, since flower displays were prideful. Now she was surrounded by dozens of roses.

Indeed, she thought, I will change.

She hadn't expected that the paparazzi would be at the hotel in Philadelphia. She had thought they would still be back in Lititz. So when they pulled up to the hotel, Amanda gasped and shied away from the window. She brushed against Alejandro as the people outside began to crowd around the SUV. Flashes went off as cameras were shoved close to the windows.

"Easy, Princesa," he murmured. "We shall get you inside and settled into a room. Then it will calm down."

"Calm down?"

"You can move about the hotel freely."

She blinked. Hotel, she thought. She had never stayed in a hotel. She was nervous. What if she got lost? What if people stared at her? What if . . .

He put on his dark sunglasses and took a deep breath. "You wait for the doormen to open the doors. They will escort us inside and away from the paparazzi. Don't say anything to those people, and if they touch you, don't respond. Let the doormen handle it. They deal with this a lot," he said.

"Touch me?" The thought horrified her.

"To get your attention," he explained patiently.

When the door to the vehicle opened, Alejandro stepped out and, after straightening his suit jacket, reached his hand down to help Amanda out of the car. Hesitantly, she took his hand. Once outside, she was too aware that there were at least fifteen camera people stealing her image. Beyond them were screaming fans, mostly young girls clamoring for Alejandro's attention. Amanda frowned and stared at them, remembering their visit to Intercourse, in Pennsylvania, a few weeks back when the crowd had started to recognize him.

The girls continued to scream and jump up, waving their arms in the air, anything to get his attention. Alejandro paused, looked at them, and nodded in acknowledgment. But he did not smile or stop to sign autographs or for photo taking. Instead, he placed his hand on the small of Amanda's back and guided her through the crowd. There were five steps, and he held her elbow. He could tell that she was overwhelmed. Between the people and the noise, it was a new and not necessarily pleasant experience for Amanda. And he understood.

She wandered over to the doorway that led to her own private bathroom. It was dark in the room, and she left the door open as she turned on the water. The countertop felt cool to her touch. Marble. The floor was cool, too. No hardwood floors or area rugs made from old clothing to cover them.

She splashed cold water on her face. Her eyes stung. She had cried herself to sleep the night before, hugging the strange, fluffy pillow to her chest. It took an hour, but she eventually found her sleep, although it hadn't been a restful sleep. She had awakened several times throughout the night, listening to the strange noises of Philadelphia that penetrated through the windows.

When she went back into the main room, Amanda took a deep breath, trying to decide what to do next. Get dressed, she told herself. Just like any other day.

The clothing that she had packed the day before seemed inadequate. Just three everyday dresses, her Sunday dress, and a nightgown. That was all she had. So she decided to wear her blue dress. As she pinned it shut, she smoothed down the fabric and glanced in the mirror.

It was a large mirror with a thick wooden frame painted gold. She had never seen a mirror like that before, and as she saw her reflection, she had to catch her breath. Is that really me? she wondered as she walked toward the mirror. With her bare feet and loose hair, she barely recognized herself. Usually, she only looked in the small mirror Mamm had hung in the washroom to make certain her hair was tidy. She hadn't ever seen herself from head to toe. The image took her by surprise.

She was thin, almost too thin. Certainly she had lost weight over the past few weeks from the stress of living under the microscope of the media. When they had taken an interest in her relationship with Alejandro and found her father's farm, Amanda had been too nervous to eat.

Her face looked gaunt, her cheekbones too high, and her skin too tanned. She wasn't certain how that had happened because she hadn't been outside too much during the past few weeks. Her dark eyes looked lifeless and scared, lacking the sparkle that she had always had. For a moment, the image of herself made her want to cry all over again.

Indeed, she realized, I am plain.

When they had first arrived inside the hotel, two men greeted Alejandro and escorted them through the main lobby, away from the peering eyes of the other hotel guests. Amanda stared as they walked, too aware that people were whispering to each other and pointing at her. Only this time, she realized, it wasn't simply because she was Amish. It was because she was Amish and with Alejandro.

She cowered behind him, shielding herself from their gazes with his body.

When he realized that she was no longer next to him, he stopped walking and she bumped into him. He laughed lightly and turned around.

"Princesa? You are all right?" He reached out and put his arm gently around her shoulder. "I thought we had lost you."

She shook her head and lowered her eyes. His arm on her shoulder felt light yet heavy at the same time. She was too aware that people were staring. She thought she saw someone take a photo. *"Nee,"* she whispered shyly, wishing people would just go away.

Taking off his sunglasses with one hand, he touched the bottom of her chin with his finger and tilted her face so that she had no choice but to look at him. When their eyes met, he smiled. "You will get used to this, Amanda."

She glanced at the people. "I could never get used to this," she replied softly.

He chuckled and tapped his finger against the tip of her nose. "We shall see about that, Princesa. We shall see," he teased. He looked up at the small crowd of hotel guests who stood a safe distance away, gawking at the scene. He smiled at them, a kind smile, but one that also warned them to stay away.

A man began speaking to Alejandro in a language that Amanda didn't understand. Immediately, he put on his sunglasses again and continued walking, talking rapidly in Spanish to the man. Back and forth they volleyed, their singsong words sounding musical and fluid. Ignoring the people who watched them, Amanda tried to listen to the words. She understood nothing.

They stood before an elevator, one of the men pressing a button. When the doors opened, Alejandro escorted her inside the wood-paneled box. The other two men joined them, and the elevator rose up to the top floor of the building.

"Princesa," he said softly, switching back to English. "They will bring your suitcase to your room. I have it adjoining mine so that I am nearby if you need me. It's a secured floor, so only people who have rooms on it can access it."

"Secured?"

He glanced at the two men. "From paparazzi," he explained. "And these two men will also be nearby. They are my security guards when I travel."

"Security guards?" What type of life, she wondered, does he really live? If she had pondered with curiosity about his life at some point, now she knew she was thrown directly into the middle of it. "Are we in danger?"

"No," he replied, a simple answer that needed no further explanation.

When the doors opened, Alejandro took her arm and led her down the hallway. There were mirrors and paintings on the wall. She glanced at them, but Alejandro seemed determined to get her to her room. No time for exploring now. She wondered if she'd have time later to stare at those beautiful pieces of art that hung on the wall.

"This is your room," he said as he opened the door for her.

He stood back and let her walk through the doorway. He did not enter behind her, giving her the privacy that she needed and that he had promised her. "We will only be here two nights. We can talk more tomorrow about what will happen next."

She glanced at him over her shoulder. "What happens next?"

He laughed at the surprise on her face, realizing that she hadn't thought much further than the moment when he had come to rescue her and take her away from the paparazzi frenzy on her father's farm. "Well, we aren't in Lancaster County anymore, no?"

She smiled, glancing around the room. *"Nee,"* she conceded.

"So we must come up with a plan, *sí?*"

"Ja," she answered.

"Now I have some things to do. I will be next door, Amanda," he said, pointing toward a door by the dresser. "It locks on both sides. I will keep my side unlocked in case you need me."

"Need you?"

He raised an eyebrow that peeked up from behind his sunglasses. "In case you get scared or lonely," he responded.

And with that, he shut the door and she was left alone in the middle of the strange room in an even stranger city. Left alone to realize that she had stepped far outside of her world in what she feared was a rash decision. Perhaps she should have left her community for Ohio. Perhaps she should have just permitted the bishop to have her sent away. Perhaps she never should have left with Alejandro.

"What have I done?" she asked out loud, grateful that no one else but herself could hear the doubt in her voice.

The loud ring of the phone on the desk made her jump. She turned away from the mirror and stared at it, wondering who would possibly be calling her. Immediately, she realized that it had to be Alejandro. No one in her family knew where she was yet. In fact, she realized, she herself didn't even know where she was.

She padded across the thick white carpet. It felt soft and warm under her bare feet. The floors at her parents' farm were all made of hardwood with throw rugs scattered throughout, except in the kitchen, which was a cream-colored linoleum. None of their rooms had anything like the plush carpet that tickled her toes right now.

By the fourth ring, she reached for the phone and lifted the handset to her ear. For a moment, she hesitated. It felt strange to answer a phone in a room instead of visiting the phone shanty by the barn. *"Ja?"* she said into the receiver.

"You are up, *sí?*"

She smiled. Her heart fluttered, and she bit her lip, happy to hear the excitement in his voice. "Alejandro!"

He laughed. "Of course it is Alejandro, Princesa. Who else would call you this early? Who else knows where you are?" Still chuckling, he didn't wait for a response. "Now, Amanda, I imagine you are hungry, no? So I want to take you to breakfast. There is a dining room downstairs with a lovely menu."

Breakfast, she thought. In a hotel, with Alejandro. Butterflies in her stomach and more heart flutters. It was all innocent; she knew that. But it would certainly be something to cause raised eyebrows from the bishop and elders at home.

"I . . . I could eat something, *ja,*" she replied shyly. She had never had food at a restaurant with a man. Only courting couples did that. She felt nervous, knowing that just because it was courting in Lititz, did not mean that it was courting in Alejandro's world. And he certainly wasn't about to let her starve, so it was only natural that he would ask her to breakfast.

"*Bueno!* Then I shall knock at your door in just a few minutes to get you," he said before bidding her good-bye.

She hung up the phone and stared at it. Communication is so much easier in the world of the Englische, she thought. With her family and friends, plans had to be made well in advance. Of course, she could use a neighbor's telephone to make and receive phone calls, but the inconvenience of walking to another farm, leaving messages, and trying to connect with people made it easier to just make plans after church service or to visit in person using a horse and buggy. Now, in the world of the Englische, the telephone sat right there, on the desk, and Alejandro Diaz had just called her to invite her to breakfast.

The feeling of butterflies returned to her stomach as she moved away from the phone and chewed on her fingernail. Her eyes wandered back to the mirror, and she saw herself, standing before it. Indeed, she looked Amish in her blue dress held together with straight pins instead of zippers or buttons. Her dark hair was hidden beneath her white heart-shaped prayer *kapp*, the strings hanging over her shoulders. She shut her eyes and waited for the knock on the door, realizing that, for the first time in her life, she wished that she wasn't plain.

Chapter Two

When the elevator opened, Amanda hesitated before stepping outside the doors. There were three people standing on the other side, and they stared when they saw Amanda.

"Good morning," Alejandro said politely and gave her a soft touch to indicate that she should get off the elevator so that the others could step inside to travel to their desired floor.

"Viper!" the one woman gasped. And then their eyes were on Amanda, mouths open and speechless to be standing before the woman who had been all over the media and news the previous evening.

He smiled but didn't stop for further discussion. Amanda kept staring back at the people, stunned by their boldness. They were unabashed in how they gawked at her. Alejandro had to reach for her hand to force her to move.

"Princesa," he mumbled with a stern tone. "*Vamos*, no?"

That caught her attention and she looked at him, not understanding what he had said. *"¿Vamos?"* she repeated inquisitively. "What does that mean?"

He winked at her. "Let's go."

She blushed and hurried after him, embarrassed that he had to prod her along like a child.

When she had been little, she didn't often leave the farm. Her mother usually left her in the care of her grossmammi *whenever she had to run errands. Mammi Lovina, as she was called, would watch Anna and Amanda when Mamm had to go to the store for dry goods or cloth to make new shirts or dresses. But there had been one time when Mamm had surprised Amanda. Anna was older and had been at school. Aaron was still a baby, so he stayed at home. Today, Mamm had announced, Amanda was going to go with her to the store.*

It wasn't as if she hadn't been to a store before that day. She had been to many stores. But this was a special store, one that was in the center of Intercourse, Pennsylvania. It was farther away and that meant a long buggy ride, just Mamm and her. With all of the chores on the farm and people who often came visiting, having one-on-one time with Mamm was a rare treat. Amanda hadn't cared if the drive took five times as long if it meant she had her mother all to herself.

Unfortunately, the drive hadn't taken five times as long. Before Amanda knew what had happened, they had pulled up to the hitching rail outside of the store. There were lots of cars in the parking lot and plenty of people wandering down the sidewalks. Different kinds of people from those Amanda was used to seeing at the other stores. And she couldn't help herself from staring.

She stopped walking as her eyes took in the sight of Englischers with their short pants and white kneesocks, floral dresses and large handbags, baseball caps and sunglasses, open-toed shoes and sneakers . . . it was almost comical to Amanda, who couldn't tear her eyes from them. She wanted to ask her mother why they dressed so funny, but when she turned to get her mother's attention, she saw that Mamm was already at the door to the store.

Mamm turned around and noticed that Amanda wasn't with her. Putting her hand on her hip, Mamm called out in a loud voice, "Let's go!" Amanda had blushed, embarrassed that, on this very special day, she might have given her mother a reason to prod her along and perhaps regret having invited Amanda to join her.

In the restaurant, they were quickly escorted to a private table at the back of the large dining room. There was a window nearby, but the sheer curtains created light with privacy. Amanda sat near the window and peeked out. No one noticed her from the outside, and for that, she was grateful.

Alejandro motioned for the waitress to bring them coffee as he placed the white cloth napkin across his lap. He watched her staring outside and smiled at the innocence and look of wonder on her face.

"Amanda," he said softly. "We need to talk, yes?"

Letting the curtain fall shut, she turned to look at him. Talk? she wondered. What on earth was there to talk about? But from the expression on his face, she realized that he obviously had an idea of what needed to be discussed and was intent on doing just that.

"I want to talk about what we are going to do," he said when he saw that he had her full attention.

She sat there, silent, trying to anticipate what he would say.

The waitress set down two cups of coffee, smiling at Alejandro and glancing nervously at the young woman seated across from him. He smiled back and waited until she left before continuing his conversation with Amanda.

Two packets of sweetener and a three-second pour of cream later, he stirred his coffee before lifting the mug to his lips. Truth was that he, too, hadn't slept well the previous night. He had sat up, watching the news, disgusted that most of the channels had reported something on how Viper had rescued the distressed Amish girl. There was video, still photographs, and interviews with people who had watched them go into the hotel. The Internet was buzzing, people were tweeting, and the world was tuned into this most unusual story.

Several times, he had paused the DVR and stared at the image of Amanda on the screen. She was young, that was true, but she was a beautiful girl who responded well to the camera lens. There was very little that she could do about that, and he suspected her photogenic nature added to the public's desire to know more. They lived in fantasy, and this one was a doozy. A fantasy brought to life through the world of social media and television, the twenty-first-century way that allowed people to live vicariously through the gossip channels.

He knew what needed to be done, and he knew that he could do it. He just wondered if Amanda could.

"I have to leave soon," he started to say as he placed his coffee mug carefully onto the table.

"Leave?" The word came out high-pitched, a squeak. She hadn't expected him to say that.

He nodded. "*Sí,* Princesa. I have commitments. Tour dates."

She sat back in the chair and stared at him. Tour dates meant travel. Travel meant people and other hotels. Other hotels meant . . . She didn't know what that meant. "Alejandro?" she asked.

He frowned as he studied her face. She was so young and so fresh. Sitting across from her at the restaurant did not feel strange to him. He could still see her at her father's farm, weeding the garden that day with her broken leg, laughing as they made homemade ice cream, dancing awkwardly in his arms. Indeed, he told himself. *She can do this.*

"You will come with me," he stated.

A wave of mixed feelings flooded through her. Relief that she would not be abandoned in this strange world. Fear for what she would face. "I will go with you," she said, her words soft and barely audible.

"Amanda," he said firmly and waited until she looked at him. "We have to construct a plan, no? I have come for you, and I promised to protect you. But what is the goal? Is it to return to the Amish or are you leaving for good?" He paused, but not long enough for her to answer. "Perhaps you don't have that answer yet, but in order to do either, you need to face the world. And you will do that by being by my side on my tour."

She stared at him, digesting his words. She wasn't certain what "on my tour" meant, but she did understand what he meant when he said "by my side." She felt her heart flutter inside her chest, wondering what his intentions were but too scared to ask.

"You will have to face the media, Amanda," he said solemnly. With his accent, the name came out soft and gentle: *Aman-tha.* "It will be uncomfortable at first, but I will help you. For a while, the attention will get worse."

"Worse?" She couldn't imagine that it would get worse. It simply didn't seem possible.

"*Sí*, worse," he confirmed. "They are already showing video of you on television."

At this announcement, she gasped. Television? Her? "Why?" she demanded. "Why do they care? I'm just . . . just . . ." She didn't know how to finish the sentence. So she didn't. "They have already ruined me."

He laughed, his laughter causing several people to turn and look at them. The whispering started. They could both hear it. "You are not ruined, Princesa. I have seen ruined. Believe me when I tell you that, despite everything, you are still you."

"I am not me anymore," she proclaimed and lowered her eyes. She hadn't felt like herself for a long time. Too many conflicting emotions and changes in her life. Now she was seated in a strange restaurant across from this man who had swooped in to rescue her. She had no idea what the future held for her, but she knew that it was a different future from anything she ever could have imagined.

Despite the eyes watching their every move, Alejandro reached across the table and took her hand in his. He lifted it to his mouth and, slowly, his eyes still on her face, pressed his lips to her skin. The action startled her, and she looked at him, wondering why he would do something so intimate and in public.

"You are still you, Amanda," he said. "You will always be you."

The color flooded her cheeks. Quickly, she pulled her hand away, too aware of people watching them.

"Get used to the eyes, Amanda," he purred. "They will watch, and we will give them what they want until they lose interest and move on. Ignore them, live our lives, and show them that they cannot ruin us."

And she suddenly understood. It was an act. She wasn't certain if she was disappointed or pleased to know that he was orchestrating everything. He was in charge of what people saw. From the moment he had picked her up at her father's farm to their arrival at the hotel to this moment, this beautiful moment when he kissed the back of her hand, it was an act for the public to see. But it was also an indication of what was ahead. He was training her, and she was scared.

"I can't give them that," she whispered.

"Sí," he said, smiling. "You can and you will . . . if you want the ability to choose your future. To choose whether you'll return home or stay; you will give them what they want."

She lifted her hand to her face, her finger curled over her lip and her elbow on the table as she pondered his words. He was watching her, his blue eyes sparkling at the challenge he had just set forth. Acting, she thought. Could it free her? Could she return to Lancaster, she wondered, if she gave the public what they wanted? If she went along with Alejandro's plan and advice? She had trusted him enough to leave the farm with him. She had no choice but to trust him now.

In a moment of recklessness, she reached across the table and, with the briefest of hesitations, took his hand, a reversal of the situation. To her delight, he hid his own smile at her gesture. Tilting her head to the side, she hid the wisp of a smile and blinked her eyes. *"Ja,"* she said. "I can do that, Alejandro. I can try, anyway. But only if you help me."

He caressed her hand, staring into her eyes, just long enough to let her know that he understood. "I promised your father that I would take care of you," he whispered. "I will not hurt you, Amanda. I will help you make that choice . . . to get to the place where you can make that choice. I got you into this," he said. "I will get you out of it."

"*Danke,* Alejandro," she said and meant it. She knew that she didn't have to worry. Viper might have one face for the world at large, but Alejandro was not someone she had to fear. Of that she was certain.

Withdrawing his hand, he smiled at her. "*Bueno!* Now that we have resolved that, let me order you a breakfast, a breakfast that will welcome you to your new world," he said with a mischievous twinkle in his eyes, his lips lifted at the edge, just slightly. "Today, you will enjoy an Englische breakfast!"

There was a new energy about him. One that surprised her. How quickly, she thought, he transitions between the public face and the real Alejandro. It was as if he turned a switch, moving seamlessly from one world to another. But always, she thought, with complete composure and polished sophistication. He behaved differently than he had at the farm—more aware of his surroundings and deliberate in his conduct. It was definitely a stronger and more calculated image that he was projecting, something that she immediately recognized as such, and at that moment, she promised herself that she would try to mirror his actions.

He spoke to the waitress, then handed her the menu. When the waitress disappeared, Alejandro reached for his coffee mug again. There was still steam lifting from the hot liquid. He shut his eyes as he sipped it. "That's good coffee, Princesa. Have you tried it yet?"

She shook her head. She had forgotten about the coffee. It wasn't something that she normally drank. Not wanting to appear rude or unappreciative, she took a sip from her own coffee.

"Did you sleep well, *sí?*"

The question surprised her. Again, color flooded her cheeks. That was a very intimate question, she thought.

He noticed the blush and chuckled to himself. "I ask only because you are in a new place and yesterday was a stressful day, Princesa. I do not mean to inquire in any other way."

Her cheeks reddened even more. "I slept, *ja*. But it's such a big room and so . . ."

He looked at her inquisitively, wondering why she had hesitated. "So what?"

"So bright!"

Again, he laughed. "I imagine that it is rather different for you. Those big windows can let in the morning sun and brighten the room." He laid his arm against the back of the booth where he sat. "Just wait until you see Miami," he said. "The sunrises there are spectacular. And the sunsets in Los Angeles! Magnificent!"

"Miami?" She hadn't thought about that, hadn't given much worry as to where she was going with Alejandro or what the arrangements would be. She knew that he lived there . . . in Miami. She must have known that she would be visiting his condominium. Mayhaps even stay there. The idea that all of this was real suddenly frightened her. "Los Angeles?"

He noticed the apprehensive look on her face. It was as if he could read her mind. "Amanda," he said, leveling his gaze at her. "I left Los Angeles to come here for you. I flew here as soon as we spoke on the phone. I canceled some very important meetings and interviews. I have no choice but to return there, Princesa. Not to mention that I start my West Coast tour in a few days." His tone was serious and stern yet gentle at the same time. "We will fly out tomorrow."

The color drained from her face. "Fly?"

He raised one eyebrow at her question. "*Sí,* fly. That is how we get to Los Angeles."

"I'm not allowed to fly," she whispered.

"What do you mean you are not *allowed* to fly?" he asked, an amused look on his face. "Of course you are allowed to fly!"

Amanda chewed on her bottom lip, staring at Alejandro with large brown eyes. She didn't want to upset him, but the bishop didn't allow the people to travel by airplane. It was forbidden. Indeed, long-distance travel was only permitted by bus, train, or boat.

"The bishop has never allowed us to travel by an airplane," she responded slowly.

"Well," Alejandro said, drumming his fingers on the tabletop. "I don't think the bishop is here to stop you."

"I've never been on an airplane." Truth was that she had never even considered such a concept. Flying? In the air? Traveling around the country? "I'd be too scared, Alejandro."

"Ay, mi madre," he muttered, shaking his head. He rubbed the bridge of his nose and said a few words in Spanish.

"I'm sorry." And she was. She hadn't meant to cause him any angst. Hadn't meant to upset him. But the idea of getting in a plane terrified her.

"We can discuss this tomorrow, no? I don't want to argue today," he finally said.

Argue. It was an ugly word. People in the Amish community rarely argued. In fact, Amanda was surprised when Alejandro said the word. It rolled so easily from his tongue, a word that she couldn't remember ever having used. Her parents had never argued. Sometimes the elders in the community had a discussion over the Ordnung and what should or shouldn't be banned. But argue! It was disrespectful to argue. The wife answered to the husband. The husband to the church. And the church to God. There was nothing to argue about when the community was structured properly.

"I should think I don't want to argue ever," she whispered. She lifted her eyes, surprised to see Alejandro staring at her. If he had heard her, he gave no indication. "I will fly, Alejandro. But I will be scared."

He nodded his head. "I understand, Princesa. But I will be there with you. And I told you that I will let nothing bad happen to you."

The waitress who approached the table, with two plates of hot food in her hands, interrupted their conversation. She smiled at Alejandro and glanced at Amanda before she set down the plates on the table.

Amanda stared at the strange concoction before her. Two round pieces of bread with what looked like eggs on top and a golden and creamy sauce dripping down the edges, barely hiding the pink hint of meat. Asparagus was on the side of the plate.

"What is this?" she whispered. "It's not breakfast food . . ."

He laughed at her. "Eggs Benedict. It's my favorite!"

She frowned. "Eggs what?"

"Eggs Benedict," he repeated, kissing his fingertips. "It is *delicioso!* You will like it, I promise."

Not wanting to sound ungrateful, she didn't question him further. It certainly wasn't what she was used to eating for breakfast. Mamm always made scrambled eggs, toast, breakfast meat, and potatoes. Sometimes, in the winter, she would serve hot cereal. But never anything as fancy as what was set before her now.

"Today, Princesa, I must meet with two radio stations for interviews. Mike arranged it when I changed my plans," he said, as he cut the food delicately.

"Mike?"

"My manager," he explained. "During the tour season, I visit local radio stations whenever I can." He glanced up at her. "For marketing. The more I market, the more songs sell and the more people want to attend concerts. It's a cycle."

"What will I do?"

He wiped the corner of his mouth with his napkin and sat back against the seat. "Well, I have arranged for someone to take you shopping."

"Shopping?"

"*Sí,* shopping for clothes."

Amanda frowned. "Whatever for? I have plenty of clothes."

His eyebrow raised, and his mouth twisted into a hint of a smile, the corner lifting ever so slightly. "Amanda," he started slowly. "We will be traveling to many different areas, and you will be all over the media. The best way to not call attention to yourself is to dress more . . ." He hesitated, searching for the right word. "More not-Amish," he settled on. "If you dress like an Amish woman, you will stand out."

Ever since she had been born, Amanda had been raised to not stand out in a crowd. As a toddler, she had worn mini versions of her mother's dresses. On Church Sundays, both she and her older sister, Anna, wore the same-colored dress to worship. Even as a baby, she wore the white prayer kapp *and had been taught quite early to never chew on the ends of the strings that hung over her shoulders.*

"Why do we all dress the same, Mamm?" she had asked when she was in her first year of school.

"It's prideful to want to be different," her mother had explained. She was at the counter, kneading some dough to make bread.

"But John Yoder doesn't wear black pants and suspenders," Amanda had confided. "He wore blue pants to school yesterday."

Her mother had laughed, her hands full of dough. "Oh, Amanda, their family is Mennonite. They aren't Amish. He doesn't have to wear Amish clothing. It's OK for him to stand out. They have different beliefs than us."

***

"Not Amish?" The thought had never crossed her mind, but she understood what he meant. If she had left the Amish, she should certainly attempt to adapt to his world. There was merit in what he suggested. "Well, there is one problem," she said with a sigh. "I don't have any money."

This time, his laugh was hearty and loud. Several people smiled and glanced in their direction. Within minutes, his cell phone would be vibrating with the tweets from several guests who would comment on Viper laughing over breakfast with Amanda, the Amish woman. But, for now, he didn't care.

"You are such a delight," he said, still smiling.

"I don't see what's so funny about that," she said.

"*Ay,* Princesa. You don't have to worry about money. It may be an issue for some people, but I will take care of you, don't worry." He bowed his head theatrically and waved his hand before her. "It is my pleasure, Princesa, to do this for you. After all," he said as he looked up at her. "I am the one who got you into this, *sí?* I promised to get you out of it."

The idea of Alejandro paying for her didn't suit her one bit. She had always been taught to be self-sufficient and to take care of herself and her family as best she could. It suddenly dawned on her that everything . . . from the hotel to the meal to the flight tickets to the new clothes she would have to wear . . . was being paid for by Alejandro.

"I'm going to have to pay you back," she said, horrified at the realization that she hadn't given thought to that part of the arrangement.

His mouth twitched, the corner lifting slightly, and he fought the urge to smile. Instead, he tapped his fingers on the table and studied her. He seemed to be considering something and working something through in his mind. Amanda gave him the space that he needed and took another bite of the breakfast, which, to her surprise, was indeed *delicioso*.

"What if you worked for me?"

She almost choked on her food. "What?"

He nodded. *"Sí, escúchame,"* he said, leaning forward so that she could hear him better. "You are acting the part, *sí?* As such, you will become part of my marketing effort. Every tweet and every photo that is taken of you and plastered on social media or the gossip news stations helps me. Even last night, the television shows that were discussing your departure from Lititz promoted my music. I will give you a salary for working for me, for helping to promote me."

"I don't want to promote you," she said solemnly. "I want them to leave me alone."

"But they won't, and you know that. So play along with it, and give them what they want while getting what you need. In exchange, I will take care of your expenses," he announced, seemingly pleased with this arrangement. And with that proclamation, the discussion was over. He looked at his watch, then glanced around the restaurant. When he spotted the waitress, he made a motion with his hand for the check. "Now finish your breakfast, and we shall get moving, *sí?* The driver is picking me up in fifteen minutes."

She looked up, surprised by the urgency in his voice. It was only eight o'clock and already he had to leave? She wasn't certain how she felt about being left alone.

"What shall I do?" she asked, feeling small and meek and not liking that feeling.

He took the check that the waitress handed to him and signed his name, which, from what Amanda could see of it, was barely more than a scribble on the paper. As he handed it back to the waitress, she hesitated and stood there for just a moment. He didn't notice at first, but as he reached for his sunglasses, he realized she was still there.

"Viper . . . uh . . ."

The dark sunglasses hid his eyes but he was clearly watching her. *"¿Sí, mamacita?"* he asked, his voice low and deep. "You want an autograph, no?" With a big smile, he nodded. "Of course!"

She looked relieved and handed him a blank piece of paper that looked like an unused check. He glanced at it and frowned, but the girl didn't seem to notice. "My name's Julie, if you don't mind," she stammered.

"I don't mind, but I think I will bring down a signed photo for you. Isn't that better?"

"Oh yes!" The excitement in her voice was more than noticeable.

"¡Bueno!"

Again, the waitress hesitated. She glanced at Amanda and looked back at Alejandro. "Do you think that . . . ?" She left the rest of the sentence unfinished.

But Alejandro had understood. He shook his head. "Not today, *mamacita.* Let's give her some space and time to adjust." He didn't wait for the woman to answer as he stood up, straightening his jacket before reaching out his hand for Amanda. Once she was standing, he placed his hand on the small of her back and guided her past the staring guests at the restaurant, immune to their looks and whispers. He hoped Amanda was able to feel the same.

Chapter Three

Within minutes, they were apart. He walked her to the door of her room and, using a flat piece of plastic, opened the door for her. He held it with one hand, his body blocking part of the entrance. "I'll be gone for most of the day," he said. The thought left her feeling very alone. She gave a short intake of breath, not wanting to complain or to show him the fear she felt.

Still, he noticed.

He had smiled at her, understanding the feeling. "You will be just fine, Princesa. Relax and enjoy yourself. When Lucinda calls for you on the phone, you must answer it and be ready. She is a whirlwind, but the best." With that, he leaned over and placed a gentle kiss on her forehead, his arm rubbing against hers as he guided her into the room.

And then he was gone.

At first, she hadn't known what to do. She wasn't used to being alone and without any specific chores. She had never had "nothing" to do in the morning.

For the first thirty minutes, she paced the floor in the hotel room, her mind in a whirl. She wondered what was happening back at her parents' farm, how they were dealing with her departure. With her absence. Her heart seemed to rip in two as she glanced at the clock, watching the time and knowing that at nine o'clock, her father was mucking the dairy barn and her mother was probably washing clothes.

She missed them already and it hadn't even been twenty-four hours.

She continued pacing until ten o'clock. That was the time when the personal shopper would call the room. He had given her very specific instructions: Amanda was to take the elevator and wait for the woman at the concierge's desk. He had even shown her exactly where to meet and introduced her to the young man in a black suit who was to ensure that Amanda was delivered safely and without issue to the care of Lucinda, who, Alejandro had requested, would assist Amanda in his absence.

When the phone had finally rung, Amanda felt grateful for the noise. She was tired of silence, of having nothing to do. She was weary of the voice inside her head that kept telling her she had made a mistake. That one voice berated her until another voice reminded her that the bishop had wanted her sent to Ohio. The church had viewed her as a problem, and in a move that surprised even her, he felt that banishing Amanda was the only way to address the issue.

"Hello?"

"Amanda Beiler?"

"Ja," she said.

The voice on the other end was high-pitched and very sophisticated. It was a cultured voice without any hint of an accent. "Viper instructed me to call you from the concierge's desk. I will wait for you here, and then we can get started," the woman said. "I'll see you whenever you are ready."

When Amanda left the room, she wasn't certain what to do. She shut the door behind her and paused, wondering if she was supposed to lock it. Then she realized that the key was left on the dresser by her suitcase. She tried to open the door, but it was already locked. First mistake, she scolded herself. She hadn't thought that through, and now because of her mistake, she had no way of getting back into the room.

Thankfully, she was alone in the elevator. She stood there, staring at the buttons, trying to remember which one Alejandro had instructed her to push. Her brain felt full already from all the new decisions that she was facing. She finally decided on "L," which was the last button at the bottom.

When the doors opened to the lobby, she breathed a sigh of relief. She knew exactly where to go and did all that she could to stare straight ahead, ignoring the people who gawked at her. Certainly it was unusual to see an Amish woman in such a fancy hotel. What made it more unusual was that they all seemed to know that she was there with Alejandro. She hurried over to the concierge's desk and said a silent prayer of gratitude to see a tall, blond woman already standing there waiting for her.

"Amanda?" the woman asked, holding out her hand.

Amanda nodded and let the woman shake her hand. "You are Lucinda, *ja?*"

The woman raised an eyebrow at the lilt in Amanda's voice. Pursing her lips, she studied Amanda for a moment, her head tilted to one side. "I can see potential," she said, mostly to herself. "Yes, a lot of potential, but we have our work cut out for us today."

"Potential?"

Lucinda exhaled and nodded toward the door. "Let's talk in the car. I have a driver waiting for us. It's best to hurry and avoid the paparazzi."

The word sent a shiver down her spine. Were they still out there, waiting like they had been at her parents' farm? She didn't ask the question that was on her mind. Instead, she followed Lucinda obediently, knowing that if Alejandro entrusted her care to this woman, she should, too.

Indeed, there were reporters outside of the hotel. Security had set up a slight blockade so that there was a distance from the entrance to where the reporters were waiting. Lucinda didn't pay any attention to them and hurried past the crowd toward the car that was waiting for them. Amanda, however, stopped, just for a moment and stared at the reporters. Their cameras began to flash as they took her photograph. Several people had larger cameras, probably videotaping her as she left the hotel.

"Amanda," Lucinda called from the car. "It's best to come along now."

Inside the large sedan, Amanda was surprised to see two men seated in the front. She didn't ask who they were, realizing that she was giving herself completely over to these strangers who Alejandro had entrusted with her protection.

"Why are these people still so interested?" she asked innocently.

Lucinda lowered her sunglasses and peered over the top to stare at Amanda. She was studying her as if trying to assess whether Amanda has seriously asked that question. "You don't know, do you?" she finally asked, slipping her glasses back on and turning to look out the window. "You are quite the innocent, indeed."

Her tone upset Amanda. No one had ever spoken to her in such a condescending manner. "Perhaps if someone would explain it to me," she said, not liking how strong her own words sounded.

Lucinda noticed it, too. With a sigh, she turned back to face Amanda. "Viper is not a typical man, Amanda. He is a star, a celebrity. That means that millions of people follow his every move. Millions."

Amanda laughed. "Millions? Whatever for?" She couldn't fathom so many people being interested in Alejandro.

"Millions," Lucinda repeated. "I understand that you are rather . . . provincial . . . but you need to start understanding that you have left your world to enter his. A world where over twenty-six million people follow him on Facebook, thousands of women follow him around the world, hoping for just once to have him glance at them the way he looked at you yesterday when you arrived at the hotel."

Amanda gasped. "What do you mean?"

"All of those photographers? They sell those photos to newspapers and magazines and television stations. They make a living off following you and capturing moments like this," Lucinda said as she reached down for a folded newspaper. She handed it to Amanda and watched as the young woman tried to make sense of what she saw.

It was two photographs. The first was of him standing beside her at her parents' farm, as they were getting ready to leave. Her head was bowed, and she had a slight smile on her lips. He stood behind her protectively, helping her to face the cameras as they walked to the car. The second photograph was of Alejandro reaching down for her hand to help her get out of the car when they had pulled up to the hotel. Indeed, he was watching her with a look on his face that she hadn't noticed at the time. With his typical skewed smile and a raised eyebrow, he looked amused, but there was something else in his expression.

"I . . . I don't know what to say," Amanda said and pushed the paper back at Lucinda. "I didn't ask for any of this."

"No, no you did not," Lucinda replied. "But you have what women can only dream about as they live their plain lives, envious that you have left yours. Frankly, they are fascinated that, for some reason, Viper has fallen for you."

Fallen for you. Amanda didn't respond. Instead, she looked out the window and watched as the buildings seemed to fly by. She remembered that day in the buggy when the crowds had finally realized that he was in her town. They had barely escaped a mob scene. The emotion of the moment and the realization that he would have to leave had left both of them breathless, embraced in what she could only remember as a kiss that expressed everything that they both felt. Then he had left her and she had to face the cameras and the reporters on her own.

But he had come back to get her.

All it had taken was that one sentence to the media. He had seen it and flown halfway around the world to get her. It wasn't just a sense of obligation on his part. No, Amanda realized, her heart racing inside her chest. Indeed, he felt something for her and, despite her own reluctance to admit it, she had fallen for him, too. Her decision to leave the farm had not been entirely to protect her family. There had been a self-serving element to that decision.

"Oh my," she whispered.

"Exactly," Lucinda said, her voice a bit softer than it had been just moments ago. "Now you have to change, my dear. Perhaps not who you are, for that is what intrigues him, but your public image. You cannot be seen with the sexiest man in the world wearing . . ." She hesitated, her eyes rolling up and down as she assessed Amanda. "Amish clothing."

"I get it," Amanda said drily. She wasn't certain that she cared for this Lucinda very much yet knew that she had no choice but to go along with her for now. She had agreed to do this, and at that very moment, she knew that she had nothing more to lose.

If there was anything that Amanda disliked more than helping at market on Fridays and Saturdays, she couldn't begin to imagine what it was. Her older cousin had just had a baby and couldn't help her husband with weekend days at the market in Maryland.

For some reason, Amanda had been volunteered to accompany her cousin's husband and two of his siblings to Maryland twice a week for the summer, until other arrangements could be made.

It wasn't the work that Amanda despised. No, indeed, she found the interactions with the Englischers fascinating, with their odd way of dressing and lack of manners when they spoke. It made her thankful that she was not of their world, that was for sure and certain.

What she despised was the drive. She would have to get up and leave the house at four in the morning in order to get to Maryland in time to set up for the opening at nine. The hired driver of the van would arrive exactly at five minutes past four, never a minute early or late. The drive was long and boring, too many people crammed in the van. She didn't understand why Anna hadn't been volunteered to go instead of her. After all, Anna was older.

When she finally mustered the courage to ask her mother why, she noticed that her mother took a deep breath, clearly disturbed that Amanda had questioned her on the matter. "Amanda," she started. "Not that I have to explain such a thing to you, but don't you realize that your sister is of courting age?"

Amanda frowned. "What does that have to do with anything?"

"If your sister is going to be exposed to young men, I'd much rather they be from our own backyard than from Maryland!"

It had taken a while for Amanda to fully understand the implication. When she finally got it, she accepted the fact that she had a summer of early-morning risings on Fridays and Saturdays and never complained again.

They spent the next few hours perusing through stores at Rittenhouse Square. Amanda was amazed at the variety of shops and the myriad of small boutiques. She had never imagined such a place existed. Lucinda directed the staff, taking charge of all of the decisions. Dresses were brought out by the armload, mostly black sheath dresses that Amanda thought were just a little too short for her liking. But Lucinda insisted that she try them on, each and every one of them.

Like a child, Amanda did as she was instructed, changing from dress to dress, permitting Lucinda to examine each one she tried on with a scrupulous eye. For reasons unknown to Amanda, some dresses were rejected while others were given a nod of approval.

"Not too fancy," Lucinda scolded the woman at the Nicole Miller store. "And don't bring me red again. Too bright and seductive!"

"How's this one?" Amanda asked as she emerged from the dressing room.

"Dear, you need to take off the white hat."

Amanda frowned. She didn't like the way the woman said that. "It's a prayer *kapp*, not a hat."

"It needs to go."

"Nee."

From her reaction, it was clear that Lucinda was not used to hearing that word. She stood up and walked over to Amanda. Circling her, like a predator surrounding its prey, Lucinda examined Amanda, every inch of her. "This dress is perfect for you. Subtle and sleek, with a hint of sophistication," she said. "But, you wear a prayer cap, and you ruin the image." The way she said the word *kapp* made it sound like a dirty word. "It must go."

"I'm Amish," Amanda insisted.

Lucinda exhaled sharply in a mocking way. "I read up on your culture, Amanda. I understand the Amish dress code." Amanda cringed at the term: "dress code."

"But I can assure you that I am also aware that you are Amish only by birth, not by baptism. Take it off." She started to walk away but paused, glancing over her shoulder. "They will put it in a box for you, Amanda. Give it to the saleswoman."

The next stop was at Burberry. More black dresses, thankfully some that came down to her knees. One dress was white, pure and brilliant white. It was tailored and flared out at the waist. Amanda stared at herself in the mirror, shocked at the color against her skin. The only time she had worn white had been on Church Sunday when she wore her white apron and bib, so carefully starched and ironed, but never had she worn anything that revealed the curves of her waist and hips.

The final purchase at Burberry was a long black trench coat. Amanda glanced at the price tag, gasping to see that it was almost $2,000. Clearly, she thought, that must be a mistake.

"Lucinda," she whispered as she handed the coat to her. "Did you see this?" Amanda pointed to the price tag.

"What about it?"

"That's so much money!"

Lucinda laughed. "Oh, you are *so* provincial." Reaching out to the salesperson, Lucinda nodded toward the register. "We'll take this one, too."

When it came time for accessories and shoes, Amanda almost cried. Lucinda insisted on heels, forcing Amanda to practice walking in the shoes, despite her own resistance. The shoes felt awkward, as though she was walking on her tippy-toes and was going to plummet forward at any given moment. Her calves felt on fire, and the tips of the shoes pinched her toes.

"I can't wear these," she pleaded with Lucinda. "Please don't make me do it."

Rolling her eyes, Lucinda waved her fingers, indicating that Amanda must continue practicing. "You cannot wear flat black shoes from Walmart with dresses worth twenty thousand dollars, Amanda. Let's be reasonable!"

Twenty thousand? Amanda stopped walking and turned away from Lucinda. The tears flooded her eyes, something she definitely did not want Lucinda to see. Had it truly only been twenty-four hours since she had left the farm? Was there to be no time to adjust? Just complete immersion into this new, strange world? Despite her trying to hide them, the tears began to fall down her cheeks, and she stopped walking, pausing to cover her face with her hands.

"Now what?" Lucinda snapped. She approached Amanda and saw the glistening tears on her cheeks. "You can't cry. It will make your skin blotchy! That will be horrible for photographs!"

Amanda turned again so that her back was to Lucinda.

"OK then, we'll get shoes that are not quite so high. Just stop crying," Lucinda sighed and called out for the salesclerk to bring more shoes but different ones. An hour later, they left the Coach store with plain boots, the compromised high heels, and one pair of open-toed glitter shoes that she could wear with the Burberry dress at any fancy dinner.

It was three o'clock when they returned to the hotel. Lucinda accompanied her to the room, pausing at the concierge's desk to request a new key for Amanda, and after the bellboy brought up the purchases, she instructed Amanda how to care for them. Each item was carefully hung up in the closet, paired with matching shoes.

Before she left, she handed a small bag to Amanda. "Alejandro will be taking you out to dinner tonight. Reservations made for seven thirty. I suggest the Nicole Miller sheath with the angel sleeves. And since the weather is nice, you don't need stockings, but you will, certainly, need what's in here."

And then she was gone.

No parting words. No warmth. Her job was done, and Lucinda needed to return to New York City. It was too obvious that "provincial" did not quite appeal to Lucinda, a woman from Manhattan who shopped on Fifth Avenue and dealt with far more sophisticated women than Amanda would ever aspire to be. Her displeasure in Alejandro's selection of a woman to accompany him on his West Coast tour was clearly evident. But it wasn't her job to approve or disprove. Just to make over the image of Amanda.

Once again, she was alone. She stared at the closed door, feeling a wave of fear wash over her. She had four hours until Alejandro would be back.

She opened the bag she was still holding in her hands and peered inside. There were several smaller bags that contained Chanel makeup, Angel perfume, and Oribe hair products. One bag contained a razor and other small toiletries. Sinking onto the edge of the bed, she stared at the contents and felt dizzy. She had to shut her eyes and concentrate on her breathing.

I can survive anything.

The words echoed in her head. Had she truly said that to Alejandro just last month, the day that he had finally left the farm?

I want to experience more.

Well, she scolded herself. You may get more experiences than you ever bargained for, Amanda.

She didn't know how to approach this evening, didn't know what Alejandro expected. After what Lucinda had told her earlier that day and the realization that this was not all innocent, she felt herself in a panic, as if trapped in a cage with no way out. She had nowhere to go, and deep down, she wasn't certain that she wanted to go anywhere, anyway! The conflict of emotions battled within her and she felt torn.

The phone rang and she jumped, startled from her turmoil of thoughts. She hurried over to it and lifted the receiver. "Hello?"

"Viper asks that you turn on the television to channel 6," a male voice said.

She looked around the room. Television? She hadn't even noticed one in the room. "Is there a television?"

A chuckle. "Open the doors to the armoire, if there is one." A hesitation. "A big chest," he clarified.

She found a large chest in the corner, and when she opened the doors, she saw a large flat-screen television. "Oh!"

"You found it, yes?" Another chuckle. "Now turn it on. There should be a button either in the front or on the right-hand side of the panel." She did as she was instructed, and when the screen flashed and moving pictures began to dance on it, she gasped. “Good, good,” the voice soothed. “Now look for the channel button and click six.”

She searched for the button and finally found one that had “CH” next to it. Afraid that she might break the television, she pressed the button once. The number *4* displayed on the screen. She pressed the same button twice more and saw it change to *5* and then *6*. “I think I did it,” she said, amazed that she had just done something so technically challenging. “Why am I watching this?”

The man laughed. “You’ll see. Enjoy.” Another hesitation. “And Viper will be back at the hotel for you at seven.” Then the receiver went dead.

Amanda stood there, the phone in her hand as she stared at the moving pictures on the screen. Bright colors, music, voices, words. She was amazed and horrified at the same time. The sins of worldliness, she thought. “Oh my,” she whispered and gently placed the phone receiver back in the cradle. She took a few steps back and sat on the edge of the bed, staring at the television, mesmerized.

And then she saw him.

Alejandro.

There was a woman in a green shirt with black slacks seated in a tall chair. Alejandro was seated next to her. He wasn’t wearing the same clothing as he had been earlier that morning. Gone was the suit. Instead, he had on tan slacks with a crisp pleat down each leg and a white long-sleeve shirt, over which he wore a darker brown jacket. His shirt was unbuttoned at the top, and she could see the necklace of Santa Barbara that he wore.

He looked relaxed. And happy.

“Viper, I understand that you just flew in from Los Angeles the other day but are heading back there tomorrow for your West Coast tour,” the woman said. Her legs were crossed at the knee and she wore tall black heels. Amanda had a hard time imagining how anyone could walk in such high shoes.

"*Sí,* it was unexpected, but I'm always glad to visit Pennsylvania. *¡Mi gente!*" He laughed, his eyes sparkling and the woman looking quite pleased with his jovial mood. There must have been other people watching the interview, as Amanda heard people cheering in the background and applauding. She realized that he was being interviewed in front of an audience.

"You recently spent quite a bit of time here in Lancaster County, isn't that so?"

He nodded. "I did, *sí.* I spent some time with a very special young woman and her family in Lancaster."

Amanda's heart froze in her chest. Was he actually going to talk about her? Them? On television?

Give them what they want, he'd told her earlier that morning. Clearly, that was his plan.

"And now?"

"Well," he said, shifting his weight in the chair as if uncomfortable with the question or not knowing how to respond. He chuckled and tugged at his shirtsleeve. "I'll be flying back tomorrow with a little bit of Pennsylvania with me," he finally said, his tone light and happy.

The interviewer laughed. "What happened to 'single, bilingual, and ready to mingle'?"

"I'm still bilingual," he teased.

"But not so single or ready to mingle?"

"Aw, you remember that?" He laughed and lifted his finger to rub above his lip. The audience laughed with him, devouring his every word.

"You didn't answer the question, Viper," the interviewer teased, wagging a finger at him in a mock reprimand.

"Let's just say that I'm ready for my next few tour stops. I love the West Coast," he said, diverting her question but smiling into the camera and winking.

Amanda covered her face with her hands, embarrassed. What would people think? She replayed his words in her head and realized that, with a great degree of cleverness, he had said nothing but insinuated everything. Was he expecting their relationship to become something more? Was she?

She watched the rest of the interview, but the interviewer focused more on his recent album and tour dates, his inspirations for his songs, and his plans for a next album. After his ten-minute interview, the show switched to commercials and that was the end of Viper's part in the afternoon talk show.

Stunned by what she had just watched, she hurried to turn off the television. She was replaying the interview in her head, scared and excited at the same time. She had never watched a television show before, outside of the few times she had been to stores run by Englischers and caught a glimpse of a television on behind the counter or hanging from the wall or above an aisle. Frankly, she had never given them much thought.

It was amazing to her that, right now, Alejandro was somewhere else but had also just been in the room with her. Truly magical in nature, she decided. Yet, she also knew the danger of such worldliness. It separated families and exposed them to more of the world than they needed to be privy to. Right now, as far as she knew, hundreds of thousands of people had watched that interview and heard him basically tell them that he was no longer "single," insinuating that she was his girl and was traveling by his side.

But I am, she thought, the realization strange and surreal.

Unlike the Amish way, Alejandro didn't want to hide their relationship. Yet, Amanda didn't really understand what their relationship was. True, he had basically come out and admitted the fact that she was going to be traveling with him. The insinuation that he was no longer single . . . well, she couldn't quite figure that one out. Of course, he had kissed her that day and he had flown halfway around the world to rescue her. In a way, how else could she look at it? She knew that the Englische world had a different way of courting. Perhaps, she thought, this is courting among the Englische after all!

When she had turned sixteen, she had gone to her first singing. It was held at a neighbor's farm after Sunday worship. Sister Anna accompanied her and for that Amanda was grateful. She hadn't really wanted to go, but her mother had insisted. It was expected, her mother had explained. With that, there was no further argument from Amanda.

It wasn't the singing that Amanda dreaded. It was the post-singing ritual of young men asking if a particular girl would ride home in their buggy. She knew that it was one of those situations when nothing good would come from it. If a boy asked her, she'd have to say yes or risk offending him. That might set off a firestorm of gossip and make other boys fearful of asking her. However, if she said yes, she risked the boy thinking that she was interested in him. She could quickly find herself having just turned sixteen and courting someone she didn't particularly care for!

Of course, there was another potential situation. No one would ask her to ride home. She'd have to walk . . . alone and by herself. If other buggies passed her on the road, they'd know for sure and certain that she hadn't been asked by any of the boys. Other boys might wonder why and, once again, gossip would spread.

So Amanda had a plan. She had no intentions of courting an Amish boy. Not yet, anyway. They were all so plain and boring, she thought. They never seemed to talk or have much to say. They certainly didn't make her heart flutter or her pulse quicken as she imagined from the few romance books she had read.

The plan was to leave early, sneak out, and walk home before the buggies left. No one would see her and no one would know. Yet, when it came time to do so, she felt a hand on her arm and, with a heavy heart, knew that her plan had been thwarted.

It was Benjamin Yoder, and he had been waiting at the door, looking for the opportunity to ask her for a ride home in his new courting buggy. Amanda hesitated, probably long enough for him to realize that she wasn't thrilled at the prospect of being seen in a courting buggy.

Unlike other Amish girls, Amanda was not one to bow her head and go along with the order of things. She tended to question the reasons behind decisions and study the world around her.

"That's fine, Benjamin," she said reluctantly. "For the company and all, I reckon."

He didn't reply to her reluctant acceptance but led her through the summer night toward his awaiting buggy. He put out his hand to help her up. She barely touched it. When he sat next to her, he slapped the reins on the horse's back and the buggy jerked forward. For the next fifteen minutes, neither spoke, merely listening to the sound of the wheels humming along the road and the horse's shod hooves clapping against the macadam.

By the time the phone rang again, she realized that she had been pacing the room and it was close to five o'clock.

"Hello?"

"Princesa!"

It was Alejandro. His enthusiasm was contagious, and immediately she smiled as she turned away from the desk, the cord wrapped around her waist as she stared out the window. "Alejandro!"

"Did you see the interview?"

Her cheeks flushed. "I did, *ja!*"

"And you are blushing right now thinking about it, *sí?*"

She didn't respond.

"I thought so," he said, chuckling. "Don't read too much into it, Princesa. It is . . ." He hesitated, searching for the right words to explain it to her. "It's what they want. It is our plan, *sí?* To get you back home . . . wherever we decide that is."

She was glad he couldn't see her reaction to his words. No one had ever spoken to her like that. He cared about what she wanted and had determined that it was a joint decision. She could tell that he, too, was as perplexed as she was. Yet, he cared enough to decide the future with her, not for her.

"Now, Princesa," he said, his voice low. She could tell that other people were surrounding him by the way he sounded, muffled and soft. He didn't want others to overhear their conversation. That much was obvious. "I will be at the hotel for you in . . ." He hesitated, and she knew that he was checking his watch for a time. "Two hours from now. You relax, take a nice warm bath, and get dressed in whatever Lucinda told you to wear. Tonight we will go for dinner and an evening of dancing, *sí?*"

"Dancing?" She was horrified at the thought.

But he laughed at her. "*Sí,* dancing. Nice dancing." Again, he lowered his voice. "Like that day at the farm. Slow and beautiful." He paused. "Like you are today and will be this evening."

"Alejandro," she breathed, wishing she could tell him to slow down and stop, but the way that her heart raced told her otherwise. If she had questioned whether she had fallen for him before, his gentle words pulled her further down that abyss of emotion that she had never felt until this day. "I'm . . ."

"You what?" he asked breathlessly from the other end of the phone.

"I'm not like those women!"

Silence.

And then he chuckled. The sound of his laughter teased her on the edge of the phone, but there was no hint of malice. *"Ay, mi madre,*

Princesa," he murmured. "If you were, you would not be where you are tonight."

"Alejandro?" She didn't understand what he meant, but he didn't have time to explain it to her.

"I shall see you in two hours. You be yourself and let me handle the rest, *sí?* That is all that I ask." And with that, the conversation was over and the phone went dead in her hand.

Chapter Four

She was waiting for him in the lobby when seven o'clock chimed on the imposing grandfather clock near the reception desk. She wasn't certain where, exactly, she was supposed to meet him, but she couldn't spend another minute in the room alone. She was nervous, standing there near the main entrance, looking around as she fidgeted in her new shoes. Lucinda had merely shaken her head at her final choice of black shoes, telling her that higher heels were more in style. But Amanda had insisted, telling Lucinda that she needed to be able to walk after all.

She had followed his directions and taken a long bath in the big Jacuzzi in her room. She had put bubble-bath salts into the water and had laughed when the bubbles overflowed over the edges. She had washed her hair, using the fancy products that Lucinda had left for her, and when it came time to dry it, she had tried to figure out how to use the hair dryer on the wall. She had never used one before but had heard about them from her friends. It was something unusual, different, and, in her opinion, unnecessary. But she was determined to give it a try.

To her surprise, her waist-length hair looked silkier and fuller than ever before. She stared at herself in the mirror, letting her hair sway back and forth until humility got the best of her. Quickly, she pinned it back into a bun, shocked at the fullness and size that it had become . . . just from using the Englischer products.

Now, as she stood in the lobby, her feet hurting in the shoes that pinched her toes and her legs stinging from having used that terrible razor that Lucinda had left her, she felt like a duck out of water. What am I doing here? she asked herself for the hundredth time.

And then she heard him.

Rather, she heard the murmur of the people in the lobby as he approached her, a group of men surrounding him. He was in the lead, but he was not alone. He wore a black suit and a black shirt, all of a shiny satin-type material. In his coat pocket was a handkerchief of red, the only color on his person. He wore his dark sunglasses, despite the fact that it was not bright inside the hotel and the sun was setting outside the tinted windows.

When she turned to greet him, she had no words.

Nor did he. For a moment, he hesitated, stopped in his tracks. Quickly, he composed himself and continued toward her, acting as if he had not noticed the transformation. With the form-fitting black dress and the relatively high heels, with her hair pulled back in a tight bun, with the hint of blush upon her cheeks, she was just . . . beautiful.

"Amanda," he murmured as he embraced her in a light yet not intimate hug. "You are magnificent."

She didn't respond.

He held her at arm's length, admiring the transition. "Dios *mío,*" he murmured, his eyes glistening with approval as they traveled down her body, taking in her new dress and shoes. "Had I only known . . ."

She tilted her head and stared at him. "Had you only known what?"

He lifted his chin and smiled at her, just a hint, expressing his pleasure. "If I had only known that you were so lovely, I would have kept you on the farm so that I would not have to share you with the world." He paused and, after just a few seconds, leaned forward to brush his lips against her cheeks, first the left, then the right. "I would share you with no one, Princesa."

"Oh," she whispered, her voice light as a breath of air.

"But tonight," he said, glancing over his shoulders at his companions, "I share you with everyone." He held her hand and lifted her arm in the air. "I introduce you to Amanda, the most famous Amish woman in the world," he pronounced. The men nodded in approval, and Amanda shut her eyes, feeling a mixture of pride and humiliation at the announcement.

"Never you mind, Princesa," he whispered in her ear. "These men are here to protect both of us. They are on our team, *sí?*"

"If you say so," she responded slowly.

It was a dream. From the ride in the caravan of black SUVs to the restaurant to the way that they were greeted, everything felt distant and fuzzy, as if she were asleep back at the farm and imagining the entire evening. Alejandro was nothing short of extremely attentive to her, ignoring the gawking fans and stolen photos from the people in the restaurant. When people asked for his autograph, he obliged. When they asked for hers, he gestured them away but always with a smile.

The dinner took place in a dark restaurant with candles burning on the table and crystal candelabras hanging overhead. He ordered for her, teasing her with an appetizer of oysters and a lobster dinner. When it arrived, she had laughed, remembering that night in the hospital when he had surprised her with a seafood feast, alarmed that she had never seen a cooked lobster before that night.

As he had done that evening, he split the lobster and fed her forkful after forkful. She had delighted in the attention and his pleasure in seeing her blush.

"You color the most beautiful red when you are embarrassed," he had whispered.

"I'm not embarrassed," she replied but didn't even sound convincing to herself.

"And now you lie," he replied, enjoying the easy banter back and forth. "But it is a pleasant lie, one that shows me your heart."

She couldn't stop herself from changing the subject. "What did that interview mean today, Alejandro? Why did you want me to watch it?"

"Um," he said, wiping at his mouth with his napkin. "You saw, *sí?* It was a good interview, don't you think?"

This time, she laughed. "I have never seen television before or an interview. Both were amazing, *ja*. But I don't understand."

He switched from one mode to another, transitioning as if nothing had transpired. "That is what you will need to get used to, Princesa. More of that type of attention. We will face the media in such a way, headfirst. Eventually, by giving them everything . . . which is nothing . . . they will move on."

Nothing. The word stabbed at her heart, and she felt a wave a disappointment. Was that what this was? A complete act? Nothing?

"What is wrong?"

He had noticed her reaction. She couldn't hide it. It was never her way to avoid such confrontation. That simply wasn't her way.

"I am nothing?"

He looked alarmed and reached for her hand. "That's not what I meant, Amanda."

"What did you mean, then?" She licked her lower lip, feeling emboldened by his stare. "I am not used to this, Alejandro, and you know that I . . ."

"You what?"

"Well," she stammered. If confrontation wasn't her way, discussing emotions was not an Amish way either. But she knew that she had to move forward and take the plunge to tell him what she was thinking. "You know what I felt that day in the buggy. I am conflicted right now. Torn between being petrified and excited about what you are doing for me."

Releasing her hand, he leaned his elbow on the table and rubbed at his upper lip with his finger, studying her and her reaction. She wished that she knew what he was thinking and prayed that she hadn't been too forward. His eyes darted around the room, as if trying to see who was nearby and might overhear. When he determined that it was safe, he took a deep breath and moved closer to her. "You are not nothing to me, Amanda. If you were nothing, I would not have returned for you. Surely you know that."

She chewed her lower lip and averted her eyes.

"But I am making you no promises. I will not dishonor you, not in the way that would make you unacceptable should you choose to go home," he continued. He waited until she looked at him. "I respect you too much for that."

She inhaled sharply. She remembered far too well *that* particular conversation from the day on her parents' porch. On the one hand, it clarified his expectations. There were none in regard to dishonoring her virtue. Of that, she could feel confident and safe. Yet, on the other hand, she once again found herself feeling a tinge of disappointment. What made her so different from the other women that he had been with? What made him so willing to spend the evening with them but not with her?

He hesitated and frowned, contemplating how to tell her the rest. "But I must tell you that the world will not believe that our relationship is . . . innocent, and I will not try to convince them otherwise. It is, indeed, what will be necessary to satisfy their need for gossip so that they can move on. I thought I had made that clear."

Understanding better, she nodded.

"Now," he said, his jovial nature back and the solemn Alejandro disappearing. "Let's enjoy tonight, *sí?* After all, we don't know what tomorrow brings." He clapped his hands and, to her surprise, a woman appeared. "Wine, I think. A nice cabernet. Whatever is the best in the house."

She leaned forward and whispered, "I can't drink wine!"

He frowned, but there was no malice in his expression. "A taste of wine will not hurt, Amanda. Even Jesus drank wine. Remember," he said, leaning forward, "I will let nothing happen to you. I am here to protect you."

When the glass of red velvet liquid was set before her, Amanda stared at it, horrified. Wine? Alcohol? She had never even contemplated such a thing. But when Alejandro raised his glass toward hers, lingering expectantly, she followed suit and, with a trembling hand, raised her own.

"Cheers, Princesa," he announced, knowing full well that people were watching them. "Cheers to an amazing new adventure for both of us." He sipped at the wine and set his glass down on the table.

Following his lead, she sipped at the liquid, feeling it burn down her throat. At first, she didn't like the taste. There was a fruity taste to it, but if she didn't like it initially, she found that a second sip helped change her mind. It was different, and she would be careful. But it was lovely, nonetheless. And Alejandro was correct, after all. Hadn't Jesus's first miracle been turning water into wine at the wedding feast he attended with his mother at the little village of Cana, in Galilee?

"That's my girl," he purred, smiling at her from behind the dark glasses that shielded his eyes.

She began to feel more brazen, more comfortable with the dark ambience and isolation. She took another sip of wine and tried to enjoy how it slid down her throat. Within seconds, her body felt lighter. "Why, Alejandro?"

"Why what, Princesa?"

"Why did you come for me?" He didn't answer right away, so she continued. "This is a lot for you, I can see that. It's a lot for me, too. I have much to learn and if I learn it, you might not like what you see," she said.

"Shh," he responded, placing a finger to his lips with a gentle shake of his head. He set his wineglass down on the table and reached his hand across the table for hers. "Let's not speak but dance." He didn't wait for her to answer as he stood, reaching for her to take his hand. With his crisp black pants and shirt, he was dark as he stood before her. Dancing, she thought. Another banned Amish activity. Yet it wouldn't be the first time she had danced with him, and the memory of that afternoon at the farm caused her to feel as if butterflies fluttered in her stomach.

She couldn't help herself as she reached out to accept his hand. Carefully, so that she wouldn't fall, she stood. "I don't know how to dance, remember?" she whispered into his ear.

"You will tonight," he replied and led her onto the dance floor.

The room seemed to fall silent when they walked onto the floor. He pulled her into his arms, mindful of the fact that she was wearing higher shoes than usual. He cradled her in his arms and held her tightly. Nestling his lips against her neck, he murmured, "Just follow my lead, Princesa."

She didn't know what that meant, but as usual, she trusted him.

He moved slowly, his arms draped around her in a way that held her to his body. She had never been this close to anyone before this evening. If she hadn't been so aware of people watching their every move, she would have probably fled. But all of those eyes watching Amanda dance with Alejandro forced her to continue moving across the floor. He held her tightly, his body towering over hers in a way that was both protective and seductive at the same time.

She shut her eyes and tried to remember that memorable day in the *grossdaadihaus* when he had tried to teach her how to dance. She could feel his body move against hers, the emotion of the moment causing her blood to race and her knees to feel weak. He was strong, that was for certain. But he was also very gentle in how he held her. There was no force in his movements, and he glided across the floor, taking her with him in a way that could only be elegant because of his physical beauty on the floor.

"Oh," she whispered in his ear.

"Tranquilo," he responded. "They are adoring you. Let them, Amanda. For you are beautiful and deserving," he said, his breath caressing her ear.

Beautiful and deserving. Those were two words she had never heard in regard to herself. Beautiful was in the eyes of the Lord, not people. And deserving? Of what? She had been taught from the earliest age that deserving was only reserved for those who followed God. She didn't feel as though she was following God right now, not after having tasted wine and especially how she was being held in the arms of a man who was clearly not her husband.

"I can't do this," she whispered.

"¿Qué?" He pulled back from her but did not loosen his hold. "What?" he repeated in English. "What is wrong?"

"This is too much, Alejandro," she replied softly, avoiding his gaze. "It's too much too soon."

He nuzzled against her cheek. "I will not do anything to you, Princesa. You are a gift from God. I will cherish it and never abuse it."

Gift from God? His words tore at her. Did he realize what he was doing? Or how she felt? She tried to back away, but his hold was too tight. "Alejandro, I'm not comfortable like this," she said.

"Shh," he whispered. "Stop and enjoy the moment." He continued to hold her and move across the dance floor. Every eye in the restaurant was upon them. She could feel the heat of their stares. "This is what they need. They need to see that you are no different than they are," he murmured softly.

His words caressed her ears as his breath brushed across her neck. She tried to do as he instructed, following the movement of his body against hers as they danced, slowly and with simple steps. The way he directed her across the floor, holding her in his arms and, with the slightest of pressure, silently telling her where to move, was like a floating dream.

It was a dream. She simply could not believe what was happening to her. Just two days before, she didn't know whether he was going to show up at the farm. She certainly did not imagine that he would whisk her away into a magical world that she didn't even know existed. A world of fancy stores and personal shoppers, and evenings of candlelit dinners with music and dancing.

"You are crying?" he asked, pulling back in surprise.

She shook her head but couldn't hide the tears starting to invade her eyes.

"*¿Por qué,* Princesa?" When she looked at him, he smiled and, with his thumb, brushed the tears away. "Why?" he asked in English.

"This is too much to take in," she whispered, tucking her head down into his shoulder. "I . . . I just feel overwhelmed."

He stopped dancing and placed his finger under her chin. Tilting her head, he stared down into her eyes. "Remember the goal," he whispered and, gently, leaned down to just lightly brush his lips against hers.

Her knees felt weak, and she had to cling to his shoulders to keep from stumbling in the high heels that pinched her toes. He seemed to sense this and kept his arm tight around her waist.

"Whether you return or stay, it will be your decision, my Princesa," he said softly, the corner of his mouth lifted in a hint of a smile. No one could hear the words except her. To the casual watcher, he was whispering sweet words of love. Amanda realized that, yet again, he was playing the fans and, indeed, giving them what they wanted. "Not theirs," he finished; then, releasing her waist, he held her hand and led her back to their table.

Chapter Five

The following morning, he asked her to his room. He had called on the telephone at seven in the morning. With a brisk and cheerful hello, he had instructed her that she should join him for breakfast; when she was ready, she could knock at the door separating their rooms.

Unlike her room, he explained, his was a suite. He had called for room service to deliver breakfast, rather than face the staring guests who, by now, were clamoring downstairs, lingering in hopes of spotting Viper and Amanda together.

She had knocked hesitatingly at the door of his adjoining room. To her surprise, another man opened it and greeted her. She recognized him from the previous evening and seemed to recall that his name was Carlos. She was quickly learning that Alejandro was rarely alone. He had a small group of men who surrounded him, usually in the background, in order to keep the mass of fans and onlookers away from him.

She smiled a silent greeting and dipped her head as she walked past him.

"This way, Amanda," he said and led her through the sitting area and into a large sunny room with a balcony. In the center of the room was a round table covered with a white cloth and fresh flowers in the center. White roses, she noticed, and simply gorgeous.

"*¡Buenos días,* Princesa!"

Startled, she turned toward the open doors that led to the balcony. He was standing there in white slacks and a salmon-colored shirt, unbuttoned so that she could see the top of his white undershirt. He wore his sunglasses, hiding his eyes from her, and held a tall fluted glass of something yellow with bubbles.

He walked toward her and set the glass on the table. Then he gave her a friendly embrace, kissing her cheeks in the customary greeting of Cubans. "You slept well, *sí?*"

She nodded.

"Good, good," he said, smiling. "And you look lovely. Again." He held her at arm's length and spun her before him. She felt like a doll on display, not quite certain that she liked the feeling. "Lucinda has a theme, I see. Black. Plain and simple yet smart." He clucked his tongue. "And very becoming." He reached for his glass and raised it to his lips, peering at her from behind his sunglasses as he said, "Today is a big day for you. You will fly across the land to the most beautiful state in the country. California!"

Her heart palpitated at the reminder.

"Now, let's sit and eat." He guided her toward the table and, ever the gentleman, pulled out a chair for her.

"What time is this plane ride?" she asked, her voice trembling at the thought.

He sat beside her and laid the napkin across his lap. "We will leave for the airport soon after breakfast. I want to prepare you for what will happen, Amanda." He reached for the silver dome that covered the food and lifted it. "Something simple today for you. Eggs and bacon."

She smiled and blushed. "I'm not used to this."

"Get used to it, Princesa," he said, setting the dome aside. "This is what you wanted to experience."

"You said I would hate you."

He laughed. "Oh, that will come, trust me. Which is why I want to prepare you."

She served herself from the plate of eggs. "Prepare me for . . . ?"

He cleared his throat and placed his elbow on the table. "There will be a scene at the airport. My people already warned me that crowds are gathering, waiting for our arrival at Philadelphia International. We have a private jet taking us to Los Angeles, so we won't have to worry about the actual flight arrival, but getting to the plane will be a mob scene, probably worse than anything you have experienced so far."

The color drained from her face. "Will it be safe?"

"Sí," he said. He glanced at Carlos. "*Mi gente* will be there protecting us. So will the airport security." He leveled his gaze at her. "They will be taking photos, shoving, and doing everything they can to attract our attention. Especially *your* attention. I will be beside you, and the security detail will keep them away. But just be prepared, Amanda. And it will be even worse in LA."

Her appetite was gone.

"Why?"

He shrugged. "It's part of the role, Princesa. Here, look at these." He reached down and pulled several newspapers and pieces of paper from the floor. Every single one of them contained a photograph . . . a photograph of her. Her and Alejandro. Photographs of her shopping. Photographs of her waiting for him. Photographs of him admiring her in the lobby. And photographs of them dancing.

"Where did you get these?"

"Some were from the newspapers. Otherwise from the Internet. People are devouring you." He leaned back in his chair and smiled at her. "You are a media sensation."

She frowned. "I thought you said it would die down."

Again, he shrugged. "It takes time, Amanda. Enjoy it while you can. You are topping the charts as a bona fide celebrity." He winked at her. "Take the good with the bad." He reached for the serving bowl of food to dish some onto his own plate. "I wouldn't be surprised if you miss it later. The life and the attention," he clarified. "Should you choose to return to Lititz."

"Did you miss it?" she asked. "When you were at my parents' farm?"

He laughed, a hearty laugh. "*Ay,* Princesa, you are good. Very good, *mi amor.*" He glanced at his cell phone, which vibrated on the table next to his plate. Without thinking, he reached for it as he answered her. "*Sí,* I did miss it. Only I didn't realize it until after I returned for you." Then, the phone to his ear, his attention was diverted to the person on the other end of the call.

Speaking rapidly in both English and Spanish, Alejandro seemed to forget that she was there. He punctuated things that he said with his free hand in the air, as if making a point to the person on the other end of the phone, even though no one but Amanda could see him. His animation and ability to switch back and forth between the two languages amused her, and she found herself listening, trying desperately to pick up a few words here and there.

But she understood nothing.

When he set the phone back on the table, he stared at her thoughtfully, drumming his fingers on the tabletop.

"What is it?" she asked.

"Good news and bad news," he said slowly. "The paparazzi have left your parents' farm."

She clapped her hands and smiled. "That's fantastic news, Alejandro! It worked! My parents won't be shunned, and they can go back to living again!" She looked relieved and the glow in her eyes spoke volumes. "This has all been worth it!"

He pursed his lips as he watched her. "That was the good news," he started. "The bad news is that they are sending a police escort to take us to the airport."

Her happiness quickly drained. "A what?"

"Police escort. They need police to accompany our car when we leave. The sidewalk outside of the hotel is jammed, and there are people waiting outside of the airport. News crews, too. It's not just the paparazzi anymore, and that means it will take a bit longer." He didn't look pleased with this news. "It also means that it will be even worse than I thought."

He spoke over his shoulder in Spanish, and the young man, Carlos, hurried over to his side. She listened to them speaking, amazed at the singsong quality of the language. It was beautiful and so very different from both English and Pennsylvania Dutch with lots of *essh* sounds that reminded her of a wind through the high branches of a tree back at the farm.

"*¡Bueno!*" Alejandro said and nodded at Carlos. "That will work, *sí*."

When Carlos left, Amanda leaned over and lowered her voice. "Who *is* he?"

He glanced in the direction from where Carlos had just disappeared. "Carlos?" He folded his napkin and set it beside his plate. "My personal assistant when I travel. At home, I have Rodriego, but on the road Carlos is better suited for dealing with security detail and logistics. Speaking of which, he will pack up your things and send them to the airport separately. We should get going now."

He paused, just for a moment, after he stood up. Reaching into his pocket, he pulled something out and, with a smile on his face, handed it to her. "I almost forgot. Something for you to put in that handbag that Lucinda most certainly had you buy. Gucci, I imagine, knowing Lucinda."

Amanda reached out and looked at the small rectangular device that he handed to her. "What is it?"

"Your very own gadget to play with," he said, chuckling at the way she held it, so delicately, as if it was going to hurt her.

She tried not to smile as she studied it. "A cell phone?" she looked up at him, a look of wonder on her face. "Whatever would I need that for? I don't have all of those people to speak to like you do! It won't even be used! No one will call it!"

He wagged a finger at her. "Someone will call it."

"Who?"

"Me!"

She laughed at the expression on his face. "Well, in that case," she replied, staring at the shiny glass on top of the phone. "I suppose you will have to give me lessons on how to use this . . . this contraption!"

"Later, *sí,*" he said, guiding her back to her room. "Now we must get going, Princesa."

If Amanda had thought that he was exaggerating about the crowds, she realized that he had probably downplayed it more than anything else. She could see the crowds outside the door before they even approached it. Through the smoky glass, crowds of people were waiting, their arms stretched over their heads with cell phones poised for that one photo opportunity that they knew was headed their way.

She clutched at his arm and stopped walking. "What are they waiting for?"

He leaned over and whispered in her ear, "Us."

Her free hand flew to her open mouth while her other hand clung to his. He took a deep breath, straightening his jacket and pushing his sunglasses back on his nose. Wrapping his arm around Amanda protectively, he nodded to the security guards at the door. With that, the doors were open and a roar came from outside.

"Vámanos," he said softly and headed toward the throngs of people waiting outside, guiding her along the way.

Arms were outstretched. People were screaming. Girls and women, she realized. It was mostly girls and women. They were reaching out to touch him, to touch Viper. Others were reaching out to her but Amanda had no idea why. Clearly, they were not interested in her.

One of the security guards quickly positioned himself to Amanda's right, protectively putting his body between her and the crowds. She cowered closer to Alejandro, thankful that he still kept his arm wrapped around her. She felt safe and protected in his embrace. Without a doubt, Alejandro would not let anything or anyone harm her.

Ahead of them, someone kept the path clear to where the sedan was waiting, door open. Alejandro paused by the door and waited for Amanda to get inside. She stumbled and fell against the car, but he reached out a hand to steady her. Within seconds, he was seated next to her and the door was slammed shut. The car hurried away and the crowd was left behind.

Amanda turned in the seat and stared out the back window. The people were still jumping up and down, screaming and taking photographs with their cameras and phones. Outrageous, she thought, as she settled back into the seat next to Alejandro, wondering why anyone would act so crazy for a silly photograph.

It wasn't the first time that a car had cut off her father's buggy, and as far as Amanda knew, it certainly wouldn't be the last. She never could understand why so many thousands and thousands of tourists flocked to Lancaster County to gawk and stare at the Amish. Even worse, she couldn't understand why some people, themselves residents of Lancaster County, treated the Amish so poorly, teasing them, mocking them, and even endangering their safety.

Without fail, there were several accidents each year involving cars driving too close to the buggies. Horses and people were injured and died at an alarming rate. Young locals liked to speed past the buggies and cut right in front of them, spooking the horses and often running them off the road.

True, the majority of the people were kindhearted and good to the Amish. But it only took one or two who harbored malice in their hearts and souls to ruin the lives of many.

It was a fact that the Amish could scarcely go anywhere during the tourist season. There were crowds of people in the stores and along the back roads, their cars moving slowly in order to roll down the window and take photographs of any horse and buggy they encountered. Walking was a hazard, too. Cars would stop and blatantly take the Amish pedestrians' photos with no regard for the wishes of the subjects to not have their photographs taken.

Amanda had often wondered what was so boring in the lives of the Englische that they found the plain and simple ways of her family and neighbors so interesting. She finally guessed that the Englischers didn't lead such exciting lives after all. They just wanted to live vicariously through others.

If anyone had ever mentioned to her that she would be thankful to be seated in an airplane, she would have laughed and told them they were *ferhoodled* out of their mind! In fact, she never would have imagined herself sitting in an airplane. It just wasn't something that was done.

Oh, she knew of a few young people who flew during their *rumschpringe*; there were even a couple that went overseas, much to their parents' chagrin and disapproval. Such behavior was, however, to be overlooked during those years, before taking the kneeling vow and settling down to raise a family. But Amanda had never even considered that she might be one of the few who embarked on airline travel.

However, after the mob scene at the airport, she didn't care. True to his word, Alejandro had never left her side. The crowd was thick and loud, pushing and shoving, doing anything they could to attract Viper's attention, to touch him, to get a photograph with him. With Amanda by his side, it was even worse. He couldn't protect himself and her at the same time. He had chosen her.

The guards had helped keep the crowd away, and slowly, they moved toward the security check. Thankfully, they were whisked into a private security room, where, to Amanda's dismay, there were issues because she didn't have any photo identification. It had been an extra twenty minutes gaining special permission based on religious grounds to bypass the security check to be escorted by the guards to their own personal gate that led to the private plane.

"How do you put up with that?" she exclaimed as she sank into the leather seats.

He laughed at her. "You'd be surprised, Princesa. That is what motivated me to keep climbing the charts."

She didn't understand what he meant but didn't feel like asking for an explanation. Despite it only being late morning, she was exhausted. Her brain was overwhelmed, and every nerve in her body felt as though it were on fire. She barely gave a second thought to the fact that she was sitting inside an airplane.

Until the time came to take off.

Alejandro instructed her to put on her safety belt and told her about the process. Still, when the moment came in which she felt the engine accelerate and the plane began to race down the tarmac, she squeezed her eyes shut and clutched at his hand.

"It's going to be fine," he reassured her in a low voice. "I do this all the time, Princesa. Nothing to be worried about at all."

Within minutes, the plane had not only lifted off the ground but was leveling off, high above in the sky and heading away from the sun. She finally released her death grip on his hand and, hesitantly, peered out the window. Her insides jumped as she looked down upon the earth.

"Alejandro!" she gasped. Small puffs of white clouds cast shadows over the patchwork of farmland beneath the plane. She could see roads with tiny little cars traveling on them. She could see houses and trees. And when she looked toward the horizon, she thought she just might have seen a sliver of heaven. "It's . . . it's magnificent!"

"God has made a beautiful world for us to live in," he replied, placing his hand on her shoulder and leaning over to peer out the window. "And he made man smart enough to engineer the aircraft so that we can appreciate it."

"Look, Amanda!"

She turned from where she was walking to see what her younger brother was staring at that made him call her back. He had kneeled down and was examining something in the tall grass. She could tell by the serious look on his face that he had found something wonderful and wouldn't move until she hurried over there to see it.

"What is it, Aaron?" she asked patiently as she approached him.

He looked up and smiled, then pointed back toward the ground. "Have you ever seen anything so amazing?"

Kneeling beside him, she had looked to where he pointed. There was a simple rock. It wasn't especially beautiful nor of any particular shape. Just a rock. Grayish in color and about the size of her fist. But there was a crack in the rock, a deep opening, and from inside that crack grew a plant.

It wasn't just any plant. It was a Johnny-jump-up that had found a way to grow from within a rock. Its green leaves, almost heart-shaped in nature, clung to the rock, and from its center emerged one single flower. It almost looked like a small butterfly with the outer wings deep purple in nature, the middle wings lavender, and the tail a pale yellow.

It was amazing, indeed.

"God sure has made a beautiful world, ain't so, Amanda?" Aaron had said, careful not to disturb the flower in its quest for life.

Indeed.

The beauty of God's touch could, indeed, be found everywhere, whether at thirty thousand feet above the ground or within a simple little rock, half buried in a small mound of dirt, Amanda pondered. She had never really thought about that before. Her world had been limited to Lititz in Lancaster County. While she appreciated the beauty of God's work that surrounded her, she had no idea how that beauty extended beyond the boundaries of the Amish and in what form.

She slept during the flight, and for that, she was grateful. Emotionally and spiritually, she was exhausted. Someone gave her a pillow and blanket, so she snuggled against the back of the seat and let herself drift away to a place that was familiar and comforting: her dreams. She dreamt of the farm and of springtime. She dreamt of milking cows and helping with hay baling. She even dreamt of Church Sunday and the singing, so full of splendor for God.

But then, her dream changed.

She was walking through a field of growing corn, the baby stalks of green brushing against her bare legs. She could hear the wind whispering through the crop as it waved like a sea before her. Behind her, she heard someone call her name. When she turned to look, it was her mother and *daed*, waving to her from the porch. They were calling her home. In the distance, she heard a horse and buggy rattling up the road.

"Amanda," someone called.

She turned to look in the direction of the new voice. It was deep and masculine with a hint of an accent. The sun was setting over the hill, casting an orange glow so that all she could see was a shadow . . .

a shadow of a man standing at the crest, the corn brushing against his legs and waist. He wore different clothes, not Amish clothes, that was for certain. His hands were behind his back and his legs spread in a forceful, commanding stance.

"Amanda, it's time," he called out and reached a hand for her.

She glanced back at her parents and, in doing so, the wind blew her prayer *kapp* from her head. It floated through the sky, and for the longest moment, she watched it. Should she go grab it, something that would surely take her farther from the man, or should she forget about it and run in his direction?

"Amanda?"

She looked back at the man, and the sun dipped low enough over the horizon so that she could see it was Alejandro. He kept his hand outstretched, patiently waiting.

With just the smallest hesitation, she turned and walked up the hill toward him, ignoring the calls from her parents at the bottom of the incline. With a smile on her face, she picked up her pace and began to run toward Alejandro. He stretched out both of his arms and laughed, watching her as she ran.

And then she was snuggled against his chest, his arms wrapped around her. He leaned down and kissed her cheeks, in a chaste and innocent manner yet speaking volumes of what he felt.

"Amanda?"

Her eyes fluttered open. She was leaning against his shoulder, and he was caressing her back, his arm draped around her shoulder. Startled and embarrassed, she sat up. "Where's the corn?" she mumbled, still waking up from her dream and trying to piece together reality.

"Corn?" He chuckled. "You were dreaming, Princesa."

The memory of the dream flooded through her, and she moved away from him. "I'm so sorry."

"You are beautiful when you dream," he whispered.

"Viper," someone said from behind them.

It was Carlos.

"Landing in ten minutes, and the car is waiting. Plus, Mike has you scheduled for an interview on *Entertainment Tonight* at three o'clock and with Sue Jarrell at four thirty. Tomorrow's rehearsal is at eleven a.m. and the pre-show VIP gathering is at six in the evening."

Alejandro nodded, but Amanda's head was spinning.

"You have meetings this afternoon?" She glanced out the window, surprised to see that the sun was still shining brightly in the sky. "But it's so late."

"Time change. There's a three-hour difference between Philadelphia and Los Angeles, Princesa. We'll leave directly from the airport for the interviews," he explained. He leaned forward, his forehead almost touching hers. "I want you to go with me."

"To an interview?" she gasped. She wasn't exactly sure what that was. Why would anyone want to interview him? Why should he want her to go, too? "Whatever for?"

His mouth lifted in a half-smile. "I want them to meet you and for you to see. You wanted to experience my world, *sí?* I'm not holding anything back." He paused before he added, "Your decision must be informed."

She frowned at his words.

He tilted his head and reached for her hand, which he lifted and then brushed his lips against while staring at her. "Plus, I want you with me. You are most . . ." He paused, searching for the right word with his lips lingering just inches above her hand. "Refreshing."

Then, without another word, he settled back into the seat, his sunglasses covering his eyes and masking his expression as the plane began its descent. The plane rattled and shook, the pressure dropping in the cabin. He seemed oblivious to the descent but not to her fears. Through it all, he held her hand.

Chapter Six

The noise was tremendous. She stood in the wings of the stage, peering out at the crowd that had filed into the Staples Center. In her simple black skirt and white silk blouse, she could have been anyone. Most people didn't notice her as they bustled by, occasionally bumping her arm. She would apologize, but no one paid any attention to her.

The stage was full of equipment and speakers, lights and props. She couldn't even begin to imagine what she was looking at for she had never seen anything like it in her life.

"Amanda," a voice said in her ear. "Alejandro wants you back in the waiting room to meet some people."

She turned around and stared at the woman by her side. With a headset on and a clipboard in her hand, she looked official, so Amanda nodded and followed her behind the stage and through a passage that went under the seats. As she walked, several people began screaming, and she heard her name being called out.

Startled, Amanda looked up and saw a crowd of young girls hanging over the railing and waving at her. They were jumping up and down, calling out her name. Several of them held up their cell phones and took photos of her, still screaming out her name. They were smiling and laughing, happy to see her and take her picture. Not certain how to respond, Amanda finally waved back but continued walking, following the woman with the clipboard.

"There she is!" Alejandro said as he greeted her with a friendly kiss on the cheek. He left his arm draped around her shoulders as he turned for her to be introduced to the three people in his waiting room. "Amanda, this is Janice Lobell, a reporter for LatinRapper.com. She wanted to meet you."

Amanda frowned and looked at him. "Latin what?"

He laughed. "LatinRapper.com. It's a website that shares information about Latino artists." He leaned over. "I'll show you later, *sí?*"

The tall, olive-skinned woman was dressed in a tight-fitting red dress and wore sparkling high heels. Her hair hung down her shoulders in long, swooping waves. Amanda couldn't help but stare at her. With heavy makeup and full lips, she was truly beautiful. "It's nice to meet you, Amanda," she said, her voice heavy with accent, and extended her hand. "How do you like Los Angeles?"

Amanda moved closer to Alejandro. "It's very nice," she said. "But busy. I've never seen so many cars."

Both Janice and the two men behind her laughed. Alejandro smiled, his arm still around Amanda's shoulders. "It's been a long two days, that's for sure."

"Oh *ja,*" Amanda admitted. "Why, we flew halfway around the world! And then all those interviews!" She turned to Alejandro, a concerned look on her face. "I'm surprised you can keep going!"

Janice glanced at Alejandro and said something in Spanish. He nodded and lowered his eyes, smiling. Amanda wondered what had transpired between them and longed to understand this mysterious language that permitted secret dialogue.

For the next five minutes, Alejandro and Janice talked, switching between English and Spanish. From what Amanda could understand,

Janice asked questions about his songs and the leg of the tour that he had just finished.

"And then we head to San Francisco for a concert at the Bill Graham Civic Auditorium, then over to Las Vegas for a concert at the MGM Grand Casino before heading back to Miami."

"Las Vegas?" Janice raised an eyebrow and glanced at Amanda. "That should be interesting for Amanda. Quite a far cry from Pennsylvania, no?"

Amanda glanced at Alejandro. "What is this Las Vegas?"

Janice answered for him. "A lot of crazy things happen in Vegas."

With a short laugh, Alejandro gave Amanda a gentle squeeze and kissed the top of her head. "We'll see how crazy Amanda gets." Another laugh. "After all, what happens in Vegas stays in Vegas!" The small group of people laughed with him, but Amanda didn't understand any of that conversation.

She had felt that way about many things during the day, just as she had felt that way about many things in her life.

It was the fall foot-washing ceremony. Amanda was not permitted to attend. She had stayed back at the farm with Aaron, entertaining him since neither one of them had taken their baptism yet. Only baptized members could attend the foot-washing ceremony, which was followed by communion.

"Why, Amanda?" Aaron had asked as they played with the latest batch of kittens that lounged in the sun. "Why must we stay home?"

She didn't have any answer for him. "It's just the way. Until we take the kneeling vow, we aren't permitted to attend."

Aaron had poked a thin stick at one of the kittens. It rolled onto its back and reached for the stick with its tiny white paws. "Are you going to take the kneeling vow?"

She shrugged. "I reckon one day."

"Anna did."

Last spring, Anna had become a baptized member of the church. Amanda had watched with a mixture of awe and surprise. Anna was very young to take the baptismal vow. Most young women and men waited until they were courting someone and ready to settle down, since baptized members could only court other baptized members. Usually couples became members just before they announced their wedding during the next season. But that wasn't always the case.

"She did, ja,*" Amanda confirmed.*

It had been a gorgeous Sunday. The air had been crisp, and the leaves of the trees were at their autumn peak. Red, orange, yellow. The windows of the room over the barn were open and a cool breeze brushed across Amanda's face. She was happy that she was able to sit by the window because the room was packed full of people and, despite the weather being cool, the closed confines of the room were warm.

She had watched her sister kneel before the bishop, her hands covering her face as he spoke to her in High German, asking her the baptismal questions. She looked so young, too young to be committing her life to the Ordnung. Amanda's eyes drifted from the four youth who were taking their baptism, and she stared outside, watching the trees in the breeze. For a moment, she wished she were outside, watching the clouds from the side of a stream.

"Why haven't you taken yours yet?"

Amanda didn't have an answer to that either. She just knew that she wasn't ready and wouldn't be for a while. She couldn't understand why she wanted to wait. But like a lot of things she didn't understand, she knew better than to question it.

"Amanda," Alejandro said as he led her away from the people. "I have Mario and TJ ready to take you to the front so that you can watch the concert." He grabbed a bottle of water from a man walking by and thanked him in Spanish. Turning back to Amanda, he forced a smile, but she could tell that he was somewhere else. "I need to get ready now, so it's best that you go with them."

She bit her lower lip and stared at him. There was something different about him. He had changed since they had landed in Los Angeles the previous day. She had noticed it immediately. The way he moved, the way he spoke to others. He used more Spanish words and touched people a lot. His posture was very calculated and sophisticated, always standing in a way that, if someone wanted to take a photo, he was prepared.

Yet, he was still himself. Generous and kind. At the concert hall, he was always asking if everybody was having a good time or if they needed anything. He always took a moment to speak to anyone who happened to be in the waiting room or asked for his attention. And, without doubt, the most amazing thing to Amanda was the way his mere presence took over the room when he entered. Just by simply being there, he commanded attention. People would stop and stare, always smiling.

The previous day she had accompanied him to the two interviews. Everywhere they went, there were crowds of people. Not as many as at the airport, true. But girls and women screaming and yelling, some even crying, when he would get out of the limousine at their stops. He always took a moment to smile and wave at the gathered crowds, then reach down for Amanda's hand as he helped her out. She kept her eyes lowered as she followed him, glad that he walked ahead of her. Twice, he had stopped and let a group of girls take his photo while Amanda waited nearby. Once, he had pulled her into the photo to the delight of the crowd.

The night before, he had left her alone in the hotel. He had to make his appearances, he explained, and the places where he was going were not places he wanted her to see. She hadn't quite understood that but didn't ask. She was tired and wanted to sleep. So she had merely nodded and accepted his instructions that she should be ready in the morning for breakfast at nine o'clock.

After breakfast, they had been driven over to the Staples Center. Alejandro had ignored the group of people who swarmed upon him, waving them away, as he showed her the stage and where she would sit later that evening. She had felt her heart race, and she shivered in awe of the fact that she was standing there, in Los Angeles, getting ready to watch Alejandro perform that evening.

"Who are all of those people?" she had asked.

"My tour manager, the stage manager, my publicity folks . . . you name it, they all are here," he had said lightly. "And, for now, you will go with Carlos back to the dressing rooms. Lucinda has sent some more clothes for you with instructions of what to wear and when. I need to speak to *mi gente* for a while, *sí?*"

The afternoon had flown by with yet another interview and preparations for the evening concert. Now she saw that Alejandro was completing his transition into Viper. He disappeared into his private dressing room to get changed, and she was left in the hands of two of his security guards.

"One minute!"

Amanda turned and saw a woman rushing toward her, armed with an arsenal of brushes, intent on quickly checking Amanda's hair and makeup. While Amanda started to back away, the woman was persistent. It had been a two-day battle with this woman, Beth. Amanda refused to wear her hair down, much to the dismay of the stylist. However, she had lost the battle with the makeup.

"Can't have you looking tired and pale for the photos," the woman had argued.

Alejandro had laughed at the standoff between Amanda and Beth, watching with amusement as he stood to the side. When Amanda looked at him, pleading, he merely had smiled in that mischievous way with which she was becoming all too familiar. "I think you are doing just fine, Princesa."

Now, as she was getting ready to follow Mario and TJ, she turned to look at Alejandro one last time. To her surprise, he was standing in a circle with the members of his band and the stage crew. They were holding hands, heads bowed, and she knew that he was leading them in a prayer. She stopped walking and watched him, something fluttering inside her as she observed this most intimate and surprising moment. She hadn't seen this side of Alejandro since their walk on the farm so many weeks ago when they had talked about his patron saint, Santa Barbara, and worshipping God. There was something magical about seeing him in prayer, engaging others in thanking God for his grace.

"Amanda, you are ready?"

She looked up at the tall man next to her. Mario was much taller than her and quite stern looking. She felt safe in his shadow. "I reckon so," she answered softly and followed him as he led her down the corridor and toward a tall black curtain that blocked the activity behind the stage from the fans.

When Mario pulled back the curtain for her to pass through, she heard a noise. At first, it was subtle. Then it grew louder. It surprised her and she looked up, trying to identify what the noise was. She stood there, staring, and slowly realized that almost every seat in the stadium was occupied. The people were screaming and yelling. The roar that she heard had been the noise of the people. And those who sat in the seats near the side of the front stage were screaming and yelling for her.

As TJ and Mario guided her to her seat, in the fifth row by the stage, people took her picture and reached out to touch her arm or shoulder, trying to get her attention. She wasn't used to being touched and tried to avoid them. Mario and TJ tightened their circle around her when they noticed her discomfort. Finally, she was able to sit and take a moment to digest what she was seeing.

All of this, she realized, was for Alejandro. When he had told her and her parents that he was a singer, an artist who traveled the world, she never would have imagined that it was like this. She was fascinated with the volume of people, with their apparent adoration for Alejandro, and all the noise. How could one man, one single man, create such fervor among so many people?

"Is it true?" Aaron asked her. "Did he really die for our sins?"

Amanda laughed at her younger brother. "Who?"

"Jesus!"

Ah, she thought. He had been paying attention at church service yesterday. She had watched him, sitting next to her father on the other side of the meeting room. He was squirming and wiggling around on the hard bench. Three hours was a long time for a ten-year-old boy to sit, especially when the sun was shining so brightly outside, beckoning him to come and play.

At the service yesterday, the bishop had been selected to preach. He had spent the majority of his sermon focusing on the power of Jesus, how he had died to save the world from sin. He was the Son of God, sacrificed by his own father in order to save the world. The lamb whose blood was shed in order to give hope to the world. Those who believed in Jesus could enter the gates of heaven and spend eternity with God and their loved ones.

"Yes, he did," Amanda said. "And we have to be forever grateful for his sacrifice."

"Why?"

She wasn't certain how to answer that question. It was what she had been told for as long as she could remember. "Vell," *she started to explain. "Think about all that he gave up for us. He gave up his life, his privacy, his future. He gave up everything to teach us about how to have a relationship with God. And then, when asked, he gave up his life so that we could all live."*

It was easy to tell that Aaron didn't understand. She wasn't certain she understood either. But, deep down, she knew that something powerful had happened two thousand years ago when Jesus had walked the earth, preaching to the masses, performing his miracles, and giving all of himself for others.

When the concert was over, Mario and TJ quickly escorted Amanda through the crowd toward the curtains that led backstage. Her mind was reeling from what she had just watched. It was amazing and horrifying at the same time. The way in which the people adored him had shocked her. After all, the worship of idols was forbidden by the Commandments.

And it wasn't just the people, she realized. It was the women. Both young girls and young women reached out to touch his hand as he performed and moved about the stage. Sometimes, he would reach down and quickly grasp their hands. Other times, he didn't.

She noticed many of them held up signs. "Marry Me, Viper" and "I Want a Viper Bite" were typical phrases carefully written on the boards. Every once in a while, Alejandro would point at someone in the crowd and grin. That would cause the crowd in that area to scream even louder.

Yet, none of that affected her in the way Alejandro did. He had transformed into Viper, the singer and stage artist. He moved across the stage in a way that was almost catlike. She barely recognized him as her Alejandro. And as she listened to the girls screaming and crying, reaching out for his touch, she realized that, indeed, she was considering him as "hers."

His music was beautiful, poetry set to music. Some of the words were shocking to her, telling stories of intimacy and physical attraction that brought the color to her cheeks. She was glad that no one could see her in the shadows from the stage lights.

Now there was a flurry of activity behind the stage. People were moving quickly, packing up equipment, and tearing down the stage props. Amanda was escorted past the people and back toward the room where some more people were gathered. The band members were drinking beer, and there were several young women back there, dressed in high heels and short skirts. Amanda avoided them as she looked for Alejandro.

He wasn't there yet.

She stood by herself, watching with fascination as the people laughed and talked. There was a high energy in the room, adrenaline that pulsated from each person. It was contagious; she, too, felt more alive than she ever had before in her life.

When he entered the room, he had showered and changed. He wore his beige pants and an open white shirt. People clapped him on the back and shook his hand. Several women hugged him. He took a moment to take a photo with the young women, who flushed at his attention. But then he left them and his eyes roamed the room, searching for someone. Searching for Amanda.

When their eyes met, he paused and waited as if gauging her reaction to what she had just experienced. He lowered his sunglasses, peering at her over the top, one eyebrow arched in an unspoken question as his blue eyes beseeched her.

She couldn't respond. The memory of him, singing and performing onstage, still burned within her. She could still see the lights above the adoring fans, hear the music. Her breath escaped her and she could only stare at him, amazed at his beauty and grace. And then she smiled.

That was enough.

In four strides, he crossed the room and reached for her. The gesture startled her, but she didn't mind as he pulled her into a tight embrace. He wrapped his arms around her and held her close, his lips brushing against her ear. "Did you like?"

It was all that she could do to nod her head. The feelings that had built up inside her made it difficult to find the words to express what she had just experienced.

He pulled back, his hands on both of her shoulders, and he stared into her face. "Is that a yes, Princesa?"

She flushed, her cheeks turning crimson, and she lowered her eyes. She was afraid that he would be able to see inside her soul if she didn't look away, as the emotions that had just flooded through her were too strong and unexplainable for her to even understand.

For in that moment, she knew that she could never return to the farm in Lancaster County. She knew that she only wanted to be with Alejandro. She knew that she loved him.

Chapter Seven

When she awoke, she found herself lying on a bed in the back of the tour bus. It took her a minute to place herself, to remember where she was. The tour bus, she reminded herself. Not at home in Pennsylvania. Not at the farm. She sat up and lifted her hand to her head. No, not at the farm. In fact, she imagined she was as far away from the farm as was possible.

The previous evening, they had left Los Angeles around midnight and driven straight through to San Francisco for the concert that evening. It had taken a while for the energy to die down after the show in Los Angeles. People lingered, laughing and talking as they drank Corona beers and ate pizza.

Even though it was late, Amanda had found herself wide-awake, her mind still alive after having watched Alejandro perform. Her ears rang from the loud music and the screaming fans. Her heart was still pounding at the realization of how she had truly felt. But, even more so, she was in awe of this amazing man. He was so comfortable, mingling amid the lingering crowd, keeping her within arm's length and always checking to make certain she was all right. It was a whisper in her ear or a caress on her arm. His attention heightened her senses, and she began to relax as she watched him move through the people.

Mario was the one who walked up to Alejandro and said something to him that Amanda couldn't understand. With a simple nod, Alejandro turned to her and smiled. There was weariness about him, the energy suddenly depleted. "It's time, Princesa," he said. "We are to leave now."

"Leave?"

He had taken her hand and started following Mario out of the room. "The bus is waiting and security has the exit ready for us." He paused to say good night to a few people; then, with a final wave at the crowd in the room, he led her into the hallway and down the corridor.

A large gold-and-black bus was on a ramp that led out from under the stadium. It was unlike any bus that she had ever seen. The inside wasn't just seats. Instead, it was like a small house with a sitting area, two leather sofas, and a large flat-screen television. He walked past the sofas and through a narrow opening, which, to her surprise, was a bedroom. He took off his jacket and tossed it on the back of a chair.

"I'm exhausted," he had said, sitting down on the bed.

Uncertain where to go, she had stood in the doorway and watched him. He still wore his dark sunglasses and reached to take them off. He set them on the small table next to the bed. He looked tired and rubbed at his eyes. *"Ay, mi madre,"* he mumbled. "Exhausted."

Crossing her arms across her chest, she smiled. "I can't imagine why."

He looked at her, surprised by her teasing tone. "Is that sarcasm I detect?" Yet, he understood and smiled, a tired smile. When he had stared at her, his blue eyes sparkled, despite his weariness. Tilting his head to one side, he pursed his lips as if contemplating something. "Come here," he said, holding out his hand.

A look of panic crossed her face. "Alejandro, I . . . I can't . . ."

He chuckled. "*Ven aquí,* Princesa. Come here," he repeated. "I told you that you have nothing to fear from me. But there is nothing wrong with my wanting to hold you. I'm tired, and I want to sleep." His eyelids drooped as he stared at her. "And I want you in my arms," he said, his voice low and husky. "I promise you that is all." He motioned with his hand, indicating that she should take it in hers. "Come," he commanded again in a soft voice.

She bit her lower lip, uncomfortable with his request. His hand was in the air, waiting for her to take it. The look on his face was bewitching, and she couldn't tear her eyes from his. As if mesmerized, and with just a slight hesitation, she took a step into the room and reached for his hand.

To her surprise, he had grabbed it and pulled her onto the bed. Laughing as she cried out, he wrapped his arms around her, tucking her body under his as he nuzzled his lips against her neck. He ignored the look of panic on her face as he gently kissed her skin. "You have seen it all, Amanda. This is my life," he murmured. "And you are doing fantastic. I know it must be hard for you."

She wished she could tell him that the hardest part was how it wasn't half as difficult to adapt as she had thought it would be. "Alejandro," she said and squirmed in his arms. He was stronger than she was: escape was impossible. "This . . . this isn't right . . ."

He leaned back, his body hovering over hers, and stared into her face. His eyes flickered back and forth as he took in her every feature. "You are most beautiful, Amanda," he said and leaned down, slowly and gently, to brush his lips against hers. "And there is nothing wrong with this. A kiss. I told you before that you have nothing to fear from me."

He loosened his hold on her but didn't let her break free from his grip. Indeed, he kept her curled against his body as he sprawled out across the bed. "Just this," he whispered. "This is what I want." He sighed, his breath caressing her ear. "It's nice to have someone waiting for me, Amanda. Someone who wants nothing from me . . . for once."

She began to relax, the tenseness of her body easing as she realized that, indeed, all Alejandro expected of her was to be herself and to let him be himself. As his breathing slowed, she listened to the gentle sound of sleep fall over him. And he slept, deeply, with his arms protectively wrapped around her, his chin resting atop her head.

It had taken her a while to feel comfortable, wondering how this would rate on the scale of sins according to the Ordnung. But she also knew that many Amish communities still practiced bundling, the young couple spending the night together with a board separating them. It was a way for couples to get to know each other and, she reasoned, was not so different from this.

So it surprised her when she awoke to find herself under the sheets, her shoes on the floor by the door. She was alone. There was no sign of Alejandro. From the stillness surrounding her, she could tell that the bus was no longer moving.

With bare feet, she padded into the sitting area. She passed by a mirrored cabinet and glanced at her reflection. It was shocking to see herself. There were dark smudges under her eyes, and her hair was falling loose from the bun. She quickly hurried to the sink and did the best she could with washing away the day-old makeup and fixing her hair.

As she finished, she heard the door to the bus open. Turning toward the front of the bus, she heard his footsteps before she saw him. He greeted her with a smile and a kiss on the cheek. "You are up! *¡Bueno!*" he said cheerfully. He was wearing freshly laundered tan pants with crisp pleats down the front and a white shirt that was unbuttoned at the throat and neck. His sleeves were rolled up, and he looked relaxed.

"Where are we?" she asked, taking the cup of coffee that he handed to her.

"San Francisco, Princesa!" He sat down on the sofa, spreading his arms out along the back. "They have already started setting up the equipment. It arrived just thirty minutes ago."

"What time is it?"

"Seven thirty," he said, glancing at his phone. "And I must go do a radio interview. A car is picking me up in ten minutes. I thought you might like to come along," he said.

She didn't respond right away. She was still wearing the same clothes as the night before and had nothing to change into for facing a new day.

"Let me rephrase that, Princesa," he said, smiling at her. "I would love your company."

The look on his face made her smile. "Why is that, Alejandro? All those years, you did this alone. Now you want my company?"

He set the coffee down and stood up, approaching her slowly. When he stood before her, he took a deep breath and reached for her hand. It was small and delicate in his, and he lifted it to his lips. "Amanda," he breathed. "There is something about you . . . I just cannot explain it."

She tilted her head, part of her wishing that he would kiss her. His voice, his smile, the sparkle of his light-blue eyes. All of it was more than she could handle. "Try," she said, her own voice a breathless whisper.

Lifting his eyebrow, he stared at her, surprised by her tone. "You are full of surprises, *sí?*" Tracing a line along her cheek, he brushed his finger across her lips. "You make me feel . . ." He sought the right word. "Alive."

"Alive?" His choice of words surprised her. She raised an eyebrow, amused. "I should think that your entire lifestyle is very much alive," she said.

"My lifestyle is busy," he corrected, reaching up to teasingly tap his finger on the tip of her nose. "But it is *you* who have given me new life." Then, to her delight, he did lean down and kiss her, his lips soft against hers. "And now," he murmured. "You must get changed to accompany me, *sí?*"

As always, he had planned ahead. Someone had left a suitcase of her clothing by the door of the bus. He left her, just for a moment, to retrieve it and then carried it into the bedroom for her, leaving her alone to change her outfit and get ready for the morning round of interviews.

She wasn't certain that she would ever get used to the crowds that waited for Alejandro outside of the buildings wherever he went. Hordes of people, usually screaming women, waiting and jumping and taking photos. When the limousine had pulled up at the first building, security was already waiting for them, holding back the mass of admirers that blurred together into a wave of noise.

When the car door opened, Alejandro ducked his head and got out first. He straightened his shoulders and waved to the crowd, smiling and posing for their cameras. Then he turned back to the open door and reached down for her hand. She hesitated as she took it. She didn't like the photos, didn't like the noise. But as she stepped out of the car, a roar went up around them.

"Smile," he said out of the corner of his mouth, putting his arm around her waist and waving, once again, to the crowds.

At first, Amanda didn't understand. Then, after repeating his words to herself, she realized that he wanted her to smile at the crowd. She tried to force a smile as he guided her down the cleared walkway toward the entrance of the tall building. Her eyes trailed away from the people, and she glanced up at a large building down the street. She lifted her eyes, craning her neck as she stared up, into the sky.

That was the photo that would be published on the front cover of the newspaper the next day: Viper staring at Amanda as she searched the heavens, her face in awe of the buildings, and his in amusement at her.

"So, Viper," DJ Scott said into the microphone. "I see you brought your private entourage with you today."

Amanda was sitting on a high stool next to Alejandro. She felt uncomfortable with the large microphone in front of her and certainly didn't want to talk to this loud, rambunctious man seated across from her. With messy hair and tattoos on his neck, DJ Scott may have impressed San Francisco listeners, but he did nothing for Amanda.

She reached her hand up to press the little plastic earphone that was in her ear. It was awkward and unnatural to have something stuck into her ear like that.

"I know people are curious about Amanda, so I thought she should come along with me," Alejandro said, laughing as DJ Scott lifted his sunglasses and raised his eyebrows. "And she's not my private entourage."

"Really?" DJ Scott twirled his chair so that he was facing Amanda. "And what, exactly, is this lovely lady to you, Alejandro?"

Amanda frowned and narrowed her eyes. Why had Alejandro insisted that she come with him?

"Well," Alejandro said, clearing his throat. "She is traveling with me, *sí?* She is my . . ." He paused and glanced at Amanda. When he saw that she was glaring at the disc jockey, he chuckled. "My good friend."

DJ Scott laughed into the microphone. "You have an awful lot of 'good friends,' Viper. Never seen one travel with you."

Alejandro grunted and shook his head at the disc jockey, indicating that a change of subject was in order. "About our show tonight, *sí?*"

DJ Scott lifted his hand. "Wait a minute, Viper." He turned his attention back to Amanda. "I'd like to hear from your friend about what she thinks of California. From what I understand, she hasn't been here before."

They both turned to look at Amanda. She glanced over at Viper and lifted her shoulder. He motioned toward the microphone, indicating that she should talk into it.

"Hello?" she said, leaning toward it.

Both men laughed.

"Just answer the question, Princesa," Alejandro coaxed softly.

She questioned him with her eyes. Had someone actually asked her a question?

"What do you think about California?" he repeated softly.

"I just talk?" she asked.

DJ Scott lifted his sunglasses off his eyes and stared at her, amused at her innocence.

"*Sí,* into the microphone," Alejandro said gently and moved the microphone closer to her.

"Ja vell," she said. "I haven't seen much of San Francisco yet, but the buildings are tall."

"The buildings?"

She nodded. "*Ja.* And there are a lot of them, like in Los Angeles."

"People come here for the views of the bay and the beaches, yet you are admiring the buildings?" DJ Scott laughed. He glanced over at Viper and smirked. "I understand you were at Viper's concert last night. What did you think?"

"Oh, it was rather loud and the people screamed a lot," she said. "Especially the women."

Both DJ Scott and Alejandro laughed.

"But the music . . ." She paused and chewed on her lower lip. For a moment, she was back at the stadium, seated before the stage and watching Alejandro transform into Viper. She could hear the beat of the music, feel the heat of the lyrics, and sense the life that exploded around her. "I have never heard anything like that. It was . . ."

Alejandro raised an eyebrow, curious as to what she would say.

"It was so . . . alive."

DJ Scott laughed, his amusement increasing at the woman who sat before him. He glanced at Viper and nodded his head, as if silently communicating his approval. "Alive?" he repeated the word she had used. "I've heard Viper's music called a lot of things but never 'alive.'"

She tilted her head and looked at him. "Doesn't it make you feel as if you are on top of the world? Like when we flew out here, I felt the same way. I thought his music was every emotion rolled into one. It was energetic. It was romantic." She hesitated before she added, "It was even spiritual."

"Spiritual?" He spat the word as if it were dirty.

Ignoring his tone, she nodded her head. "At my church, we sing to God. We honor him through hymns. Our songs tell stories and teach lessons. It is a way to pass along our traditions. To connect with the Lord. To keep our community together. His music is no different, *ja?*"

DJ Scott sat back in his seat, his mouth hanging open. For the first time in a long time, he was speechless.

Alejandro laughed. *"Ay, mi madre,"* he managed to say. "Princesa, you have done it!"

She looked alarmed. "What did I do?"

"Floored DJ Scott!"

DJ Scott shook his head, trying to regain his composure. He took a deep breath and turned his attention back to Viper. "Well, I'm not quite certain of how to respond to that," he managed to say. "A spiritual Viper? Seems like you may have lost your venom!"

Alejandro rolled his eyes but chuckled. "That remains to be seen."

The rest of the interview focused on the Viper tour and where they were headed over the next few days. It was news to Amanda that they were going to Las Vegas the following day and then, after two nights of performances, that they would return to Los Angeles for an awards ceremony where Alejandro would be performing.

"Male Artist of the Year," DJ Scott said, shaking his head. "Sure have come a long way from the streets, haven't you, my friend?"

Alejandro sighed. "Long way is right, *amigo*. No more fighting in clubs or battling with the boys on the streets."

"When will you be headed back to Miami?"

"Next week," Alejandro said. "It will be good to have a week in my city. Party with *mi gente*!" He said the last part with a great flourish, and DJ Scott laughed at him.

Amanda glanced at him. Miami? She hadn't thought about that. His home. Her heart fluttered at the thought. What would happen when he was home, without the interviews or the concerts? She wondered what he did during his spare time. What would she do?

"Amanda? Have you finished piecing that quilt top yet?"

She rolled her eyes.

Her mother took her silence as an affirmation that the task wasn't finished. "Are you daydreaming again?" She clicked her tongue several times as she hurried over to see what Amanda was doing. "Idle hands and idle minds . . ." she complained when she saw that Amanda hadn't been finishing the task.

"I know, I know," Amanda said. "I'm sorry, Mamm. I was thinking about the garden for this spring. I can't wait until the warm weather returns. This cold is just . . ." She searched her memory for the right word. "Well, just downright cold! Makes me want to sleep until it warms up!"

*"*Ja, *mayhaps you want to sleep, but you need to finish piecing that quilt top. You know we're having folks over to start on your sister's wedding quilt."*

Amanda frowned. "She's not even courting anyone yet!"

Her mother stopped and turned to look at Amanda. "She needs to fill that hope chest. One day it will be your turn, and she'll most likely reciprocate!"

Bending her head to the material in her hands, Amanda continued working on the quilt. It wasn't what she wanted to do. She'd much prefer being able to daydream or just go take a nap. But there was no such thing as downtime on an Amish farm. Even in the winter, there was quilting or crocheting to do when the other chores were finished.

She just didn't see what was so evil about idle hands or idle minds. Even the Lord gave the people a day of rest.

The rest of the day was a whirlwind. More interviews, more driving, more crowds. She met people, shook their hands, and just as quickly forgot their names. Everywhere they went, there were photographs taken of Alejandro with fans, alone, sometimes with her. She didn't care for any of it but found peace in the small gestures that Alejandro made. He always made certain she was taken care of and never alone for long. He included her by keeping her by his side and occasionally putting his arm around her waist, and always had a soft word of reassurance to whisper in her ear.

People seemed to smile wherever they went. Everyone greeted Alejandro as if they knew him. At a local television station, a young woman was charged with escorting them through the building. She seemed to gush with enthusiasm, introducing Alejandro to everyone she passed.

It was around two in the afternoon when Alejandro finally collapsed next to her in the limousine. He reached into the ice bucket for a bottle of water and twisted off the cap. He handed it to her, then reached for another.

He sighed and drank from the bottle before leaning back into the seat and rubbing his eyes.

"You are tired, *ja?*"

He glanced at her, then shut his eyes again. "*Sí,* tired."

"You have a long night ahead of you," she pointed out. "Can't you rest?"

Another sigh as he glanced at his watch. "Need to grab a bite to eat, then get over to the stadium. Sound check before the meet and greet at six."

She wondered how he could keep going like this. At every stop, he was on. Viper. Smiling, laughing, cheerful, and polite. The same questions from different people. The same sound bites to give them answers. And always the photographs and crowds. They would travel that night in the bus, leaving San Francisco for Las Vegas, where they would do it all over again. The only good news was that they were staying in a hotel in Las Vegas, and he told her she could sleep late on both mornings.

"I have to let you know that my manager, Mike, is going to be in Los Angeles," Alejandro said, glancing at his cell phone and scrolling through several messages. "He's taking us to lunch."

From his tone, she sensed that there was an underlying message to his words. "Is that a good thing, then?"

Alejandro shrugged. "He's a marketer. That means he looks at everything as an opportunity," he explained, but she didn't really understand what he meant. "And then, Miami!" He smiled to himself, a distant expression on his face as he thought of his Miami home. "A little R & R by the pool, *sí?*"

"R & R?" She didn't know what that meant but figured it must be something right *gut* from the smile that stayed on his face. He looked happy, and she found herself wanting to reach out and touch his hand, to hold it, and feel his arms around her.

"Rest and relaxation."

"Like a Sunday?" she asked, tucking her legs under her as she sat next to him in the limousine.

He laughed. "Like a Sunday, *sí,* only it will be a few days of Sundays strung together."

She pondered that for a moment. She couldn't remember ever having days off, doing nothing. *Idle hands* . . . "What do you do with a string of Sundays, Alejandro?"

Turning his head, he stared at her, his tired smile still on his face. His eyes studied her face, and before she knew it, he'd reached out and brushed his thumb along her cheekbone. The gesture startled her, and she jumped. Yet, rather than pull away, she pressed her cheek against his hand, shutting her eyes and enjoying his touch.

"You are so beautiful, Amanda," he whispered. His eyes flickered over her, taking in her beige long skirt and white silk blouse. Their outfits were matching, and that amused him. With her hair pulled back, she looked older and sophisticated. "Beautiful, *sí*. But inside and out." He leaned over and gently kissed her on the cheek, an affectionate kiss to compliment her innocence. "We will do whatever you wish, Princesa," he finally responded. "But we shall definitely have a fiesta with music and people, food and drink, dancing and singing!" This last part, he said with more energy and life. "We shall celebrate Amanda, the most famous Amish woman in the world!"

"That sounds terrible!" she said, making a face at him.

Once again, he laughed at her. "I suppose it does, *sí?* Well, we shall find *something* to celebrate." His phone rang, and he glanced at it. He checked the caller ID and sighed. "Excuse me, Princesa. I must take this call."

While he conversed on the phone in Spanish, she turned and stared out the window. Buildings flashed by, and she found herself admiring the different types of architecture. Unlike Los Angeles, San Francisco seemed to be full of old-fashioned character, reflected throughout the small buildings skirting the roads they traveled. Some of these roads were hilly and as the car reached a crest, she would enjoy a plunging view of the beautiful San Francisco Bay and marvel at the blue waters of the Pacific Ocean.

Amanda had never seen an ocean before this day, and she caught her breath. She wished that they could go to the beach. She wanted to feel sand under her bare feet, the cool water on her toes. It never crossed her mind to make such a request. She knew that Alejandro had a busy afternoon ahead of him. As for herself, she was tired, too; the jet lag of crossing the country and sleeping in strange places had taken its toll on her. She turned away from the window and shut her eyes, feeling the familiar sting of weariness.

She knew it was past suppertime at home. Her parents would have eaten already, and her father was most likely finishing his evening chores. She wondered if they missed her, and she made a mental note to call them on that strange phone that Alejandro had given to her the other day. Even if she only left a message, she would feel better for reaching out to them to let them know that she was fine, surviving in the world of the Englische.

Englische, she thought, leaning her head against Alejandro's shoulder. When she did, she felt him shift, and he stretched his arm around her, pulling her against him. If this was the world of the Englische, she thought, it wasn't as bad as she had imagined She was surprised at her own ability to adapt, to follow Alejandro's guidance. While she missed some things about the farm, she also felt that her senses were heightened as they traveled from place to place.

She found that she was even looking forward to the concert that evening, although her ears were still ringing from the previous night. In her mind, she could still see Alejandro on the stage, singing and dancing to entertain all of those adoring fans. He was truly a different person onstage, his clothing soaked in sweat by the time the concert was over. She knew that he gave the audience everything he had during the show, and she admired him for how hard he worked.

When they arrived back at the stadium, Alejandro walked her to the bus and told her he'd return before the show if she wanted to take a short nap. Then, with a quick kiss planted on her lips, he turned and hurried to a small group of men waiting for him by the entrance. Inside the bus, Amanda watched from the window as he embraced several of them, clapping them on the shoulders in a gesture of warmth and familiarity. Without looking back, they walked through the open doors and inside the building.

She *was* tired, but she couldn't sleep. Her mind was in a whirl, overstimulated for sure and certain. She sat on the sofa in the front of the bus and sighed as she looked around. One week ago, her life had been so different. True, she had been at the farm and the paparazzi had been ruining the lives of her family and community. But never could she have imagined how much her life would have changed in just a few short days.

From Philadelphia to Los Angeles to San Francisco, and next to Las Vegas and then Miami? Some of these cities she had never even heard of! There were new sights and sounds, smells and foods. Even the mobs of people interested her, despite Amanda not fully understanding the crowd's fascination with Alejandro. Or with her, for that matter.

At one of the radio stations that morning, she had caught sight of several magazines and newspapers on one of the tables. They were opened to different sections and pages, but all were about Alejandro. He had laughed when she pointed it out and just mentioned that the people were probably reading them to catch up on the latest gossip before the interview. But then her eyes fell on the photos of herself.

"Alejandro!" she had gasped, reaching for the paper. "That's me!"

He had glanced up from his cell phone and peeked over her shoulder. "*Sí,* it is," he said, returning to his text messages. "You are America's darling right now, Amanda. Get used to it."

She didn't think she could ever get used to it.

"Why does everyone stop and stare at us?" Aaron had asked her when she was driving the buggy to the general store for an order of food for her mother. Mamm needed flour, sugar, pickling spices, and beans, so Amanda had offered to go in her place. Once Aaron had heard that Amanda was hitching up the horse to the buggy, he had scurried out of afternoon chores to help her, begging and pleading to ride along.

Now, as they were driving down the road, he had asked the question that had perplexed Amanda for years. Why did the tourists find the Amish so fascinating? Why did so many people clog the streets of Lititz and the surrounding communities each spring, summer, and fall?

Even driving the horse and buggy down the road was an issue. Some tourists grew irritated when they were slowed down on their journey because of the buggies. The winding roads of Lancaster County were not conducive to passing other vehicles, especially during the tourist season. So when they finally could pass, they often tried to cut off the buggies as if retaliating for the delay in their busy day.

"Oh, Aaron," she said, smiling. "We're just different from them."

"So they stare at us?"

Amanda laughed. "Don't we often stare at them with their silly clothing and funny hats?"

He giggled at that. "Ja, *that is true."*

"Don't worry," she said. "You get used to it eventually, and at some point, you stop noticing it."

Amanda managed to take a short nap. It felt strange to sleep during the day. The only time she had ever done such a thing was on those rare occasions when she had a cold in the winter or a summer flu.

In the bedroom that was at the back of the bus, she had shut the curtains, and with the room so dark, sleep had finally overtaken her. It was a deep sleep, and when she finally awoke, she couldn't clear her head to fully wake up. It took her a moment to remember where she was and what she was doing there.

San Francisco, she thought as she awoke.

She stretched as she got out of bed and opened the curtains. She could barely make out the blue sky overhead. The bus was behind a gated barrier so that the general public could not disturb the crew of the traveling Viper show.

Amanda rubbed the back of her neck and made her way to the bus door. She just wanted to feel the sunshine on her face. She wasn't used to being inside so much. She was starting to feel as trapped as if she were back at the farm, cowering inside the house as she hid from the paparazzi.

Outside, she covered her eyes from the blinding brightness of the sun. Even though it was starting to dip in the sky, it was still strong, especially after she had just awakened from a nap. Shutting her eyes, she lifted her face toward the sun and felt the warmth on her skin. For a moment, she was transported back to the farm and standing in a large field, the cows grazing nearby and the sound of a buggy rolling down the street at the end of the lane.

"It's her!"

She snapped out of her daydream and looked in the direction of the voices. People were gathered by the gate and taking her photo. Amanda frowned and looked away. The solitude of the moment was gone, just like that.

Uncertain about what to do, she wandered away from the gate and toward the open doors through which Alejandro had disappeared earlier. The guard nodded his head and let her pass without asking any questions. Inside was a corridor with doors along each side. She could hear music coming from the end of the hallway, so she walked in that direction.

Inside the stadium, she stood by herself among the empty chairs. On the stage, the band was tuning their instruments, and she could see Alejandro talking with several men and a woman. She sat down in a seat and smiled to herself as she watched him interacting with the people. A touch on the arm for one, his head tossed back in laughter at another.

"Check! Check! One, two, three, four!"

She saw Alejandro lift his hand to his ear and tilt his head. He nodded and said something to the man next to him, then he walked away, toward the center of the stage. He was in command, totally in charge as he directed the different people, and then, with a wave of his hand, the music started and he began to sing to the empty stadium.

She watched him, curious about how it felt to stand there, before the thousands of seats, and know that in just a few hours every seat would be occupied by an adoring fan. Shutting her eyes, she remembered the evening before with the music and the people and the lights. It had been magical, and she saw that Alejandro had a true gift from God. He touched people's lives in a way that she had never imagined possible. Through music, she realized with amazement. Music.

Yet, at the same time, she was beginning to see that it was more than just the music. It was also the man. From the way that he moved onstage to how he interacted with people one-on-one, Alejandro was always on and always performing. Nothing was too much trouble. He'd pause for photographs and autographs and just a kind word for someone on the streets.

As the song ended, she noticed Carlos cross the stage and whisper something to Alejandro. He waved his arm at the band and said something that Amanda couldn't hear. Within minutes, Alejandro was walking off the stage and grabbing a bottle of water that Carlos handed to him.

She felt something vibrate in the pocket of her dress. Her cell phone. She reached for it, turning it over in her hands as she looked at the screen. A message was there from Alejandro.

```
Where are you?
V
```

She frowned, wondering how to respond. She pressed several buttons but nothing happened. It asked for a lock code, and she couldn't remember what Alejandro had told her the number was.

"Stupid thing," she mumbled, starting to stand up so that she could try to find him. She certainly didn't want to cause him any unnecessary worry.

It vibrated again.

```
I see you.
Stay where you are.
I'm coming.
V
```

She looked around, wondering how he had found her. But she didn't question his instruction, so she sat down, the cell phone back in her pocket. She really needed to get him to spend time with her so that she could figure out how to use it.

"What are you doing sitting here by yourself, Princesa?" he asked as he emerged from the hallway behind her. He smiled as he crawled over the seat and sat next to her. "Wow," he said, looking around. Kicking his feet up so that they rested on the back of the chair in front of him, he put his hands behind his head. "I don't see this vantage point too often! Impressive."

She followed his gaze. He was staring at the massive stadium and the seats, empty now. The stage was large and oppressive in such a setting. Later, when the seats were filled and Viper was dancing and singing on it, the stage would be exciting and powerful.

"This is all for you," she said, her tone matter-of-fact and without a hint of bravado. "I wonder, though, how that makes you feel."

He frowned at her question, his eyes narrowing as if in deep thought. "I ask myself that question frequently," he admitted. "Grateful? Appreciative? Humbled?"

"Really?" She turned to face him, for his choice of words had surprised her. "I'm glad to hear that."

Now it was his turn to raise an eyebrow. "Why is that, Princesa?"

For a short moment, she looked around at the stadium. In her mind, she could imagine the people cheering for him as he entertained them. While this was a whole new world for her, she also could sense the dangers that came with it. "I can imagine that all of this attention could really change a person," she said. "Maybe some people take it for granted after a while."

"Hmm," he replied, nodding his head slowly as if thinking about what she had said. "It has been known to happen, *sí*."

Suddenly, she turned to him, facing him as she asked the burning question on her mind. "So how do you keep it balanced, Alejandro? How do you stay humbled?" The question was asked with innocent curiosity, and she could see from his expression that he wasn't exactly certain how to respond.

Finally, he did, with two simple words: "I remember."

"You remember? You remember what?"

He took a deep breath and exhaled slowly. "Everything, Princesa. I remember everything, and that keeps me focused on doing what I do for the people who love the music." He stretched his one arm over his head and laid it casually across the back of her seat. His eyes continued to study the empty arena. "I remember the struggles. I remember the poverty. I remember how hard my mother worked to put food on the table. I remember the street fights, the hustling, the things I don't ever want to tell you about."

"You can tell me anything," she said softly. "I'd never judge you."

"Not these things," he said firmly. "But I also remember that one thing got me through all of that. One thing got me to where I am today. One thing is all that matters above all others."

She waited for him to share that one thing with her. But he remained silent. "What is it, Alejandro?"

He chewed on his lower lip, casting a quick glance at her before he nodded his head, as if agreeing with himself to share it with her. "God."

Chapter Eight

The MGM Grand Hotel in Las Vegas was unlike anything she could have ever imagined. It was large and bright, with lights and sounds and people everywhere. With security guards walking beside them, Alejandro guided Amanda through the lower lobby and casino to the elevators. People were sitting at the slot machines, feeding coin after coin into them before pressing buttons. Lights rang, bells chimed, and voices surrounded them.

Some people looked up and noticed the small entourage walking through the casino. Others didn't bother. They were too interested in the blinking lights and clanging beeps of the machines before them.

A few people approached Alejandro, begging to take a photo. He obliged a few of them, posing with the fans flanked on either side. Amanda waited patiently beside the security guards and simply shook her head when people asked to take her photo. Some respected that. Others paid her no attention and took the photograph anyway.

The night before, they had arrived at Las Vegas at three in the morning, having taken a private jet from San Francisco right after the show. Faced with a seven-hour drive ahead of them on the bus,

Alejandro had preferred to fly to Las Vegas, especially later at night when they would be less noticed by the guests at the hotel.

He had all but carried Amanda from the car to the hotel. She was exhausted, leaning against him. She had never stayed up so late nor had she ever felt the bone weariness that overcame her body.

They were staying in the Skylofts, a private two-floor loft with sweeping views of the city. He had led her up the stairs to the bedroom, and she collapsed on the bed, curling her legs up as she nestled into the pillow. She had heard him chuckle as he took off his tie and tossed it onto the lounge chair next to the bed. She simply didn't care. She needed sleep.

When she had awoken in the morning, she was surprised to find him sleeping next to her. Somehow he had managed to remove her shoes and get her under the sheets. But she was completely dressed in the long skirt and white silk blouse that she had worn the day before. He, however, was wearing a sleeveless white undershirt, his one arm over his head as he slept.

She had watched him for a moment, her heart swelling at the sight of Alejandro asleep in the bed next to her. She noticed his tattoos on his arms, so many of them. Words in Spanish, musical notes, and even an image of a snake. She reached her hand out to touch them, gently tracing a line along the dark-blue ink. She hadn't remembered him joining her. Frankly, she knew that there was another bedroom, and she wondered why he hadn't slept there.

Quietly, she had stolen out from under the sheets and got out of the bed. She glanced at the clock on the dresser, surprised to see that it was almost noon. She felt guilty for having slept away half of the day. She wondered if she should wake up Alejandro but decided against it. Surely he was overly tired, too.

She had wandered around the suite, peeking over the railing to the open sitting area beneath her. Everything was very large and grand but also very contemporary. Another first, she thought. She wasn't certain if she liked that type of decorating, being used to more country furniture, which was comfortable and homey. She felt as if this room looked cold and sterile.

By the time Alejandro had awoken and hustled down the stairs, she had already showered and changed and was snacking on a platter of fresh grapes that someone had left on the long table in the dining area. He smiled at her as he straightened his red handkerchief in the pocket of his black shirt. "You slept well, *sí?*"

She had nodded, smiling back at him. *"Sí,"* she teased.

"¡Ay!" He had laughed and walked over to her, leaning down to kiss her forehead. "You are beautiful this morning, Amanda."

"Afternoon," she had gently corrected.

He had responded by glancing at his watch and caught his breath. "I see that. We must go before we are late."

"Go?"

"Sound check, quick rehearsal, dressing, then the VIP meet and greet," he had said, hurrying to a leather bag on the sofa. Amanda hadn't noticed it there earlier. He opened it and reached for his phone, quickly checking the text messages.

Now, as they walked through the MGM Grand, Amanda couldn't help but stare at the strange people and machines, seeing the lights blinking and listening to the noises. There were no windows in the casino, and most of the people sat alone. She couldn't imagine why anyone would want to use those slot machines, relying on chance.

The room over the barn was filled with people, all of their eyes focused on the five men standing before them. Just the week before, one of their ministers had passed away. It had been unexpected, a simple heart attack in his sleep. A peaceful way to be called home to the Lord.

At the next church service, the members were selecting a new minister. Each member had walked up to the bishop and whispered into his ear the name of a person who they recommended for the task. A short tally would produce five to seven candidates who would be called to the front of the room.

The bishop had five books on the table. The Ausbund. It was the hymnbook used by the church for singing, the oldest-known hymnbook in existence. Inside one of the books was a slip of paper. The five candidates had to choose a book and peer inside. The one who found the paper was now the new minister, a lifelong position that affected both him and his family. It was often a position that was met with tears of humility at the great burden that lay ahead.

Amanda had sat next to her mother, peering at the men. Each one was sweating and pale, nervously shifting his weight as, with a trembling hand, he reached out for one of the books. The first three men opened the book and nothing fell out. There was a sense of relief on their faces while the other two men began to glance at their wives.

The fourth man reached out to take a book, hesitated, and changed his mind. He grabbed the other book and opened it.

A single piece of white paper fluttered through the air and to the ground.

Silence in the room.

The new minister had been selected by God. It was his will that had led the man to select that particular book.

The new man fell to his knees and covered his face, weeping.

The rest of the afternoon passed no differently from the previous day in Los Angeles. At the VIP meet and greet, Amanda stood to the side of the room, looking at the lines of people who had paid hundreds, if not thousands, of dollars just to meet Viper and have their photos taken with him. She couldn't help but watch with a mixture of amusement and curiosity as Viper greeted each person individually and shook their hands, asking them for their names. He addressed them by their name during the rest of the conversation and answered any questions that they had. Some of the women would jump into his arms, kissing his cheeks and holding his hands. Viper would laugh, hugging them back, and on two occasions, he kissed them back, chastely on the lips.

The shyer people, mostly younger fans, would stand in silence before him, their mouths hanging open as they faced their favorite singer. For those fans, Viper would ask them questions such as where they lived and what grade they were in. When they walked away, three of the younger girls had tears of joy streaming down their faces.

What she noticed about his interaction with the fans was the fact that he had something to say to everyone. He made each one of them feel comfortable and important in his presence. His ability to maneuver among the fans, adapting to what they wanted, was amazing to Amanda. She couldn't imagine being so at ease among strangers. She also couldn't believe that this was Viper, a caring man who focused equal attention on each of his fans before the show, a show when he would sing songs about things that were intimate and inappropriate at times, songs that sometimes used language that she had never heard spoken before, and about relationships with women that were as unchristian as could be.

Still, she watched him with adoration in her eyes and love in her heart.

Even more surprising was when a few of the fans approached her, shyly at first, as they whispered to one another and stood before her. Amanda noticed them staring at her and turned her attention from Viper.

"Hello," she managed to say. "Are you having a right *gut* time, then?"

One of the girls, who couldn't have been any more than thirteen, glanced at her friends. "We were hoping that we could have a photograph with you," she asked. Clearly, she was the spokesperson for the others.

"A photograph?" Amanda couldn't imagine why they would want such a thing.

They nodded their heads.

"Vell," she said slowly. At least they had asked, she told herself. "I reckon that it would be all right," she acquiesced reluctantly.

The girls smiled and hurried to stand next to Amanda, but the next problem became clear. Who would take the photo? If one of the girls took it, they would not be in the photo.

"¡Ay, mi madre!" The cheerful voice that approached them could only be Viper. "I see that you ladies have found my Amanda, no? You have talked her into a photo with you? *¡Muy bien!* Let me take the photo, then!" The girls flushed and handed their cameras to him. With great theatrics, Viper began to take their photos and asked them to pose, teasing them as he took photo after photo.

Amanda laughed at his antics, and the three young girls were ecstatic at the attention that Viper had given to them. Some of the other people in the room were recording Viper in action while a few others tried to get into the photos. Before long, he was no longer the center of attention as everyone was clamoring for a photo with Amanda.

By the time that the meet and greet was over, Amanda felt as though she had made new friends, even if she would never see them again. She had been hugged by the younger girls and fawned over by the older ones, who asked her questions about traveling with Viper.

Alejandro took her hand when it was time to leave. He kissed the back of it, then lifted it into the air, a gesture of departure from the gathering in the VIP Lounge. Then, with a broad smile and a wink, he said his good-byes and led her out of the room into his own private dressing room.

When the door shut behind them, he turned to her, his eyes staring at her and assessing the woman before him. For a moment, she panicked. Was he upset that the fans had shifted their adoration from him to her? She hadn't asked for their attention; that was true. But she also knew that this was his show.

He took two strides toward her and reached out, grabbing her by the back of her neck. It didn't hurt, but it was forceful. And it startled her.

He pushed her backward, her back against the wall. With wide eyes, she stared at him, frightened for the briefest of moments. His eyes looked different. They glowed so bright that she wouldn't have been surprised if flames erupted. With his hand still on the back of her neck, he stared down into her face, his expression unreadable and void.

"Alejandro?" she questioned, trying to get a reading on him.

He responded by lowering his mouth onto hers, his lips crushing against hers as he kissed her with a fierceness that reminded her of that day in the buggy, oh so long ago. Unlike that kiss, this one did not end. It lingered and was full of passion that she had never even dreamed of feeling. She felt him pressing against her, trapping her against the wall. Yet, she didn't feel threatened. She felt exhilarated.

When his lips finally left hers, he trailed them along her cheek and down her neck, until his breath was warm against her ear. "Dios *mío,* Amanda," he mumbled. "What are you doing to me?"

She wanted to respond, but her knees felt weak. She was glad that he still held her neck, her body crushed against his. Without that, she might have stumbled from the sheer emotion of the moment. She felt his lips against her ear, and without being able to stop herself, she tilted her head back and shut her eyes. Everything tingled, and her breath was coming in short waves.

"You are so pure," he said softly. "So good. Our worlds are so different and yet . . ." He pulled back and stared down into her face. His thumb traced a line down her cheek and lingered by her lips. "You are finding a way to fit in without even trying. My God," he whispered and leaned his forehead against hers. "You are everything!"

"Alejandro . . ." she started to protest.

"Shh," he said, pressing a finger gently against her lips that were slightly swollen from his kiss. "Don't say it. Don't downplay what just happened."

Not understanding what he meant, she questioned him with her eyes.

"Don't you see?" Alejandro said, laughing as he placed both hands on her cheeks, holding her face gently. "They adore you, and you connected with them! You didn't even try, Amanda. Do you know how special that is? You have a magnetism about you that draws them in."

"That is good?"

He laughed again and nodded. "Perhaps you'll understand one day. But for today, let's share the victory."

His happiness was contagious, and she found herself smiling at him. He kissed her again, this time gently and without making her feel trapped. Although, she realized with a blush covering her cheeks, she hadn't really minded when he had pressed her against the wall. She had been in his arms, and his kiss had told her all that she needed to know, giving her more than she had ever dared to feel.

The knock on the door interrupted the moment. "Security," a voice called out.

Alejandro sighed as if reluctant to open the door and release her into their care. When he did, she felt more at ease, recognizing Mario and TJ waiting to escort her from backstage to the special seats reserved in the fifth row just for them.

"Take care of her," Alejandro instructed Mario as she left the dressing room.

***

The audience at the MGM Grand was just as energized as the crowd from the previous evening. Her entry to the VIP section at the front of the stage created a stir among the audience, and Amanda walked closer to Mario and TJ, grateful for their presence. A few hands reached out to touch her arm as she walked to her seat—an invasive gesture that took her by surprise. But after she was seated, a security guard on either side of her, the attention of the fans returned to the stage.

When the moment came for the concert to start, Amanda felt her pulse quicken again, anticipating the power of his music and the beauty of his dance moves.

The lights dimmed and the crowd began to roar. Amanda tried to make out Alejandro at the top of the stage. It was too dark. Yet, when the lights flashed back on, there he was, standing on the tall platform, his hands modestly crossed behind his back, and his head bent down. He wore a black silk shirt and black slacks—everything dark about him, even his sunglasses, which helped to shield his eyes from the bright lights.

The noise from the audience was deafening. Overhead, on either side of the stage, his image was projected on large screens. She stared at those images, realizing that, indeed, Viper was larger than life. Under the heat of the lights, she could see beads of sweat starting to dot his forehead. By the end of the performance, he would be soaked in sweat, drenched. She knew that from having watched him the night before.

And then the music started, and he began to sing.

Once again, she was amazed at how he transformed. Gone was her Alejandro. In his place was this new man: Viper. Viper, who danced and sang, moved down the stage, jumping onto platforms and reaching out to touch the extended hands of the fans. He laughed. He pointed. He even lifted his glasses and winked at the ladies. He was an entertainer, and they loved every minute of it. In return, she could tell that he was feeding off the energy from the crowd. It was a mutual love affair.

"We should leave now," Mario shouted into her ear. "The last song is next, and he will want to leave right away." Without another word, he touched her elbow and guided her through the dancing people, many who recognized her and took her photograph while they exited.

Once they had slipped through the draped black curtain and passed security, she felt Mario's hold on her arm loosen. He was more relaxed when the crowds weren't around.

She waited in the dressing room, sitting on the sofa and playing with the label on a bottle of chilled water that TJ had handed to her. The dressing rooms weren't as nice as the ones in Los Angeles, a bit smaller and rather plain. She saw that his next outfit was already hanging up, ready for him to get changed into after showering.

Almost ten minutes passed before she heard the door open, and then he rushed in. As she suspected, he was drenched in sweat and looked exhausted. She started to go to him, but he shook his head and held up his hand to stop her. "Give me a minute, Amanda," he said, his voice thick and hoarse. He walked past her into the small bathroom and shut the door behind him.

She heard the shower run and knew that he was washing away the show from his skin. Her heart broke for him, knowing that he must certainly be decompressing after such an energized performance. She took his clothes from the rack and carried them over to the bathroom door, leaning against it while she waited. After a few minutes, the water turned off and she could hear him moving about in the bathroom, sighing as he dried the water from his body.

Softly, she knocked on the door and said, "I have your clothes here, Alejandro."

"Gracias, mi amor."

He opened the door, and she handed the clothes to him, glancing away when she saw his bare arm reach for the hangers. While she had seen the tattoos before, it surprised her when she realized that his one arm was covered in blue ink from the elbow to the shoulder and along his back. She hadn't noticed all of them before, even at the farm, for he always wore long sleeves or an undershirt. Of course, she had seen the ring of music notes that circled his wrist and his one arm, but she hadn't given any thought to the rest of his body and whether he had any more tattoos.

When he finally emerged, he looked fresh and bright, full of energy again. He smiled at her and held out his arms, encouraging her to give him a hug. Holding her, he sighed into her ear. "That's better, *sí?*"

She smiled, even though he couldn't see.

"Did you enjoy the show, Princesa?"

She pulled back and stared at him, her eyes searching his face. "You give them everything, don't you?"

Her response startled him, and he blinked, repeating her words in his head. "I never thought of it that way but *sí,* I think you are right."

"It must be exhausting," she said simply.

He laughed. "Exhausting and exhilarating at the same time. But all that matters to me now is that you enjoyed it!"

"Of course!" she exclaimed. "How could anyone not enjoy it?"

"*¡Bueno!*" He clapped his hands. "Now, we can go party in Vegas, Princesa! I want to show you the bright lights and crazy world that is Las Vegas!"

"I should think you'd want to collapse and sleep!"

He laughed at her. "*¡Ay,* Dios, Princesa*!* No one sleeps in Vegas!"

If she had thought that he was joking with her, she quickly realized that, despite the late hour, Alejandro was more than correct. With security guards trailing them, Alejandro managed to maneuver through the crowd and escape with Amanda into a waiting car. She wanted to ask where they were going, but he gave her a playful tsk-tsk and shook his head.

The driver pulled away from the MGM Grand, and Amanda glanced out the window. That was when she saw it: Las Vegas at night. The buildings were lit up, so the sky was as bright as if it were daytime.

People were everywhere: walking on the sidewalks, crossing the streets, entering and leaving the casinos. As the car pulled past the Luxor Hotel, Amanda gasped at the brilliant beam of light that shot upward from the top of the glass pyramid into the sky.

He laughed at her expressions, her hand pressed against the window as she took in the bright lights and fancy buildings. The car made a turn and drove down another road until they were heading back down the main strip past Caesars Palace, the Mirage, Treasure Island. Alejandro said something in Spanish to the driver and, immediately, the car was pulled to the side of the road.

Alejandro opened the door and helped Amanda out, ignoring the looks from people who were on the sidewalk. He grabbed her hand and hurried across the street so that she could see the pirate ship battle that was just getting ready to begin. He smiled at the people as he moved through the gathering crowd, ignoring their dropped jaws as he positioned himself close enough so that Amanda could see.

"Stand here," he said in a low voice so that only she could hear him. He pulled her in front of him, his arms wrapped protectively around her shoulders.

When the lights flashed onto the ships and the show began, Amanda gasped again and reached up to grab his hand. He laughed and pulled her closer so that her back was pressed against his chest. Neither one seemed to notice the people who began to take their photographs and crowd around them. Instead, they watched the show, oblivious to the attention they were drawing.

The show was almost over when Alejandro began to make his way through the crowd back toward the car, holding Amanda's hand tightly in his own. "*Ven aquí,* Princesa," he murmured into her ear. "It's time to go back to the MGM now that you have seen Las Vegas." He glanced at the crowd. The people were growing excited, and more were taking photos of them, not the pirate ship reenactment. "Besides, I have a special surprise for you back at the suite."

***

Her sister seemed extra happy on Monday morning. She was smiling to herself as she set the table for breakfast. Amanda had helped her father and Aaron with the morning milking, but now, as she washed her hands in the kitchen sink, she noticed the extra spring in her sister's step.

"What's gotten into you, Anna?" she whispered when her sister reached into the cabinet by the sink for glasses.

Anna tried to hide her smile. "I don't know what you mean."

There was no time for Amanda to ask another question as the kitchen door opened and Aaron ran into the room, his cheeks flushed pink and his eyes sparkling. "I'm so hungry!" he said, hurrying to wash his hands. "I sure hope we have biscuits this morning!"

Their mamm *laughed at his enthusiasm. "When do I not have biscuits? Ever happened before?"*

"Sundays!" he replied and his two sisters laughed.

It wasn't until the breakfast dishes were cleared and Aaron was off to school that Amanda had a chance to corner her sister upstairs. "I see that smile," Amanda said. "What are you so happy about?"

Anna bit her lower lip, trying to contain her happiness, but she finally burst out laughing and grabbed Amanda's hand. "You won't ever tell?"

Amanda shook her head. "Nee, *never."*

"Menno Zook brought me home last night after the singing!" Anna exclaimed with a bright smile on her face.

Even Amanda had to gasp at that one. "Menno Zook?" He was the youngest son of Jacob Zook and the last of the Zook kinner *at their farm. It was one of the largest farms in their church district, and since he was unmarried, Menno was an attractive prospect to many a single Amish girl.*

"I was just as surprised as you are! Menno! Can you imagine?"

No, Amanda thought. She couldn't imagine.

If Menno Zook had asked to take Anna home in his buggy, he had something serious on his mind and that was most certainly marriage. It dawned on Amanda that since Anna was almost two years older than she, her sister was almost of the marrying age. In a few years, she would certainly be married, and that meant Anna would leave the house and start her own family. Without Anna around, Amanda would have to do more chores, both inside and outside of the house. Plus, she realized, it would be lonely without Anna.

But as it had been established by the Ordnung some five centuries ago, when her Amish ancestors' beliefs stemmed from the Anabaptists', Amanda needed to fight those thoughts of a personal nature and reflect more on what would make her own sister happy and wholesome. Indeed, feelings of jealousy or envy, if entertained for more than an instant, could easily lead to lack of modesty and to nonconformism; and modesty and conformism were but the two most important pillars sustaining the community. Such were the ways of the Amish.

So instead of saying what she was really thinking, Amanda merely smiled and said, "That's just wunderbar, *Anna."*

When he opened the door and stood back, waiting for her to enter first, she immediately noticed the soft music playing in the background of the suite. Then she noticed the table. It was set with white linens and crystal glasses. At one end, there were two place settings with silver domes covering the plates. In the center of the table was a tall candelabra, the burning candles casting a soft glow. There were people in the room, and from what she could tell, they appeared to be waiting for Alejandro and Amanda.

"What is this, Alejandro?" she whispered.

"It's dinner."

She laughed at him. "It's after midnight!"

He raised an eyebrow and tilted his head toward the table. "I don't see a clock in the room," he teased. "Now, let's sit, Princesa. I think you will be most pleased."

Taking ahold of her arm, he led her across the room and pulled out a chair for her to sit. She felt uncomfortable with the two servers standing there, watching them. But Alejandro appeared oblivious, not even noticing them standing in the background. After she sat down, he took his place next to her at the head of the table. "It's practically a home-cooked meal, no?"

At the same time, the two men approached the table and simultaneously lifted the silver domes. The large white plates underneath were covered with huge red lobsters that were still steaming from being cooked.

"Alejandro!" she gasped and stared at him with wide eyes.

"¿Sí?"

"Lobster?"

He tapped his chin with his finger as if deep in thought. "I seem to recall a young lady who was rather smitten with lobster in New York City and Philadelphia not so long ago."

She burst out laughing at the expression on his face. "You are too much!"

Plucking the linen napkin off the table, he snapped it by his side and laid it across his lap. "You think so?"

She shook her head, still smiling as her eyes danced. "Oh *ja,* I know so!"

He reached across the table and took her hand, holding it for a moment as he stared at her. There was something about his expression, something deep and thoughtful. She felt her heart skip a beat as his fingers entwined with hers. "I would give you this every night," he said softly, his eyes studying her face. "It's yours for the asking."

Her mouth opened, just slightly. She wanted to say something. But no words came out. Instead, she chewed on her lower lip and gently withdrew her hand from his. Delicately, she reached for her own napkin and placed it across her lap, never breaking his gaze. "I would never ask anything of you," she whispered.

One eyebrow arched, and he nodded his head, a hint of a smile playing on his lips. "And that, *mi amor*, is exactly why I would give it to you." Then, taking a quick breath, he pursed his lips and glanced at the plates before them. "For now, I suggest that we get started on these wonderful lobsters. Do you need help opening the claws?"

It amazed her how he could switch like that. One moment, his sultry eyes and soft, gentle voice caused her heart to palpitate and her blood to race through her veins. Yet, just as suddenly, he could turn it off. The only problem was that she couldn't. She felt her heart still racing and knew that her cheeks were flushed. Instead of answering him, she nodded her head and let him reach for her plate.

She watched him crack open the claws, and with a mischievous gleam in his eye, he dipped the meat into the butter and held it out for her. When she reached for it, he tsk-tsked and shook his head. "Remember New York?" he said, a playful tone in his voice. "Shut your eyes, and I shall feed you, Princesa."

"Alejandro . . ." she started to say, but the impish smile on his face stopped her from continuing. Trying to calm her nerves, she did as he commanded, closing her eyes and waiting.

"Now open your mouth, Princesa," he said, his voice husky and deep, an obvious edge to it.

She wanted to argue, to stand her ground. But she remembered, too well, how she had felt in New York City. It seemed as if it had been so long ago instead of just a few short months. She remembered how her world had collapsed when he left. How much life had changed as she sat in the Skylofts, the candles flickering, the music playing, and Alejandro waiting for her to accept his gift.

She opened her mouth and felt him place the lobster on the tip of her tongue. The decadent taste of the lobster heightened her senses. It didn't help that he watched her until she finally swallowed.

"It's good, *sí?*" The words came out like a breath of air, and immediately she opened her eyes. He was watching her, his eyes glowing with excitement.

"I . . . I don't know what to say," she whispered. "This is all too much."

"Nonsense." He dismissed her with a casual wave of his hand. "This is nothing."

"That's not what I meant," she replied. "I feel . . ." She couldn't finish the sentence.

"You feel what, Princesa?"

"Overwhelmed," she admitted. "Everything that is happening is so different, so over the top, so . . . busy and fast."

He shrugged. "I live a fast life, Amanda." Lifting up the lobster claw, he snapped it in half. "But you knew that, didn't you?"

"I never imagined . . ."

He stopped her in midsentence. "How could you have imagined? But the amazing thing is, Amanda, that you are adapting quite well and I think that is what, deep down, bothers you." He shut his eyes as he ate a piece of the claw meat. "*¡Ay, qué rica!*"

"I think I should say good night," she said and started to stand up.

He frowned. "You are upset?"

"Tired," she lied, knowing that God would forgive her this one little lie.

Chapter Nine

When the limousine pulled up in front of the building in Los Angeles, Amanda peered out the window and gasped. The path from the car to the front doors of the all-glass building was lined with a wide red carpet. Both sides of the carpet were roped off with thick gold cords supported by copper posts, and behind them stood crowds with cameras already flashing at the couple's arrival.

Security people wearing black suits lined the carpet for crowd control, and a man wearing a tuxedo and white gloves opened the door to the limousine.

Alejandro looked at Amanda and gave her an encouraging smile before he slid on his sunglasses and stepped out of the car. The people roared and flashes of lights twinkled randomly from the crowd. He straightened his suit jacket and waved to the people. Then, to their delight, he held up his finger as if indicating for them to wait for a moment as he ducked his head back into the limousine.

"Ready, Princesa?" he asked. "This will be a fun night, I promise."

When she placed her hand into his and slid her body on the seat toward the door so that she could step down onto the curb, she heard it. Another roar. It was as if the noise were a wave flooding the waiting fans.

Tonight, she wore a long gown that was both black and beige. The bodice was black and hugged her top, the design flowing down to her tiny waist. The bottom part of the dress was layered in a beige fabric that sparkled. But the most beautiful part was the black lace that ran from the bodice into the skirt, like branches from a weeping willow brushing down her sides.

When she had seen the dress earlier in the day, she had balked. "I can't wear that!" she had exclaimed, horrified at the prospect of wearing something so revealing.

He had laughed at her. "Why ever not, Princesa?"

"It's . . . it's . . ." She hadn't been able to find the words to express what she was feeling. No sleeves? Low cut? Sparkling fabric?

"It's gorgeous," he had said, finishing her sentence for her.

"Indecent," she had snapped, pointing at the neckline. "I believe *that* was the word I was looking for!"

Again he had laughed, clearly amused by her reaction. "For seven thousand dollars, I hope it is not too indecent."

"What?" she had exclaimed when she heard his declaration. She couldn't imagine anyone spending that amount of money on a dress. It was wasteful and much too worldly. "That's outrageous!"

And yet, she was now standing on the red carpet, her hair pulled back in her customary bun at the nape of her neck, wearing that very same indecent dress and all too aware that it showed off every curve of her figure and was, indeed, gorgeous. It was a feeling she had never felt before, and as she watched Alejandro's eyes rove up and down her body, she blushed knowing that she was enjoying this more than she should.

With a moment of planned hesitation, Alejandro stepped aside and let the fans and paparazzi take her photograph. Flashes from the cameras temporarily blinded her, and she flinched as her eyes started to see black spots wherever she looked.

She heard him laugh, and he took a step toward her. He put his hand on the small of her back and leaned down to whisper in her ear. "Now you know why I always wear my sunglasses, *sí?*"

She looked at him and smiled at his little joke, which caused him to laugh again.

That was the photo that went viral on social media: the Amish woman in a $7,000 evening gown, smiling softly at the superstar in his black silk suit, laughing in delight at her reaction to something he had whispered.

As they walked down the red carpet toward the building, which was lit up and crowded with people, Alejandro paused in certain places to wave to the fans. Amanda would stand a step behind him, allowing his adoring fans to have their photos of Viper.

"Viper!" someone called out in a large roped-off area. "A moment of your time!"

He glanced over and lifted his chin in acknowledgment. He reached for Amanda's hand and led her in that direction. A woman stood there with a microphone while a man behind her, with a camera on his shoulder, filmed Viper's approach.

"You're looking dapper as ever this evening," the woman gushed into the microphone as she stood next to Viper.

He twitched his shoulders and smiled at her. "*Gracias,* Kaitlyn!" He took a step to the side and pulled Amanda closer. "Have you met Amanda yet?" The way her name rolled off his tongue sent a shiver up her spine, despite the fact that it was hot outside.

The woman turned to Amanda, her eyes wide and glowing. "You know that I haven't, but I'm delighted to meet the young woman who has captured the hearts of America."

Amanda blushed and averted her eyes.

Viper laughed at her modesty. "And mine," he added, his voice teasing but seductive.

Kaitlyn raised an eyebrow and glanced into the camera. "No speculation there, Viper!" They both laughed while Amanda blushed and took a step backward. Kaitlyn quickly changed the subject, as she knew her time was limited. "You are up for a big award tonight, Viper. How are you feeling about that?"

Amanda frowned and looked at him. An award? She had known that it was an award dinner, but she didn't know that he was receiving one.

"*Sí,* a big award. I'm honored," he said, laying his hand flat on his chest and taking a slight bow, the motion sincere. "Without my fans, I wouldn't be here. So, in fact, this award would be for all of them."

When they finally continued down the red carpet, Amanda reached out to touch his arm. He glanced at her. "You are up for an award?" she asked. "For what?"

"Male Latino Artist of the Year."

"But you don't paint!" she exclaimed with a smile, teasing him.

He laughed at her, happy with her gentle teasing, which he took as a subtle indication that she was feeling more comfortable in her new environment *"Ay,* Princesa.*"* He shook his head, clicking his tongue as they approached the door. "That, I most certainly do not." He leaned over and pressed a soft kiss on the side of her head, then gestured for her to walk before him into the building.

Once inside, she was surprised to see hundreds of people, the men wearing fancy suits or tuxedos and the women in gowns both long and short. People smiled at them as they walked through the crowd, and a few stopped to exchange a handshake or even a friendly hug with Alejandro. And all of those people stared at Amanda, waiting for an introduction. Within thirty minutes, she estimated that she had met twenty of them, none for whom she could remember a name. The one thing that did stick in her mind was the way that the men raised an eyebrow when they met her and how several of the women had all but sneered at her, clearly not impressed or not wishing to show their own envy of Amanda's position in Viper's life.

"*Ven,* Princesa," he murmured in her ear. "We must take our seats."

They were escorted to a special section of the dining hall. Round tables were covered with white cloths, and three-foot-high vases were filled with gorgeous white flowers. The people who were nominated for awards were seated toward the front so that they wouldn't have to walk as far to accept the award, should they win.

There were several other people already seated at their table when they arrived. Alejandro greeted all of them and introduced Amanda. He would whisper in her ear that the younger man, Justin Bell, was nominated for New Artist of the Year, while the woman at his side was an actress on a television show for children and teenagers. There were also three other couples at the table, including another Latino—a rapper known as Dricke Ray, and two African American singers who Viper apparently knew very well.

All of their dates looked like models with long legs and wavy hair that hung down their backs. Their makeup was heavy yet beautiful. For the first few minutes, it was all Amanda could do not to stare, feeling inferior in her own appearance.

Pride. The word whispered through her mind, and she immediately felt ashamed. She had never cared about her appearance before now. How quickly she had forgotten all that she had learned throughout her life! What was important was not how she looked, but that she honored God. Even in Los Angeles, she could continue to honor God and not give in to the worldly ways of the Englische.

Or could she? She glanced around the room at the crystal chandeliers and magnificent floral arrangements. Where was God in all of this? She felt lost, and for the first time that day, she realized that she missed home.

"Amanda," Alejandro purred into her ear. "Have a sip of your champagne."

She turned to look at him. "My what?"

He handed her a tall fluted glass with a pale, bubbling liquid in it. At the bottom was a juicy red strawberry. "Champagne," he said. "You will like it."

Obediently, she took the glass and stared at it. "Is that a strawberry?" she asked, amazed. "I've never seen such a thing!"

Several people at the table snickered, and Alejandro laughed. "It is good," he insisted and urged her to take a sip.

When she did, she immediately noticed the bubbles. They tickled the back of her throat and almost made her want to sneeze. The taste of the liquid was not fruity as she expected, although she did taste something sweet about it. To her surprise, she did like it. "It is *gut!*" she said, smiling at him. "It's different but right *gut!*"

He touched her free hand and lifted it to his lips. "Just sip it, Princesa," he whispered.

"Charming," Dricke said and leaned over toward Amanda. "You are liking Los Angeles, no?"

She nodded her head. "Oh *ja,*" she said. "It's ever so much better than that Las Vegas!"

Several people at the table laughed at her statement.

"And why is that?" Dricke said politely.

"I don't think gambling is good," she admitted. "Those people should be at home with their families, not sitting in front of those noisy machines losing their money."

"Ah," Dricke said. "But some people find that to be entertainment!"

Amanda frowned. "How odd! I see nothing entertaining about giving away your money!"

Again, the people at the table laughed. Or, rather, the men laughed and the woman with Justin Bell laughed. But the other women rolled their eyes and looked away. It was clear that they didn't care much for Amanda's innocence and saw nothing amusing about her fresh perspective on what they so often took for granted.

"I agree with you!" the woman next to Justin Bell said. Her name was Celinda Ruiz. She had large brown eyes and thick black hair. The smile on her face was the only genuine one that Amanda had seen come her way from a woman that evening. Immediately, Amanda knew that she liked Celinda, and for the first time, wondered if she might actually find a friend in this strange world of Alejandro's.

For the next hour, the four-course meal was served by men wearing white gloves, who greeted each guest by name. Amanda was stunned when the waiter called her Ms. Beiler; she whispered to Alejandro, wondering how he knew who she was.

"They all know who everyone is here," he responded quietly so that no one else would overhear. "That's their job. To make us all feel like VIPs . . . very important people," he explained.

It was after the plates were taken away and the tables cleared that the award ceremony began. Amanda watched in earnest from the beginning but soon lost interest as to what was happening on the raised stage in the front of the room. She watched the people, instead. Polite applause for each named nominee, and loud bursts of applause for the winners. Those who did not win smiled and accepted their loss with grace, while those whose name was ultimately called seemed to act surprised and humbled by the honor of receiving the award.

When it was time for the MC to announce the Latino Artist of the Year, Amanda was surprised to learn that Dricke Ray, seated to her left, was also up for that award. She glanced at him, then at Alejandro, wondering if they felt competitive toward each other. That was one reason that the Amish didn't have competitions like this. It set one over the rest, which could cause resentment.

However, she saw no indication that Dricke Ray or Alejandro held a grudge against each other.

"And the winner of the Latino Artist of the Year is . . ." A moment of silence filled the room while the MC struggled with an envelope.

He opened it and glanced down at whatever was written on the paper inside before he smiled and leaned into the microphone. "Viper!"

The room all at once burst into applause, and Alejandro smiled for the photographers who hurried to take his picture. He leaned over and placed a soft kiss on Amanda's cheek before he stood up. Dricke Ray stood, too, and gave Alejandro a friendly embrace before Alejandro strode toward the stage, pausing to shake hands with two other people along the way.

Amanda watched as he climbed the steps to the podium, shook the hand of the MC, and accepted the small crystal statue. He glanced at it, then smiled at the crowd.

"Gracias," he said, and the applause died down. "*Gracias* to *mi gente* for this award." He held it up, his eyes taking it in for a long, drawn-out moment. It was clear that he was moved by the honor of receiving the recognition of his peers and the industry. "For this honor, I especially thank God, who led me down this path and showed me the way from the streets to the stage. And I couldn't have gotten here without my fans. Without my fans, there would be no Viper." He paused and glanced around the room until his eyes fell on Amanda. And he smiled. "Life has a funny way of changing in a moment's notice. Embrace change and enjoy life, *mis amigos*. I do!" He lifted the award up. *"¡Muchas gracias!"* he said, thanking them one more time before he stood back from the podium and waved at the crowd.

He was escorted off the stage, and the MC was soon announcing the nominations for the next category.

It was almost thirty minutes later before he reappeared. He sat down next to Amanda and reached over to take her hand in his. She smiled at him and whispered, "Congratulations!"

He squeezed her hand and returned the smile. "Not bad for a little *chico* from Cuba, no?" She could tell that he was pleased as well as a little overwhelmed. His humility did not go unnoticed.

After the awards dinner, Alejandro informed her that they were invited to an after-hours party. She wasn't quite certain what that meant. Hadn't they just spent the night at a party? But from the eager look on his face and the way that the other men at the table were talking with him, she knew that it was important to him.

"Did you enjoy yourself tonight, Amanda?"

Amanda turned around and found Celinda Ruiz standing behind her. She was adjusting the back of her dress and smiling, her teeth brilliantly white and her face glowing. Amanda imagined that Celinda was much older from the sophisticated way she carried herself. But, once again, she found herself drawn to Celinda.

"It was right *gut, ja,*" she said softly.

"I love your accent," Celinda said and touched Amanda's arm in a friendly gesture. "It's so . . . so . . ."

"Amish?" Amanda offered.

Celinda laughed. "Actually, I was going to say honest."

Amanda blushed. "I'm ever so sorry. I just don't know how to talk to such worldly people," she said, her eyes downcast. "It's so much to take in. Everything is so different."

Linking her arm with Amanda's, Celinda led her away from the small group that had gathered in the lobby while they waited for their cars. "Amanda, you are doing fine," Celinda said. "Trust me. I grew up in this business, and I know it can be hard. To come from your background and be thrust into the limelight?" She shook her head. "It's remarkable, really. I think that's why the public is so fascinated with you."

They stopped walking by one of the windows. Outside, crowds still gathered behind the cordoned off entrance to the building, the darkness lit up from the glow of the fans holding their cell phones in the air in the hopes of capturing a photo of a celebrity. As people began to leave, the mob clamored for their photographs. For a moment,

Celinda stared outside as she stood next to Amanda. They watched the crowds and the flashing lights.

"You know," she started slowly, "you and I are similar."

This surprised Amanda and she turned to look at her new friend. "I cannot begin to imagine how!" she exclaimed, but she was smiling.

Celinda nodded. "Oh yes. We are both in the spotlight, not just because of who we are but because of who we love." She paused for a moment and lifted her chin, obviously aware that someone was photographing her with Amanda. "Justin and I have been dating for over a year. I'm the most hated woman among teenage girls in America." Despite the harsh words, she laughed. "You, on the other hand, have captured the attention of Viper, the hottest Latino singer in the world. Yet, surprisingly, you remain the darling of America. But that might not always be."

"I don't really know what that means," Amanda confessed.

"It means people like you. The fans," she explained. "And that's good. But remember, they might like you today, but it could change without any notice. Be careful."

The warning was not ominous, but it gave Amanda a moment to pause and think. How could these people like her so much when they knew nothing about her? Yet, according to Celinda, they could just as easily stop liking her for no apparent reason.

"Why do they hate you?" Amanda asked, her eyes wide and curious. *Hate* was a word she had never really heard used before, not among her community.

Celinda shrugged and glanced over at Justin, who was talking with five young men. "I suppose because I have him, and they don't. It ruins the fantasy for these girls." She looked back at Amanda. There was a soulful look in her eyes. "It's all about the fantasy. I've been to Justin's concerts, and the young girls actually weep during his performances. Can you imagine?"

Certainly, Amanda could not.

"Justin having a girlfriend ruins the fantasy," Celinda stated matter-of-factly.

"Amanda." He had approached her from behind, and she heard him breathe her name before she felt his hand touch her shoulder. She looked up and smiled when she saw Alejandro standing there. He was holding his award, and despite his dark sunglasses hiding his eyes, she knew that he was staring at her. "You are ready, no?"

"Ja." She nodded.

They parted company with Celinda and headed toward the door. Once again, they found themselves on the red carpet and walking toward the limousine that was parked at the end of it, waiting for them in order to take them to the after-hours party.

But Amanda was tired. She sat next to Alejandro in the limo and, taking a deep breath, ventured to ask the question that was on her mind. "Do you think I might return to the hotel room, Alejandro? I'm ever so tired, and I don't think an after-hours party is something that's for me."

For a moment, he didn't answer. She could see a muscle tighten in his jaw. Disappointment. Still, as he stared at her from behind his glasses, she could feel his resolve breaking down. It was his turn to sigh. He reached up and took off his glasses. "You know that I have to go, *sí?*"

"Sí," she said sincerely.

"¿Sí?" The corner of his mouth twitched as he fought a smile. "Did you just say *sí?*"

"I did," she said, just as amazed as he was.

"No . . . *ja?*" When she didn't answer, he laughed. "You have changed, Amanda Beiler. I will get you speaking Spanish yet!"

"I don't think one word is any indication that I could ever be fluent in Spanish," she said, but her tone was light. "You speak it far too fast for me to pick up anything."

He reached over and brushed his fingers across her cheek. "I was glad you were there tonight," he said as his eyes studied her face. "Everyone was enthralled with you, Princesa." The way that the word *enthralled* rolled off his lips sent a shiver down her spine. She shut her eyes and felt him lean forward to softly brush his lips against hers. "I will miss your company tonight," he whispered.

She didn't respond.

The driver dropped him off first, and Alejandro reluctantly left her alone in the car. She heard him instructing the driver to not only drop her off at the hotel but to escort her safely inside. Then he leaned into the open car door and stared at her for a moment. "I don't like leaving you, Princesa," he stated. "You will text me when you get to the hotel room, *sí?*"

"Ja." She nodded, not entirely certain she'd be able to figure it out. But she would try.

With a wink and a smile, he shut the door and disappeared into the night, the tinted windows of the car shielding her from the flashing cameras of the paparazzi and adoring fans that fawned over Alejandro. Within minutes, the limo was moving again and she was alone in Los Angeles, the farthest place on earth from Lancaster County, Pennsylvania. She leaned her head back against the seat and, after kicking off her shoes, sighed.

The question floated through her mind: Do I miss the farm? In many ways, she did. She missed the quiet of the early-morning hours with birds chirping and the creaking of the metal windmill. She missed the noise of the cows chewing their cud while they waited to be milked. She missed the smell of freshly cut grass and freshly baked bread.

Yet, she had to admit that she was enjoying her adventure. New sights, new sounds, new smells. Alejandro's attention also added another degree of excitement to her life. He was attentive and kind, gentle and protective. She felt safe near him, even when her heart pounded so fiercely inside her chest when he was near.

Danger, she warned herself. Yes, as much as she felt safe near him, she also knew that she was in danger. Her heart was in danger. Her future was in danger. Her ability to possibly return to the Amish way of life was in danger. She shut her eyes and sighed. It worried her that she was adapting so quickly to life with Alejandro among the Englische. How would she ever return to her family's ways?

Chapter Ten

It had surprised her that she had awoken alone in the hotel room. True to his word, Alejandro had arranged for her to have an adjoining room, her own private space next to his suite. She had half expected that he would venture into her room when he returned at night, perhaps crawl into bed to hold her as he had for the past few nights.

But when she awoke, not only was she alone, but the door between their rooms was shut. Someone had closed it during the night.

The sun was just cresting over the buildings and casting an orange glow in the room. She padded over to the window and pulled back the shades. It was a beautiful morning with not one cloud in the crystal-clear blue sky. She wanted to feel the sun on her face and breathe in the fresh air. A walk, she thought. Just a short one while Alejandro was sleeping.

Fifteen minutes later, she was dressed and riding the elevator downstairs. It was quiet that early in the morning, and she told herself that she would just walk down the street a little bit, get some exercise. She missed the long walks down the lane at home, whether to a neighboring farm or to visit a friend. Although, she admitted, she hadn't had much ability to do that during the past few months since her return from Ohio.

On the street, she looked around and decided to walk away from the sun. Cars drove by, but the roads weren't too busy. It felt good to be alone and walking, just her thoughts to occupy her.

She wondered at what time Alejandro had returned to the hotel. The previous evening, when he hadn't returned by midnight, she had found her phone and couldn't figure out how to turn it on. After struggling with it for a while, she had finally carried it downstairs to the front desk and asked someone for help. Several people had smiled at her while one man gave her a quick lesson in how to use the smartphone.

"Just type his phone number here," he instructed.

"*Ja vell*, I don't know his phone number," she had replied.

The man had tried to suppress his smile as he showed her how to find it in the contacts list on the phone. It was easy to find since it was actually the only number listed in the phone. "After you select it, just type your message using the keys."

"Those little things? How do I do that, then?" she asked, still not understanding what he meant.

"Look, the easiest thing to type is a heart. Click the left bracket key and the number three. Just use your finger to push the small buttons," the man had said.

"Oh help," she muttered, trying to do as he instructed. When she finally did it, she stared at the strange figure: <3. "How is *that* a heart?" she had asked the man.

"Trust me," he had laughed. "Now click 'Send.' That little button at the bottom."

"Like this?" she had asked, doing as he instructed.

The phone made a soft pinging noise, and the man nodded. "Sent! Congratulations on sending your first text!"

She frowned, staring at the phone. "A bracket and the number three make a heart? That seems like Englische foolishness to me," she mumbled, still not quite understanding.

Yet, seconds later, she had heard a louder ping and a message flashed across the screen:

<3 back at you, Princesa.
LOL
V

She started at the noise, delighted that something had happened with the phone, but as her eyes tried to decipher the message, she looked back at the man. "I don't understand," she said and turned the phone around so that he could read it.

The woman behind the counter had taken the opportunity to stare over the man's shoulder and began to giggle. "He replied to you, dear!"

"He did?" Amanda had flipped the phone back around and stared at the message. "I can't read that."

"He sent you a heart back and signed it 'LOL,' which means laughing out loud. I imagine the *V* stands for Viper," the man had explained.

The woman raised an eyebrow. "Perhaps LOL stands for *lots of love*," she teased. The man had cast a stern look at the woman and she took a step backward.

"So it's in code?" Amanda had asked. "How am I supposed to know what he meant, then?"

Several of the guests were returning from their evening out and had stopped to watch the scene. They laughed at her delight in receiving a text and chuckled when they overheard her comments.

That had been at midnight. Now it was seven in the morning, and she was alone, walking the streets of Los Angeles while he slept in, having most certainly returned home later in the early-morning hours.

It was too beautiful of a morning to sleep in, she thought as she lifted her face to the warmth of the rising sun. Ahead of her was a park with tall palm trees and walking paths. She headed in that direction, happy to see some wide-open green spaces with pretty flowers and birds. She walked along the pebble-stone paths, listening to the crunching noise under her shoes.

When she saw a park bench ahead, she sat down and quickly kicked off her shoes. She missed walking barefoot as she had on the farm. Shoes were too constricting, especially these that Lucinda made her wear. Chunky heels made her feel as though she was walking on her tippy-toes, and the front of the shoes pinched her toes. Barefoot is better, she thought as she leaned down to pick up her shoes.

She carried her shoes in one hand as she walked along the path. Several early-morning joggers ran past her, most of them smiling at her and one even greeting her with a happy "Good morning!"

It felt good to walk, unrestricted by people crowding her or wanting to take her photo. It felt even better to be outside and alone with her thoughts. She watched several squirrels foraging in the mulch under a tree. One stole a nut from another, and they began chasing each other on the ground until disappearing up the trunk of the tree.

"Hey! Aren't you that Amish girl?" someone asked from behind her.

Amanda turned around, startled to see a young man and woman in jogging attire behind her. They were running in place but stopped when she faced them. At first, she didn't respond. She hadn't given much thought to being noticed without Alejandro beside her. He seemed to travel with crowds of people following him.

"You are her!" The woman looked at the man beside her. "It's her!"

"I best be going," Amanda mumbled and started to walk away, heading back in the direction from which she had originally come. But she could hear the people behind her talking to someone else who was walking by. Before she knew it, there was a small group of people following her, just five people, but they were murmuring and pointing at her.

She should have known better and she berated herself as she hurried along the path. She had thought no one would notice her. She had thought she could handle being alone in a big city like Los Angeles. Now she was being followed by a small group of curious people, which, when she glanced over her shoulder, was creating more of a stir among others.

"Just one photograph!" someone called out.

Amanda quickened her pace, fighting the urge to cry. She just wanted to get back to the hotel, back to the safety of her room. She said a quick prayer to God, hoping that he was listening and it was his will to answer.

"Need some help, ma'am?"

She looked up, both surprised and relieved to see a police officer walking toward her. Never in her life had she interacted with a man of the Englische law. But under the current circumstances, she was more than willing to ask for assistance. "I just want to get back to my hotel," she said softly, avoiding his eyes. "I didn't want to cause a scene."

The officer glanced over her shoulder at the gathering crowd. They had stopped thirty or so feet back, but one was taking photos with his smartphone while the others whispered and pointed. "I suppose I can help get you there," he said, raising an eyebrow at the crowd before he began to escort her in the direction she indicated.

It took ten minutes to walk back. For Amanda, it was the longest ten minutes of her life. She didn't want any trouble, nor did she want to cause a big scene. She had merely wanted to go for a walk, to be alone with nature for just a short time. Now she wished that she had never left the hotel.

The officer escorted her to the front doors and, with a smile, wished her well.

With a sigh of relief, Amanda hurried into the hotel and started to make her way across the lobby. But she felt something on her arm, a soft touch that held her back. Startled, she looked up and saw a man in a dark suit holding her arm. "Miss Beiler," he said. "Please permit me to assist you."

Without waiting for an answer, he started to walk toward the elevators. She noticed that he leaned toward his shoulder and said something; then, after a brief pause, she heard the word "Affirmative." A quick glance at his ear told her all that she needed to know: security with a wireless phone in his ear. She had seen plenty of security men at the concert the other night wearing the same earpiece.

Once the elevator doors opened onto her floor, the security guard walked her down the hallway and passed her own door. She was about to point out that they had missed her doorway when another door was flung open and Alejandro stepped partially into the hall. He was wearing a long black robe, and his face looked pale and tired. His eyes were red with dark shadows underneath. She had never seen him look so sickly.

"¡Dios *mío!*" he said angrily, reaching out to grab her arm and pull her into his room. *"Gracias, amigo,"* he said to the man before quickly shutting the door to the room. Once it was closed, he whirled around to face her, his eyes glaring as he stared through her.

"Alejandro?" she asked, backing away from him. "What's . . . what's wrong?"

"Where . . . have . . . you . . . been?" he said, forcing himself to speak slowly with an even tone.

She didn't understand the look on his face. She had never seen him look so angry. "I . . . I just went for a walk," she offered.

"A walk? A *walk*?" He threw his hands up in the air and turned away from her, muttering in Spanish words that she presumed would be unfit for her ears if spoken in English. *"Ay, mi madre,"* he shouted and then spun back to face her. "Do you know how worried I have been? Do you, Amanda?"

Tears sprang to her eyes. "You were sleeping," she whispered.

"Of course I was sleeping!" he shouted. "I didn't get back here until after four in the morning!" He took a step toward her, his eyes still fierce and glaring at her. "Then I get awoken to find out that you are wandering the streets of Los Angeles at seven in the morning! Alone!"

"I . . ."

He held up his hand to stop her. "No, no more words. I have been worried about you, Amanda. There is no excuse for you to leave this hotel on your own. Ever!"

"I'm an adult," she said, lifting up her chin defiantly.

"An adult?" he snapped, his eyes flashing as he hissed the word. "Was it not only a week ago that you were living on a farm in Pennsylvania? That you had never flown in an airplane or stayed in a hotel?" He raised one eyebrow at her and reached out to cup her chin in his hand. "You might be an adult in the Amish world, but you are not an adult in *this* world, Amanda. Not yet. What's more, you are mine to protect." He pressed his lips together, grimacing as if the thought pained him. "I promised your father, no?"

"Is that such a horrible thing?" she asked, her eyes wide with fear at his words.

Some of the anger left his eyes but not the fire. For a moment, he didn't respond but merely looked into her face, his own expression softening. His hand slid from her chin to the back of her neck as he pulled her toward him. "A horrible thing?" he murmured. "To protect you?" He pursed his lips as if thinking hard on the question. "It is a horrible thing, *sí*," he admitted.

She gasped, horrified at his words.

But then a hint of a smile crossed his lips. "Horrible because what I'd like to do is anything but protect you and keep you safe," he murmured, his thumb caressing the side of her neck beneath her ear. “But I made that promise,” he whispered and leaned down to kiss her. It was a soft kiss that countered his anger from just moments ago. When he pulled back, he stared into her eyes and whispered, “Don’t scare me like that again.”

She lowered her eyes, ashamed that she had made him worry.

“Now,” he said, dropping his hand from her neck to reach for her hand. “I need to sleep, Princesa. And you shall stay with me so that I don’t have to worry about you wandering off again.”

He didn’t wait for her answer as he led her toward the double doors that opened into his bedroom. On the way, she released the shoes that she was still holding in her hand, listening to them softly thump onto the floor as she crossed the threshold into the bedroom.

Chapter Eleven

They were sitting outside at a fancy Beverly Hills restaurant on North Canon Drive. Amanda sat next to Alejandro while his manager, Mike, sat on the other side of the table. It was close to three in the afternoon, the lunch date having been postponed because Alejandro had slept until after noon, his arm tucked firmly around Amanda as if to reassure himself that she was still there.

Now Amanda sat there as if on display, a plain white silk blouse and dark skirt the only thing visibly Englische about her. Everything else screamed Amish: the way her hair was pulled back into a bun at the nape of her neck, the way she sat next to Alejandro, nervous and rigid, the way she looked at him when a question was asked of her as though afraid to respond on her own. She had even kicked off her uncomfortable shoes under the table.

"So this is the young woman, eh?" Mike said, staring at her, studying her, assessing her. "I see the beauty," he said, turning his gaze back to Alejandro. "But the shyness . . ."

"She's right here," Alejandro said casually, raising one eyebrow as he reached under the table for Amanda's hand. "And she does speak English."

Amanda blushed and averted her eyes.

"I wasn't aware that she spoke at all," Mike retorted in a not-very-kind tone. "I haven't heard her say more than two words."

"Mike!" Alejandro snapped, his tone sharp and his expression suddenly fierce. "Be careful, here."

The warning hit the mark, and his manager nodded, glancing over at Amanda once again. "I apologize, Amanda," he said unnaturally. "You must forgive me."

This time, Amanda rolled her gaze to meet his and narrowed her eyes. She didn't like this man. She knew that at once. It was his eyes, she thought. They are hollow. "And why is that?"

He shrugged. "I'm not used to seeing Viper with a lady friend." He reached for his drink and started to raise it toward his lips. "At least, not a serious one."

No, she thought. She didn't care for him one bit. He was not a good person and certainly not acting in Alejandro's best interests. She exhaled sharply and met his gaze, refusing to cower under his steady stare. "As his manager, I imagine you are pleased when Alejandro is pleased, *ja?*"

Mike looked surprised. *"Ja?"* He looked at Alejandro. "What is that? Some Amish word?"

Alejandro caught his breath, and quicker than Amanda could see, he reached across the table and grabbed Mike's arm. He held it in a tight grip as he lowered his voice. "I'm not telling you again, Mike."

Shaking Alejandro's grip from his arm, Mike rubbed the spot and shook his head. "Look, I'm all for this, Alex. The media and the fans are crawling all over this story. But I'm warning you," he said. "Singers that settle down . . . well, you have a choice. Love over fame, my friend. Keep milking the media all you want, but I warn you, *amigo*, against making that choice. It could be fatal to your career. You are risking it all."

Alejandro shook his head, lifting his hand to his temples and rubbing them. "Dios *mío,* Mike," he mumbled. "You're really pushing me today."

Sensing that the lunch was going nowhere fast, Mike tried to salvage it by changing the subject. "On a good note," he said, clapping his hands together, "sales are up, and we just confirmed next spring's lineup in Brazil, Bolivia, and Costa Rica. Now we're working on the summer dates for the US."

The conversation quickly shifted back onto safer ground as the topic changed from Amanda to concerts and recording dates. Amanda found herself lost, drifting into her own thoughts.

She knew right away that this Mike was not a man who held Alejandro's best interests at heart. No, indeed, he was definitely more concerned with his own interests, and that probably meant his wallet. Mike was just like the others . . . only wanting things from Alejandro. That tore at her heart, knowing how alone Alejandro must truly feel, especially when traveling away from his friends and family.

Now everything was beginning to make sense. She understood his worry from the morning when he had awoken to find out that she had wandered away from the hotel. She was the only person he trusted to look out for his own best interest, and in turn, she could trust him with the same. His worry had been over the top, but at least she understood why. He cared.

By the time that the lunch was over, Amanda was ready to leave. It was almost four in the afternoon, and despite having a decent night's sleep, she felt tired. She knew that they were scheduled to fly to Miami the following morning; she was looking forward to some stability for the next few weeks. While she didn't know what to expect in Miami, she was hoping that it would be a bit slower-paced with a lot less people around.

"It was nice to finally meet you," Mike managed to say as they were leaving.

She responded with a silent nod and walked behind Alejandro as they exited the restaurant.

Once in the backseat of the car, Amanda turned her face toward the window, hoping against all hope that Alejandro wouldn't mention that horrid man's name to her. However, once they were settled and the car was moving, he wasted no time in apologizing for his manager.

"He means well," he said, although his tone didn't sound too convincing. "He's just all about the business."

"*Ja*, I saw that," she said with a hint of sarcasm in her response. Then, embarrassed by the use of the word *ja*, she looked away again. She had never felt ashamed of her upbringing until she had met that man. With a touch of guilt, she realized that she hoped she wouldn't have to meet him again.

"I'm sorry if that was"—he paused, searching for the right word—"uncomfortable, Princesa. That was not my intention."

She frowned and stole a glance at him. She could see the sorrow on his face. Despite the lazy morning spent in bed—his arm tucked around her while she listened to the soft noise of his gentle snoring—he still looked tired. The last thing he needed was for her to make him feel worse, she thought. "I felt like I was on display for his approval," she finally said.

"You don't need his approval," he said, reaching his hand out to rub her shoulder before pulling her close to him so that her head rested in the crook of his arm. "You only need mine."

A laugh escaped her lips as she tried to pull away, but he held her tight, pressed against his body. "Is that so?"

"*¡Sí!*" he teased. "No one else's but mine." A sigh escaped his lips, and she felt him lean his head back. "And now, I think we should visit Rodeo Drive, shop a little, so that when you return to Miami, you have everything you need."

Everything I need? She wanted to laugh. In the short time she had spent with him, she had more than she had ever owned in her life.

"There's nothing that I need, Alejandro," she reprimanded gently. "You know that."

He kissed the side of her head. "Then let me spoil you, Princesa, and shower you with gifts of beauty, perhaps a pretty necklace to shine as bright as your eyes." He stopped talking for a minute, then said something in Spanish to the driver, who nodded in response. They exchanged a few more words, then satisfied, Alejandro settled back into the seat. "A necklace, *sí*. A woman can never have enough jewelry."

At this, Amanda laughed again. When he glanced at her, she shook her head and smiled. "I don't have any jewelry, and it never bothered me before."

One eyebrow arched over his eye, barely visible from behind his glasses. "Well," he said. "Let's change that, *sí?*" When she made a face at him, indicating her distaste for such worldly things, he nuzzled at her neck and lowered his voice. "Let me spoil you, Amanda. It gives me much pleasure to do so."

"I don't think we need to buy that, Elias," her mother said. "It's so expensive, and we can make do with what we have. Also the upkeep . . ."

*Her father shook his head. "*Nee, *Lizzie," he said. "With Aaron almost old enough to drive by himself, we should be looking for a new mare that he can handle alone. You know that my horse is too much for him." He smiled at his son. "Besides, I think Aaron would like to have his own horse, ain't so, son?"*

Amanda smiled as her eleven-year-old brother lit up and nodded his head eagerly. Then, to her surprise, Aaron glanced at her and grinned. "Mayhaps Amanda would like to go along?"

His invitation warmed her heart. She had an especially close relationship with Aaron, despite their five-and-a-half-year age difference. She reached out and touched his arm. "Nee, bruder," *she said. "I think this is something special for just you and* Daed.*" She hated to turn him down, but she also could tell that her father was looking forward to introducing Aaron to the horse auction, a father-and-son bonding time.*

She had attended plenty of horse auctions with her father throughout the years. It was quite exciting to listen to the chant-like voice of the auctioneer and watch the young men lead the horses back and forth along the enclosed aisle. The horses would prance, trotting and pacing, as if showing off for the audience.

Her mother was still not convinced. "I just don't know, Elias," she said, shaking her head. "It's so much money and such a big responsibility, ja?*"*

*Elias placed his hand on Aaron's shoulder, staring down with pride into his son's face. "*Vell, *Lizzie," he said. "A man can spoil his son a little,* ja?*" He smiled. "It gives me pleasure to do this for my boy."*

And with that, it was decided. Secretly, while a little jealous of that special bond her brother shared with her father, Amanda was also pleased. Aaron was such a good boy and so obedient to their parents that he deserved a special treat, and with all of the responsibility he faced in years to come when he would take over the farm, having his own horse to tend was a good start. If anyone deserved to be spoiled a little, it was Aaron, she thought, as she watched them walk out the door and head toward the barn to hitch up the horse to the buggy and set out for the auction.

Along Rodeo Drive, Alejandro walked beside her, pointing out and commenting on the different stores. The street was lined with tall palm trees. Each store looked fancier than the next. At one point, he motioned toward a street and told her that he had a condominium down that way, on the outskirts of Beverly Hills.

"You have a home there, too?" she asked. "Then why do you stay at a hotel?"

He shrugged. "It's easier sometimes when I'm not here for long periods of time. Next month, I'll be back for a week or so, and I'll stay at the condo."

She didn't understand that. It seemed wasteful to have a place to live in a city but not use it when he was in town.

As they strolled along the street, people were stopping and staring. Amanda tried to ignore them but noticed that they were taking photos, too. However, unlike in the other places they had traveled, people here seemed to respect their privacy and didn't swarm them. At least that was a relief, she told herself.

"Ah," he said. "Here we are." He stopped walking at the corner and gestured toward the white building with tall, dark windows with white shades covering the top half. "Shall we enter, *sí?*" As if on cue, a man opened the door and gave a slight bow as Alejandro led Amanda through the glass entrance.

Inside the store, Amanda had to pause. The ceiling was high with recessed lights. However, hanging from the center of the room was a crystal chandelier that cast a soft golden glow against the walls. Throughout the room, there were displays of jewelry that sparkled, catching rays of light.

"Good morning," a woman greeted them. She paused, staring first at Alejandro, then at Amanda. It was clear that she recognized him. "Welcome to Cartier's, sir."

He nodded and reached for Amanda. "We're looking for something for the lady," he said, smiling pleasantly, his eyes darting around the room. "Perhaps a necklace," he said and looked at Amanda. *"¿Sí?"*

She wasn't certain how to respond. She had never owned a piece of jewelry. Jewelry was worldly and not of the Amish community. Still, she couldn't help but stare at the different displays, her heart pounding inside her chest. She had never seen anything as beautiful as the jewelry on display at this store.

The woman led them farther back into the room and away from any prying eyes of other customers. Alejandro locked his hands behind his back as he strolled along the different displays, gesturing toward a couple of pieces that appealed to him. Watching him move through the store, she was amazed at how comfortable he was. She, on the other hand, felt extremely out of place. The opulence of the store with its marble accents and crystal-stemmed sconces hanging from the walls was intimidating to her.

"*Ven aquí,* Princesa," he said, gesturing for her to join him at one of the displays. Once she was at his side, he pointed at the necklace that the saleswoman had placed on a velvet board. "That is beautiful, no?"

"It's eighteen-karat white gold with forty-eight diamonds," the woman explained. "The two rings symbolize love entwined."

Amanda blushed and turned her back slightly so that the woman couldn't hear her as she whispered. "That's too much, Alejandro."

But he laughed. "Too much? *¡Ay,* Princesa*! ¡Qué dulce!*" He pulled her close to him and hugged her, kissing the top of her head. "For you, the royal treatment, no?" He nodded toward the woman, indicating that she should put the necklace on Amanda.

The woman walked around the corner and stood behind Amanda, slipping the cool necklace around her throat. The two entwined rings lay against her chest, and the chain pressed gently against her neck. "It's adjustable," she explained. "You can make it longer or shorter if you'd like."

Amanda reached up and touched the two rings. It felt strange to wear something against her throat. Yet, there was something magical about wearing a necklace, something so forbidden among the Amish. She glanced at Alejandro, who was leaning against the counter, watching her with an amused look on his face. He smiled when she turned to face him.

"*¡Perfecto!*" he exclaimed. Then he motioned toward the mirror. "Go see how beautiful you are."

Beautiful. There was that word again. She didn't think she would ever consider herself beautiful, no matter how many times Alejandro said it to her. Embarrassed, she stood there, uncertain of what he wanted her to do. Then, hearing him laugh, she felt him approach her and place his hands on her shoulders.

"Here, Princesa," he said softly. *"¿Permiso?"* He didn't wait for her approval before turning her gently toward a mirror. He stood behind her, his hands still on her shoulders as he gazed over her head into the reflection that stared back. "What do you think?"

She blinked and stared at the mirror. But her eyes were not on the necklace. Instead, she was looking at him. His blue eyes sparkled, his sunglasses resting on top of his head. He was staring at her, their eyes meeting each other in the mirror as they stood there.

"Beautiful, *sí?*"

She lifted her hand up and touched the necklace once again. It felt cool under her fingertips. "I have to trust you," she said. "I don't know about these things, but *ja*, it is beautiful to me."

"As are you to me," he said quietly and leaned down to brush his lips gently against the side of her neck, his eyes still locked on hers.

Amanda blushed a deeper shade of red, too aware that the saleswoman was looking the other way but smiling.

Chapter Twelve

She stood in the foyer of his condo and stared up at the high ceilings overhead. Everything was bright white, and all the floors were made of marble. It was pristine and immaculate, shiny and bright. Doorways opened to several large rooms filled with sunlight from the walls of windows. Off to one side of the foyer was a semicurved staircase, covered in soft white carpet, with a white wooden banister and railing that led to the second floor.

From the outside, the building did not look impressive. Not compared to the mansions that surrounded it, all with massive iron gates and security guards. As they had driven through those neighborhoods, Amanda had gasped at the size of the houses. Each one was more beautiful than the next, with majestic entrances and impeccable landscaping.

"I'm just not here enough for a house," he had explained, almost apologetically. "But I think you will be comfortable enough, *sí?*"

There were doormen stationed at the entrance. They greeted Alejandro with a somber nod when they opened the front door for them. Alejandro had guided her to the elevator and protectively held the door for her as she stepped inside, despite the fact that there was a man standing there to unlock the elevator and take them to his floor.

The penthouse.

Once the doors opened and he guided her through the door to the condo, she had taken one step into the foyer and felt her heart begin to pound inside her chest. Alejandro stood in the doorway, leaning against the frame as he watched her. His expression gave away his amusement at her reaction.

"You live *here?*" she asked.

He shrugged, trying to act modest. "When I'm in Miami, *sí*. This is home."

"Oh help," she muttered. "It's like a castle!"

He laughed and entered the room. "Let's not get carried away," he said and reached for her hand. *"Ven aquí,* Princesa,*"* he said as he led her through the doorway. "Let me show you around so you can feel at home."

The layout of the condominium made it feel like a house. It was simple and made sense, she thought. For a man who rarely stayed in Miami and, on those few occasions, rarely entertained in his place, the emphasis was clearly on the outdoor area, which included a covered cabana with multiple small rooms that could open up, facing the pool. There was a formal dining room, which Alejandro confided he had rarely used, and a pristine gathering room that ran the width of the penthouse, having French doors that opened to the large indoor and outdoor patio.

"I could never feel at home here," she said quietly, her eyes wide as she took it all in. "It's so huge! I'd get lost!"

He stopped walking and turned to face her. There was a sad look on his face, and she wondered what she had said to get such a reaction from him. She didn't have to wait long to find out for he immediately put his hands on her arms, holding her at arm's length.

"Princesa," he said. "That breaks my heart." He placed a hand on his chest and tilted his head. "Tell me that isn't true."

She laughed at him. "That I won't get lost? I'm sure I will!"

He shook his head. "No, no. The other part. That you will never feel at home here."

Ah, she thought, suddenly realizing what she had said that upset him. Her cheeks flushed, and she looked away from under his steady gaze. "I am not sure of what I meant, Alejandro."

He removed his hand from his chest and took her chin in it, tilting her face up so that she had to look at him. "Promise me that you will try," he said softly. "It is important to me that you feel comfortable here."

He showed her around the back patio, pausing for her to look over the four-foot wall and admire the view of the Atlantic Ocean. Indeed, it was spectacular, and she could barely stop staring at the beautiful blue ocean. On the other side of the patio, there was a cabana by the far side of the rooftop pool. She noticed plush outdoor lounge chairs, with colorful pillows, and a bar in the cabana. She even saw a chandelier hanging from the ceiling and an open door leading to a bedroom in the back. She wanted to ask about that, why he would need to have a bedroom by the pool, but thought better of it. She might not like the answer.

Back inside, he showed her where the kitchen was and introduced her to the housekeeper, Señora Perez. She was an older woman who gave Amanda a once-over and then, deciding that she fit the bill, quickly embraced her, kissing the stunned woman on both cheeks and saying something in Spanish.

Alejandro had laughed and shook his head, replying in Spanish before he led Amanda through the rest of the condo.

There was a large media room on the first floor. Alejandro told her that this was where he worked on new songs when he was in Miami. He also had an office next to the media room with double French doors that opened to the outside patio. Everything was immaculate, large, and bright. The floors were either a white marble with veins of brownish-gold running through them or plush white carpets, which, he told her, were replaced at least once a year or whenever they became soiled.

Holding her hand, he led her up the staircase. She chewed on her lower lip, still staring at the large, open ceilings and massive white woodwork that lined the walls. In all of her life, she had never imagined such a place existed. Her heart began to palpitate, and she felt the urge to run. Where am I? she asked herself, trying hard to remember the smallness of her parents' farm. The difference between there and this amazing masterpiece of a home was unfathomable, and she had to eventually push the memory of the farm out of her mind in order to focus on what Alejandro was saying to her.

There were six bedrooms upstairs. She asked why he needed so many, and he mentioned that, often when he was home in Miami, he'd have family or friends stay over. He winked when he added, "We will have a big party tomorrow night, and many people will stay, *sí?*"

A party? That meant more people, new faces and names, odd questions and different languages. It meant loud music and people dancing, something she wasn't comfortable doing. It meant people drinking and laughing over things she didn't always understand. No, she didn't like the sound of a party at all.

When he opened the double doors to the largest bedroom on the floor, she had to catch her breath. The back wall was all windows, overlooking the back patio and the pool. The carpet was thick and white, just like downstairs, and the walls were covered in a cream-colored fabric. Silk, he explained. There was a large four-poster bed with the same cream-colored fabric for bedcoverings. A lounge chair by the wall of windows beckoned to her. She could imagine sitting there, watching the sunrise in the morning, and crocheting her blankets or doilies.

The room was, in a single word, gorgeous.

"This is my bedroom," he said, his voice dropping a tone.

Something in his voice caused her to turn around and look at him. He was watching her, waiting for her reaction. Lifting her chin, she faced him and asked, "Where will I stay?"

For a moment, he didn't respond, merely looked at her with his eyes narrowed, as if searching to find her soul. The look on his face made her catch her breath for she knew, immediately, what he was thinking. A shiver ran down her arms and she felt chilled, with a mixture of fear and excitement.

"I should like for you to stay with me, Amanda," he said at last.

"I can't do that," she managed to say. "I . . . It's just not proper."

"You stayed with me on the road," he pointed out, one eyebrow perfectly arched as he questioned her.

"Ja," she said, nodding her head. And the guilt she had felt over that. Now that they were on more permanent ground, she knew that she had no choice but to remain true to her upbringing. "But that was different. This is a home, not a hotel."

"I fail to see the difference," he responded patiently.

Squaring her shoulders, she took a short breath and leveled her gaze at him. "Alejandro, I am not sleeping with you," she heard herself say, shocked that the words actually rolled off her tongue so easily. "You told me yourself that you respect me too much for that. And you know full well that I am not like that anyway!"

He lifted his hand to his chin and rubbed it between two fingers, assessing her. He seemed to be thinking, and she gave him that time. Her heart was pounding, shocked at herself for having said something so bold to him. Despite the drastic changes in her life, she knew better than to change her own values and expectations. She refused to lose that piece of herself. Not now, not ever.

He sighed and glanced toward a door in the corner of the room. *"Entiendo,"* he said, relenting to her demand. *"Ven aquí,* Princesa. If you will not stay with me, I will have you stay next door." He crossed the room in five long strides and opened the door. Stepping back, he waited for her to approach him and peek through the open doorway.

It was a smaller room with a large bed and two chairs instead of a lounge chair. The nightstands were not the same dark wood as in his room but a brushed white, more feminine and less formal. She noticed that the bedcovering was also more feminine, cream on white with flowers. There was a private bathroom near an inner wall where another door led back to the hallway. Clearly, this was a room for female guests, which, she didn't fail to note, was attached to his room.

"That's much better," she said, trying to sound stronger than she felt.

He saw through it and reached for her arm. She turned to look at him, surprised by the gesture. For a moment, he said nothing, just stared at her. That smoldering look in his eyes made her catch her breath. She had seen that look before . . . after the VIP meet and greet. When he had kissed her with such force and passion that she had nearly lost her senses.

To her surprise, he took a step closer and placed his hands on the sides of her cheeks, holding her face tenderly in his grasp. "I know you want me," he murmured.

"Alejandro," she started to say. His words shocked her. She could feel the heat from his stare, and it was so strong that she felt her knees would buckle.

"You know I want you, too," he continued, his voice almost a soft purr.

"Please stop," she whispered, horrified at his words. She knew what he was suggesting, and it made her feel very uncomfortable. There was a line in the sand of their relationship, and he was crossing it.

"How long will this continue?" he whispered, touching her lips with his finger.

She tried to back away. "Have you stopped respecting me, then? That you would say such a thing!"

He clenched his jaws but pulled her close so that her small body was pressed against his. "*¡Ay, Dios!*" he said softly, shaking his head. "You are so pure, Amanda. So pure and so good," he said. He took a deep breath and exhaled, his breath caressing the back of her neck. "I could never stop respecting you," he sighed. Then, with the greatest of reluctance, he released her and turned away, facing the open doorway. "So I will give you a few minutes to get comfortable, and when you are ready, I will meet you downstairs. I need to make some calls, Amanda. Then perhaps we can relax by the pool, *sí?*"

He didn't wait for her reply but disappeared through the doorway. When the door shut behind him, she heard the lock turn. She leaned against the wall and covered her face with her hands, fighting the urge to cry. Her heart pounded against her chest, and she was glad for the wall to hold her up. Otherwise, she feared she would have sunk to the floor on her knees.

How had everything gotten so out of control in such a short period of time? she asked herself.

Her thoughts were interrupted when someone knocked at the door that led to the hallway. Trying to shake the feelings that she had over her strange encounter with Alejandro, she hurried to the door and opened it. A man was standing there. He smiled at her and, with her permission, entered the room with her luggage.

"Viper told me to bring these here," he said. "My name is Rodriego. If you need anything, you just ask." He set the bags down by the large armoire in the corner and opened the doors to the piece of furniture. Inside, there was already folded clothing on the shelves. He gestured to it as he explained, "Lucinda sent some clothes ahead for you. We took the liberty of unpacking it for you."

Amanda blinked and stared at the folded clothing. "For me? Whatever for? I already have enough."

Rodriego smiled as he walked over to the closet. "There is more hanging in here. Should take you through a few weeks, no?"

Following him, Amanda peeked over his shoulder at the large walk-in closet. She was amazed to see shoes on the shelves and dresses hanging from the two rods. "Oh help," she mumbled. "I couldn't live long enough to wear all of those clothes."

This time, Rodriego laughed. "Oh, I think you'll find that you will, Miss Beiler." He stepped away from the closet and started toward the door. For a moment he paused, then turned back to look at her. "It's been interesting to follow the stories about you and Viper. From what I know, you will be a welcome addition to the household." And then, without another word, he disappeared.

For the next few minutes, she stood in the closet, looking at all of the clothing. Dresses with no sleeves, long gowns for events, even small bathing suits hanging on special hangers. She pulled one out and stared at it, trying to figure out how one would actually wear such a small garment. Was that the top or the bottom? she wondered, holding up one part to her body. A bikini? Rolling her eyes in embarrassment, she shoved the hanger back on the rack and hurried out of the closet.

She was standing on the porch, the afternoon sun gently warming her face as she stretched to pull the clothesline so that she could unpin her pale green dress and fold it. Holding it in her hands, she lowered her nose to inhale the fresh scent of the outdoors imbued in the clothing. There was nothing like freshly laundered clothes, she thought as she set the dress on the top of the basket at her feet.

"Amanda," her mother said from the open door. "Don't forget to put the laundry away, ja?*"*

"I won't, Mamm,*" she replied. As if she would forget, she thought wryly.*

She carried the basket into the house and headed upstairs. The steps creaked under her bare feet. At the top of the stairs, she went into her parents' room and set the basket on the bed. She started to sort the clothing on their bed, setting the different dresses in neat piles alongside her father's and brother's work pants. When she had five neat piles, she began to hang the clothing up.

The dresses were hung on simple wire hangers and placed on the pegs in the wall. Three dresses in her mother's room, two in Anna's, and two in Amanda's. For her father and brother, she put their black trousers on the pegs directly, hanging them from their shoulder straps, two pairs for each. Their white shirts were neatly hung beside the pants but, like the dresses, they were placed on hangers.

She left the empty laundry basket on the floor of her mother's room and, glancing quickly at the wall, smiled. Laundry was done for a few days, a task that she disliked while doing it yet felt satisfied when it was completed. Freshly laundered clothing always looked bright and welcoming when it hung against the plain white walls of their bedrooms. It was at times like these that she was glad she wasn't Englische with excessive clothing. Three dresses. That was all she needed after all.

Shutting the door behind her, Amanda hurried back downstairs to see what else she could do to help her mother.

She wandered out to the pool, her bare feet on the warm concrete floor. The air smelled of the sea, a salty smell she had never encountered before. It was moist on her skin, and she felt the dryness of the heat almost immediately. Hoisting up her skirt, she stepped into the pool, her feet and ankles submerged on the first step. Immediately, she felt cooler, and after glancing around to make certain she was alone, she stepped down one step farther and sat on the side of the pool.

She hadn't been swimming in years. When she was younger, she had visited a neighbor's pond on hot summer days, splashing around in her dress until she was soaking wet. While she knew how to swim, she wasn't particularly fond of it. She preferred to sit on the edge of the pool, her feet dangling in the water. She watched the ripples she created as she wiggled her toes, amazed that such a small movement could disturb the entire surface of the pool.

"¿Señorita?"

The voice startled her and Amanda jumped, turning around to see Señora Perez walking toward her, carrying a tall glass with ice in it. With a smile, the older woman handed it to Amanda and gestured for her to sip it. She did. Iced tea, but not the same type of tea that she was used to at home, the meadow tea. It was sweeter and with more of a lemon taste than of mint. Still, it was refreshing.

"Danke," Amanda said, embarrassed at having been served by this woman. She was used to being the one cooking and serving food, not the other way around. "It's right *gut,*" she said and wondered if Señora Perez understood English. The older woman smiled and nodded, then scurried back toward the house.

A strange life, she thought. For the past week, she had traveled to five cities: Philadelphia, Los Angeles, San Francisco, Las Vegas, back to Los Angeles, and now Miami. She began to realize that, for Alejandro, the road was his home. He lived out of suitcases that other people packed for him. He dined in restaurants or in hotel rooms, eating food that other people cooked for him. He certainly never was served good home-cooked meals. Even more disturbing was that the people who surrounded him clearly cared more about their own self-interests than him, even though she suspected their success was strictly based on his achievements.

No wonder he had wanted to come to the farm, she thought. And an idea formed in her head. She would enlist the help of Rodriego and Señora Perez if she had to, but she wanted to do something special for Alejandro, and she knew just what it was.

"You are relaxing, *sí?*"

She craned her neck around and smiled when she saw Alejandro walking toward her. He had changed and wore colorful swim trunks and a sleeveless white cotton shirt, a towel draped over his shoulder. He tossed the towel onto a lounge chair and walked toward her, kneeling behind her and wrapping his arms around her.

That familiar rush flooded through her veins, and she shut her eyes, leaning back against him.

"Do you know, Princesa," he said into her ear. "It is a nice feeling to look out my window and see you sitting here. I had to join you."

She started to pull away. "Oh no!" she exclaimed. "You said you had calls to make."

He laughed at her, releasing her as he stood up. "They can wait, no?" Then, before she could respond, he took off his shirt, tossed it on top of the towel, and dove into the pool, barely skimming the top as his body glided under the water. When he reemerged, he shook his head and turned around to look at her. "Ah," he said, grinning. "That is good. Time to relax for a bit, *sí?*"

She looked away, not used to seeing a bare-chested man.

"Come in, Amanda," he said, walking through the water to where she sat.

"I can't," she responded, watching him carefully. "I don't really know how to swim."

This amused him, so he raised an eyebrow. "No?"

"No," she said. "Not very well, anyway."

He stood before her and placed his hands on the pool wall beside her. Water from his chin dripped onto her skirt, which was bunched up by her knees. She glanced down at it, noticing wet droplets on the fabric. He followed her eyes. "Ah, you are getting wet! You should have put on a bathing suit!"

This time, Amanda laughed. "You mean that tiny little thing hanging in the closet? No thank you."

"I should like to see this 'tiny little thing' on you, Princesa," he teased, that all-too-familiar mischievous tone in his voice and gleam in his eye.

She tried to hide her laughter. "I'll be happy to show it to you," she teased back. "It's on a hanger in that monstrously obscene closet!"

Her words struck him as funny, and he tossed his head back, a full-blown belly laugh echoing through the backyard. His eyes glowed, and he shook his head. "Monstrously obscene, *sí?*" Shaking his head, he backed away from her and dipped down into the water, his shoulders glistening with the water. "Women would kill for that 'obscene' closet, and yet you mock it?"

A simple shrug of her shoulders was her reply. "Not this woman. At home, I had three work dresses and one for church. That was sufficient." She paused as if thinking before she continued, "That amount of clothing that is in that closet? Why, no one could live long enough to wear it! You Englische put too much emphasis on clothing."

"You tell that to the fashion designers who are already calling, trying to get appointments with you so that you can wear their clothing to concerts and events," he said before he dropped beneath the water and began to swim laps in the pool. He swam with his face in the water, his legs kicking and splashing as his arms paddled through the water with long, graceful strokes.

She couldn't help but watch him. He was poetic in the water, as if he had been born in it. His muscles rippled, and when he dove under the water, she caught her breath, hoping that he was all right. Then he was swimming back toward her, each stroke bringing him closer. He did this ten times, back and forth, taking a breath of air every eight strokes. She counted, mesmerized by his actions. She had never seen anyone swim quite like that.

When he finished, he stood near her in the shallow end and shook his head, droplets of water splashing her and causing her to jump. He laughed and, once again, pushed through the water to lean against the wall next to her. "You like, *sí?*"

"Oh yes!" she gushed. "I just wish that I could swim like that!"

He cocked his head and looked at her for a moment. "You do?"

"Ja!" she said, nodding her head.

In one quick movement, he reached out and grabbed her, pulling her off the side of the pool and into the water. Screeching, she clung to him, her clothes instantly wet and sticking to her body. He continued laughing, holding on to her as she dug her nails into his arms, afraid to let go.

"Alejandro!" she gasped. "Why did you do that?"

"You want to learn to swim," he started, relaxing his grip on her but holding her nonetheless. "You must get into the water, no?"

"My clothes are soaked! Probably ruined!" she protested, looking down at the blouse, which, to her dismay, was clinging to her body. A blush covered her cheeks.

He walked backward, holding her as he did so, which pulled her deeper into the water. "You said you could never live long enough to wear all of those clothes," he teased. "Now you will begin to do just that!"

Despite her discomfort, she couldn't help but feel an overwhelming sense of excitement about being in the water, her clothes clinging to her and his arms holding her so that she didn't drown. She stopped fighting him and put her arms around his neck, feeling totally safe in his arms and liking the feeling of his attention.

She chewed on her lower lip for a second, staring up into his face. He was smiling, that half-crooked smile that made him look so mischievous and on edge. His eyes met hers as he continued to walk backward, his arms protectively wrapped around her waist.

"Kiss me," she breathed, shocked that what she was thinking was actually spoken aloud.

He, too, seemed stunned by her request. His expression changed, a flash of surprise, and then without further encouragement, he leaned down and pressed his lips against hers, holding her tight to his chest as he honored her request.

She kissed him back, becoming lost in the sensation of his passion and knowing that she was entering a place completely different from where she had originated. Gone was her shyness. Gone was her discretion. All that she knew was that this man, this gloriously wonderful man, was kissing her; their bodies pressed together, and she felt as if her body were on fire, despite the fact that she was surrounded by water.

"*¡Oye, amigo!*"

They both looked up at the sound of a man's voice. Alejandro took a deep breath, glancing back at the beautiful young woman in his arms. *"Lo siento,"* he murmured. Then, without missing a beat, he smiled over her head at whoever was approaching. "Miguel! Eduardo!" He released Amanda from his hold but kept his hand around her waist. "*¡Bienvenido, mi gente!*"

Behind the two men came three others, all wearing shorts and unbuttoned shirts. Alejandro made his way to the pool stairs, bringing Amanda with him. As he climbed up the stairs, the water dripped from his body, and he reached for his towel. He hesitated, then held it open for Amanda, instead of using it himself. He wrapped her inside the warm towel and whispered in her ear that she should go change. Introductions could be made later.

Obediently, she hurried past the small group of men, avoiding their eyes for she knew that they had most certainly witnessed that kiss in the pool.

***

She hadn't meant to walk into the kitchen at that precise moment. She had been outside, helping Aaron with his new horse. Her brother was still too small to properly groom the horse and certainly not without someone being nearby to oversee him.

But Amanda had wanted to get something from the kitchen. Sugar cubes to spoil the horse. She hadn't realized that her mother and daed *were in the kitchen, sitting at the table and talking. Only they weren't talking.*

She stopped in the doorway, catching her breath as she saw her father and mamm *kissing. In all of her years, she couldn't remember ever seeing her parents show any signs of affection toward each other. That was reserved for private time and behind closed doors. Feeling guilty, she realized that this was their private time, and they had indeed been behind closed doors until she had walked in.*

Quietly, she backed out of the room, hoping that they would never know that their daughter had walked in on them at such an intimate moment. Still, as she hurried back to the barn, she smiled to herself, loving the fact that there was still passion between her parents, a passion that stole kisses in the kitchen when the curious eyes of their children were nowhere around.

By the time she had changed and gathered the courage to return downstairs, music was playing in the backyard and the men were lounging around the pool, cocktails in hand. More people had arrived, both men and women. She was stunned to see women in tiny bikinis, lounging by the pool, some with the straps to their tops hanging down by their sides.

Standing in the shadow of the overhang, she watched as several men swam in the pool while Alejandro stood in the middle of another crowd of men, laughing and speaking to them in Spanish. He had a glass in his hand with a clear liquid. She knew that it most likely was not water.

"¡Ay, Princesa!" he called out and waved to her, gesturing that she should join him.

Reluctantly, she padded across the patio. She wore a simple dress, sleeveless, with small flowers on the white fabric. It hugged her waist but flowed from her hips. She felt conspicuous with her bare arms and the V-shaped neckline. As usual, she wore no shoes, preferring to be barefoot whenever she could as she had often done at home in Pennsylvania.

"I want you to meet my friends," he exclaimed, reaching for her hand and pulling her close.

After the introductions were made, Amanda stood by his side, feeling extremely uncomfortable and wishing that she was anywhere else but here. The men were switching back and forth between Spanish and English, their accents thicker than Alejandro's and harder for her to understand. The women were off to the side, sunbathing, although Amanda thought their skin was already a beautiful golden-bronze color.

"So you are this famous Amish girl, *sí?*" the one man named Miguel asked, sidling up to her. He shook his hand in the air, as if shaking something off it. *"Ay,* Dios *mío,* Viper," he said. *"¡Qué rica!"*

"Hey!" Alejandro said, but his eyes twinkled. *"¡Basta, papito!"* The other men laughed, and Amanda moved closer to Alejandro, feeling her heart in her throat and immediately not liking these men at all, despite not understanding what they had said.

"¡Oye, chicas!" Alejandro called out, looking at the women. "You OK over there, *sí?*"

One of the women waved her hand absentmindedly, indicating that she was fine while the other two women ignored him. It was only when Amanda looked closer that she noticed they were wearing small earbuds and listening to music.

To Amanda's dismay, the group of people continued to grow with more revelers arriving throughout the afternoon. By the time the sun was beginning to set, there was a full-blown gathering, over twenty-four people, around the pool. The music grew louder; the women disappeared and came back, having changed in the cabana. It was clear from how comfortable they were at Alejandro's place that they had been there many times before.

Amanda managed to excuse herself and retreat into the shade of the indoors. She felt lost and alone, despite all of the people who had descended upon Alejandro. This is his life, she thought. His friends. She felt out of place and wished that those people would just leave. But immediately after that thought crossed her mind, she regretted it. After everything Alejandro had done for her, she thought, she was ashamed to feel so ungrateful, especially when he was clearly having a good time.

In the kitchen, Señora Perez was preparing food. Amanda stood back and watched, wishing she knew Spanish and could offer her help. It was apparent that Señora Perez was used to impromptu gatherings at the condo when Alejandro was home. She didn't even blink an eye at the extra work that had just been forced upon her.

"May I help you?" Amanda finally said, not being able to continue standing there and watching.

To her surprise, the woman looked up and smiled. "No, *gracias*. It's fine, but thank you, *mamacita*."

She spoke English! Amanda was thrilled. She rushed forward and leaned against the counter. "Please let me help," she implored. "I feel so helpless and would feel ever so much better if I could do something."

"*El señor* will no like," the woman said, shaking her head.

"Nee," Amanda countered. "I want to. Please." She reached out and took the tray of appetizers from Señora Perez. "Please," she pleaded one last time, to which, with a sigh of defeat, Señora Perez relented.

Through the open door, Amanda carried the tray. She could at least bring the food outside, she thought, finally feeling useful. In all of her years, she couldn't remember not working. Every day, there was something to do: cooking, cleaning, laundry, animal care, gardening. *Something.* At least when they had been traveling, she had accompanied Alejandro to his meetings and interviews, to the meet and greets and concerts. She wasn't certain if she would ever get used to doing *nothing*, not like those women on the lounge chairs.

She made several trips, carrying the prepared food to the large table that was near the pool. No one seemed to notice. Alejandro was dancing now, laughing with his friends and even singing. From the shadows, she watched him, seeing that the women were now more engaged with the men. They had used the bedroom in the cabana to wash and get changed. All of them looked like they could have been movie stars, with high heels and small dresses that hugged their overly tanned bodies.

One woman danced closer to Alejandro. She had blond hair that hung in long, loose waves over her shoulders. When he saw her, he wrapped his arm around her waist and pulled her close. Their bodies moved as one to the Latino music in a way that Amanda had never even imagined. She felt a twinge of jealousy as she watched them, too aware that Alejandro was dancing with another woman, their bodies pressed against each other. It was indecent, she thought, while at the same time too aware that she was also wishing she could dance like that . . . both physically and emotionally.

It was clear that the party wasn't going to end at any time soon, and Amanda didn't want to be a part of it. Quietly, she retreated back inside and stole upstairs. She entered her bedroom, leaving the lights off, and moved over to one of the chairs by the window. For a long while, she sat there, watching the people downstairs, seeing Alejandro mingling with everyone, enjoying himself far more than she had seen him do in the past week while traveling.

It dawned on her that, indeed, he was home, and she felt further from it than ever.

Letting the curtain fall back, she walked away from the window and began preparing for bed. She heard the familiar ping of the cell phone, and, surprised to hear anything at all from the device since only Alejandro knew the number, she looked around the room for it. It was on her night table. Someone had put it there, plugging it in for her so that it would be fully charged.

Picking it up, she saw that Alejandro had sent her a text.

Are you coming back down, Princesa?
Are you OK?
V

She smiled and walked back over to the window. When she pulled the curtain back, she wasn't surprised to see him standing so that he could see her. She glanced down at the phone and tried to remember what the people at the Los Angeles hotel had shown her. How was she supposed to send him a message again? she asked herself. Then she remembered:

<3
A

She glanced out the window and, a few seconds later, saw him glance down at the device in his hand. When he saw her message, he laughed and looked up at the window. She raised her hand, pressing it against the glass, to which he responded by lifting his own and waving back at her. Then, satisfied that she was well tended, he turned back to his guests.

She watched only for a few seconds, not liking the way that the woman with the long blond hair, the one with whom he had danced earlier and had introduced to her as Maria, kept lingering near him. Jealousy, Amanda said to herself, scolding herself for feeling such an emotion. It was ugly, and she didn't like the feeling. For the last time that night, she turned away from the window and made her way to the bed.

Sleep, she thought. Perhaps sleep would cure the foreboding feeling that had started to swell inside her chest.

Chapter Thirteen

The next day, it was well past noon when he emerged from his room. She had been outside, weeding the potted plants that surrounded the outdoor living area, when she heard him call out for her as he exited the kitchen through the open patio doors. She leaned back and peered around the corner, smiling when she saw him approach.

He was wearing freshly laundered white linen slacks with a crisp crease down the front of each leg. His white linen shirt was rolled up at the sleeves and unbuttoned down part of his torso. The tan leather belt matched his tan leather loafers. Her eyes were drawn to the tattoos on his arms, wondering what had ever possessed him to deface his own body, despite the intricate details of the design.

"Guder mariye!" she sang, greeting him with a bright, sunny smile. "Or, in your case, afternoon!"

His eyes were hidden behind brown sunglasses, but she could tell that he had stayed up late the evening before by the drained look on his face. "What are you doing?" he asked, kneeling down beside her.

"Gardening!"

"Why?" He looked perplexed, not just at her answer but at her enthusiasm.

"There were weeds, and some of the flowers needed to be deadheaded," she explained.

He brushed his hand against her arm. "I have a gardener who should be doing that, no?" He stared at her shoulders. "You will get burned, Princesa. You must wear sunblock."

"What's that?" she asked innocently.

"A protective lotion for your skin," he responded, standing back up and reaching a hand down for her to take. Helping her to her feet, he leaned over and gently kissed her cheek. "You will burn your beautiful skin or get freckles, like me." He pointed to his cheeks where a few freckles could barely be seen. "I must go visiting some businesspeople in Miami, Amanda," he said, changing the subject. "You may come along with me, if you'd like."

"Nee, nee," she objected. "I love gardening and would so much prefer to stay here, Alejandro." When she saw the look on his face, she quickly added, "If that's fine with you, that is."

"Sí," he said dismissively, waving his hand at her last remark. "But I would prefer that you do something else that is more exciting and less laborious."

"Laborious?" she repeated, stressing each syllable of the word. "But I like doing this."

He raised an eyebrow. "It makes you happy?"

"¡Sí!" she said lightly, smiling impishly at him. "It makes me happy!"

A low growl escaped his throat, and he reached for her waist, pulling her toward him and leaning down to nuzzle her neck. "I like when you speak Spanish," he purred into her ear. A shiver ran up her spine, and she had to catch her breath. "Perhaps I will teach you more than *sí*," he said, and then, after a pause, he peered down into her face. "On the other hand, *sí* might come in handy with you."

The color flooded to her cheeks, and he laughed at her modesty.

"You weren't blushing yesterday in the pool," he reminded her, his voice soft and seductive. Waving a finger at her, he winked playfully. "Don't think I forgot where we left off."

"Alejandro!" she whispered, pushing gently at his chest as if to try to get away from him. But her halfhearted attempt was futile, and when he leaned down to kiss her lips, she responded in kind.

"More of that later, *sí?*" he whispered. He gave her one last chaste kiss before, quick as a flash, he released her, smoothed down his pants to avoid getting any wrinkles, and glanced at his watch. "Now, I will see you later. Put on that lotion and have fun . . . weeding." He started to walk away and then paused, glancing over his shoulder to watch her for a few more seconds.

She felt him watching her and looked up. His eyes were hidden behind his glasses, so she couldn't read his reaction. So she merely smiled and tilted her head. *"Ja?"*

He shook his head quickly, as if pushing thoughts out of his mind. *"Nada, mi amor,"* he said. "Don't forget that we have a party tonight."

"A party tonight?" she repeated, her voice a pitch higher. "What was last night?"

He laughed and started walking away, waving to her over his shoulder. She could hear him still laughing as he walked through the French doors and disappeared inside.

The church service had just ended, and Amanda was following her older sister, Anna, as the women began to prepare the food for the noon fellowship meal. The men were busy converting the benches into long tables so that the younger women could carry the plates of cold cuts, fresh bread, and bowls of salad for the first sitting to enjoy.

Amanda set plates at the table, moving slowly behind her sister, who was setting down silverware. After the first group of church members ate, it would be up to the women to quickly gather the plates and wash them for the second sitting. That was when the younger adults would eat. During the first sitting, it was the young, unmarried women's job to refill water while the older people and young mothers with their children ate.

"Aren't you eating?" her sister asked when they finally had a chance to sit down. It was almost one o'clock, but Amanda wasn't hungry. She picked at the food and stared off into the distance.

"Hmm?" she said, interrupted from her thoughts. She looked up at Anna.

"You haven't touched anything yet," Anna said, concern in her voice.

Shrugging, Amanda poked at her food. She was tired after having gotten up so early to finish morning chores before church. The service had been so long that, despite her best efforts, she had fallen asleep twice during the sermons. It wasn't that it was boring. No, that wasn't it. But she was mentally tired of the routine, the repetitive nature of every other week going to church, listening to the bishop expose the evils of the world or rebuke church members for harboring sin in their hearts.

She couldn't help but wonder if there wasn't anything else out there. Why did everything have to be the same routine, the same songs, the same gatherings? She found herself thinking about the world of the Englische and suddenly understanding why so many youths explored it during their rumschpringe. *She wondered what it would be like to experience just a taste of that world.*

It was six o'clock when he finally returned. Amanda was lying down on her bed, a cold cloth on her eyes, when she heard him enter her room without knocking.

"*¿Qué es eso?*" he asked. "Rodriego said that you are not feeling well. What's wrong, Princesa?" He crossed the room, and she felt the bed shift from his weight as he sat down on it, right next to her. His presence filled the room, and she could smell the musky scent of his cologne. "*¡Ay,* Dios *mío,* Amanda*!*" he scolded her. "You didn't put on sunblock!"

"No," she whispered. "It hurts, Alejandro."

He pressed a finger against her shoulder, watching the bright pink skin turn white under his touch, then immediately return to pink. She flinched. "I'm sorry, Princesa," he said quickly.

"How long will it hurt?" she whined, choking back the tears.

"A few days," he said and sighed. He lifted the washcloth from her face. She opened her eyes and stared at him. Her brown eyes blinked, and he frowned, despite the innocent look on her face. "Why didn't you listen to me?"

"I forgot."

He made a face at her and shook his head. "Well, you won't forget again, no?"

"No," she replied meekly, hating the burning, pinching feeling on her forehead, shoulders, and the back of her neck. "I can't lift my arms."

He chuckled and got up, taking the washcloth to the bathroom to rinse it with cold water. After shaking off the excess water, he came back to the bedroom and gently placed it on her forehead and eyes. "I bet not," he said softly.

"I've worked in the sun all my life," she said. "I never used that sun lotion before. And I've never had this happen."

"Princesa," he tried to explain. "Miami is much closer to the equator, and the sun is much stronger here. I also doubt that you wore sleeveless dresses when you gardened at home, no? You must protect your beautiful skin."

Beautiful skin? The two words almost made the pain worthwhile. She had never thought about skin as being something . . . beautiful.

She could hear him fiddle with his cell phone and heard the sound of him texting someone. She started to lean up on her elbows, but the pain stopped her. The washcloth fell from her face. "Who are you texting, Alejandro?" she asked, immediately regretting the question. She had never asked him before.

"I'm getting you some medicine," he said, setting the phone on her nightstand.

"I don't think I can attend your party," she replied, hating the thought that she might have ruined his night.

He waved his hand dismissively. "That's not important," he said. "Every night is a party in Miami. I'm more concerned about you."

It was twenty minutes later when someone knocked at the door. Alejandro opened it. Rodriego stood there and handed him a small white bag. Thanking him, Alejandro hurried back to the bed and helped her sit up, ignoring her wincing at the pain.

"I need to help you take your dress off, Amanda," he said.

"What?" The thought of him undressing her startled her. It was bad enough that he was sitting next to her on the bed.

He frowned at her. "This is serious. You need to take it off. You'll feel much better, and I can apply the Benzocaine to your skin."

She shook her head emphatically. "No!"

"Amanda!" His voice was firm, and he didn't wait for another argument from her. He unzipped the back of the dress and gently lifted the fabric from her shoulders to slide it down her arms without touching her inflamed skin. Carefully, he helped her slip her arms out, paying particular attention to not expose her breasts.

Despite the pain, she clutched the dress to her chest, avoiding his eyes.

"Stop being so modest," he said. "I'm not peeking." His voice was light and teasing, but she looked away, a tear rolling down her cheek. "Amanda," he chastised gently. "Please. You are breaking my heart."

"I'm sorry," she managed to say. "I'm embarrassed."

At this, he merely shook his head and started spraying the medicine on her back and shoulders. Immediately, everything cooled and she felt some degree of relief, although her skin still felt tight.

"Better?"

She nodded.

"Good. Now lay back on the pillows and rest, my naughty Princesa. It will feel poorly in the morning, but by nightfall, it will start feeling better." He set the spray on the nightstand and stood up. "I will have Señora Perez bring you fresh water and a painkiller, too. You need to stay hydrated." He started to walk toward the door.

"Alejandro?" she said, still avoiding his eyes.

He paused at the door, his hand on the doorknob. *"¿Sí?"*

Sitting on the bed and clutching the front of her dress, she turned to look at him. Her eyes met his, and she felt a rush of emotion. He had not once said a cross word about her having disobeyed his order. He had taken care of her. He had gotten medicine for her sunburn. *"Danke."*

The hint of a smile crossed his lips. "You're welcome," he said as he opened the door and slipped outside.

Her mother was sick. It was the flu. She had spent a good three days in bed, feverish and sweating. She couldn't eat. She couldn't do much more than sleep. Anna and Amanda had done all they could to keep the house in order and to take care of their younger brother.

At supper, their daed *was silent, often glancing at the place where his wife usually sat. It was empty, and he didn't seem to care for that one bit. It made him nervous that Lizzie was ill. By the fourth day, he couldn't take it anymore. No sooner had they finished the silent prayer over the food than he had excused himself and disappeared out the kitchen door, leaving his three children to stare after him in wonder. Elias returned an hour later with a doctor. An Englische doctor who made house calls to the Amish.*

"But, Daed,*" Anna had said, her voice a whisper so that she didn't offend the visitor. "An Englische doctor? What will the bishop say?"*

Elias had hushed his oldest daughter with a wave of his hand and led the doctor up the stairs to the bedroom.

By the following afternoon, the medicine that the doctor had left for Lizzie seemed to start working. Two days later, she was able to come downstairs and sit in the kitchen for short spells. And the following day, she managed to sit at the table for supper with the family. While her appetite wasn't back in full force yet, she managed to eat a little of the food.

Amanda was amazed at the transformation in her father. He was no longer jittery and nervous. Instead, he acted as he always had during the evening meal. But once, just once, he looked up at his wife, and when she met his gaze, he smiled ever so slightly before looking away, returning his attention to his food.

He had challenged the Ordnung by reaching out to the Englische for help. It wasn't that others didn't do it, but it was frowned upon. However, Amanda realized that her father had chosen to care for his wife over following the church. It was at that moment when she knew that her father truly loved her mother in a way that she had never really considered before.

It was a love that she hoped she'd be able to find herself one day.

It was around one in the morning when she awoke. Her skin still hurt but not as bad as earlier in the evening. She managed to sit up in bed, listening to the noise that had awoken her. Music and laughter. Splashing and singing. She got out of bed and padded across the white carpet toward the window. Pulling back the curtain, she looked outside and was shocked to see the backyard filled with people.

Alejandro's party.

If she had thought the party the previous night was large, this one was enormous in comparison. She tried to find Alejandro in the crowd but couldn't. There were too many people. For a while, she sat in the chair and watched, amazed at the festivities. Part of her felt envious that she wasn't able to participate. However, she knew that it wasn't just her sunburn that kept her from the party. It was her morals.

Women and men were drinking. Everyone was dancing. Some people were swimming, and Amanda wasn't entirely certain that the women were wearing complete bathing suits. Debauchery, she thought as she let the curtain fall to hide the scene.

The noise didn't die down until well after three o'clock. She had tried to go back to sleep but hadn't been able to do so. Twice she had gone back to the window to peer outside. As the crowd thinned, she finally saw Alejandro. He wasn't alone. That tall blond woman, Maria, was glued to his side. At one point, Alejandro had his arm around her and was singing, a small crowd standing around them and laughing, cheering him on.

Disgusted, Amanda forced herself to go back to bed and covered her head with a pillow. She hadn't cared for that Maria the night before. Maria had barely greeted her when they were introduced before she slipped into Spanish, purposefully excluding Amanda from the conversation. Now she knew that she couldn't trust her at all.

She heard his door open and glanced at the clock. Four in the morning. It was so late, but she was wide-awake. She sat up in bed, listening to him moving around in the room next door. His phone rang. Then, his voice muffled; he was talking to someone.

Curious, she got out of bed, grabbed her simple white robe, and made her way to the door that separated their rooms. When she heard him end the call, she hesitated. She wanted to talk to him, to ask him about that woman and the people. But she didn't want to appear too bold.

A soft knock on the door surprised her. Frowning, she reached for the doorknob, but the door opened before she could turn the handle.

"You are up?"

"Ja," she said, pulling her robe close to her chest, ignoring the pain on her shoulders. She reached her hand up to make certain that her hair was still pinned back. "How did you know?"

He smiled and leaned against the door frame. "Your light shone from under the door," he stated.

She blushed. He had known she was up and probably suspected she was on the other side of the door. "It's late," she said meekly.

Reaching out his hand for her, he beckoned her to come close. She resisted and he laughed. "Amanda," he said. His words sounded strange and the expression on his face was different. Serene and peaceful but also relaxed. "Come stay with me tonight," he said. "I promise . . ."

She shook her head. "You know that I can't."

Taking her hand, he ignored her protest and pulled her into his room. "You can, *sí,*" he said, his eyes dancing at her. "I just want to hold you, to sleep with you in my arms."

"Alejandro . . ." she protested. "That's just not proper."

He waved his other hand at her. "There's nothing improper about it." He pulled her farther into the room and toward the bed. "I need you," he implored. Kicking off his shoes, he sat on the edge of the bed and pulled her close. "I missed you tonight," he said, leaning his head against her stomach.

Not knowing what to say or do, she put her hands on his shoulders. She could feel the muscles beneath his silk shirt, immediately hating the thoughts that started to flood through her mind. "You shouldn't have missed me," she said. "You were surrounded by your friends."

He sighed, relaxing against her. "But it is you, Amanda . . . you that I wanted near me. You aren't like them. You don't want anything from me." He paused. "You're simply . . . perfect." His voice grew quiet, and Amanda pulled away. She helped him into the bed and pulled the sheets up, covering his chest. He held her hand and, with bloodshot and weary eyes, tried to look at her. "Stay with me."

"Go to sleep, Alejandro," she said gently.

When she heard his breathing deepen, she released his hand and smoothed the sheets over him. For a moment, she stood back and looked down at him, sleeping in the bed with a peaceful look on his face. Leaning over, she gently brushed her lips against his forehead before she turned off the light on the nightstand and tiptoed back to her own room, carefully shutting the door behind herself so as not to wake him from his much-needed slumber.

Chapter Fourteen

The next few days seemed to fall into a similar routine. Amanda would awaken early, spending the cooler morning hours in the garden, where she weeded and tended to the flowers. By the time that the sun rose high in the sky, she retreated back inside and spent time in the kitchen with Señora Perez.

They seemed to have developed a mutual friendship. Señora Perez gave up trying to chase Amanda out of the kitchen, and Amanda won her over by baking fresh bread or cookies. By the time Alejandro would strut downstairs, always freshly showered and dressed impeccably, the kitchen would greet him with warm smells reminiscent of Lancaster County.

Amanda would sit with him while he ate his breakfast, despite the fact that it was usually eleven when he emerged from upstairs. She brought him fresh coffee when he finished his first cup and always cleared away his dishes. In the afternoons, he usually disappeared into town, visiting friends and business associates.

At night, people would show up and there was always a party. One night, he had told her he was going into town to his favorite nightclub, Bongos. He hadn't asked her to join him, and she wondered why. But she knew better than to ask. Nightlife and nightclubs were part of his job. She was better off staying home.

It had been a week when she noticed that he was up earlier than usual. He wore simple white cotton pants and a white undershirt when he emerged from his office instead of the stairs. He carried a coffee mug in his hand and greeted her with a warm kiss on the cheek.

"You're up already, then?" she asked, surprised.

"Sí," he said, reaching for the coffeepot. "I have a new song that I'm working on. I'll be staying home today."

She hadn't heard him come in the previous evening. She had gotten used to their routine and slept through the nights. Miami was his home. It was where his friends were, and he had to socialize. She knew that, and it didn't bother her. In fact, she was glad that he was comfortable leaving her home alone. She crocheted in her room before going to bed at nine o'clock.

Having Alejandro home during the day would be a new experience for her.

He started walking back to his office but paused and glanced over his shoulder at her. "And I'd like to take you to dinner tonight."

That was another surprise. "Just us?" she asked.

He tried not to smile at her enthusiasm. *"Sí,"* he said. "Just us. Somewhere fancy and nice, so I can pamper you. You've been in this condo all week. Need to get you out, Cinderella."

Amanda looked over at Señora Perez, who simply smiled and turned around as Alejandro left the room. But not before Amanda caught that look on the older woman's face. It was the look of amusement and knowing, a look that could come only with years of wisdom.

"What does that mean?" Amanda asked, hurrying over to Señora Perez's side. "What should I wear?"

Señora Perez shrugged her shoulders, still smiling. "You have many clothes, no? Find something beautiful and fancy for him."

Amanda pouted. "That's not much help, Señora. I don't know what fancy means!"

"Ay, Dios *mío,"* Señora Perez said, but her eyes were glowing. "That sleeveless black dress is beautiful, no? But go outside and get some color here!" She reached her hand out and touched Amanda's collarbone. "Too white!" She glanced at Amanda's legs and pointed. "There, too!"

Twenty minutes later, Amanda padded outside in a one-piece bathing suit. She refused to put on the two-piece suits, finding them insanely immodest. Making certain to cover her body with the sunblock lotion, she was determined to avoid a sunburn this time.

She sat on the edge of the pool for a while, dipping her legs into the water. Her mind wandered back to the farm in Pennsylvania, and she wondered what her parents were doing. She knew that she had to write to them. It was something she had put off doing. Still, two weeks had flown by quickly, and she felt guilty for not having contacted them.

Two weeks, she thought. That's it? It felt like a lifetime. So much had changed. She had changed. And she found that she didn't too often think about Lancaster County or the Amish way of life. It wasn't that she discredited it. No, that wasn't it. It was just so easy to adapt to Alejandro's way of life, at least most of it. He had made it easy to adapt and to change. One gleam from his eye could make her knees melt. One word of praise made her entire day brighter. Even when he was gone, he would text her, to check on her and to let her know that he was thinking of her. And, always, she responded the only way she knew how: <3.

It was hot, so she decided to go into the pool. She knew she'd be fine in the shallow end. It was no different from the pond she went swimming in as a child. Glancing around, she made certain that no one was watching before she pushed off from the edge of the pool and slipped into the water. It felt cool against her hot skin, and she ducked down to get her hair wet. Her bun felt heavy, and she wanted to take the pins out to let her hair down. But she knew better than to do that.

For the next twenty minutes, she waded around the pool, enjoying the tranquility and the peace in the backyard. Then, knowing that she needed to get out, she climbed up the three steps and reached for her towel. That was when she saw him. Holding the towel in front of her, she dabbed at her face to dry the droplets that fell. But she kept staring at him.

He was inside the door of his office, one arm stretched above his head as he leaned against the door frame. With his sleeveless T-shirt that clung to his chest, she could see every muscle. He looked relaxed as he watched her and deep in thought. She wondered how long he had been standing there, staring at her as she was in the pool. She wondered if he had seen her in the bathing suit, which hid nothing of her body from his eyes. Realizing that he must have, a deep blush covered her cheeks, and she buried her face in the towel.

When she looked up, he had retreated back inside, and once again, she was alone.

Aaron and his cousin were playing in the stream in the back paddock. Their pants were rolled up, and they were barefooted as they stomped through the flowing water. A little farther downstream was a small pond where the water collected. The boys liked to build dams in the stream, watching the water back up until it cascaded down the rocks, making a small waterfall.

Amanda stood on the lawn and watched them for a few minutes. She could hear them laughing as they splashed each other. Her father walked over and stood beside her, quietly taking in the scene. When she glanced at her father, she was surprised to see a tear in his eye.

"Daed?" she asked.

He smiled and wiped at it. "Such a beautiful boy, ja*?"*

Without another word, her father turned and walked back to the barn to finish his afternoon chores.

***

It was seven o'clock when she walked down the stairs, careful to hold on to the railing so that she didn't fall in those high-heeled shoes that Lucinda had sent to her. He was standing at the front door, talking with Rodriego, but when Rodriego glanced over his shoulder, Alejandro turned to see what he was looking at.

Both men stood there and stared.

Amanda paused and pursed her lips, feeling uncomfortable under their steady gaze. She averted her eyes and continued down the stairs, counting as she went so that she didn't trip along the way. At the bottom of the stairs, she stopped and looked up, once again, at Alejandro.

"Ay, mi madre," he whispered and crossed the floor toward her. "Amanda," he breathed, reaching out to take her hands in his. He held her hands out to her sides and let his eyes travel down her dress. "You are gorgeous!"

No one had ever said that to her. No one had ever looked at her that way. She felt her heart beat, wondering if it was sinful to feel pleased that he was so appreciative. She had taken almost an hour to get ready, wanting to look especially nice for Alejandro. He had worked all day. She had only seen him those two times: once in the kitchen and then again when he had been watching her by the pool.

He laid his arm across her shoulders and gently guided her toward the front door. "The car is ready, *sí?*" He didn't wait for Rodriego to answer as he reached for her hand and helped her down the front steps toward the car that was waiting in the driveway.

She paused. There was no limo or large SUV tonight. Instead, it was a small black car, low to the ground, which looked like only two people could sit in it. "What is that?" she asked.

"You like?" He seemed pleased with her reaction as he walked her to the passenger door. Opening it, he helped her get inside.

Once he was next to her, she turned to him, her eyes glowing. "It's so small!"

"It's a Porsche!"

She laughed. "A what?"

"A Porsche! It's my fun car!" He laughed with her.

"I didn't even know you could drive!" she exclaimed.

At this comment, he tilted his head back and laughed even louder. *"Ay,* Dios," he said, shaking his head as he reached for the key and turned it on. The car started, the engine sounding like a soft hum. "You are too much, Princesa."

He moved the stick shift into first gear, and the car lunged forward as he took his foot off the clutch and sped out of the driveway. Amanda squealed and put her hands out, pushing against the dashboard, which only made him laugh again, only louder this time. He shifted the car into second gear, speeding down the road even faster.

Once he approached the main road, he slowed down and glanced over at Amanda. "You like, no?"

"No!" she said, but her eyes said otherwise. She was excited by the speed and his daring maneuvers on the road. "You are a crazy driver!"

"You are the one seated next to me," he teased. "I think you might be the crazy one!"

"Mayhaps!" But she laughed at him, enjoying his attention and his games.

The restaurant was on Ocean Drive in the heart of Miami. Amanda was amazed at the brightly lit buildings and the long streets lined with palm trees. She stared out the window as he drove through the streets until he pulled up in front of a dimly lit building with a waterfall by the front entrance.

A man opened the door for Amanda, and she carefully stepped out of the car. Alejandro walked around the back of the Porsche and gently took her elbow, ignoring the people who stopped and stared at the iconic couple. Several people took photos, which caused Alejandro to stop and smile, even shaking their hands and chatting with them.

Amanda stood by his side, amazed at how he simply moved through people, so comfortable and casual, as if it was the most natural thing in the world to talk to strangers. She admired that characteristic of him and longed to be able to do the same. But she knew that she was too shy to ever be able to converse with strangers in such a manner.

Chapter Fifteen

She was waiting at the studio, sitting on a stool, while the crew was buzzing around Alejandro. They were filming pieces of a video for one of his songs, other footage having been taken from his recent concerts in California.

The activity was mesmerizing, and she watched everything as if it wasn't real. Women in skimpy dresses were clinging to Alejandro, music blasting in the background while Alejandro put his arms around them, laughing and nuzzling at their necks. Amanda knew it was for show, but it stung, nonetheless. At one point, he pulled a leggy brunette into a hug and trailed his finger over her lips before leaning down to kiss her.

Amanda looked away.

"Cut!"

Alejandro looked up and, with a smile, released the woman, saying something in Spanish to her that made the girl laugh.

The director of the video approached Alejandro, and for a moment, they discussed something privately. She watched, noticing that Alejandro took off his dark sunglasses and hung them from the front of his shirt, nodding as he started to follow the director. They disappeared behind a glass door, and she could see them staring at something on a screen. Alejandro pointed at the monitor, and the director nodded.

The day had started out like the past few days, with Alejandro getting up early and disappearing into his private recording studio next to his office on the first floor. In the afternoon, he had taken her shopping in Miami or for walks on the beach, always with someone trailing them to make certain that crowds wouldn't bother them. At night, he would take her to a nice restaurant, showing her off to the people of Miami. It had amazed her each morning to find out that the newspaper had photos of them with blurbs about where they had dined the night before. When they had returned to the condo, Alejandro would excuse himself and retreat, once again, to his recording studio.

He worked hard, and she recognized that he had a passion for his music. Sometimes she could hear music coming from the studio, but that was usually when someone had opened the door to bring Alejandro a drink or someone stopped by to visit him.

He spent countless hours on the phone, e-mailing, texting, and calling people. Most of the time, he spoke in Spanish, and Amanda would return her attention to whatever she was doing . . . crocheting or reading.

On one of their outings, he had insisted on buying her a small handheld device that he called an e-reader. He told her that she could read books on it, countless numbers of books. She had never been much of a reader, not from lack of desire, but because she never had much reason to read. Within days, however, Alejandro had introduced her to a new world. She devoured as many books as she could, disappearing into the worlds of Jane Austen and the Brontë sisters.

She carried the device everywhere with her.

"We need to reshoot that scene," someone called out.

Amanda snapped out of her thoughts and looked up. She wasn't certain what that meant, but she didn't think it sounded good. When she saw the women going back onto the set and taking their places,

Amanda sighed. She didn't fancy looking at Alejandro when he kissed that woman again.

"This time, darling," the director said to the woman, "he's going to slide your strap down and kiss your shoulder. We need that intimacy." The director didn't wait for her response before he turned around and yelled, "Places, everyone!"

The music played, and everyone repeated the dancing and laughing as they had before. Alejandro was singing, his body moving in a way that Amanda couldn't imagine. He was like poetry, dancing and flowing with the music, his arms pumping in rhythm to the beat. He was beautiful to watch, and she found herself mesmerized, despite knowing what was going to come.

When he reached for the woman and took her in his arms, she felt her stomach churn, but she couldn't look away. Once again, he ran his finger over her lip before lowering his mouth onto hers, and then true to the director's word, his hand moved to her shoulder, and in one fluid movement, he gently slid her strap off and moved his lips along her skin, the hint of a smile on his face. The woman leaned her head back, her eyes shut as if enjoying his touch.

A tear fell from Amanda's eyes.

"Cut! Perfect, people!"

And it was over.

A neighbor boy had picked up Amanda and Anna to take them to the singing. He was a distant cousin, and since the sisters did not have an older brother to take them to the singing, he had volunteered. Amanda had sat in the back of the buggy, eager to arrive but scared nonetheless.

Singings were a time for youths to socialize. At sixteen, Amanda was allowed to enjoy a more relaxed time in her life. Rumschpringe. *The time when youths who were raised Amish could experience more of the world, free from the restrictions of the Ordnung and church. Simply put, rules didn't apply to the youths during this period of time that ended when they took their kneeling vow and became baptized members of the Amish church, a lifelong commitment that could only end in one of two ways: death or shunning.*

The singing was being held in a large room over a barn at a farm two miles from their own. Earlier that day, the g'may *had held church at the same location. Every two weeks, the church was held by a different family in the church district, giving each family in the* g'may *the opportunity to host a church gathering at least once a year.*

After the singing, each young man would often ask a young woman if he could take her home. This was the time for young people to socialize in private with someone who attracted their attention. By courting this way, they could get to know each other without the risk of inappropriate behavior so often found among the Englische.

Amanda knew that a young man probably wouldn't ask her home. She was, after all, only sixteen and far from a marriageable age. But she had hopes that, mayhaps, Joshua Esh might ask.

She had known Joshua Esh since she was a young girl. His family owned a large farm on the other side of their g'may*. He was older than her, true, but they had always gotten along when they had the opportunity to socialize after church or at gatherings. He was tall with curly brown hair and big blue eyes. As a younger son, he would eventually inherit the Esh farm, which was well established and, from what Amanda could see, very well maintained. The Esh family had a good reputation among the church members. More important, whenever she saw Joshua Esh, she felt a flutter in her stomach.*

It was at the end of the singing when her eyes began to rove around the room, seeking out Joshua Esh. He was standing with his friends, his supper gang, the boys he hung around with when his work was done. At one point, she thought she saw him look at her and smile, but she couldn't be certain.

"Amanda," Anna hissed. "Stop that."

She looked at her older sister. "Stop what?"

Her sister narrowed her eyes at her and lowered her voice. "I know what you are doing," she whispered. "If he's going to ask you, it's up to him. Don't make cow eyes at him."

Flushing, Amanda looked away. "I'm not making cow eyes," she said defensively, but she suspected her sister was correct.

It was almost time for the singing to end. Some of the young men were starting to approach the young women, and slowly, the crowd began to thin out as couples left the barn and headed toward the buggies.

Joshua was looking around the room. Amanda saw him and straightened her back. She held her breath when he started to walk toward her. Oh, she thought, if only he asks me! She tried to act natural as she stood with her friends, Emma and Hannah. Out of the corner of her eye, she could see him walking toward their group. Her heart began to beat faster and her palms started to sweat. What would she say to him in the buggy? What would they talk about?

"Hannah," he said as he approached the group, sparing a shy smile to the other girls. "Might I have a word with you?"

And just like that, Amanda knew. He wasn't interested in her at all.

She was quiet on the way back to the condo later that afternoon. It had been a busy day with people, noise, and music. Alejandro hadn't spent much time with her. He was constantly surrounded by other people who demanded his attention. She had sat in the shadows, watching with conflicting emotions. On the one hand, she wished that she was back at the condo. It was so peaceful and removed from the rest of the world. She liked being home and tending the plants. She had even started a small container garden with some vegetables at the back of the patio with the help of Rodriego. Yet, she loved being near Alejandro . . . just not caring for the visual of him taking another woman into his arms. Still, she recognized that this was all part of the game of the music industry.

"You are quiet, no?"

She glanced at him but looked away. "Tired," she offered meekly, knowing that it wasn't entirely true.

"Hmm," he responded, pondering her explanation. He studied her from the back of the town car that was driving them home after a long day of work. "I think that's not it, Amanda."

She kept staring out of the window.

"Princesa," he said, shifting his weight so that he was looking directly at her. "You have to understand that it is all make-believe."

"I . . . I know that." But her voice gave away some of the doubt. If that was make-believe, perhaps other things were, too. Perhaps everything was make-believe, including her being at his side. Was everything planned for image building and sales?

His hand touched hers. "It's what the fans want."

She looked at him. "Is that it? The fans?" She raised an eyebrow in question. "They want to see you practically making love to a strange woman?"

"They would, *sí,*" he admitted truthfully, his expression somber. "But that was hardly making love, Amanda."

"Then what was it?" she demanded. The woman had been barely dressed in his arms, and he had held her, his hands on her bare skin. The image flashed through her mind, and she had to look away.

"Acting."

She hated that word. Acting meant lying, she had come to realize. Even their own interactions in the face of the public were nothing more than acting. She noticed that he changed whenever the paparazzi and the public were around. He was much more open and friendly toward them, posing with them as if he was happy to do it. She knew that he enjoyed the interactions, but she also knew that he was busy and tired. Still, he always made time for the fans when he was able to do so.

Even more disarming was how he treated her. The gentle caresses, the sweet words in her ear. Was it mostly for the benefit of the public? How much of that was acting?

Behind the scenes, he had been more reserved at home when it came to her. When they had first arrived in Miami, his attention had disarmed her while, at the same time, excited her. But since he had started working on his music, he seemed to be in a different world. He worked in private in his office and studio. He spent more time away from her. Alone. It worried her.

He lived a fast life. There was no denying that. The work, the travel, the people, the parties. He had expressed such an interest in her, but she also knew that, in his world, intimacy was a fleeting fancy. He had told her that much when he was on the farm back in Pennsylvania. He had also told her that he respected her too much to sleep with her, not that she would ever have done such a thing. Perhaps he was bored of her. Perhaps it had all been an act, she thought despondently as she stared out the car window.

Still, her mind remembered his kisses.

She realized that it had been several days since he had approached her with any sort of intimacy on his mind. Just like her mother had always told her: "Best leave kissing for marriage."

Back at the condominium, Alejandro helped her from the car. Once inside the condo, he excused himself to go into the studio once again. She watched him leave her, standing in the foyer, and felt the all-too-familiar pang in her chest. She had no idea what she would do if he no longer wanted her to stay with him. Where would she go? Returning to Pennsylvania seemed more and more like a far-fetched reality to her. Besides missing her parents, she didn't miss much else, not even the familiar routine of her day-to-day chores.

Wandering into the kitchen, she saw Señora Perez busy with the beginning of preparations for supper. Amanda sighed and sat down at the granite counter, leaning her elbow on it and staring out the back window.

"¿Qué pasa, mamacita?" Señora Perez asked.

Amanda glanced at Señora Perez, then shrugged. "I don't know," she admitted. "But I'm sad."

"Sad? No sad!" Señora Perez waved her finger at Amanda. "No!"

"*Ja*, sad," Amanda said. "I feel lost."

It took a moment for Señora Perez to interpret in her head what Amanda meant. *"¿Por qué?"* she asked in Spanish before quickly switching to English. "Why?"

Another shrug. "I don't think he cares for me anymore," she said sadly.

At this, Señora Perez hesitated, then laughed. "Oh, *mamacita*," she said, waving her hand. *"¡No es verdad!"* Quickly, she repeated what she had said in English. "It's not true! He adores you, *mamacita*. Adores you!"

Amanda raised an eyebrow. "Adores me?" she repeated, not believing what she heard.

"Sí," Señora Perez said, placing a hand on Amanda's arm. "I have never seen *el señor* so happy in the five years that I have worked here." She smiled and patted Amanda's arm twice before she returned to her work.

Happy? Amanda wondered about that. What was it that truly made Alejandro happy? Was it being Alejandro or being Viper? She was having a hard time balancing the two personalities. And to hear that he adored her? Could it be true? He was so busy, always working, rarely relaxing. Was it possible that this man, this incredible man, could possibly have deep feelings for her? Feelings that she knew she felt but sometimes had difficulty showing. It wasn't in the nature of the Amish to be demonstrative of affection. If only she knew how to let him know, to show him how she felt.

And then, her idea from the week before hit her. She had wanted to do something special for Alejandro. Perhaps tonight would be the right time. She had wanted to make him a special dinner, home cooked and served to him in the dining room that he never used. She wanted to wait on him, the way she would have if they were back in Pennsylvania with food that was made fresh and wholesome, not from a restaurant or store.

She confided in Señora Perez, who merely looked at her in a strange way but with a smile on her lips. The look of wisdom. She nodded her head and held up her hands as if saying, "The kitchen is all yours." Within minutes, Amanda was opening the refrigerator and cabinets, pulling out food and setting it on the counter. She had a new purpose, and it gave her the energy and enthusiasm to continue.

It was close to seven thirty when Alejandro emerged from his studio. He looked tired and was rubbing the back of his neck when he walked into the kitchen. The lights were down low, and he saw candles flickering from the dining room. He looked around, surprised to not see Señora Perez hovering nearby but Amanda, smiling as if she were the cat who had swallowed the canary.

"*¿Que es eso?*" he said. Then, as if remembering that she didn't speak Spanish, he repeated his question. "What is this?" He sniffed at the air and looked at her, his blue eyes large and wide, bright and gleaming. "What is that smell? *¡Qué rica!*"

"You like?" she asked.

"*¡Sí, sí!*" He smiled and, despite his weariness, approached her. "What did you do? That is definitely not Señora Perez's cooking!"

Amanda stretched out her arms, gesturing to the kitchen. "I made you supper, Alejandro! A home-cooked meal so that you can relax, not go out, and have some good food." She wanted to add *for once* after that, but kept it to herself.

"You cooked?" That seemed to please him, and he leaned against the counter, crossing his arms over his chest as he studied her. "What other surprises do you have for me, Amanda?" he asked, smiling. "That is perfect for tonight. You must know me very well."

If only I did, she thought. But she blushed at the compliment and lowered her eyes. "I know you are working so hard. I wanted to surprise you. To do something nice for you for a change."

He rubbed his cheeks with his hand, his eyes still studying her as she stood there, proud of her achievement. There was something knowing in his expression, and when it dawned on him, he nodded his head. "I see," he said solemnly. "And you have, Princesa."

Like an eager child, she led him into the dining room and had him sit at the head of the table. She had set it with his best china and had even asked Rodriego to help her pick out a bottle of wine from Alejandro's wine cellar so that she could pour him a glass. He watched all of this with an amused expression on his face, taking in her enthusiasm and joy at serving him.

When she had finally served the food and sat beside him, he lifted his wineglass toward her in a silent toast. Then, after sipping it, he handed her the glass. "Please," he insisted. "One taste."

Reluctantly, she took the glass. Not wanting to spoil his good mood and attention, she did as she was instructed and tasted the wine. It was different from the wine he had given to her in Los Angeles, but she noticed that it was stronger and deeper in flavor. If it wasn't wine, she thought, I might even like it.

She had cooked him a simple meal. Baked chicken, mashed potatoes, green beans, and salad. But it smelled good, the meal filling the room with the fragrance of home-cooked food.

"I've been busy, *sí?*" he said, his voice serious as he watched her.

She nodded. "*Ja*, but that's your life."

He didn't respond right away.

Happily, she dished out his plate and set it before him, sitting back to watch as he ate. But, to her surprise, he didn't move. Instead, he continued to watch her, his smoldering blue eyes seeming to drink her in. She glanced around, curious as to what he was looking at. "Alejandro?"

Leaning forward, he pushed his plate away and reached out for her hand. When she placed it in his, he pulled so that she had no choice but to move from her seat and onto his lap. He wrapped his arms around her and maintained her gaze. "I'm sorry," he said softly. "I'll make it up to you."

She tried to laugh. "I don't know what you have to make up."

"Sí," he said. "You do. But you don't understand, Amanda." *Amantha.* She loved how he said her name. His thumb caressed her shoulder and the gesture sent shivers down her spine. "I have fallen into my regular routine and forgotten that this is all new to you, no?" He waited for a reaction, but she had none. "My video is recorded, and my new song is finished. I have time now. I will make it up to you."

"Alejandro . . ." she started to protest.

He lifted his finger and pressed it to her lips.

It reminded her of earlier in the day, the gesture he had made with the woman during the video, and it chilled her. He noticed and tilted his head, narrowing his eyes as he studied her reaction.

"Ah," he said. "That really bothered you today, no?"

She shrugged, wishing she could deny it, but that would be a lie.

"You were jealous," he stated simply. Then, when she said nothing, he smiled. "That is good."

"Good?" she asked, surprised by his reaction.

"*Sí*, good! You were jealous of that other woman." He was smiling now. "You care."

His words shocked her. Had he ever questioned that? Had he ever doubted how she felt about him? She wished that she felt brazen enough to tell him, to let him know that her heart sang whenever he was near her. But that was not her way. It was the way of the man to make the move, not the woman. She looked away from him, but he chuckled and forced her to look back at him.

"That is good that you care," he said softly, his voice thick and husky. "I care, too." She blinked and met his gaze, questioning him with her eyes. "*Sí*, I care more than I want sometimes, but I cannot deny that I care." His smile softened his words.

"More than you want?" she asked, blinking her eyes in wonder at what he meant.

He gave a small shrug. "It's true. My life is not one that warrants one woman, Amanda. It isn't easy to feel so strongly for one woman when there are so many others throwing themselves at me."

His words stung, but she knew that he was speaking the truth. "Like Maria?" she asked innocently.

"Maria?" he asked, startled by her question. "Maria is an old friend, Amanda. Nothing more."

"But . . ." She wanted to ask him about the other night when Maria had been hanging on him. The words, however, wouldn't come. "I . . . I can go back to Pennsylvania," she said instead.

He laughed. The sound reverberated in the room, and he pulled her close to him, hugging her tightly. *"Ay,* Dios *mío,"* he said, breathing in her scent. Pulling back, he held her face in one hand and shook his head. "That is the very last thing I want."

"Really?"

He smiled and gently kissed her lips. "Really," he reassured her. Then, tilting his head at her, his eyes sparkling, he nodded toward the food. "Now, let's have some of this wonderful food that you have prepared, no? You have worked hard, and I am hungry."

For the next thirty minutes, they had laughed and talked, sharing stories about their youth and life before they had known each other. Amanda listened to Alejandro, enthralled to hear about his years living on the streets of Dade County, fighting with other boys, and stealing to get food just to survive. It contrasted sharply with his current lifestyle as well as with her own upbringing. Even the poorest Amish family was cared for by the community, if need be.

They were almost finished with dinner when Rodriego entered the dining room, excusing himself as he hurried to Alejandro's side and whispered something in his ear. Amanda watched as Alejandro stiffened and shut his eyes, murmuring a few words under his breath. Then, wiping his mouth with his napkin, he nodded and said something in Spanish to Rodriego.

"What's wrong?" she asked.

He shook his head and gestured with his hand for her to stay seated while he stood up. "One moment, Princesa," he said. But his voice was strained and his jaw clenched tight. "I'll be right back."

Without another word, he left the room. She stared after him, immediately alarmed that something bad had happened. His reaction and expression told her that. She pushed her plate away and sank into the plush dining room chair, waiting and trying to ignore the heaviness that filled her chest.

He wasn't gone for long but returned with a serious face. His eyes flickered at her but immediately shifted away. The stress was clear in his expression, but Amanda waited patiently, knowing that he would tell her what was bothering him when and if he wanted to.

Sitting back down in his seat, he took a deep breath and lifted his hand to his temples, rubbing them. *"Ay,* Dios *mío,"* he said under his breath. Still, Amanda said nothing. He reached for his wineglass and finished it in one solid gulp. As he set the glass down, he looked at Amanda and shook his head. "I'm so sorry, Amanda."

"What is it?" she finally asked.

"Tomorrow . . ." he started but could not complete the sentence. She imagined the worst and braced herself for what was coming. Silence. It was as if he was hoping she would fill in the blanks for him, but she couldn't. He sighed. "That was my mother on the phone. We must go to her tomorrow." He paused and reached for the wine bottle to refill his glass. "She insists."

"Your mother?" Amanda asked, her voice cracking as she said it.

"*Sí*, my mother," he repeated.

"I didn't know she lived here!"

He nodded but avoided meeting her gaze. "*Sí*, on the outskirts of Miami. I may have mentioned it once . . . back in Pennsylvania."

Immediately, Amanda moved into action. *"Ach vell!"* she said. "Of course we must see her! And I must make something! What shall I bring? A dessert? Some bread? Alejandro, help me here!"

He lifted his hand to calm her down. "Easy, Princesa. I don't think you understand."

"Of course I do!" she said. "Your mother!"

He chuckled and shook his head. "*Sí, mi madre.* Mami is . . ." He hesitated, searching for the right word. "She is different. A strong personality, Princesa. She has opinions and isn't afraid to express them."

"But she is your mother," Amanda repeated, pointing out the obvious. "Family is important!" She looked at him, but all she received in response was another sigh. He seemed reluctant, and for the briefest of moments, she wondered if he was ashamed of her. "Is it me?" she asked.

"¿Qué?"

"Is it me that you are afraid of? Will I embarrass you?"

He shut his eyes for a long moment, leaning back in the chair while he did so. She waited for an answer, too afraid that she might have been correct. But when he opened his eyes, he reached his hand out for her again, and when she took it, he stood up and pulled her into his arms. "Never," he whispered and nuzzled at her neck. "I would never be embarrassed by you. I told you," he said. "You are perfect."

"Only God is perfect," she retorted.

"OK," he teased. "God and you."

"Alejandro!"

But his laughter made her smile, despite the poor taste of his joke.

"Come," he said softly, tugging at her hand. "Let's go dancing tonight."

"Dancing?" She shook her head. "You know I don't know how to dance."

He didn't listen to her but led her out of the dining room, ignoring her protests. Instead of stopping, he took her outside and made her stand near the cabana. He disappeared inside, and moments later, she heard music. Soft, beautiful music with a rhythmic beat to it and a tinny sound. When he came back to her, he was moving his feet and hips in rhythm with the music.

"Salsa!" he said proudly, dancing around her, his body moving as if connected to the music. He clapped his hands and reached for her. She laughed at him, amazed at how fast he could move his feet. "Come, Princesa. Learn to salsa with me."

"Salsa sounds like a food!" she quipped back but took his hands.

He pulled at her, trying to get her to move her feet as he was doing. She laughed, stumbling as she tried, so he placed his hands on her hips, moving them back and forth so that she could feel the rhythm. "That's right," he cooed when she started to relax and move. "Now your feet. Pretend you are skating on ice a little. Good girl!" She felt ridiculous but enjoyed the expression on his face. He was enjoying teaching her this dance, that was for sure and certain. "Now, move your arms a bit. Like this, *sí?*" She tried to imitate him but felt foolish.

He let go of her hips and began to dance on his own, circling around her with his feet twisting and turning as he moved. Then he reached for her again, placing his hand on her waist and holding her one hand in his other. He gently pushed and pulled at her waist as he danced around the patio with her. Amanda stumbled more than danced, but Alejandro was a forgiving dance partner. At one point, he twisted her around so that she dipped under his arm and spiraled. When she stopped, he pulled her into his arms and laughed.

"Not bad, Princesa," he said. "You might make a good *cubanita* after all."

"Cubanita?" she asked, repeating the word.

"Little Cuban mama," he said and brushed his finger against the tip of her nose. "You are certainly beautiful enough."

She blushed and looked away. "Don't say such things," she whispered, despite liking it.

"*¿Por qué no?*" When she didn't respond, he chuckled to himself, amused at her modesty. "Sweet Amanda," he said. "You don't know what you have, do you?"

No reaction.

The music switched to a slow-moving song. He held her tight and moved in time to the beat. She began to relax and laid her head against his shoulder. Shutting her eyes, she listened to the slow rhythm of the music and felt him guiding her as they danced.

What is sinful about this? she wondered.

As if reading her mind, Alejandro cleared his throat before he spoke. "You are adapting quite well, Princesa." His voice sounded husky and gruff. "Not too many thoughts of home?"

How often did she think of home? There were moments, glimpses of her past that continued to peek into her present. She missed her mother and her father, that was for sure and certain. She missed the animals on the farm. But Alejandro kept her busy and his life was so full, so exciting and vibrant. While she would have liked spending more time with him in the evenings, she understood that he needed to work and, for Alejandro, that meant going out to the clubs.

"Some," she finally admitted.

"Thoughts of returning?" he asked, the same gruffness in his voice.

She pulled back and looked up at him, her eyes searching his face. What was he thinking? she wanted to know. Was he worried? Even in the dim glow of the outside lights around the pool, she could see his blue eyes, so clear and transparent yet so full of everything about him. Her heart started to beat rapidly, and she suddenly knew why the Ordnung forbade dancing. It was moments like this that they wanted the youth to avoid. Moments of closeness that could lead to intimacy. *"Nee,"* she whispered.

He pulled her into his arms and hugged her, his body pressed tight against hers. She could feel the power of his muscles and the heat of his skin. Her pulse quickened, and she knew that she had to retreat. Her will was strong, and she wouldn't give up the core piece of her Amish upbringing, although she also sensed that Alejandro respected that enough to not ask her to make a choice.

"I . . . I should go clean up the kitchen," she said when he released her.

He laughed, shaking his head. She was trying to escape, that much was obvious. "Don't you dare, Princesa. Señora Perez will do that in the morning."

"Well then, I . . . I guess I'll . . ." Her voice trailed off. She didn't want to hurt his feelings, but she needed to get away from him, away from the powerful feelings she felt when he held her and touched her.

As if understanding her dilemma, he placed a finger on her lips and shook his head. "Don't say it. I understand. And"—he glanced at his watch—"I must be going out. I have to meet Eduardo and Little Juan for a while tonight. And we have a big day tomorrow."

She looked at him with wide eyes. *"Ja?"*

"You will meet *mi madre*, the formidable Alecia." He smiled and shook his head, laughing to himself. "What she will do with you, I have no idea. It should be quite interesting."

Amanda frowned. She wasn't certain what that meant but knew better than to ask him. The only thing Amanda knew was that family was to be respected and honored.

Chapter Sixteen

She wore a modest blue dress with her hair tied back in her customary bun at the nape of her neck. Rather than the fancy high heels, she wore flat sandals with blue stones on the front. It felt funny wearing sandals; she was so used to being barefoot. Whenever they went out at night, she wore those dreaded chunky-heeled shoes that Alejandro loved so much, but she always felt as though she might fall.

He had driven the Porsche to his mother's house, which was located just twenty minutes away. Prior to arriving, he had sighed and stopped the car at a store, slipping inside to pick up a large bouquet of flowers. Several people recognized him, and he paused long enough to have his photograph taken with them. Amanda watched from inside the car, amused at how he could transform. During the car ride, he had been quiet and deep in thought, but once the fans recognized him, he was all smiles and laughter.

As he got back into the car, several people noticed Amanda and took photos of her, too. She waved, knowing that was what Alejandro would want her to do. The people smiled and cheered, snapping photos as Alejandro pulled out of the parking lot.

His mother's house was in a secluded area, but the surroundings were not as grandiose as at Alejandro's condo. Her home was a redbrick house with white pillars, very different from Alejandro's beautiful penthouse condo with walls of windows and breathtaking views of the Atlantic Ocean. There was a tall fence surrounding his mother's house with a gate at the entrance. Alejandro pulled up to it and rolled down his window, punching a code into the number pad. As the gates slid open, he glanced at Amanda and gave her a supportive smile.

"¿Listo?"

She looked at him, not understanding what he'd said.

"Ready?" he translated, laughing. But it was a forced laugh. She could tell that he was uncomfortable as he put the Porsche into first gear and drove through the gate.

There were other cars in the driveway, and she heard him exhale. Clearly, she was going to be meeting more than just his mother today. She felt her own nerves begin to tense, feeding off Alejandro's pulsating energy. She didn't know why she was nervous, except that he was, too. It was rubbing off on her. That was for certain.

When the door opened, Amanda stood behind Alejandro. He was wearing simple khaki pants with a black short-sleeve shirt. He plucked his sunglasses from his face and hooked them over the front of his shirt, stepping back to place his hand on her waist and guide her through the front door.

"They'll be out back," he said, his voice flat.

The house was much simpler than Alejandro's home. It was colorful and bright with photos on the walls. She paused to glance at them. Alejandro. Children. Photos of what she imagined was Cuba. She saw one of Alejandro with the hint of a beard and a baseball cap tilted sideways on his head. He looked young and fierce, a scowl on his face.

He paused, letting Amanda absorb what she saw before he cleared his throat, indicating that it was time to move on.

The doors were open to the outside, and there were at least thirty people standing around the pool, talking and laughing, drinks in their hands. Instead of short, skimpy outfits, the women were dressed more modestly. Unlike the parties at Alejandro's condo, these people were all Latino . . . Cubans, most likely. And from the way that they all quieted down when Alejandro walked in, quickly assessing her, she suspected they were family.

Alejandro took a deep breath before he walked down the steps to the patio, his arm still protectively around Amanda's waist, gently pulling her along beside him. The group of people remained silent, watching and smiling as Alejandro approached.

There was a shift in the crowd as a woman walked forward. She was a small woman with dyed black hair that was pulled back from her face, similar to how Amanda wore hers. Her face was wrinkled and round, with large blue eyes that stared first at Alejandro before turning toward Amanda.

She stopped in front of the couple and lifted her chin, one eyebrow raised slightly, a gesture that Amanda realized was so typical of Alejandro. And she knew that she was standing before his mother, while the rest of the crowd watched for the introduction of Alejandro's lady friend.

"Bienvenido," she said simply to Amanda.

Amanda glanced at Alejandro, not certain what his mother had said.

"Mami," he started. "May I present Amanda Beiler?"

His mother glanced at him, narrowing her eyes slightly before she turned back to Amanda. *"Sí,"* she said and leaned forward, kissing Amanda on both cheeks. "I have heard much about you."

Amanda didn't know how to respond. She felt strange with all of these people staring at her. It dawned on her that these people had known Alejandro for most of his life. They'd known him during his troubled years living on the streets of Miami, when he dealt drugs and fathered children that he didn't even know. They knew him in ways that she never would, saw sides of him that she never wanted to see. For some reason, she began to sweat between her shoulder blades and her hands started to feel damp.

"Unfortunately," his mother said, scowling at Alejandro, "not from my son."

"Ay, Mami," he said, shaking his head. "Why do you have to be like that?"

She lifted her chin and stared directly at him. Indeed, Amanda could tell that she was a formidable woman, one who was proud and strong, not despite her past struggles but because of them. *"¡Sí!"* she snapped. "I read about this woman in the papers? Disgraceful."

He mumbled something under his breath in Spanish.

"A woman lives in your home?" She tsk-tsked under her breath, shaking her head. For the first time, Amanda felt ashamed. She knew exactly what his mother must have been thinking. What everyone most likely was thinking. Color rose to her cheeks, for she hadn't looked at it that way.

"Oh no!" Amanda said softly. "It's . . . it's not like that." There was a sense of urgency to her tone, an urgency that caught the attention of the people standing nearby who watched the introduction of Amanda to Alecia.

His mother turned her gaze to assess Amanda. "Then how is it? There is no chaperone? And this is my son, no?" The way she stressed the words *my son* hinted at an underlying meaning that caused Amanda's cheeks to darken in color.

Alejandro stiffened next to her, and immediately Amanda realized that she had put him in this situation. She had caused this rift between his mother and him. "I am not like that," she whispered, lowering her eyes.

"Oh?" This intrigued the mother and her look softened. "Then what are you like, Amanda Beiler?"

"Mami . . ." Alejandro started, shifting uncomfortably next to Amanda, but his mother held up her hand, stopping him in midsentence.

Everyone was watching, listening. Now Amanda understood why Alejandro had been reluctant to bring her to meet his mother. There was silent judgment amid false accusations. "I . . ." She didn't know how to explain it. Finally, she reached for his mother's hand and held it in her own. "Your son saved me, Señora Diaz. He saved my family, too." She looked up at Alejandro and smiled, feeling as if she had to somehow protect him from the accusations. "He is a good man with a very large heart to do this for me. My own church was going to send me away or shun my family."

"Alecia!" Someone called, walking toward her from the crowd. It was an older man, who placed his broad hand on Alejandro's shoulder. "Perhaps it is time that you introduce us to this young friend of your son, no?"

For a moment, Alecia stared at Amanda, her blue eyes searching Amanda's dark ones. She glanced down at the hand that held hers, and after a brief hesitation, Alecia almost smiled. The corner of her mouth quivered, another facial expression that was so similar to Alejandro's.

"¿Mi hijo? ¿Un buen hombre?" Her eyes danced at the words. Amanda didn't understand what she'd said. But whatever it was caused his mother to relax. She clutched Amanda's hand, squeezing it gently. "If you think so," she said, "then you must be one very innocent woman."

"Mami!"

His mother looked at Alejandro, her eyes sharp and fierce. "Don't ruin that in this girl. I can see from her eyes and hear from her words that she is . . ." His mother hesitated. "Different. Don't spoil it, Alejandro Christian!"

He looked away.

Alecia pulled Amanda away from her son, still holding her hand, and guided her toward the crowds of people. They were watching her, still smiling and eager to meet her. Apparently Amanda had passed his mother's inspection, for she introduced the young Amish woman to aunts and uncles, cousins and family friends. They all greeted her with handshakes and smiles, some even reaching out to embrace her.

Alejandro moved away from the masses and made his way to a group of three men who greeted him with warm hugs, slapping him good-naturedly on his back. Amanda was relieved to see that he looked more relaxed now. Apparently, she thought, his mother must have approved.

It was a hot summer day when the family arrived at the Beiler farm. Amanda stood on the porch, her bare feet dry and dusty from having worked outside all morning, helping her father and brother with the dairy before spending an hour in the garden. It hadn't rained in a while, so she had to water the plants by carrying a large bucket back and forth from the faucet in the barn.

Aunts, uncles, and cousins arrived by buggies, parking them along the lane. The women carried baskets of food into the house while their husbands unharnessed the horses and led them to the barn and pasture.

Outside of the house, Amanda and Aaron had set up tables with benches and folding chairs to accommodate the fifty-plus people who descended upon the farm. It was always gut *to see the family and very rare to get everyone together.*

Her mother's family was large. She had nine brothers and sisters. Only five showed up as the others either lived too far away or had other plans that weekend. Among the cousins, there were at least thirty who arrived, ranging in age from five years old to thirty-five. Some of the older ones brought their own children. Within an hour, the front yard was alive with kinner *racing around and laughing while the older adults lounged in the shade and talked.*

The women were in the kitchen, preparing the noon meal. Amanda found time to sit quietly on the porch, a cold glass of meadow tea in her hands as she watched the activity. She saw her sister, Anna, talking with three of their cousins, young women who lived in the neighboring church district. Anna looked at home among the cousins, despite the fact that they did not see one another very often.

Aaron walked up to her, slipping quietly onto the bench beside her. "Why aren't you joining them?" he asked innocently.

She glanced at her younger bruder *and leaned over, nudging him gently with her shoulder. "Sometimes it's nice to just watch,* ja?*"*

"Watch?" he asked.

*"*Ja, *watch," she responded. "This is our family, and I like to watch how they interact. Family is so important, Aaron. I think we are blessed to have such a right* gut *one, ain't so?"*

He followed her gaze and tried to see what Amanda saw. The power of family was lost on Aaron. He was too young. "I'd rather be playing ball, I reckon. More fun than just sitting here."

She laughed at him as he slid off the bench and ran back to join his cousins who were throwing the ball to one another in the front yard. One day, she thought, as she turned her gaze to watch him. One day he will understand.

The fiesta at Alejandro's mother's house lasted until the sun had set. After hours of eating and drinking, laughing and talking, everyone was reluctant to leave. But Alecia signaled that it was time to wrap up the event by announcing that she was tired and going to bed soon. While she suggested that the family could stay, no one did. They knew it was time to say good-bye and part company.

Alecia started to walk out but paused by Alejandro. She stood before him, looking him over with a critical eye before she nodded her head. "I will walk you and Amanda out," she announced. It was time for them to go, she was saying.

Tucking her hand into the crook of Alejandro's arm, Alecia walked beside him, Amanda trailing obediently behind, pausing to say goodbye to two of the cousins who were nearby. She could hear Alecia talking to her son, her words low so that no one could hear. Amanda didn't have to try, for the words were in Spanish and she wouldn't have understood anyway.

At the door, Alecia turned to Amanda and placed her hands on the young woman's shoulders. She spared her a soft smile and leaned forward to kiss her cheeks. "You keep my son the way you see him . . . as a good man, *sí?*"

Alejandro made a noise, and Amanda didn't have to look to know that he was rolling his eyes. She never broke her gaze with his mother as she nodded. "I will try," she said truthfully, although she wasn't certain whether that was possible. Clearly, Alecia had a different perspective of Alejandro than Amanda did, a perspective that came from years of knowing her only son.

"That's a good girl," Alecia said, a slight smile on her lips. One last time, she turned to Alejandro. Waving a finger at him, she scowled. "Remember what I said! No ruining this!"

"*Ay*, Mami," he groaned, rolling his eyes again.

His mother reached up and pressed her hand against his cheek. "And you!" she said firmly. "You call your *madre* more, *sí?*" She kissed him on the lips, a maternal gesture that surprised Amanda. Then she turned and walked away, heading for the stairs without so much as a "good night" to the rest of the family.

He was silent on the ride back home. Amanda gave him that time to reflect and think. She knew that it had been a strenuous day for him and he needed to be alone. She wondered if he would retreat to his studio when they returned home or if he would disappear into the Miami nightlife as he so often did. She sensed he needed relief from the stress of the day.

Back at the condo, he was still deep in thought as he went into the living room. She stood in the doorway, watching him as he went to the bar and poured himself a drink. Vodka and cranberry. He hesitated, then poured a second one and carried it over to her. She was just about to shake her head and refuse the glass, but he wasn't paying attention, and she took it, not wanting to upset him.

Lifting his drink into the air, he toasted her. "Here is to you, Princesa," he said, his face drawn and stressed. "To the only woman who has broken through my mother's shell of resistance." In one motion, he swallowed half of the drink and turned away from her, walking over toward the sofa to sit down. He held the glass in his one hand and raised his other hand to rub at his eyes. "Dios *mío,*" he mumbled.

Confused, Amanda stepped into the room, wondering whether she should just retire to her bedroom. She had never seen him like this, tough and hard, fierce and emotionless. She wondered whether this was the real Alejandro or if it was just the result of having spent time with his mother and extended family.

"What's wrong?" she quietly asked.

He sighed, sipping again at his drink before he leaned forward and set it down on the glass coffee table. "*Nada*, Princesa. Nothing is wrong."

"But you seem upset . . ."

He shook his head and forced a weak smile for her. "Just the opposite," he said. "I have never been happier."

She didn't quite believe him.

After a few minutes of silence, he gestured for her to join him on the sofa. She obliged, setting the untouched drink on the table next to his. He reached for her hand and lifted it to his lips, softly kissing her fingertips. "You are perfect, Amanda," he started, immediately silencing her protests with his other hand. "You win everyone over. It's an art that took me years to perfect."

His words worried her. She had never tried to win anyone over. She was always just herself, behaving as she was raised to be: honest and truthful. Did he think it was an act?

"I have worked very hard to build this image," he continued. "To get all of this." He gestured absentmindedly with his hand, indicating the room and everything in it. Yet, she knew that wasn't what he meant. It was much more than his penthouse condominium. It was the wealth, the adoration of fans, the image. "There is a lot at risk," he admitted. "I hadn't counted on getting sidetracked."

"I don't understand," she confessed, wishing with all of her might that she could help him. But his words didn't make sense to her. What did the evening at his mother's house have to do with his career?

"No, I imagine you don't," he said, sighing one last time. He kissed the back of her hand again and stood up, lifting her to her feet. He reached down and caressed her cheek. "I suppose it's time for you to retire, no? It has been a long day, and I must go out for a while. I won't be home late tonight as I have some recordings scheduled for tomorrow. But the following day, I have a surprise for you."

The change in his demeanor, the rapid way he could release his dark mood of reflection and deep thought to return to his regular self, startled her.

"A surprise?"

"Sí," he said. "You get up early and pack your bathing suit and a pretty dress. We are going on an adventure!" He kissed the top of her head and walked her toward the stairs. "It will be a day that you will not forget, I promise," he said. "A day to make up for today."

She wanted to tell him that she had enjoyed the day, despite the tension between Alejandro and his mother. She had enjoyed meeting his family and answering their questions about her background that was so very different from theirs. She had even enjoyed the music and the food, so spicy and different from what she was used to. But he didn't give her the opportunity as he turned and retreated back toward the front door.

Minutes later, she heard the engine of the car start and the wheels peel out of the driveway.

Chapter Seventeen

When she walked downstairs, she was surprised to see him, standing in the kitchen and giving directions to Señora Perez. They were speaking in Spanish and laughing as he pointed to things in the pantry and refrigerator, while the older woman moved about the kitchen.

"Buenos días, mamacita!" he exclaimed when he saw her. He was wearing all white, from his shirt down to his shoes. He rushed to embrace her in a big, warm hug, the comforting feeling of his arms around her a welcome greeting.

"*Gut mariye* to you, too." She couldn't help but laugh at his joyful mood. Considering how hard he worked, Amanda knew that he must be tired, especially since it was so early in the morning—at least for Alejandro.

To her surprise, he held her at arm's length and studied her, his blue eyes traveling the length of her body. "You are ready, no?" he asked, gesturing to the baskets and coolers on the counter.

"For what?"

"Your surprise!" he answered, his arms spread out as he spun around. She loved watching him, the way that the motion of his body was so fluid and supple. She could watch him for hours and often found herself envious of his ability to move. "Today," Alejandro announced, "today is your day, Princesa!"

She stood at the counter, her fingers tapping on the granite, trying not to smile at his exuberance. Today was no different from any other day, as far as she was concerned. And, while she remembered that he had mentioned a surprise, she certainly didn't expect him to make such a fuss. "My day?" she asked. "Why?"

With a mischievous smile, he placed his hands on her shoulders. Just his touch was enough to make her light-headed. "You will see! Today, Amanda, is about you," he said. "You and me! We spend the day together. No cell phones. No people. Nothing but you and me."

That *was* something different. She wanted to argue that she didn't need that, that she knew he was so busy. But the thought of having him alone, to herself, with no technology or people to interrupt them, intrigued her.

The previous day, she hadn't seen him at all. For the most part, she had spent the day alone, gardening in the morning and reading all afternoon. She had received several texts from him—little messages to let her know that he was thinking of her as he recorded a new song. Needed it completed before his next round of concerts.

Still, when suppertime came and went, she had been surprised, if not mildly disappointed, that he hadn't returned home yet. A text at nine o'clock informed her that he was wrapping things up and she shouldn't wait up for him. A long day indeed, and she had missed him.

"Ja vell," she said demurely. "That might be right nice, spending the entire day together."

He laughed and reached out to hug her, spinning her around in the kitchen, oblivious to Señora Perez's eyes. "*Ay,* Dios," he said, holding her close.

With her cheek pressed against his shoulder, Amanda inhaled and could smell the musky scent of his cologne and she shut her eyes, just enjoying his affection and attention. She didn't even care if Señora Perez saw.

"Today is a day meant for us!" He was jovial, laughing and happy in a way that she hadn't seen before. It was as if he felt a newfound freedom. And Amanda was only too happy to enjoy it with him.

They left the building in a town car, Rodriego helping to carry the baskets and coolers downstairs to the trunk. Alejandro held her hand as he led her to the car, opening the door for her to get in before he settled next to her. When the car took off, he put his arm around her shoulder and pulled her in close, kissing the top of her head.

"Are you ready for a fabulous day, Princesa?" He clapped his hands and then pumped his fists in the air. "Fabulous! Just for you!"

Amanda laughed at his enthusiasm. "I would be if I knew where we are going!"

They headed toward the sun, which had already risen over the Atlantic Ocean. The drive was short, and the air began to take on a different quality. It was cleaner and tasted of salt. The ocean. Amanda pulled away from Alejandro and leaned against the door, peering outside as the great Atlantic Ocean and miles of pristine beaches appeared.

She felt his hand on her shoulder, gently rubbing her back, and she glanced back at him. "We are going to the beach?" she asked.

"We are going to the ocean," he responded, correcting her.

"Then we are going to the beach?" she said, laughing at the twinkle in his eye and mischievous grin on his face. But he didn't respond, merely took his sunglasses out of his pocket and slid them on his face. He shifted his hips and reached into his pocket for something, then in a fluid motion, turned to look out the window while handing her something. She looked down at his hand and saw an oblong-shaped black box. "What's this?"

"Open it," he said, his voice flat and commanding.

She took the box and did as he told her. Sunglasses. Dolce & Gabbana. She pulled them out and laughed when she saw that they were black with an animal print on the temples. "Do I need these, then?"

"Sí," he said, still looking out the window, but she could tell that he was smiling.

Ten minutes later, they pulled into the driveway of a marina. The wooden docks were surrounded with boats, dozens of boats. Each one dipped and bobbed as the water lapped against its hull. Some were plain fishing vessels; others were large sailboats with their tall masts wrapped in sail covers. Farther out on the docks were larger boats, floating houses with double decks and lounge chairs in the back.

"Are we going sailing?" she asked, clapping her hands like a child. "I've never gone on a boat! Oh, Alejandro!" She reached out and touched his arm, his skin warm beneath her fingers. "This is so exciting! A sailboat!" Then she gasped. "Is it safe? Do you know how to drive a sailboat?"

"Drive a sailboat?" he repeated, amused by her choice of words. *"¡Ay, mamicita!"* He wrapped his arm around her neck, chuckling as he pulled her toward his shoulder and gave her a hug. "You are *deliciosa,* Princesa! Simply *deliciosa*!"

When the car stopped, the driver stepped out and hurried to open the back door for them. Alejandro helped her out of the backseat and said something in Spanish to the driver, who nodded and moved toward the trunk. Several men, dressed in shorts with white-collared shirts, hurried over, smiling as they greeted Alejandro.

"Mr. Diaz!" one man said, reaching out to shake Alejandro's hand. "Everything is ready! Just as you instructed."

"¡Bueno!"

The man glanced at Amanda. "May I have an introduction, sir?"

"But of course!" Alejandro took a step to the side and gestured toward Amanda. "Princesa, this is Captain Charles."

The man extended his hand toward her and bowed, just slightly, from the waist. "My pleasure, Ms. Beiler."

Hesitantly, Amanda accepted his hand, shaking it before quickly stepping backward to stand behind Alejandro. The surroundings, so unusual and surreal, made her feel small and insignificant. Such a world that existed, she thought. A world so different from Lancaster County!

In her youth, she had read about boats in stories at school. She knew about travel by sea from reading the Bible. Jesus preached to the masses in the Sea of Galilee from a boat in order for all to hear. He had even calmed a storm when his disciples were terrified that the boat would capsize and sink. She had imagined small boats, boats made of cypress wood and used for fishing. She also knew that some of her parents' friends took cruises on large ocean liners, being one of the forms of travel permitted by most bishops. But she had never imagined standing in a marina, a captain greeting her, and preparing to go sailing for the day.

So when Alejandro led her along the docks and around the sailboats, she wanted to ask why he was passing them. Instead of asking, she followed him, staring at the different vessels and admiring the tall masts and listening to the gentle lapping of the water as it caressed the hulls.

He stopped at the end of the farthest dock, in front of a massive boat. It had three levels with two back decks for sunbathing. It was long, longer than her father's dairy barn. The sides gleamed white, and two flags hung from the back: one the American flag and one with five stripes in blue and white, a single red triangle, and a lone white star. Along the back were two words painted in black: *Viper's Nest*.

She gasped. "Is this . . . ?"

He laughed, delighted with her reaction. "Let's get on board, and I'll show you around, Amanda."

Taking her hand, he led her up the gangway to the back deck and through the sliding glass door into the salon. She gasped when she walked through, amazed to see white carpet covering the floor and dark, shiny wood paneling surrounding the walls of a full living room and dining room. There were big bouquets of flowers on the table, exotic flowers that looked like the faces of birds.

The kitchen had granite countertops and a small built-in eating area. There was a full refrigerator, sink, and stove for cooking meals. The floor in the kitchen was hardwood stained a deep cherry, similar to the paneling in the other rooms.

He made her follow him up a curving staircase that led to a foyer with three doors. She peeked inside the two doors to the left and saw that they were small bedrooms. The door to the right, however, opened to a large master suite with a king-sized bed that dominated the room. The far side of the room consisted of a sitting area, while the near side accommodated a mahogany desk and some bookshelves along the wall closest to the door.

"Alejandro," she whispered.

It was magnificent; she had no words to express what she was feeling. It was overwhelming to stand in the middle of this amazing yacht. She couldn't even imagine what it cost, not just to buy but also to maintain.

"You like, *sí?*"

She didn't know how to respond. It was impressive, true. But she wasn't certain if she liked it. She felt small and far too plain amid such opulence. "I'm not sure," she admitted truthfully.

Her reaction caused him to laugh, and he pulled her into his arms, hugging her tight to his chest. "That's one of my favorite things about you, *mi amor*. Where others would be so impressed, you find yourself questioning it, no?" He kissed the top of her head before he released her. Then, clapping his hands, he motioned toward the door. "Let's go. They will bring our things in so that we can relax. Once they get started, you can change here, if you'd like."

He started walking down the stairs, and she followed, careful to hold on to the railing so that she didn't fall.

"Where are we going?"

He walked over to the refrigerator and opened it, pulling out a bottle of water and handing it to her. "The Bahamas," he said casually.

"Where is that?"

He laughed and pulled out his own bottle of water. "The islands. I want to take you swimming in the crystal-blue water of the Bahamas, Princesa." He twisted off the top of the water bottle and set it on the counter. "We won't be able to go onto the island because you don't have a passport yet. But we can anchor and swim, have some lunch, before heading back."

"A passport?"

"*Sí*, a passport. We will need to get you one at some point."

She knew what a passport was but never knew anyone who ever needed one, not in her community. International travel? The Amish simply didn't do it. "For what?"

Alejandro set the bottle of water on the counter as he replied, "To travel to different countries." Turning, he walked out of the kitchen galley and into the next room, calling out in Spanish for someone.

Amanda frowned. Different countries? She had never imagined traveling to a different country and wasn't certain she wanted to do something like that. Despite their recent travel the previous week, she wasn't comfortable flying and would prefer to keep her feet on the soil. American soil.

It took another thirty minutes for the captain and crew to finalize their preparations and start the engines. Left alone, Amanda explored the interior of the yacht, opening cabinets and doors, surprised to find everything stocked with non-perishable items and bottles of wine, liquor, and mixers. Shutting the doors, she glanced around and, in her mind, could envision the parties that must have taken place on the yacht. She could hear the music and see the dancing women in small bikinis surrounded by men in shorts with drinks in their hands. She scowled at the image and wandered outside to the back deck.

As the shores of Miami started to disappear, Alejandro reemerged. He had changed into a pair of shorts and was not wearing a shirt. Once again, Amanda was mesmerized by all of his tattoos and caught herself staring, wondering what he found so attractive about marking up his body.

It was close to ten in the morning, and he carried two drinks in his hand. He sat next to her at the table overlooking the back of the boat and handed one to her. When she raised an eyebrow, he made a face. "You'll like," he simply stated and kicked back to watch the wake of the ship.

She tasted it. It was tangy and sweet at the same time. Despite realizing that it had alcohol in it, she liked it. "What is this?"

"Cranberry and vodka," he responded. When she frowned, he rolled his eyes playfully. "Don't worry. It's light. I'll make certain you don't tumble overboard, Princesa." He stretched out his arms and smiled. "This is the life, no? So peaceful and relaxing."

She wanted to ask about the boat, wanted to know about how often he used it and how many women he had brought to it. Immediately, she glanced away, ashamed at herself for feeling so jealous of his past.

One of the crewmen emerged from the glass doors, carrying a tray of food. He set it down on the table where they sat. Without a word, he turned to leave, but Alejandro said something in Spanish to him. Moments later, music was playing in the background.

The sun shone on her face and Amanda shut her eyes, enjoying the warmth of the rays as they caressed her skin. By now, she had acquired a nice tan after days spent outside, gardening and relaxing by the pool. She still put on her sunblock every morning but was less afraid of getting burned.

The wake from the boat mesmerized her. She found herself watching it, drawn to the gentle noise of the motor and the whitecaps of the wake. In all of her life, she had never imagined something as magnificent as this boat, cutting through the ocean as it headed away from land and toward this place Alejandro called the Bahamas.

They were camping. It was the annual vacation spot for Amanda and her family. Every year, they would arrange for someone to tend to the dairy for two days so that they could take the horse and buggy to Elias's brother's farm outside of Strasburg, where the family would gather to cook outside, play volleyball, catch up on the latest news, and relax.

Amanda was never certain that such outings were meant for her mother to relax. After all, Mamm still helped with the cooking of the meals and the washing of the dishes. But for Amanda and Anna, it was two days of being able to enjoy visiting with the cousins and not work.

Amanda particularly liked to spend her time sitting on a log by the fire at night. The flames would dance and crackle, casting a spell on her. In the background, she could hear her family singing a hymn, their voices lifting in unison as they sang about the love of Jesus for humankind. Amanda knew that she should join them, but the fire held a fascination for her.

In the flames, she could see the years of persecution that the Amish and Mennonites had faced. She knew from reading the Martyrs Mirror, *that mammoth book that outlined over four hundred years of persecution, that many of the Anabaptists were tortured and burned at the stake. Amanda stared into the fire, trying to imagine such a fate.*

Even more, she tried to imagine how she would react if pressed. Would she have had the strength to stand by her beliefs or would she have renounced her Anabaptist heritage in order to escape such a horrible death?

"Amanda!"

She looked up from where she sat and saw Anna waving toward her from where she stood with the others. "Coming," she called back, and with one final glance at the fire, she quickly stood up and returned to join her sister and cousins.

The islands completely amazed her. They looked like floating pieces of land, surrounded by small, narrow lips of sand upon which the crystal-clear waters came to rest. When the boat finally anchored near a small island, Alejandro instructed her to go change into her bathing suit. It wasn't a question but a command, and despite feeling awkward, she did as he said.

She had packed as he had told her, and once in the master suite, she found her bag placed on the floor near the desk. The bathing suit was a one-piece, brightly colored with pink, blue, and green, the colors against a background of black and with a gold clip in the front. When she slid it on, she glanced in the mirror and turned from side to side. Her skin was dark from the days spent by the pool. The bathing suit pattern made her look even thinner than she already was. Still, she didn't like how it exposed the shape of her breasts and the curve of her hips. She reached into the bag for the matching cover-up and slipped her arms into it before exiting the room.

"*¡Ay, qué linda!*" he said when she rejoined him outside. He kissed his fingers and gave her a sultry look. "Lucinda is outdoing herself with your wardrobe, Princesa. You look . . ." His eyes rolled over her body and sparkled. "Magnificent!"

Knowing that compliments were hard for her to take, he gave her a chaste kiss on the forehead before taking her hand and moving toward the back of the boat. She saw a small boat tied up to the stern, and Alejandro gestured toward it.

"Where did that come from?" she asked.

He pointed up above toward the top level. "It was there, Princesa. Next to the hot tub."

"Hot tub?" She hadn't explored the upper deck, but now that she craned her neck, she saw that there was another sitting area up there near where the captain drove the boat. "I didn't see up there," she said.

"Later, Amanda," he said softly. There was something different about Alejandro. He wasn't as jovial as usual, his expression more serious. She wondered if something had happened while she had changed. Had he received a phone call? An e-mail? "For now, let's enjoy this moment in the boat. I want to take you swimming." He held out his hand, indicating that she should take it to step down into the boat. Without question, she did as he wanted and took a seat in the back of the small boat.

She watched as he untied the dingy and stepped in before releasing it from the back of the yacht. He moved deftly in the boat, as if he was at home on the water, balancing himself against the rolling motion caused by the gentler waves. As he moved toward the small outboard engine, his muscles rippled and she had to look away.

With complete confidence, he steered the small boat away from the yacht and toward the island. He peered over her shoulder and the bow of the boat as he steered, maneuvering it through the water with expert precision. When they approached the island, he slowed the boat down and stopped the engine.

"Let me toss the anchor," he said, but his mind seemed elsewhere.

After securing the boat, he turned to Amanda and forced a smile but continued to avert his eyes. *"¿Listo,* Princesa?"

She nodded, confused as to this rapid shift in his mood. She watched as he tossed his sunglasses into the boat and, without a word to her, dove off the side of the boat into the crystal-clear water. When he emerged, he bobbed in the water and shook his head, droplets splashing everywhere.

"*¡Ay!* It's perfect! Come in, Amanda!"

Reluctantly, she took off her bathing suit cover and eased her way off the side of the boat and into the water. It covered her head, and for a moment, she felt as if she was drowning. She kicked with her legs, and as her body rose to the surface, she felt his arms reach for her waist. Gasping for air, she suddenly found herself in his arms.

"You all right, Princesa?"

She nodded. *"Ja, sí."*

He laughed, the tension from before suddenly vanished. "You are a fish, no?"

"I think not," she sputtered, relieved to have his arms supporting her.

Gently, he released her and swam farther away. "It's gorgeous here," he said. "The water is just right."

She managed to tread water, watching him as he swam. She didn't want to stray too far from the boat, knowing that she was not a strong swimmer. Still, she couldn't stop watching him, amazed at his movements in the water. Poetic, she thought, too aware that she was watching him with a racing beat in her heart.

He swam back to her and pulled her into his arms. Before she could say a word, he covered her mouth with his, kissing her with a fierceness that was completely unexpected. Salty water dripped onto her face and his arms crushed her with a force that caught her off guard. Their legs brushed against each other as they treaded water, but it was Alejandro who kept her afloat.

"Ay, Amanda," he breathed into her neck, holding her tight. "What have you done to me?"

"Me?" she asked, breathless from his kiss.

"¡Sí, tú!" He stared into her eyes, holding her face between both of his hands. "I'm lost."

"Lost?"

He shook his head as if pushing thoughts away. "Never mind," he mumbled, slowly starting to pull her through the water back toward the boat. "This island is safe. We can go closer and eat lunch on the beach. No one patrols here, so you are fine without a passport."

He helped her into the boat, then pulled himself into it. Water dripped from his head as he pulled up the anchor, then started the engine. He steered the boat toward the beach and pulled the engine up from the water as they neared it. Effortlessly, it glided into the sand, and in one easy motion, he jumped from the boat and pulled it ashore.

He reached inside for the basket with one hand and then for Amanda with his other hand. "Come, Princesa," he said. "Let's pretend we are stranded on an island, just the two of us, with no pressure from the rest of the world," he said lightly, but there was an edge to his voice.

"Is something wrong?" she asked, concerned that something had happened.

He lifted her hand to his lips and kissed it. "Nothing is wrong," he said. "In fact, everything is just perfect." They stood on the edge of the beach, and he set the basket down in the sand. "Go swim, Princesa. Play in the water while I prepare our picnic. Remember," he said, "this is a day just for you."

She was standing in the master bedroom suite, having just changed from her wet bathing suit. Her hair was wet, and she used one of the plush towels from the bathroom to dry it. In her bag, she had packed a brush, so she took the time to brush her hair. It was long, so long that she had to brush it over her shoulder. In the typical Amish tradition, she had never cut her hair, so it hung beneath her waist, long and straight but thick.

Picking up the towel once again, she rubbed her hair so that it wasn't so damp from the seawater. She could smell the salt, and the texture felt different. It would take a long time to dry; she knew that from experience. But she could pin it back into a bun, despite it being damp.

He cleared his throat, and she spun around, surprised to see him leaning against the door. She hadn't heard him climb the stairs, nor had she known that he was watching. There was a strange look on his face, a blank expression and his eyes looked distant. Immediately, she backed away and put her hands on the sides of her head, her mouth forming a perfect *O* from surprise.

"Alejandro!" she gasped. "You can't see me like this!"

He crossed his arms in front of his chest, watching her like a cat spying a mouse. He was amused. "Why ever not?"

"My hair!"

At this, he tilted his head and raised an eyebrow. "Your hair?"

She tried to pull her hair back, to hide it from him. When he realized what she was doing, he stepped into the room and stopped her by taking ahold of her hands. She looked away, embarrassed to the point of tears. "Please stop," she whispered.

"I've never seen you with your hair down, Amanda," he said, his voice low and husky. "No, perhaps once. In the hospital, no? I think you look beautiful with your hair down."

She shook her head, wishing he would just turn and leave. "You don't understand," she managed to say.

"Then explain, *sí?*"

A tear fell from her eyes as she turned to look at him. "Only my husband should ever see me with my hair down," she whispered.

At first, he didn't respond. He reached up and wiped away the tear, studying her face. His eyes flickered back and forth as he stared at her eyes, her nose, her lips, then back to her eyes. Something shifted in his expression, and the tension from earlier suddenly vanished as he took a deep breath and smiled.

"What if he just did, Amanda?"

His words were lost on her but only for a moment. She frowned and blinked twice, trying to understand what he had just said. She didn't want to presume that she understood, and she wasn't even certain if what she heard was what was said. "I . . . I don't . . ."

He placed a finger against his lips. "Shh," he whispered. "Listen to me, Amanda." He removed his finger and, gently, bent down to kiss her lips, lightly and with control. "I cannot imagine my life without you. When you are away from me, you are all that I can think about. Yesterday, when I was in the booth recording . . . it was terrible. I couldn't concentrate, could barely sing. I was distracted by thoughts of you." He ran his hands down her shoulders and caressed her arm. "When you are near me, I just want to disappear with you, to be alone with you and to hold you. Without you, I am not complete; I am lost and have no idea who I am."

Her heart began to pound. What was he saying?

"I want to be with you, for always. I want to make love to you, to sleep next to you, to wake beside you," he purred. "I want to be a better man because of you. You worried once about how much you would change after leaving the Amish, and I told you that, *sí*, you would change, but you would live." He smiled and stared into her eyes. "But you have also changed me and shown me what living is all about. And I don't want to live one more minute without you by my side."

"By your side?" she repeated softly.

He leveled his gaze at her, tilting his head slightly as he paused, taking a deep breath before he nodded his head, just slightly, and added, "By my side, *sí*, but also as my wife."

Wife? The word rang in her head. *Wife* was a big word. *Wife* meant forever. *Wife* meant no other woman. *Wife* meant children and a future.

Wife also meant that she could never return to the Amish or that way of life. She would forever be a part of this new world, one that she had barely tasted for not quite three weeks. Could this truly be happening?

"I . . . I don't know what to say," she replied hesitantly.

He placed his hands on her shoulders, holding her at arm's length. "Tell me that you love me as much as I love you," he said. "Surely you know that I do, *sí?* That I am so in love with you that I can barely see straight . . . that I can barely breathe unless I know you are nearby or waiting for me."

"Oh," she whispered.

He smiled at her. "Is that all you can say? 'Oh'? I have just proposed to you, Amanda. I want to marry you."

Images of the farm flashed before her eyes. The gentle peace of living among her family and church members. The sounds of the horses pulling buggies down the road. The laughter of children playing outside after church service. The sight and smell of freshly laundered clothing hanging to dry on lines that stretched from the corner of the porch up to the edge of the barn. With one word, she realized, it would be gone forever.

But as she refocused on Alejandro's blue eyes, staring at her, she knew that she had no choice. There was never any doubt that she loved him and that she would have to decide the future of her life. The two different worlds could certainly not coexist, that was for certain. Or could love make it work? Was that enough?

"Yes," she said, her voice barely more than a whisper. "Yes, I will marry you, Alejandro."

To her surprise, he let out a loud whoop and lifted her into his arms, spinning her around. He was relieved, and with a touch of astonishment, she realized that he had actually feared that she might turn him down, say no to his proposal. And as he laughed, she felt tears fall from her eyes, tears that blended both joy and apprehension, and she laughed with him.

Chapter Eighteen

"Are you out of your mind?"

Alejandro frowned at his manager as they faced off in the recording studio. He hadn't expected such a reaction from Mike. "I believe such news is usually met with the word 'Congratulations,' no?"

Mike shook his head, rubbing his forehead as if he had a sudden headache. "My God, Alex," he mumbled. "Is she really worth throwing it all away for?"

"¿Por qué?" Alejandro demanded angrily. He had hoped for support and understanding, not such a negative reaction. Not from his manager. "Why is it 'throwing it all away'?"

In a swift movement, Mike leaned forward and swiped his hands at the newspapers that he had brought with him and laid on the table. Papers went flying. "That's why! That, my friend, is why!"

Alejandro glared at his manager. "The fans?"

"Yes!" Mike roared, his voice loud and fierce. "Yes, the fans! They don't want a married Viper! They don't want to see Viper settle down!"

"They adore Amanda," Alejandro objected. He picked up one of the papers and pointed to the photo. It was from the previous day when they had returned in the evening from the day at sea. Photographers had been camping out at the marina, waiting for their return. Alejandro had given the owners permission to let the paparazzi wait rather than chase them away. The photo was of Alejandro helping Amanda off the boat, his hand clutching hers and a smile on both of their faces.

"They adore her today," Mike said, his voice sounding exasperated. "Today while she is perceived to be your little pet, your flavor of the month with such an air of innocence. But you wait and see what happens if you marry her. They will turn on her, and they will turn, my friend, on you!" He said the last part while pointing a stiff finger at Alejandro.

Alejandro waved his hand at Mike. "Now it is you who is out of his mind," he said, laughing. "They will never turn on her nor will they turn on me! She is America's darling, and you know that."

Both of Mike's hands flew to his face, and he rubbed at his eyes in frustration. He turned his back to Alejandro and paced the room for a few steps, muttering under his breath. Finally, he turned around and stared at Alejandro. "Why marriage? Why so soon?"

"I love her," Alejandro stated with a simple shrug of his shoulders.

"Bah!" Mike retorted. "Love! I've seen it before with you. Convenient amnesia, Alex. My advice? Keep her under your wing; sleep with her if you must. Just don't cross that forbidden line and marry her, Alex. We've worked so hard to keep you uncommitted in the eyes of the public, to keep that bad-boy image. Don't ruin it by becoming a family man."

"Sleep with her?" Alejandro said, a sneer in his voice. "Sleep with her? Is that what you think this is about? Sex?"

Mike dropped his hands to his sides and stared at him. There was an incredulous look on his face. "Isn't it always?"

For a moment, the look in Alejandro's eyes frightened Mike. He glared at Mike, his eyes narrow and sharp. His chest rose and fell in rapid succession as the blood raced through his veins. "She is the only person who asks absolutely nothing of me, Mike," he said between clenched teeth. "She loves me for who I am, not for what I can do for her . . . which is more than I can say for you!"

"You pay me to manage your career." Mike pointed his finger at Alejandro again. "Not to coddle your emotional whims or needs for the ultimate conquest . . . to bed an Amish girl!"

With that, Alejandro lunged forward and grabbed his manager by the collar, shoving him against the wall. "Don't you ever talk about her that way again," he hissed. "And perhaps you should remember what you just said. That I am the one who pays you! You work for me, and not the other way around." He took a step backward and shoved Mike away. "I can replace you, Mike, and will not think twice of doing so if I ever hear you speak disparagingly of Amanda again!" He shuddered. "That is my future wife you speak of, Mike. I will not have it."

Without another word, Alejandro left the room, slamming the door behind him.

He didn't return home until later in the evening. She was sitting outside, reading one of her books when he returned. He strolled onto the patio, a bouquet of flowers in his arms and a grin on his face as he greeted her.

"How is my beautiful fiancée?" he said as he walked down the steps from the kitchen that led to the patio.

Setting the e-reader aside, Amanda jumped to her feet and ran to greet him, smiling at the flowers. "You're back!"

He pulled her into his arms and hugged her, being careful not to crush the flowers. *"Ay, mamacita,"* he murmured. "You missed me, no?"

"Are those for me?" she asked innocently but knowing full well what the answer would be.

"These?" He glanced at the flowers. "No, they are for my other fiancée. Have you seen her?"

She laughed and took them. "Then we best be getting them into water for her, *ja?*"

He followed her into the kitchen and watched as she opened cabinets, looking for a vase. "I need to go to Los Angeles next week for a few days. I'd like you to come along," he said as she filled the vase with water.

"Oh?"

"Sí," he said. "I am performing live on a show. You will go, no?"

She made a face at him and laughed. "Of course!"

"And we will need to make an announcement," he said quietly.

At that, she looked up, surprised. "I have no one to announce it to, Alejandro. I already wrote a letter to my parents today. I thought they should hear it directly from me before they hear it from the newspapers."

He nodded, understanding the wisdom of her decision to send them a letter. "And we will need to make arrangements," he continued, his words stilted and sounding odd. It was strange to think of Alejandro speaking about their wedding. It was all so new to her. "What do you think about before the holidays?"

She realized that by the word *arrangements*, he actually meant the wedding itself. It dawned on her that her idea of a wedding would be very different from his. She knew that Englische couples often married in churches and threw elaborate parties. The brides wore fancy white gowns with veils. "I . . . I don't know what to say," she admitted.

"During the holidays, I have a busy schedule," he explained. "Jingle Bell concerts, Times Square for New Year's. We'll be traveling quite a bit, and then I have several concerts in South America. It would be better to not wait, no?"

It was late September.

"I don't know anything about Englische weddings," she said quietly, suddenly feeling awkward. At home, the weddings were announced, and everyone knew what to do. Preparation was usually made in two to three weeks, but it was always the same. Nothing fancy.

"Hmm," he said thoughtfully as he studied her expression. "I see where that could present a problem." The seriousness of his tone made her look up at him, the color draining from her face. To her relief, he laughed and reached out his hand. "Come here," he commanded, holding his arms out for her. She let him pull her into his arms and hug her, loving the protective feeling of his embrace. *"Ay,* Dios,*"* he said softly. "What would I ever do without you, Princesa?"

"I'm sorry," she apologized, feeling that it was necessary, but that only caused him to laugh.

"For what, Princesa? For being you? That is why I love you so much."

I love you. Those words sent a thrill through her. She had never imagined hearing those words and especially not from a man like Alejandro. No, she thought, she had never imagined a man like Alejandro in her life, period. He was the fabric that dreams and fantasies were made of, not a man who wandered into the life of a plain and simple Amish girl from Lancaster County, Pennsylvania.

"Oh, Alejandro," she sighed, feeling the too-familiar sting of tears in her eyes. "I . . ."

He looked down at her. "You what?"

"I just can't believe this is happening," she said, her words choked as she tried to hold back her tears.

He wiped the tears away and gave her a tender smile. "It is happening, Princesa. And I would have it no other way," he replied. He pulled her into another embrace, rocking her back and forth gently, still smiling as he held her. "You've got *mi corazón* . . . my heart, Princesa."

The moment was interrupted by the ring of his cell phone. He reached into his pocket, and mouthing "I'm sorry" to Amanda, he answered in Spanish. He was animated and his hands began to make gestures as he spoke to whoever was on the phone. Quietly, Amanda returned to the flowers, fluffing the stems, and then she carried the vase to the foyer so that she could set it by the entrance on the bombé chest.

She looked around, realizing that this was to be her home with Alejandro. She was no longer a guest but his fiancée. The realization struck her, and she caught her breath. This magnificent condominium, ten times the size of her parents' farmhouse, would be "home." She wondered if she would ever be able to think of it that way.

The night before had been magical. After he had proposed to her, they had sat on the back of the yacht, holding hands and staring into the clear, star-filled sky. Neither spoke. There were no words. At one point, he turned to her, smiled, and leaned over to kiss her.

"What was that for?" she had asked shyly.

"For agreeing to become my wife, Princesa," he had replied. He brushed his fingers along her shoulder and smiled softly at her, his voice low as he said, "For making this little *chico* from Cuba the luckiest man in the world." Shutting his eyes, he sighed and held her close as he breathed in her scent. *"¡Qué tranquilo!"*

The yacht had pulled into the marina at nine o'clock. Despite the darkness and late hour, Amanda had been surprised to see the paparazzi there, smaller in number than she had grown used to from before, but enough of them to make her shy away and hide behind Alejandro. He had laughed at her and held her hand, teasing her as he helped her disembark onto the deck.

Now she stood in the center of the hallway, her arms wrapped around herself, feeling completely overwhelmed. How had all of this happened? And so quickly. Oh, she had known that she loved Alejandro during the summer at the farm. When he had left, she had felt that her world had collapsed. Still, she had not imagined that she would walk away from the only life she had ever known to become his wife, a wife to a celebrity in a world that she was still only just beginning to learn about. Would she ever be able to adapt to that world?

Chapter Nineteen

They were to spend seven days in Los Angeles, he had told her. Most of these days were spent at the studio, filming another music video and discussing with his team the holiday concerts that he was scheduled to perform. He was also doing some charity work at a local school for Hispanic children. His days were busy, and although he tried to include Amanda as much as he could, she also spent several days alone at the condo.

She didn't mind. She was amazed at the size and grandeur of his two-bedroom Los Angeles "hideaway," as he called it. She realized that it was one of the first times in her life that she had been alone in a house. At the farm, there was always someone there. At Alejandro's Miami home, Rodriego and Señora Perez were there, as well as the other part-time people who floated in and out during the day. It was nice to be alone, to read her books or write letters.

But at night, he always came back, took a shower, and changed into a freshly pressed suit, eager to show her the city.

"Tonight we have a dinner," he said. "It's a media event, so there will be lots of photographers there." He was drinking a cup of coffee that he had made as he leaned against the kitchen counter. At this condo, he seemed more relaxed. Without Señora Perez to pamper him or Rodriego to manage the house, Alejandro had to do more things for himself. It surprised Amanda that he did so with such ease.

"Oh?"

He set the coffee mug in the sink as he checked his pocket for his cell phone and glasses. *"Sí,"* he replied. "And I asked Celinda to take you shopping today. A day of primping and pampering." He peered at her from behind his glasses and smiled that mischievous half-smile. "Be a true daughter of a goddess for the world tonight, Princesa!"

He laughed when her mouth fell open, stunned by his words.

"Besides," he said, strolling across the kitchen to give her a kiss before he left. "It is good for you to cultivate friendships, no?"

"I reckon," she said, not certain how she felt about spending the day with a complete stranger. Although she had enjoyed sitting with Celinda and her boyfriend, Justin Bell, at the awards dinner the other week, she felt uncomfortable shopping with someone as glamorous as that woman.

He started to walk toward the door but turned around, digging into his front pocket. "I almost forgot," he said walking back toward her. "Keep this to buy whatever you'd like." He slid a small plastic card into her hand. "There's no limit, Amanda, so don't feel awkward."

She looked at the black credit card in her hand. American Express. Under the numbers at the bottom of the card was her name: Amanda Beiler. "I can't accept this!" she gasped, thrusting it back at him. She had never even held a credit card in her hand before, never mind thought about having one in her own name. The Amish paid for everything in cash, never credit. And to have Alejandro paying for her?

But he pushed her hand away before she could give the credit card back. "Of course you can," he said and pointed a finger at her. "And you will. Celinda will know what you should wear tonight, so no arguing with her, Princesa." He gave her one more kiss, his lips lingering just momentarily over hers. "I want you to look fabulous tonight."

***

The dinner was held at a private dining club. The men wore tuxedos, and the women wore a mixture of gowns and fancy dresses. Amanda felt out of place in the simple, strapless black gown with a rhinestone clasp by her bosom. However, Alejandro had simply stared at her when she emerged from the bedroom where she had changed.

"*¡Ay,* Dios*!*" he whistled and shook his hand. "Celinda is a good shopping companion for you, no?" He stepped forward and reached for her hand. Lifting it over her head, he ordered her to turn around. The lower part of the dress fanned out, exposing her ankles and her rhinestone-studded shoes. "We may have to replace Lucinda, *sí?*"

Nothing would have pleased Amanda more than never seeing Lucinda or hearing her name again. But she didn't say anything of that nature.

Certainly, she had enjoyed her time with Celinda during the afternoon. People seemed to stop and stare wherever they went. Her composure under such pressure amazed Amanda. During it all, Celinda was oblivious to the photographers and gawking fans. Instead, she spent her time focusing on Amanda and helping her select the perfect dress for a magical evening.

Afterward, they had managed to find a quiet place to grab a quick late-afternoon lunch. Amanda was increasingly drawn to the young woman and found that, despite their different backgrounds, they had a lot in common. Amanda was looking forward to spending more time with Celinda that evening.

Amanda smoothed down the edge of the dress and smiled at Alejandro, her eyes wide and hopeful as she asked, "You like, *ja?*"

He shut his eyes and smiled, putting his hand on her waist and pulling her toward him. "*Ja,*" he teased. His voice was low and husky, with a gruffness to it that she was starting to recognize when he was pleased with her. "If only you'd say yes, I'd forget about the dinner and spend the night with you . . ." He nuzzled at her neck.

She placed her hand on his shoulder and pushed him gently away. "Alejandro!" She knew exactly what he meant, and the insinuation embarrassed her. Not only was that reserved for marriage, it was also something the Amish did not discuss so freely and openly. Yet, her embarrassment amused him and he laughed at her. "Stop," she whispered but couldn't help herself from smiling at his teasing.

There was a limousine waiting for them outside the lobby. The doorman opened the door and nodded as Alejandro and Amanda exited the building. The dining club was nearby, so it only took a few minutes to navigate the streets and pull up out front. As she was beginning to expect, there were crowds at least ten deep, taking photos and cheering at the different people who emerged from the cars.

Alejandro waved to the crowd, then reached down to help Amanda out of the limo. There was a collective gasp from the people as she stood there, her hair pulled back in her customary bun with the dress that she had bought earlier that day with Celinda. Several people behind the ropes called out her name, and Amanda turned in their direction, blinded by flashes from iPhones and cameras.

"Now I know why you wear sunglasses all the time," she said to Alejandro. To her surprise, he reached up and, removing them from his face, handed them to her in a chivalrous gesture. Playing along, Amanda put them on, and to the delight of the crowd, she turned to face the blinding cameras and posed.

Alejandro laughed, clapping his hands in amusement at her little display for the people. They cheered, too, enjoying this playful side of Amanda.

"You are simply amazing," he whispered, his eyes glowing at her as they continued walking into the dining club. It pleased her tremendously to know that he appreciated her teasing.

Once inside, they were separated as swarms of people began to vie for their attention. Alejandro made his way to the bar to order drinks while Amanda found herself next to Celinda and a group of well-dressed and sophisticated women who made her feel inferior by their style, their grace, their presence. Celinda provided a quick introduction, and Amanda immediately forgot their names. But she noticed that they were aloof and uninterested, quite different from Celinda.

"You look stunning," Celinda said softly so that the other women didn't hear.

"*Danke* for your help," Amanda replied. "Alejandro seemed pleased."

Celinda laughed. "I bet."

"Who are those women you introduced to me?" Amanda asked. "Should I have known them?"

Once again, Celinda laughed. She was a happy woman with a lot of self-confidence. Amanda found herself liking her even more. "In our world, they are rather well known. I think that they were put out by the fact that you didn't recognize them."

At this, Amanda shrugged. "Why should I know them?"

"Oh, Amanda," Celinda said, shaking her head but clearly amused. "They are famous!"

Glancing over her shoulder at the women who were now talking with two men dressed in tuxedos, she shook her head. "Not in my world," she added. "Just some fancy women, is all."

Amanda disliked going to the local market on Saturdays. The Englische tourists were always out, especially in the summer. But her mother needed some items and asked Amanda to harness the horse, ignoring Aaron's enthusiastic offer to help. "Need to get some vinegar for the beets and more rennet and cheesecloth for the cheese making this afternoon. I thought I had enough but ain't so."

Oh help, Amanda thought. Going to the market would be crazy on a Saturday morning.

She was standing in line, Aaron bouncing at her side and begging for some candy, when she saw the young girl. She was clearly a tourist and waiting for her own parents to finish shopping. Englische tourists loved to shop at Amish markets, hoping for an opportunity to engage in dialogue with them while buying Amish foods that would probably never be eaten.

The girl had long blond hair that hung down her back. She wore a white shirt, a pair of jeans, and cowboy boots. Leaning against the wall, she looked bored and reached into her pocket to pull out a tube of lipstick, which she promptly opened and rubbed over her lips. Red. As she put it away, she glanced over at Amanda and Aaron. Her expression was dull. Clearly, she was unimpressed with the two plain Amish youth before her. After all, she was beautiful and she knew it.

"Why did she just paint her lips?" Aaron whispered, staring back at the strange Englische girl.

"Because she's ugly on the inside," Amanda replied, feeling naughty as soon as she said it but smiling when Aaron laughed.

The room was crowded with people, each of the women dressed in the latest fashion, trying to outshine one another while most of the men were dressed in similar garb: black tuxedos. As she sat at the table, she looked around, shaking her head slightly at the ostentatious nature of the event.

Tall vases of flowers decorated the white-linen-clad tables. Each place setting had multiple plates and gold flatware. There were four glasses at each place, for water, white wine, red wine, and champagne. All to recognize the talents of one man: a music producer? She felt that it was beyond opulent even for this world where "too much" was the norm.

"Here, Princesa," Alejandro said and handed her the tall, fluted glass with bubbling liquid in it.

Taking it from him, she started to lift it to her lips but, as she started to take a sip of the champagne, she noticed a silver object on the bottom of the glass. For a moment, she did a double take and squinted, trying to see what it was.

"Alejandro," she whispered as she leaned toward him. "There's something in my glass!"

He raised an eyebrow at her. "Oh?"

"I think it's a bug or something!" she whispered, careful so that no one else could hear.

He shut his eyes and chuckled under his breath, shaking his head. "Why don't you look, Princesa?"

She frowned at him, wondering why he didn't care, and reached for the tall flute of bubbling champagne. Looking into it, she tried to determine what was at the bottom. It was large and round, the bubbles floating up from it toward the surface. If she didn't know better, she'd think it was a ring. "What in the world?" she asked.

Rolling his eyes but laughing to himself, he took the champagne glass from her hand and lifted it to his lips, drinking the liquid until just a bit remained. Then, he tilted the glass onto the white napkin and a ring emerged. Her heart began to pound as she realized that people were observing them. They watched as Alejandro dried off the ring and slipped onto one knee before her. He held the ring between his fingers and, as if offering it to her, lifted it ever so slightly.

There was a collective silence from the people who sat near them. All eyes were watching. She felt the color drain from her face, hating the attention but knowing that this was Alejandro's way of announcing their engagement to the world. He reached for her hand and gently slid the ring onto her finger before lifting her hand to his lips and planting a soft kiss where the jewel sat.

"Oh," she gasped, mesmerized by the ring on her finger. "Alejandro!"

"If you are going to marry me," he said softly so that no one else could hear, "I want the world to know. That is all right, *sí?*"

Too aware of the people staring at them, she forced herself to nod, shocked at the public nature of this display but understanding exactly what he was doing: playing to the fans and the media. When he stood up, he pulled her to her feet and embraced her in front of everyone. People applauded and cheered politely, quickly sharing the news with those who sat at tables farther back and hadn't been able to witness firsthand the official engagement of Viper to the young Amish girl. It would, however, be discussed on all of the gossip radio shows and entertainment channels for days to come.

Chapter Twenty

The media and the public approached the engagement from one of two perspectives. Some people felt that the engagement was rushed and, as such, a mistake. How could a man like Viper settle down with just one woman, they argued, and one as inexperienced as this Amish girl, Amanda Beiler? The other side argued that Viper had met his match in the innocence of the Amish girl. He was calming down and, as a result, getting ready to slow down at last.

Amanda shoved the magazine away, disgusted with what she had read. It worried her more than she chose to admit that Alejandro was, indeed, so experienced and known for sleeping with so many women. She, on the other hand, had only kissed one man: Alejandro. What if the reporters were right? What if he couldn't settle down with just one woman?

"*¡Buenos días,* Princesa*!*" he sang as he walked into the room.

She looked up and tried to smile, but the heaviness of her heart weighed deeply upon her. In her world, the union of two people was a time of joy and happiness. Marriage was forever. There was never any underlying speculation. Yet, she knew that in Alejandro's world, forever could have a very different meaning, indeed.

"What's troubling my beautiful fiancée?" he asked as he sat down at the table and nodded at Señora Perez, who promptly served him coffee.

Amanda glanced at the magazine. "Why do they write such horrible things?" she asked.

He reached over for the magazine and shuffled through it. When he came upon the article about their engagement, his eyes quickly scanned the words, then the photos. He didn't seem fazed as he pushed it aside. "They have to report on something, no? The truth is boring. Speculation is what sells copies of their magazine. It won't go away, Amanda."

"I reckon." But she didn't feel that way. Instead, she felt it was an invasion of their privacy. What was even more unnerving was that she didn't like how it made her feel. She didn't need to feel any more insecure than she already did. Despite loving Alejandro and knowing that he loved her, she was too aware that she was scared of what might lie ahead for them.

Three days before, they had returned to Miami. Alejandro was helping some friends mix their beats at his home studio during the afternoons, the three men sitting around a computer while listening to the music and adjusting the different levels. At night, he had shared supper with her before disappearing for the evening to visit clubs with his friends.

She hadn't minded, but she did notice that the media seemed to follow his every move, publishing photos of Alejandro at the dance clubs and wondering why he was out alone, without his fiancée. He had scoffed about it, completely undisturbed by the insinuations. Still, he saw that Amanda was bothered by such questions.

"Come here," he said and reached out for her. She obliged, and he pulled her onto his lap. Wrapping his arms around her waist, he held her close, with an all-too-familiar gleam in his eyes. "I don't like to see you upset, Princesa. This is our time. We must enjoy the moment." She didn't respond. "I have a break in my schedule, Amanda, in two weeks. Why don't we go away on the boat for a while? I'll have Rodriego do what he can to expedite that passport, and we can tour the islands for a few days?"

She shook her head. *"Nee,"* she said. She knew that he was busy. The studio was finishing his video that he had recorded a lifetime ago in Los Angeles, wanting to release it over the Internet before Thanksgiving. And she knew that he was recording a new song. "It's all right, Alejandro."

He studied her reaction, his blue eyes flickering over her face. "I see," he said simply. "You know that I won't get much of a break again until after the holidays. We have concerts in six cities on the East Coast and appearances at other events before New Year's."

Boston. New York. Philadelphia. Providence. New Jersey. Back to New York and then Baltimore. Yes, she was aware that they were going to be traveling. The thought didn't bother her. She had enjoyed more of Alejandro's attention and company when they had first left Lancaster and were on the road. Still, she shrugged. "I just feel . . ." She didn't know what she felt. Useless? Bored? Something.

"You are beautiful when you are frustrated," he said lightly.

"I'm not frustrated," she retorted, but as soon as she said it, she knew that he was right.

"I know!" he said, squeezing her tighter. "We will arrange a party with friends and family here to celebrate our engagement!"

Another party? The thought pained her. She was tired of parties and people. She didn't feel as if she fit in with these people. They liked to eat and drink, dance and sing. She felt inadequate next to the barely clad women with bronze skin and long, wavy hair who all vied for Alejandro's attention, not caring that Amanda was standing beside him.

"Two weeks from Friday!" he said happily. "And you will plan it. That will keep you busy and occupied. I will have Rodriego help you."

"I'm not so certain about that," she said cautiously.

But he insisted.

True to his word, Rodriego kept her busy, spending most of the day with her and arranging for her to meet with a party planner who could take Amanda different places . . . to taste food, to select flowers, to print invitations, to pick out decorations. Reluctantly, she went along with it, but only because Alejandro was so excited. When she saw him in the mornings, he would ask her what she had done the previous day. She'd tell him, and he'd nod his agreement with her decisions.

"You are a good event planner," he teased one morning. "It will be a fabulous party."

She wished that she felt as confident.

Everything had to be removed from the rooms downstairs. Amanda and Aaron were in charge of that. Anna was responsible for washing the baseboards and corners of each wall. Mamm was mumbling under her breath as she looked at the windowsills and shook her head.

"Anna, you see that your bruder *wipes down those sills! So much dirt, you'd think we never cleaned them!"*

Amanda had overheard her mother. "I'll do it, Mamm. I just asked Aaron to wipe down the furniture outside. Might as well give it a good cleaning before we bring it back in, after service."

*Her mother paused as if repeating what Amanda had said in her mind. Then, satisfied, she nodded. "*Gut, *Amanda.* Danke.*"*

Once a year, the church service was held in their house. This weekend was that time of year. That meant that everything had to shine, a complete cleaning of the entire house . . . although Amanda thankfully noticed that her mother was more focused on the downstairs than the upstairs. Every inch of the walls, floor, woodwork, and cabinets had to be scrubbed and cleaned. Everything had to shine with cleanliness and care. Everything had to smell fresh and clean.

Amanda was always amazed at how her mother managed to coordinate Church Sunday fellowship. With over two hundred people, more or less, attending, she had to ensure that there was enough food for everyone. She coordinated this with neighbors and friends. One family would bring the pie box, a large wooden box with shelves that contained freshly made pies for all of those people. Depending on the time of year, there would be pecan pie, apple pie, pumpkin pie, or shoofly pie. Another family would bring freshly baked bread or cold cuts. And still another family might make the cup cheese, pretzels, applesauce, or chowchow.

It took a lot of coordinating to feed so many people and to have a spotless house in which to entertain them. Amanda knew that the other women would be critical of her mother's house, maybe even find a reason to gossip about her skills as a housekeeper. It was a little game that the older women sometimes played.

"Did you see how dirty her windows were?" one might whisper, clicking her tongue several times as she shook her head in disapproval.

"Her sink drain hasn't been cleaned in years!" another might add.

Over the years, Amanda had heard it all and was determined that no one would be able to say such naughty things about her mother and her own home. If that meant two days of cleaning the first floor from top to bottom, so be it. No one would fault her mother for not knowing how to host church service, that was for sure and certain.

It was the evening of the party. Amanda's stomach was in a knot, but she knew that, at this point, it would either be a wonderful success or an amazing failure. The party planner had been helpful, guiding Amanda through food selection, table placement, and floral arrangements. Amanda suspected on more than one occasion that Alejandro's hand was behind the decisions that were made, but the seasoned Carol had always made certain Amanda thought the decisions were her own.

She hadn't seen Alejandro for more than a few minutes during the past two days. If it hadn't been for Rodriego and Carol, who kept her busy, she would have collapsed on her bed and buried her face in her hands, crying.

Ever since Los Angeles, and what she had come to realize was a staged proposal at the dinner, a proposal that fed the media and social network circuits, Alejandro had been aloof and distant. In fact, he had barely mentioned their engagement, and she feared that he might have changed his mind. Gone were the hugs and the kisses. Gone were the stolen glances and sultry looks. Instead, he was out late at night and the tabloids were having a field day with the photos of women trying to capture Viper's heart (or at least one night with him) before he settled down with his Amish wife.

Every morning, Rodriego left a stack of papers on the table at the place where Alejandro usually sat. However, most mornings, he wasn't there to look at them. His routine varied without any prediction: either he slept late or woke early to work. The contrast in his inconsistencies confused her. Her eyes would wander to the papers, seeing the photos and the circled articles on the printouts that Rodriego had gathered. Amanda never even knew whether he saw those articles, but each photo made her feel as if a lump was forming in her throat.

Perhaps the media was right, she thought as she stared out the window in her bedroom, watching the setup of tables and flowers and other decorations that Carol had told her would be "just perfect." Perhaps he can't settle down with just one woman.

Someone knocked at her bedroom door. She glanced over her shoulder at the door before letting the curtain fall back into place, then she padded across the plush white carpet toward the door. She was wearing a white robe, tied at the waist, after having taken a nice warm bubble bath in the large tub in her bathroom. So standing behind the door, she opened it slightly and peeked outside, making certain that she was hidden.

It was Alejandro.

He seemed tense and withdrawn, standing on the other side of the door. His eyes studied her face, flickering back and forth from her eyes to her lips. Yes, she thought. Something was clearly bothering him. "May I?" he asked, gesturing toward the room.

"I'm not dressed," she said softly, her heart pounding as she noticed the way his jaw was clenched.

"Ay, Dios,*"* he said and pushed the door open, gently but with enough force that she had no choice but to back away and let him into the room. He stood before her, wearing a black tuxedo that accentuated his broad shoulders and muscular chest. When he saw her standing there in the white robe, clutching it tightly at her throat, he actually almost smiled. "Is that why you said no?" He motioned toward the robe. *"¡Qué rica!"* And he laughed, reaching out to take her hand and pull her close to him. The gesture startled Amanda, and as he took her hands, she felt the robe open slightly, exposing more of her chest than she felt comfortable with.

"Alejandro," she said, trying to free her hands in order to close the top of the robe.

But he wasn't listening. Instead, he backed her into the wall and cupped her head against it. "I have a surprise for you tonight," he said softly, that deep, husky tone to his voice, the one that she hadn't heard since their engagement was announced. "I hope it makes you happy, Princesa."

"I'd be happy if you let me get changed properly and privately," she replied, her voice soft but firm. "This is inappropriate."

Again, the laugh. A deep belly laugh that she hadn't heard for a while either. "What is the difference? Explain that to me," he asked. "Between seeing you in a bathing suit and seeing you in a robe?"

She managed to free one hand and clutch at the robe. "I can't explain it. But there is."

His face was close to hers, and his blue eyes searched her dark ones. With his other hand, he traced an imaginary line along the tip of her nose to her lips. "Not for long," he whispered before he leaned forward to kiss her, a powerful and passionate kiss that left her breathless and stunned. She could smell the strong, musky scent of his cologne and felt the strength of his body against hers. The way the kiss made her feel caused her cheeks to flush, especially when he pulled away, just enough so that he could gaze into her eyes once again. "It will be a good night, no?"

And then he released her. As suddenly as his moment of passion was there, it was gone.

He turned away from her and walked toward her closet. "Lucinda sent you a dress that I'd like you to wear tonight," he said, with a gruff hoarseness to his voice. "I asked Señora Perez to hang it in your closet. It's the pale blue dress." He glanced over his shoulder at her. Once again, he seemed to hesitate, drinking her in with his eyes. When he cleared his throat, he looked away. "I think you will find it most beautiful and flattering, despite how simple it is," he added, his voice returning to normal.

Without another word, he left the room and shut the door behind him.

For a moment, she stared at the closed door, stunned by the whirlwind that had just flown in and out of the room. What had just happened? she wondered. Clearly, he was a man of many moods and ways of expressing them. After two weeks of barely seeing him, she was even more confused by his actions and words just then, more than by his weeks of silence and absence.

Downstairs, people were already gathered in the backyard. Unlike Alejandro's other parties, the people were dressed in much fancier clothing. Men wore suits or tuxedos, and the women wore pretty designer dresses. Amanda stood in the kitchen door, her hand nervously touching her hair to make certain that her bun was still in place and that no strands had come loose.

"¡Qué linda!"

Amanda turned around, surprised to hear Señora Perez behind her. "You startled me," Amanda said with a slightly nervous laugh.

"You look beautiful," she said in her thick, broken English. "But let me fix your hair." Before Amanda could protest, Señora Perez was poking at her hair, sticking something into her bun. "There! *¡Perfecto!*"

Again, Amanda reached her hand to her hair and was surprised to feel several small flowers tucked into the bun. She blushed, not used to such attention, certainly never having put flowers in her hair. "That's so fancy," she mumbled, mostly to herself, for Señora Perez was already guiding her out the door.

"There she is!" Alejandro called out. He was standing with a group of people, a glass of champagne in his hand. Leaving the people, he hurried to meet Amanda on the steps of the patio. With a grand sweep of his arm, he gave her a slight bow before taking her hand in his and lifting it to his lips. As he did this, his eyes swept over her and he sighed. "Stunning," he whispered so that only she could hear. He turned her around, admiring the flowers in her hair and the way that the dress's flared hemline danced around her ankles.

She felt as if she was on display, and it made her feel uncomfortable.

"There's Amanda," Alejandro said once again, turning back to the guests. They watched the show with a mixture of adoration and amusement at the charming Alejandro. "My future bride," he announced, lifting his arm in the air and making a broad, exaggerated sweep before her. To Amanda's dismay, the people began to applaud, and she wished the earth would open up and simply swallow her whole.

He helped her down the patio steps and guided her through the crowd and toward the cabana. She recognized his family, his mother and uncles. She saw Justin and Celinda, smiling from across the patio. She even noticed his regular entourage, Miguel and Little Juan.

Surprisingly, she didn't see Maria or her pack of friends. For that, she was grateful.

Once at the cabana, he turned around and smiled at the crowd. "To celebrate our engagement," he said loudly, "I have a surprise for Amanda. I have written a new song, and it is being released tonight. But before it is released, I wanted to sing it here . . . to Amanda . . . in front of all of you."

As if on cue, music started and the crowd began to laugh, applauding at the lively beat that surrounded them from the outdoor speakers. Amanda stood there, by herself, while Alejandro transformed in front of her eyes. For a moment, she was back at one of the concerts, listening to him sing in front of thousands of people, hearing them cheer and stare at him with complete adoration.

Then he began to sing.

"Living on the road, life on the stage," he started, his voice strong and poetic. The crowd began to clap, swaying back and forth in rhythm to the music. "Never thought 'bout love. Just living day to day." He moved away from her, dancing and laughing as the people danced with him. Even Amanda smiled, watching him as he sang and danced. He was enjoying himself.

"Singing in the booth, moving state to state. VIPs and private jets. Never thought 'bout fate." He paused and glanced over his shoulder at Amanda. "Plain fame. It was all my game. Traveling 'round the world. Never thought to change. Women come and go. Never think twice. The last thing on my mind, thinkin' 'bout a wife."

Several men cheered at that part of the song, and Amanda frowned. Alejandro moved back toward her, reaching out for her hand.

"Life has its own plan, not much we can do. God gave me my princesa. How could I help but fall for you?" He pulled her close and stared down at her face, his eyes sparkling and full of life.

"Plain fame. Not worth the name. Not if it means you won't share the same. Plain change, that's my new life, but only with my love beside me as my wife!"

The crowd of people cheered, and Alejandro put the microphone down, the music still playing in the background as he caressed Amanda's face. She tried to look away, embarrassed by so much attention, but he tilted her chin and forced her to look back at him.

"You like your wedding song, *sí?*" he asked, with that familiar sly smile on his face.

Amanda frowned. "Wedding song?"

He kissed the back of her hands, then leaned down, whispering softly into her ear, "*Sí*, Princesa. Today is your wedding." He paused before correcting himself. "Our wedding day."

Confused, she looked around at the people. They were Alejandro's friends and family, business associates, and other singers, some of whom had flown in from New York and California. Everyone was smiling. Everyone was waiting, watching for her reaction to the bigger surprise of the evening.

"But . . ." It dawned on her what he had done. And in that moment of clarity, she looked away, fighting the tears that threatened to slip from her eyes.

He pulled her into his arms, ignoring the people around them. They were smiling, all of them having been told in advance about the surprise ceremony. All of them, except Amanda. "Now you have planned the perfect Englische wedding, no?"

"Oh, Alejandro," she managed to say, choking back a sob.

Indeed, without telling her, he had helped her plan her own wedding. He had kept her busy, hiring people to assist her, but by not telling her, he had removed all of the stress and pressure of wedding planning. And even more important, he had followed several of the Amish traditions. From the three-week time period after announcing their engagement to the pale blue dress he had given her to wear, there were elements of Amish mixed with the Englische.

And suddenly, he was leading her toward a clearing on the patio where a man stood in a suit. On either side of the area were tall white vases with white and blue flowers. He held her hand as they stood there, before the people who had gathered to celebrate, and she heard a flurry of words that barely made sense to her. She was in a dream, nothing making sense, as Alejandro stood next to her, nodding at the words and making his commitment to love, honor, and cherish Amanda until death do them part.

Amanda sat next to her bruder, *watching as the bishop stood before the congregation, the young bride wearing a pale blue dress with white apron and cape and the young groom in his Sunday best. They had just sat through almost three hours of sermon and singing. Now was the time for the marriage ceremony.*

"Do you confess, brother, that you wish to take our fellow sister as your wedded wife, and not to part from her until death separates you? Do you believe this is from the Lord and that through your faith and prayers you have been able to come this far?"

Aaron shifted on the hard wooden bench, fidgeting as he sat next to her. He should have been seated with the men but had snuck over to where Amanda sat in the back with the other young, unmarried women. He was too old to be sitting with the women, but Amanda made room for him anyway.

He leaned over and whispered to her, "Will I have to do this someday?"

She smiled and touched his knee to silence him, but she nodded at his question.

"Will you and Anna?"

Amanda lowered her head. "Shh!"

"Is Anna going to marry that boy who keeps bringing her home?"

Amanda gave a quick roll of her eyes and whispered, "If God wills it, mayhaps next year."

He groaned. "We'll have to do this again next year?"

She had to stifle a giggle at his impatience. She imagined that, for a twelve-year-old boy, sitting through such a long service, on a Thursday of all days, was painful. He'd rather be anywhere but at church during the week. She had felt the same way when she was younger. But, now that she was old enough to attend singings and watch her friends pair up with Amish men, she began to feel a shift in her heart.

She watched the bride as she nodded her head to the bishop when it was her turn to answer the same questions.

Amanda knew that the wedding party would continue until early evening. There would be food all afternoon, singing of hymns, and a general feeling of fellowship as the community and family gathered to celebrate this union—a forever union. That evening, the newlyweds would stay at the bride's parents' home in order to help clean up and reorganize the house in the morning. For the next few months, they would live apart, only seeing each other on the weekends. Come spring, if they were lucky, he'd find a farm or house where they could live and begin their married life together. And, of course, by the following winter, there would most likely be a baby.

It was all so romantic, Amanda thought. If only it might happen to her one day.

Unlike with the other parties at Alejandro's condominium, people began to leave shortly after midnight. Amanda stood by his side, saying good-bye to people she had never met before and wondering whether she would ever see them again. She was dazed and in shock, her heart beating inside her chest as she replayed the events from the evening.

The song. The justice of the peace. The vows. The kiss.

It wasn't real, she thought. It was a dream. Perhaps all of it was a dream and she was still living a simple and plain life on her parents' farm in Pennsylvania, miles and miles away from the tall palm trees and blue skies of Miami, and certainly a world away from the life she had just married into.

Amanda Diaz. It didn't even sound Amish.

In all of her life, she never would have been able to imagine that this was how it would turn out. She never thought she'd leave the Amish. She never thought she'd move away from Pennsylvania. And she certainly never imagined getting married to such a man as Alejandro Diaz in front of over two hundred people of whom none was either family or friend from her side.

Everything seemed unusually quiet when the last guests finally left. Alejandro stood at the front door, his back toward her for just a moment. She watched him, wondering what he was thinking. His shoulders lifted and fell as he took a deep breath before he turned around and looked at her.

"Wife," he whispered, a hint of a smile on his lips.

"Husband," she replied playfully, despite the pounding of her heart inside her chest.

He crossed the room in three strides and pulled her into his arms. For a long moment, he stared down at her, his eyes studying her face. Then he leaned down and nuzzled at her neck. "You are so amazing, Amanda Diaz," he said, his warm breath caressing her ear. "I hope you thought tonight was perfect."

She shut her eyes, feeling the power of his arms around her. With her cheek pressed against his shoulder, she felt safe and protected. "Perfect," she whispered.

"It's not over yet," he whispered back, and she squeezed her eyes shut, fear and apprehension flooding through her. "Come," he commanded, and holding her hand while looking at her, he led her up the stairs and toward his bedroom.

Outside the bedroom, he stepped aside and pushed the door open so that she could walk through first. She hesitated, biting her lower lip and looking up at him. His eyes glanced over her head and into the room. "Go," he urged softly. "See what I have done."

The room was aglow with candles, dozens and dozens, perhaps hundreds of candles. Almost every surface of every piece of furniture was covered with white roses in an assortment of vases. The room smelled heavenly, the sweet scent of flowers mixed with the musky odor of candles. She gasped when she saw it, clasping her hands before her chest and taking a step inside the room.

"Alejandro!" she gushed, looking around. It was magnificent, truly amazing to see the white petals basking in the orange glow of the flames. "It's . . ." She glanced at him. "It's like nothing I've ever seen!"

He crossed the room toward a silver champagne bucket, and without saying a word, he popped the cork and poured two glasses of the bubbly golden liquid. When he handed the tall, fluted crystal glass to her, he lifted his own in a silent toast, his eyes meeting hers and urging her to sip her champagne.

She did.

He reached up with one hand and untied his bow tie, pulling it free from the shirt collar and casually tossing it onto a chair. "Come here," he demanded, his voice low and husky with his eyelids half lowered as he regarded her. "I want you to unbutton my shirt, Amanda."

"I . . ."

"Do it," he said.

She felt faint as she took the two steps required to stand before him. He reached for her champagne glass, freeing up her hands to touch the top button of his shirt. There were little black-and-gold buttons, and she frowned, never having seen anything like that before. "I'm not certain I know how," she said, horrified at her own admission.

He smiled, chuckling to himself. "Here," he said, handing her the champagne glasses so that he could undo the strange buttons. When they were off, he slid his arms out of the shirt and tossed it by the bow tie on the chair. He dropped the buttons into his pants pocket and reached out for the champagne glass that she was holding for him. He stood before her in his black tuxedo pants and white sleeveless undershirt, his eyes smoldering as he watched her, like a cat watching a bird before it pounces.

"Your turn," he whispered.

"I . . ." The words caught in her throat. This is not happening, she told herself.

"Your shoes," he said, trying to not laugh at the look on her face. "I meant your shoes."

"Oh," she said. It was easy to kick off the simple heels with rhinestone straps over the toes.

"Isn't that better?" he teased. He knew how much she preferred to go barefoot. If only he knew how fast her heart was beating inside her chest, she thought.

He motioned toward the side of the bed, gesturing for her to sit down. When she did, her eyes wide and staring at him, he knelt before her and took the champagne glass from her hand, setting both glasses on the nightstand among the vases of flowers. Turning back to her, he ran a finger down her arm and took her hand in his. Gently, he squeezed it, staring at the new shining ring on her finger.

"I want you to know," he started to say, an edge to his voice, his eyes still on her ring, his thumb gently playing with it. She looked down at his hand in hers, realizing that she was staring at the hand of her husband, a man who would never know the hardship of daily farmwork or milking of cows. Instead, this was the hand of a man who made magic with his voice and words, his smile and gestures, his looks and image. But he was, indeed, her husband.

"I want you to know," he began again, "how very happy you make me, Amanda." He leaned down and kissed the ring. "I never thought this day would happen." He glanced up at her. "I never thought I, of all people, would ever get married."

She wanted to say something, but the look in his blue eyes stopped her.

"You changed all of that," he said, a slight smile on his lips. "These past few weeks . . . well, they haven't been easy on me," he said. "I'm not used to waiting for and wanting someone the way I have waited for and wanted you." He squeezed her hand again. "I had to remove myself from the condo, from you, in order to protect you."

Protect her? She frowned, not understanding. "From what?"

"From me," he admitted in a low, sensual voice that mirrored the look in his eyes. "You don't know how I feel around you, Princesa. What I want when I am near you. You don't know what you do to me. And that's the beauty of it. You simply . . . don't know." He reached out and touched her cheek. There was something about the way that he looked at her, his expression so serious and pensive, as if he had something on his mind. With a slight hesitation, as if lost in thought, he gave her a soft smile. "I'm sorry for being distant. It will never happen again."

She pressed her cheek against his hand and shut her eyes. "I thought you had changed your mind," she whispered. "I was afraid you had stopped loving me."

He laughed, a deep, rich-sounding laugh. He stood up, pulling her so that she stood before him, and he wrapped his arms around her. "Dios *mío,* Princesa. I could never stop loving you," he sighed, breathing in the scent of her hair. He nuzzled at her neck and reached up, his hand gently plucking the white flowers from around her bun. He took a small step back and placed them in her hand, smiling as she glanced down at the white rosebuds.

Covering her hand with his, he gave her a gentle tug while turning her around. "Just stand in front of the mirror, Princesa," he murmured. When she was facing away from him, her back pressed against his chest, she found herself in front of a tall mirror. Her eyes stared at the reflection. What she saw startled her.

Mirror people. A man and a woman. A husband and a wife. Alejandro and herself.

He had his hands on her shoulders, bare under the fabric of the Chanel dress. He was taller than she was, and she could see him peering at her, his blue eyes dancing and sparkling in the mirror. He reached up and began to pull at the bobby pins in her hair. As each pin slid out from her hair, she felt a shiver run up her spine until she finally shut her eyes, not wanting to watch the mirror people anymore.

"Look," he said as her hair tumbled down her back. With his fingers, he combed through it and pushed some over her one shoulder. "You are beautiful, Amanda Diaz."

At his command, she opened her eyes, but she didn't look at herself. Instead, she stared at him. His hands rubbed her shoulders, the touch of his skin against hers setting her on fire.

"Qué dulce," he murmured into her ear. He lifted her hair away from her neck and ran his lips against her skin.

Fire ran through her blood, and she shut her eyes, leaning back against him as she felt his hand carefully slide the thin strap of the dress over one shoulder, pausing to caress her skin before he removed the other strap. With both of her shoulders bare, she shivered under his touch.

"Open your eyes," he commanded softly.

"No," she whispered.

"Princesa," he said, his hand moving toward the zipper in the back of her dress. She heard it sing as he gently pulled it down to her waist. The dress was loose now, and she shivered, even though she wasn't cold. She felt him hook his hands into the fabric and gently tug so that it fell down by her feet in a small puddle of blue-and-white satin. "Open now," he breathed as he traced a line along her shoulder with his lips. "See how beautiful you are."

"Alejandro." She wanted to do what he asked, wanted to please him, but she couldn't. "I . . . I just can't." She felt him turn her around again, and then his finger was under her chin, tilting her head just enough. Now that she was facing away from the mirror, she opened her eyes. "I'm scared," she whispered, staring up at him.

"Don't be," he replied. His eyes gazed down at her, standing before him in a white lace bra and panties. She saw his jaw clench, the muscles twitching for just a moment, before he put his hand on the curve of her waist and pulled her close to him. "Dios *mío,*" he murmured to himself before he lowered his mouth onto hers, the past weeks of pent-up passion unleashing at last in a kiss that weakened her knees and caused her to collapse against him, her hands on his shoulders.

He pressed her back toward the bed, guiding her as she stepped backward while still in his arms. Gently, he pushed her so that she was sitting on the edge of the mattress, her big brown doe eyes staring up at him, frightened and excited at the same time. In one swift movement, he removed his sleeveless undershirt and tossed it on the floor, his eyes still holding her gaze. But her eyes flickered, just for a second, as she glanced down at the tattoos on his arms and chest.

"Tonight," he said, walking toward her again. He pushed her back onto the bed, helping her move backward as he hovered over her. "Tonight I make you my queen, Princesa." He chuckled softly as he saw the color flood to her cheeks. Reaching for her hand, he placed it on his chest. "Touch me here," he said. "Feel my heart beat."

She could.

"It beats for you. For us. For this moment. Forever."

She felt the tears forming at the corners of her eyes.

"No tears," he said, shaking his head. "Just enjoy this moment, Amanda. And may it shine forever."

With the flickering glow of the candles illuminating the room, Alejandro took Amanda in his arms, his lips covering hers once again. She wrapped her arms around his neck, letting him guide the way and show her how to love as husband and wife. And when the moment came, she realized that, indeed, she was lost in the moment, lost in his attention, and lost in the power of his love.

Chapter Twenty-One

She awoke to the smell of freshly brewed coffee in the bedroom. For a moment, as her eyes fluttered open, she didn't remember where she was. It wasn't the farm, and it wasn't her bedroom. She blinked and tried to focus in the dim light from the crack in the curtains that covered the window.

"Buenas días, mi amor."

When she heard his deep voice, tender and soft, she started to sit up, but realized that she wasn't wearing anything. Clutching at the sheet, she covered herself and wiggled around in the direction of his voice. She saw him, sitting in the chair by the bed, sipping at his coffee while he stared over the edge of the mug, watching her with his deep blue eyes. He was already dressed in golden khaki slacks with a white long-sleeve shirt that was unbuttoned at his neck. The sleeves were rolled up to his elbows. Seeing his tattoos on his arms reminded her.

Her mind returned to the night before, hours spent in intimacy, and she sank back into the pillow, covering her head with the sheet.

He laughed.

She heard him set the mug on the nightstand and felt the mattress shift as he crawled into bed next to her. Before she could protest, his arms were wrapped around her and he was pulling her close against his body.

"Shy this morning, *sí?*" He was amused.

"Don't tease me," she whimpered softly, but she loved the feeling of his chest against her back and his arms holding her tight.

Another laugh. His good mood was embarrassing her even more, and she wished with all of her might that she could stay hidden under the sheet all day. But it wasn't to be. He pulled at the sheet and tossed it aside. "I will tease you. I will look at you. And I will keep loving you," he purred into her ear. "But not until you get up, get dressed, and get moving."

She opened one eye and peeked at him, causing him to shake his head and smile. "To where?"

He ran his hand down her bare arm, pausing to brush it against her flat stomach. "I'd prefer to stay here all day with you like this in my bed, but, alas, that is not in the cards, Princesa." He tickled her side playfully, and she tried to not laugh. "But you have a honeymoon ahead of you, and while I will have plenty of time to admire my wife's beautiful body and shower it with love, that will not happen until we are on the boat and on our way to the islands."

As he rolled off the bed and reached for the coffee mug, she sat up, clutching the sheet to hide her breasts. "Islands?"

"Sí." He nodded. "I want to relax on warm beaches, dance at the marinas, and sleep under the stars." He watched her covering herself and raised an eyebrow, amused at her modesty. "And make love to you again and again."

She blushed, her heart beginning to race as the color rose to her cheeks. Averting her eyes, Amanda refused to look at him. "Stop, Alejandro! You are embarrassing me!"

"You weren't saying that last night," he teased, watching her from the side of the bed, his lips hovering over the steaming mug of coffee with a playful smirk on his face.

Flopping back onto the pillow, she covered her face with the sheet again, but when he started to laugh, she found herself joining him.

Two hours later, she was sitting in the shade of the overhang at the back of the boat, her legs tucked up under her as she rested her chin on her hand and watched the shores of Miami disappear.

My life, she thought. This is my life now.

Alejandro hadn't been joking with her when, on that first day after picking her up from the farm, he had warned her that she would not only change but also live. She had changed, accepting the worldliness of Alejandro's life. While she missed glimpses of her former life with the Amish, she was adapting to this new world.

"Princesa!"

She lifted her head and realized that Alejandro was calling her from inside the living quarters of the boat. She swung her legs down and quickly stood up, giving a stretch before she hurried in the direction of his voice. *"Ja?"*

He was standing in front of the large flat-screen television. He waved his hand for her to join him. "Come, come," he said, his voice full of excitement. "I found a news story about us." Putting his arm around her shoulders, he leaned over and kissed her head. "Um, you smell like coconut oil. *¡Deliciosa!* I could gobble you up." He nibbled at her skin and whispered, "Save that for later, *sí?*"

She laughed at him but turned her gaze to the television. Within the next two minutes, the commercials ended and the news program came back on, displaying a photograph of Amanda in her blue-and-white dress, with Alejandro in his tuxedo singing to her. Horrified to see herself on television, she buried her face against his shoulder and groaned, embarrassed by such attention.

"America's most famous Amish girl is Amish no more," the reporter started. "Last night at a party to announce their engagement, Viper surprised everyone by turning it into a wedding. After serenading his bride-to-be with his just-released song 'Plain Fame,' Viper and Amanda exchanged vows in front of over two hundred friends, family, and fellow artists in what has been reported as a most intimate and sophisticated ceremony. We wish Mr. and Mrs. Viper the best of luck as they head for their honeymoon aboard his private yacht before his Holiday Tour kicks off."

Alejandro laughed and clicked off the television. *"¡Excelente!"* He tossed the remote control onto a chair and turned around to hug Amanda. "Mr. and Mrs. Viper," he sang. "I like the sound of that."

"It sounds terrible," she said, making a face before she shuddered and added, "Snakes."

For the next hour, they sat at the back of the boat, sipping mimosas and eating cheese and grapes that were brought out to them. She liked the bubbly taste of the orange juice mixed with the champagne, despite the fact that there was alcohol in the drink. Just a little, he had said, to give it the bubbles. They talked about their wedding, the upcoming holidays, and even about the upcoming year. With a new album being released before Christmas, the following year would be busy with promotions, concerts, and events throughout many different countries.

She didn't like the idea of flying so much, but from the look on his face, she knew that he expected her to travel with him.

"It'll be good for you to see the world," he said, plucking a plump red grape from the bowl and popping it into his mouth. "It's the best education, to see the world."

"I never had much use for education," she admitted. Indeed, as with all Amish youth, she had only completed up to the eighth grade.

"I graduated high school," he admitted. "Just not with my class. The streets were my education, but so was travel." He sipped at his drink. "Just wait until you see the beauty of South America. You will be forever changed!"

At that statement, she laughed. "My goodness, Alejandro! I think I've been through enough change already for one lifetime, *ja?*"

"What's wrong with you, Amanda?" Anna asked her sister as she pinned her apron over her dress. "Why don't you want to go to the singing?"

Amanda stretched across the bed, her arm tossed over her forehead. She managed to shrug. "I don't know," she admitted. "I just don't."

Her sister turned to stare at Amanda, one hand on her hip and a scowl on her face. "You sure do seem to like spending more time at home than with friends these days. Something is different about you."

Again, Amanda shrugged. She didn't know how to tell her sister that she preferred the simplicity of being at home, helping her mother and daed, *and just being alone. She had lost interest in the singings, especially after Joshua Esh had started courting Hannah. It wasn't that she had truly cared for him. No, that wasn't it. But she had watched the pairing up of couples and realized that everything seemed too orchestrated. So planned. So preordained. She didn't want to live a life that was so constricted. She wanted to live life, period. To appreciate the beauty of nature, to think about the world, and to dream about what might be out there, waiting for her. She wasn't made from a cookie-cutter mold. No, she realized, she was different and wanted something different. She just didn't know what it was.*

For the next five days, Amanda basked in Alejandro's undivided attention. During the day, they would tour the different islands, somewhat unknown among the locals and other vacationers. In the afternoons, she would curl up with her books on the boat, escaping to the world of the past while Alejandro checked his e-mails or made any necessary calls. At night, he would take her back onto the islands, finding some local restaurant with fresh Caribbean lobster or a fancy dining facility at one of the larger hotels so that he could dance with her afterward.

She was even getting over her shyness with him when he approached her at night in the privacy of their bedroom. The look in his eyes as he reached for her, tenderly undressing her under the glow of the moon that shone through the small window, sent chills down her spine. It thrilled her to think that she could make Alejandro look at her in that way.

But her favorite time of the day was the nighttime. After he had made love to her, he would sleep with his arms wrapped protectively around her, their skin pressed against each other, and his breath caressing her ear as he slept. She would lie awake, listening to the gentle sound of his soft snores, and smile, clinging to his arm that was across her chest. There were moments when she wanted to cry . . . the joy was overwhelming.

"Do you see the bluebird?"

Amanda knelt next to her brother, pointing to the pretty bluebird as it fluttered by the bird box on the telephone pole near the road. "She's beautiful, ja?*"*

*Aaron nodded. "*Ja, *God's creature."*

It was a ritual of theirs. Every spring, they would walk down to the end of the driveway on Friday evenings. The sun would be setting over the neighbor's farm, the sky a soft golden orange. In the distance, a buggy might be heard rattling along the road or a mule might bray. But, otherwise, it was peaceful and quiet, a time for reflection and to look for the bluebird as she flew back to the box with straw or yarn in her mouth to make her nest.

There would come a time when the bluebird would leave, usually toward the end of summer. Amanda always wondered where she went and if her babies went with her. It broke her heart to think otherwise, so she chose to believe that they flew south for the winter, enjoying one another's company until they returned north.

Those moments with Aaron were special, a time of joy and sharing that often brought tears to her eyes. Having just turned twelve, he was still enamored of nature and life, appreciating all of God's creatures. She, on the other hand, was enamored of her little brother and loved seeing the world through his eyes.

As the sun continued to set over the field and the bluebird disappeared into the box for the last time that night, Amanda stood up and reached for her brother's hand. Together, they walked back down the dusty lane toward the house.

"Good news, Princesa!"

She looked up as he breezed into the room. She was sitting on the sofa, crocheting a blanket. It was different shades of white and cream, and she was using a shell stitch. She knew that it didn't get too cool in Miami, but she could picture herself curled up with the blanket at night during the winter months, perhaps seated outside and reading one of her books.

"Good news is right *gut!*" She smiled at him, loving the glow in his eyes. "Now, mayhaps you'll share it with me?"

"The new song has hit number one, and there's even talk of a Grammy!" He reached down for her hand and plucked her from the sofa, pulling her into his arms. "Your song!"

She laughed at his joy. "You mean your song."

"Our song," he whispered, nuzzling at her neck. "I think we should go out tonight to celebrate!"

Life was a constant celebration with Alejandro. Since their return from their tour of the islands, he had been more attentive and insisted that she accompany him everywhere. Even when his friends came over to work on songs—the men sitting around the table with Alejandro focused on the laptops before them, mixing the songs and adjusting the music levels—he wanted her in the room. She'd sit in a big chair, reading or crocheting, occasionally looking up when Alejandro asked her what she thought. She'd nod her head, not quite certain what he was asking her but knowing that it was the appropriate response.

"And tomorrow we leave for New York. Our first interview on television!" He laughed and set her back onto her feet. "The world wants to meet Mrs. Viper!"

Inwardly, she groaned. The thought of being on television was terrifying to her. For Alejandro, it was nothing to be interviewed by reporters or to perform in front of thousands of people. Amanda much preferred staying in the background.

"Friday morning, we have to get up early. Performing at the *Today Show* before our interview with *The View*," he reminded her. "Don't worry about packing. Lucinda has your outfits picked out, and they'll be at the hotel." He glanced down at his phone and shook his head. Someone was calling. She watched him as he answered the phone in Spanish, turning his back to her as he walked over to the window, his voice soft and low.

Rodriego glanced at Alejandro as he walked into the room. He held a small white envelope in his hand. "Amanda," he said. "This came in the mail today for you."

She took the envelope, surprised to see the formal, loopy curves of handwriting on the front. Her mother. She felt her heart flutter and an immediate wave of dread flooded over her. She hadn't heard from her parents since she had left. Indeed, each of her letters went unanswered. So when she had written that she was getting married to Alejandro, she never expected to hear back. Certainly they were heartbroken by her decision to leave her family, to leave with Alejandro, and to leave the Amish. However, she had to remind herself that they had been prepared to send her back to Ohio in order to stop the paparazzi from bothering their community.

"Thank you," she whispered as she stared at the envelope. It wasn't very large. Whatever was inside, whatever words waited for her, it certainly wasn't more than one sheet of paper. After two months of silence, only one sheet?

He was watching her from the window and quickly ended his phone call. Pushing the phone into his pocket, he strode over to the sofa and knelt down before her. "Shouldn't you open it before you judge the contents, Princesa?"

Her eyes flickered from the envelope to his face. With a slight frown, she nodded, acknowledging the wisdom of his words, which he had spoken after observing her expression and reading her mind. Sighing, she flipped over the envelope and slid her finger along the flap to open it. As she had suspected, a single sheet of paper fluttered out. She felt his hand on her knee and spared him a quick smile before she opened the piece of paper and began to read her mother's words. They flew off the page with pieces of each sentence cutting through her like a dagger.

Received your last letter.
Disappointed in your decision.
Anna getting married in November.
Too much work on the farm.
Father selling the farm.

Amanda sighed and handed him the letter. She waited until his eyes scanned the few short lines. It was signed "Love, Mother." But the words did not express any indication that she meant it. To her family, she was a stranger now, having chosen the life of the Englische over the life of the Amish.

"We can try to visit, no?" he asked as he handed the letter back to her.

She shook her head. *"Nee."* She slipped the folded letter back into the envelope. "Not yet. They aren't ready." She met his concerned gaze. "Maybe they never will be."

He squeezed her knee, a gesture meant to comfort her as he stood back up. "Come," he said. "Let's go out for dinner and dancing, *mi amor*." He pulled her to her feet and placed a soft kiss on her lips. "Let me show off my beautiful wife to the world and spoil her with attention and love, *sí?*"

If only his kiss could quell the sadness that she felt in her heart.

"One day," her father said to Aaron, "this farm will be yours, son."

Aaron stared at his father, a concerned look on his face. "Where will you and Mamm live?"

Everyone had laughed at the innocence of his question.

The music was too loud, and Amanda wished that she could just go home. She was tired, and they had a busy day tomorrow, with leaving for New York City. But Alejandro was in his element, laughing with his friends and buying drinks for some of the pretty women who hovered nearby. Amanda didn't mind that for she knew it was part of the Viper game.

But she did mind Maria, who continued to hang around him, her hand on his shoulder possessively. She monopolized Alejandro's attention, not letting anyone else get close to him. Of course, when Amanda would approach him, Maria would quickly disappear, not even sparing a smile or a single word for Alejandro's wife.

"*¡Mi amor!*" he called out when she walked toward him. He pulled her into his arms and gave her a soft kiss. "You are ready to dance, *sí?*" He gestured toward the dance floor. Without waiting for an answer, he turned and led her onto the floor where other people were dancing, the lights of the club swirling overhead and the music pounding in her ears.

At the sight of Viper bringing his wife onto the floor, people cleared a space for him. Amanda watched him as he began to dance, mesmerized as always by the way that he was able to make his body move in time with the music. He loved to dance, and when he did, his entire expression changed. Music coursed through his blood.

He reached out for her, his arm around her waist. Pulling her close, he helped guide her to move in time with the music. Despite not being comfortable dancing in such a setting, Amanda found herself loosening up as his fingers entwined with her one hand, moving her backward across the floor. Just being near him was overpowering and filled her with energy. His enthusiasm for life was contagious, and when he began to sing in her ear, she found herself laughing, forgetting that she was tired and had wanted to go home.

The DJ changed up the music and, to Alejandro's delight, played his most recent song: "Plain Fame." The crowd cheered and made room for Alejandro to serenade Amanda—their own private concert. She stood off to the side of the floor, her eyes watching his every move as Alejandro transformed once again into Viper, performing for the crowd as he sang to her.

"Looking at you tonight, your eyes sparkling so bright, your smile and laugh stuck inside my head. When I'm on the road, or in the booth, my heart stays with you instead," he sang, crossing the dance floor, pausing to dance in front of a group of women in the crowd. Their cheers encouraged him, and he kept singing, dancing along the perimeter of the gathering until he stood before Amanda. "Fame . . . the only name of my game, until that day you came into play." He reached for her hand and pulled her back into his arms, looking down into her face and ignoring the noise of the crowd behind them. "Love over fame. Without you nothing would be the same."

The crowd pulsated with energy as they cheered, dancing to the beat and taking cell phone photos of Alejandro and Amanda as the song ended and everyone applauded. The DJ quickly began a new song, and the dance floor filled once again.

For a moment, they stood there, neither one moving. He held her in his arms, staring down into her face. From his expression, she could tell that he was pleased. His eyes flashed with that all-too-familiar sultry look as he studied her face, his breathing short and deep. His eyes dropped to her lips, and she knew that he wanted to kiss her, to hold her, to take her home.

"You ready to go, Princesa?" he asked, his voice husky and deep. She blushed, knowing what that meant.

"Sí," she said softly, lifting her eyes to meet his. "Always."

Chapter Twenty-Two

Something was wrong. She could sense it right away. The crowds in New York City were not responding in the typical way. Despite Alejandro having given an amazing early-morning performance at the *Today Show* and the crowds cheering him on, Amanda could feel that something was off.

She stood inside the studio, watching through the window. There was a security guard assigned to stand by her, a precaution that Alejandro had insisted upon, although Amanda wasn't certain she understood why.

Then she saw the signs: "I Can Be Amish Too" and "A Married Viper Is Just a Garter Snake." She shut her eyes when she saw those signs and turned away from the window.

They had arrived in New York City the previous evening. The airport had been crowded, and security had guided them through the corridors to avoid any crowds. Several people had recognized him and called out. Alejandro had waved but didn't stop for his usual photo-and-chat opportunity. Instead, he reached for Amanda's hand and led her along with the security guards.

Amanda had been tired and promptly slipped into bed, barely shutting her eyes before she had fallen asleep. She had thought she heard Alejandro chuckling at her as he switched the light off and retired to the sitting room to work on some music. That's where she had found him at three in the morning, still poring over his laptop, mixing music.

"You still up, *ja*" she had asked sleepily from the doorway. "It's three, Alejandro."

He glanced at her. "Is it?"

She had crossed the room and slid next to him on the sofa, curling her legs under her and resting her head on his shoulder. "Come to bed," she had whispered.

"In a minute."

Shutting her eyes, Amanda had fallen back to sleep, sitting next to him while he continued to work. It was four o'clock when he had finally shut the laptop and started to stand, waking her in the process. He took her hand and led her back into the bedroom. He had to leave in an hour, so rather than sleep, he had stripped off his clothes and crawled into bed with Amanda, taking her into his arms and waking her with soft kisses before he made love to her.

Now, as she stood in the studio, her thoughts flipping between the memory of his love that morning and the obnoxious messages on those signs, she could only sigh.

"Coffee?"

She turned around and smiled at the young woman who handed her a warm coffee mug. *"Danke,"* Amanda said as she took the coffee.

"I . . . I think . . ." the woman started to say but stopped, averting her eyes. "Never mind."

Amanda smiled. Most people tended to avoid her. Their attention was either on Alejandro, or they were too intimidated by her Amish past to approach her. *"Nee,"* she said, encouraging the woman to speak her mind. "Tell me what you think."

The young woman glanced through the window at Alejandro performing outside. "I think your story with Viper is amazing," she confided in Amanda. Shyly, she glanced at her again. "It's very romantic."

For a second, Amanda looked away. *Amazing? Romantic?* Those were words she had never associated with any aspect of her life. Still, she felt that familiar rush of emotion when she returned her gaze to watch Alejandro as he sang to the crowds. At one point, she thought she saw him turn to look at the window as if searching for her. She smiled, not certain whether he could see her through the tinted glass.

"I think so, too," Amanda finally replied.

Was it only six months ago that she had been returning from Ohio? Less, she realized. How much her life had changed since that time. One accident, and everything had shifted in ways she never could have imagined.

"They're ready for you," a man said over her shoulder.

Amanda glanced at him, then handed the coffee mug back to the young woman. "OK," she said, slipping her arms into the Burberry jacket and tightening the belt before she followed the man down a long corridor toward a door that led outside. Once the door opened, she could hear the noise of the screaming fans, some who were now screaming for her. The security guard gently took Amanda's elbow and led her through the break in the crowd toward the stage.

Alejandro had wanted her up there with him. He wanted to introduce her to the fans before singing his hit song, "Plain Fame." He wanted her standing on the stage so that he could serenade her in front of the thousands of people gathered in Rockefeller Plaza and the millions who were watching from the comfort of their homes.

"Many of you know," she heard him say into the microphone, "that I just released a new song." The crowd began to scream, knowing what song he was about to sing. "Many of you also know that I wrote this song about my feelings for one particular young lady." He paused. "A lady who, with the blessing of God, has become my wife." More screams and a few hisses from the crowd. He had warned her that might happen. Alejandro ignored them as he turned, gesturing to the side of the stage. "I want to introduce you to Mrs. Viper, Amanda Diaz!"

Screams. Applause. Cheers.

Taking a deep breath, Amanda walked up the stairs and joined Alejandro. With his gloved hand, he reached out to take hold of hers. He lifted it to his lips, kissing the back of her skin and smiling when she blushed. "I wrote this song for you, Amanda," he said into the microphone. "But today," he continued, waving his arm over the crowd, "I sing it for all of you!"

The crowd jumped and yelled, waving their arms as he began to sing the song. Amanda felt awkward, standing on the stage, uncertain what to do. She had never been on the stage when he was performing, and it was odd watching him as he sang and entertained the audience. Fans reached up, hoping that he would shake their hands. Their faces beamed, bright and hopeful, full of adoration for this man.

Amanda understood why.

She could feel the pulse of the music as he sang. She even found herself swaying in time to the beat, and with the encouragement of one of the band members, she began to clap along with them. When Alejandro turned around and saw her, he grinned and yelled into the microphone, a happy noise, as he pumped his arm into the air. The crowd continued to scream and yell, dancing and clapping with him.

When the song ended, Alejandro lifted his arm into the air and lowered his head, listening to the final cheers from the crowd before he walked backward a few steps, turned, and reached out his hand for Amanda. Hesitantly, she took it, and to her surprise, he pulled her into his arms and kissed her in front of all of the people.

One of the morning anchors, Marc Latner, approached the stage, a microphone in his hand as he grinned and reached out to shake Viper's hand. "That was a great show. As always," he said. He smiled at Amanda. "And it's wonderful to meet the new Mrs. Viper. Congratulations on your recent wedding."

She returned the smile but stepped backward, hiding behind Alejandro. He laughed and put his arm around her, bringing her back toward the front so that everyone could see her.

"Thank you, Marc," Alejandro said. "We couldn't be happier."

"And with a new release song that burned its way to the top of the charts, I can imagine that life is all the way around quite good!"

Alejandro nodded. "God continues to bless me, first with my success and now with my wife."

"You do seem to work a lot. Not a lot of downtime. I understand that you have quite a few shows coming up along the East Coast," Marc said.

"That's right. We're hitting the major cities over the next few weeks but will be right back here to ring in the New Year with the Big Apple!" The crowd cheered and Alejandro laughed, nodding at the people and pumping his arm in the air.

"And a new album is being released before the holidays?"

Alejandro nodded. "*Sí, sí.* And we'll begin our spring tour in South America before returning to the States for a summer series."

"As always, you are keeping yourself busy. And, as always, Viper, a pleasure to have you here."

"Thank you, Marc. It's always great to be here and to entertain the good folks at Rockefeller Plaza!"

Thirty minutes later, they were in the back of a limousine, hurrying across Manhattan to their next stop for an interview on a morning talk show. Amanda stared out the window, watching the tall buildings pass by. Next to her, Alejandro was on his cell phone, talking with Mike about some appointments the following week in Miami and Atlanta.

By the time he finished the phone call, they were pulling up at their next stop.

While Amanda was a nervous wreck, petrified about being interviewed by the panel of women, she noticed that Alejandro breezed into the building, stopping to shake hands with several people. All in a day's work, she thought with both a touch of pride and envy at his composure and confidence.

"What's life like, Amanda, married to Viper?"

She wanted to squirm in the chair, but Alejandro had mentioned to her that it was imperative to pay attention to every gesture, movement, and expression. She glanced at him and he smiled, raising an eyebrow as he waited for her response.

"It's rather busy," she finally said, and the audience laughed. "And there's always a lot of people around." More laughter.

The woman who was asking the questions sat next to Amanda on a sofa. She was an older woman and had pleasant eyes. Amanda knew that she liked her right away and felt comfortable talking to her. It made the blurry faces of the audience disappear. "A lot different from living on an Amish farm, I would say, yes?"

Amanda bit her lower lip and stared at the woman. She didn't want to talk about the Amish. She didn't want to compare the lifestyles. It wasn't fair. But Alejandro had already prepped her for that question. "Obvious differences, *ja*," she admitted. "But there are less obvious similarities."

That seemed to catch the attention of the interviewer. "Oh?"

She nodded. "*Ja*, like the sunrise in Miami." She smiled. "I love waking up early and sitting on the back patio, watching the sun light up the sky. The birds are so happy and greet the day in song. Why, I can shut my eyes and could just as well be back at the farm!"

There was a murmur of appreciation among the audience, and the female interviewers nodded their heads.

Amanda glanced at Alejandro, hoping that she was saying the right things. When he smiled his encouragement at her, she continued. "And the people. *Ja vell*, they stare a lot and steal photos. But they did that in Pennsylvania, too." She turned her gaze back to the interviewer and, with a slight shrug of her shoulders, added, "Guess it's just for different reasons now." The audience laughed again, enjoying the innocent banter of the young woman.

The interviewer turned to Alejandro. "I must say," she began, "I've seen a big change in you, Viper. I think I understand why." She leaned forward and placed her hand on Amanda's knee. "They always say that behind every good man . . ."

The audience chimed in to finish her sentence. "Is an even better woman!"

Alejandro laughed, holding up his hands in mock self-defense. "*¡Ay,* Dios*!* I give, I give!" The audience loved his reaction.

When the fervor died down, the woman turned to Alejandro. She tilted her head as she smiled at him. "What's next, Viper? From bad boy to playboy to international sensation to loving husband! The transition is pleasant to see, true, but will the fans feel the same way?"

"Aw, Barbara," he said, rolling his eyes and leaning forward so that his elbow was resting on his knee. "My fans and my music are my everything, you know that." He turned his head to look at Amanda. She saw his eyes, dancing at her, and her mind flashed back to earlier that day when she had found him working at four in the morning. She blushed and he laughed. "Only I'm sharing the victories with someone very special to me now." Playfully, he leaned over and whispered, "What are you blushing about, Princesa?" which only caused her to turn crimson, to the delight of the audience and interviewer.

"Your new song . . ." Barbara continued. "It seems to say an awful lot, Viper. You have merged two very different worlds, haven't you? Yet you admit that you are choosing love over fame. Is that an indication that you might be slowing down a bit now?"

For a moment, Amanda thought that he was going to squirm. The question took her by surprise, and she immediately worried that people might actually be thinking that he was going to slow down. If only they could see how hard he works, she thought, wishing that she could speak up and say that. But this was Alejandro's question and she knew better than to respond. *Least said, soonest mended,* her mother always used to say.

He remained remarkably composed. "We're hitting eight cities between now and New Year's, Barbara. The only slowing down that will happen is for everyone else trying to keep up with me." The audience approved of his response and clapped, a few whistling from the seats. Alejandro laughed and looked out at his fans, waving his hand at someone.

"It's a beautiful thing," Barbara said, turning toward the camera. "Seems like music might tame the cobra, but it took someone as lovely as Amanda to tame the viper."

"Celery?"

Anna nodded her head shyly. "Ja," *she admitted. "I asked* Mamm *to plant the garden with lots of celery."*

That could only mean one thing, Amanda realized: a wedding next fall.

"Did he ask you?"

The direct nature of the question caused Anna to gasp, her forehead crinkling in a frown. "Of course not!"

"Then how do you know?"

Anna shook her head and dismissed her sister with a wave of her hand. "Oh, Amanda, you don't understand. You haven't courted yet."

It was true. Despite Benjamin's attempts to court Amanda, she had been quite standoffish with him. In recent weeks, she hadn't even attended any of the singings at all. Her friends often stopped by the farm, wondering if she was unwell. Amanda just replied that she was busy and tired and didn't feel like attending that week. Secretly, she was thankful that singings only happened every other weekend after church service. It gave her more space to avoid the questions.

"He won't ask until later in the fall. But we've talked about the future, and he hinted that I should talk to Mamm," Anna said, her cheeks rosy with excitement and her eyes glowing. "You are happy for me, ja?*"*

"You haven't been courting for that long," Amanda observed drily.

"What's that supposed to mean?" Anna snapped, the glow disappearing from her eyes.

Another shrug. "You never know what can happen, I reckon." She closed her eyes when her sister stormed out of the room, roughly shutting the door as she left. Truth was that she didn't want her sister to get married and move away. Truth was that she wished she, too, could find happiness. Truth was . . .

"I don't think I care very much for interviews," Amanda said reflectively as they sat at a window table at Bryant Park for dinner.

"Why's that, Princesa?"

She thought for a moment before she responded. "It's an unnatural dialogue, isn't it? The back and the forth. It's not like how we talk to each other. It's a forced conversation, and that makes me uncomfortable." She picked at her salad. "No, I don't like them at all."

He chuckled. "That's a shame because you handled the interviews very well."

They had left the television studio and visited two radio stations for interviews as well as a thirty-minute meeting with an entertainment show. It had been a long day with people constantly around. Carlos kept everything organized, and Alejandro said that the day was flawless. But Amanda had felt that it was chaotic and out of control. No matter where Alejandro went, there were crowds of people. If they weren't surrounded by his fans, they were most certainly surrounded by his inner circle of people who handled the logistics of his life.

"Do you think so, then?"

The sincerity of her question startled him. Setting his fork down, he wiped his mouth with his napkin. "Amanda," he said. *Aman-tha.* She still enjoyed hearing him say her name. "At some point, you will need to realize that the media adores you. You were spectacular today. And the way you handled Barbara . . ." He shook his head and smiled. "She's one of the toughest interviewers, but she just doesn't make it seem that way, no?"

"If you say so."

"The social media went crazy after your interview," he confided in her. "So it's not me saying so. The numbers don't lie." He seemed pleased with that, so she was reluctant to ask him what he meant. "And furthermore," he added, "you are *deliciosa, mi amor*. When you blushed today . . ." He let the sentence trail off. *"Ay, mi madre,"* he sighed happily. "I knew exactly what you were thinking."

"Alejandro!" She glanced around, hoping that no one could overhear his words.

He raised his eyebrows and growled playfully at her, his eyelids drooping just enough that she could barely see his blue eyes. "I want to see you blush tomorrow when you think back on what happens later tonight."

Horrified at his insinuation, she wished she could be angry or offended. No respectful Amish man would ever speak to his wife like that. Yet, despite what she knew was inappropriate by the standards of her family and church, she also knew that her insides fluttered when he talked to her like that, his eyes seeing through her and his voice caressing her heart. Her head felt light and woozy, and that surreal feeling flooded over her. She had no reply or comeback to his statement, so she merely looked away, hating the heat that colored her cheeks, clearly giving away what she was thinking.

"Stop," she whispered.

He laughed and pulled her close to him, his arms wrapped around her. *"Ay, mi amor,"* he said, running his hands down the sides of her arms. "What you do to me."

Chapter Twenty-Three

Carlos was waiting at the hotel lobby when the limousine pulled up to the front entrance. A few people lingered nearby, craning their necks to see who would emerge from the long black car with tinted windows. Alejandro waited until the doorman opened the car door before he reached for his sunglasses and slid them over his nose. He got out of the car and paused to smooth down the front of his slacks before he turned to reach for Amanda's hand.

The delay was enough time for a small crowd to gather, recognizing Viper and his young wife.

He started to wave to the fans and pose with Amanda when he felt a strong hand on his arm. "Alejandro," Carlos said and leveled his gaze at him. The expression on his face said it all. Something was wrong. "There is no time. We must speak."

Without so much as a second glance at the crowd, Alejandro clutched Amanda's hand and hurried after Carlos into the hotel lobby.

An elevator was waiting for them, and the hotel staff lowered their eyes as Alejandro and Amanda walked past them.

"What's going on?" Amanda whispered, a sense of dread falling over her. Her heart began to race as a dozen different horrible thoughts flooded through her mind.

"I don't know," he replied and offered no more words.

Once in their hotel suite, Carlos said something to Alejandro in Spanish. Amanda chewed on her lower lip, feeling lost and scared. She saw Alejandro catch his breath and lift his chin at whatever news Carlos shared with him. Then he nodded his head twice and glanced at Amanda. She had seen that look before, and the blood drained from her face.

"If you'll excuse me, Princesa," he said, and without waiting for her reply, he followed Carlos into a private sitting room in the suite. She stood there, staring at the closed door, and felt the racing beat of her heart inside her chest, remembering the only other time she had felt so scared.

"Now be careful," she had warned, an edge to her voice.

"I know that," he replied sharply, a quick roll of his eyes telling her that he was well aware of how to harness the horse. "I've done this before, you know."

Amanda frowned at her brother. "No need to be sassing me, Aaron. I just don't want you hurt, is all."

He made another face as he turned back to the large horse. "Daed taught me how to do it," Aaron mumbled. "I am almost a man, ja?*"*

She shook her head and leaned against the wall, wishing that he would hurry up and finish. Her mother needed to get to the store before they closed for the day. Tomorrow was Saturday, and they needed to make an awful lot of pies for the fellowship meal that followed church service on Sunday. They were supposed to go earlier in the afternoon, but nothing seemed to work according to Mamm's schedule.

First, the neighbor stopped over and stayed far too long visiting. Then a sun shower had come and drenched all of the laundry that was hanging out to dry. Finally, Daed had needed help fixing a fence after one of the mules had broken through and was found in a paddock at the farm next door, bothering the cows. Everyone's schedule had been thrown off-kilter, that was for sure and certain.

"You sure you don't want me to help?"

Aaron glared at her. "I am done telling you already. No!"

Frustrated, Amanda turned around and walked out of the barn door into the sunshine. She stared up at the sky, shaking her head. Not a cloud up above. Where had that rainstorm come from? Hadn't been in the forecast, that was for sure and certain. Otherwise, Mamm wouldn't have told her to hang the clothes outside.

She heard the scuffle of the horse, the nervous pawing, followed by the sound of a board breaking. Then silence.

"Aaron?" She cocked her head to the side, listening, but heard nothing. She didn't want to turn around. The silence was deafening. "Aaron?" She forced herself to walk back into the barn, her eyes taking a moment to adjust to the darkness.

And then she saw him.

He was lying facedown, motionless, on the floor of the horse stall, blood slowly oozing from the side of his head.

She wanted to scream, but no sound had come out of her mouth. He wasn't moving, his lifeless body on top of a broken board. The horse was standing to the side, sweating, biting at her flank, her ears pinned flat against her head, broken blood vessels invading the white in her eyes. Two things were immediately clear. The horse was in excruciating pain, badly colicky, and Aaron had been kicked by it as the horse must have mistakenly associated him with the pain.

"Daed!" The word came out of her mouth like a choked whisper. She took a step forward, staring at the body of her twelve-year-old brother. No movement. No flutters. No noise. And she knew. He was dead.

"Daed!" This time, the word came out louder, and then she managed to scream.

***

When Alejandro returned to the room, his face was pale and tense. He avoided looking at her for a moment, waiting for Carlos to leave the suite. Once the door shut behind him, Alejandro paused, thinking for a moment, his eyes staring at the carpet under his shoes.

"What is it?"

Taking a deep breath, he looked up and stared at her. She could see the sorrow in his eyes as he managed to say, "There's been an accident, Amanda."

"Who?" But she already knew.

"Your father."

"Is he . . . ?"

Alejandro shook his head. "He's in critical care at the hospital. I have a car coming to take us there now."

She shut her eyes, saying a quick prayer to God, asking him to watch over her father. "What happened?"

Alejandro crossed the room and put his hands on her shoulders. "They think he had a stroke while in the buggy. He was driving and swerved. A car was passing and hit the buggy," Alejandro said.

Her eyes flew open and she grimaced. Always the cars passing the buggies. Always the teenagers trying to scare the horses. How many times had she cringed as the cars flew past the horse-drawn buggies? Accidents happened all the time. "Is he going to live?"

"I don't know, Amanda, but we will make certain he has the best care, the best doctors. I will fly in anyone from anywhere to care for your father."

"I have to be there," she said, her voice shaking. "I should have been there."

He shook his head. "Don't say that."

The tears began to fall. "I never should have left."

Alejandro cringed at her words. "Listen to me," he said firmly and placed his hands on either side of her face. "I don't ever want to hear that. You don't know God's plan. If you had stayed, you might have been with him. You might have been injured." He paused. "Or worse."

"It's all my fault," she moaned. "Everything. I took away everything from them. First Aaron, then Anna, now me!"

He pulled her into his arms, ignoring the way that she stiffened, trying to extract herself from his hold. "It's not your fault, Amanda."

She sat at the front of the room, the plain pine coffin resting atop a table before her. Her parents and sister were next to her, weeping as the bishop spoke about God and his plan for his children. The words didn't make sense to Amanda as she stared at the small coffin. How could this be his plan? she wanted to ask.

There were over three hundred people crowded in the room. For the past two days, these same people had come to the house, paying their respects to the Beiler family. Neighbors had helped to clean out the back room, washing it from top to bottom after the furniture was removed to the barn. That was where Aaron's coffin had been placed after the undertaker prepared and returned his body.

Amanda couldn't look at him in the house. At first, she refused to go into the room. Instead, she had sat in the living room, her hands folded on her lap and her eyes downcast, not hearing the kind words that people said to her. They tried to comfort her, but her pain was too great.

It had been her fault.

No one said it. They didn't have to. She should have listened to her instinct and not to Aaron. Her father's horse was very large and powerful. That was why Daed had bought Aaron his own horse the year before. But Aaron had insisted on trying to harness his daed*'s horse, and Amanda had given him that liberty. In return, one swift kick from the horse and Aaron had died.*

Anna and her mother had heard the scream and ran out of the house, reaching the barn first. Elias had been on the other side of the barn, so it took him longer to run to where Amanda lay, crumpled on the ground, sobbing.

Her father assessed the scene, his eyes wide and full of disbelief. When he finally saw Aaron's body in the stall, he simply said two words in an emotionless tone: "my boy." Two words. But they said it all.

Within an hour, the house had been abuzz with people. Somehow Anna had managed to run to the neighbor's house and, through her sobs, tell them what happened. The Amish grapevine took over from that point. The bishop and ministers descended on the house, neighbors flocked to the farm, and the Beiler family was comforted through prayer as their community took action in the preparation of the funeral.

As for Amanda, she watched everything as if she were floating above the room, a bystander who observed the activity. Nothing seemed real. Her twelve-year-old brother hadn't just died. The neighbors weren't cleaning out the room so that his body could be placed there in a coffin. Her father wasn't really sobbing uncontrollably as people tried to comfort him. Her sister wasn't pushing away the hand of Menno Zook, the young man who tried to comfort her. It was all a dream.

But she knew the truth.

***

She was quiet during the car ride to Lancaster. Alejandro sat next to her, watching her thoughtfully. After a while, he turned to his phone and began sending messages, his thumbs moving rapidly across the small keyboard. Twice the phone rang, but he didn't answer the calls.

At the hospital, Alejandro led her through the lobby and past the information desk. He already knew where Elias was: the trauma center.

Amanda wasn't prepared to see her father in the hospital bed, tubes in his arms and up his nose. Machines beeped and flashed next to the IV bag that dripped liquid into his arm through the tube. Her mother was sitting next to the bed, her face ashen and her eyes glazed over as she stared at her husband.

"Mamm!" Amanda rushed toward her mother and wrapped her arms around her.

"Oh, Amanda!" her mother sobbed, clinging to her daughter. "You came home!"

"Of course I did, Mamm," Amanda said, a wave of guilt flooding over her. "Alejandro told me and we left at once." She felt her mother stiffen at the mention of Alejandro's name. "He's here, too," Amanda added softly. Extracting herself from her mother's embrace, Amanda turned to look at her father. "How is Daed?"

Lizzie shook her head and fought the tears. "He's in the Lord's hands now," was all that she could say.

For a long while, they stood there, side by side, looking down at Elias. For such a vibrant, active man to be motionless and incapacitated shocked Amanda. She couldn't fathom her father being anything less than a constant blur of energy. But in a single day, all of that had changed. A stroke, Amanda thought, wondering what he would be like if he managed to survive.

The door opened, and Alejandro cautiously entered the room. He glanced at Elias but quickly turned his attention to the two women standing at his bedside. It struck him how different they looked: Lizzie with her Amish garb, and Amanda in her plain black skirt and white blouse. She had transformed into an amazing woman in the past few months and now faced the biggest trial of them all.

"*Buenos días*, Lizzie," he said softly as he crossed the room and approached Amanda's mother. "I'm so sorry about Elias."

Lizzie nodded in response but said nothing.

"The doctor is coming in," Alejandro said, directing this statement at Amanda. "I requested that we speak to him. To get an update, *sí?*"

She nodded her head and reached for his hand. *"Danke,"* she whispered.

For a long time, life was in a holding pattern at the Beiler house. Family and friends stopped by on an almost-daily basis, checking on Elias and Lizzie. The garden went unweeded. The crops remained untended. Even the barn began to grow rank with odor from the lack of attention in cleaning the manure from the bedding.

Anna did what she could inside the house, and Amanda took over outside. It was too much for the girls to handle, especially as they were dealing with their own grief. Amanda blamed herself for having left the barn. Anna blamed herself for not having been there to help harness the horse.

For the rest of the summer and into the fall, there was a black cloud hanging over the Beiler house. Neither daughter attended singings. They were too tired after taking care of all the chores. The celery plants died and any talk of a wedding was long gone. When the wedding season came and went, Anna began to withdraw, losing weight and sleeping as much as she could.

Spring came and Elias managed to find the spiritual as well as physical strength to plow the fields in preparation for planting a new crop. Lizzie walked through each day as though in a trance, slowly trying to find a rhythm to her life, despite the gaping hole in her heart. By the time the one-year anniversary of Aaron's death was upon them, the shadow of the lost child was all that remained . . . that and Anna's depression.

He carried her bag through the kitchen and into the *grossdaadihaus*. Amanda didn't follow him but stood in her mother's kitchen, looking around. Everything seemed smaller to her. She didn't remember how confining the room felt with low ceilings and dark walls. She wondered if he had noticed it when he first arrived on the farm back in the summer. If he had felt the same way, that everything was quaint in the country.

"It's cold in here," he said when he returned, rubbing his hands together. "How do I turn on the heat?"

She didn't respond but walked to the propane fireplace and turned it on. He approached her, standing behind her, and rubbed his hands down her arms, trying to warm her.

"I suspect we need to get changed, *sí?* Tend to the animals?"

She nodded.

Neighbors had been helping with the cows and horses for the past two days. But Amanda knew that they had their own responsibilities at their own farms. On their way back to the farm from the hospital, they had stopped at their neighbors' to let them know that the farm would be taken care of that evening and the following morning.

"Come," he said, directing her toward the *grossdaadihaus* so that they could change their clothing and focus on the evening chores.

It felt strange working alongside Alejandro in the dairy barn, especially without her father being nearby. She couldn't remember a time when she had milked the cows when her father hadn't been there. Alejandro seemed to shift into a different mode, quietly helping to milk the cows, muck the aisle, and drop the hay from the hayloft. She appreciated the fact that he didn't speak to her, permitting her that time to think and work through the jumble of emotions that she was struggling with.

The routine of milking the cows and carrying the buckets of fresh white milk to the refrigeration system in the back room helped her refocus her thoughts. The events of the past few years played like a movie in her mind, snippets of her life that led up to this moment. And it all came down to one decision on her part: a decision that had changed everyone's life.

Aaron.

She had turned her back for one minute, and in that instant, everyone's life had changed. One decision, one momentary lapse, and the future had been altered.

She knew what she had to do, the only way that she could make up for what had happened.

She had to stay.

"Alejandro," she said, her voice flat and emotionless.

He glanced up and noticed the distant look on her face. *"¿Qué es,* Princesa*?"*

She turned to look at him, but her eyes saw through him. Beyond him. She was looking into the new future, seeing the only way she could make this right. The past three years flashed before her eyes. She saw her parents and her *bruder*. She saw her father's pride when he watched Aaron playing in the stream. She saw Aaron's excitement from attending the horse auction with Daed. She saw Anna's smiling face when Menno Zook had brought her home and her confiding about the celery in the garden.

One moment had changed all of that: the moment she had turned her back on Aaron. Now, only one decision could change the dark future she knew loomed ahead. Unfortunately, she knew that decision demanded she not turn her back on her family again.

"I can't go back with you," she said, the words hurting her throat as they escaped her lips.

It took him a moment to digest her words, and when he did, she could tell from his frown that he didn't care for them. "What do you mean?"

Shaking her head as if brushing away her vision, she blinked and finally saw him. "I can't go back with you. Not until my *daed* is better. If I go back with you, Anna will have to come home from Ohio. If she comes home, she might never get another chance at getting married." She walked toward him, a new energy in her step.

"Amanda," he said, narrowing his eyes. "You think I'm going to leave you here?"

But Amanda ignored the beginning of his arguments and continued, her voice pleading with him for understanding. "You don't understand, Alejandro." She lifted her hand to her head, staring for a moment at the ground. Painful memories came back to her, and she squeezed her eyes shut, hoping that they would go away. "Everyone was so distant and sad after Aaron's death. The loss was more than anyone should ever have to be burdened with."

"You can't stay here alone!"

Amanda opened her eyes and lifted them to look at him. She had to make him understand. "It took so long for my parents to heal. They were destroyed. They could barely function. It was Anna and me who held it together. She and I worked so hard trying to keep this place together." Amanda grabbed at his arm, holding it tightly. "Don't you see? She missed out on one opportunity. Menno Zook didn't wait. She almost lost her sanity over it. I won't have her miss out on another chance. She deserves some happiness in her life. If Jonas Wheeler wants to marry her, she needs that same time that God gave me to find you, Alejandro." She paused and chewed on her lower lip. "I know how this works for the Amish. If she comes home to take care of my *daed* and the farm, she won't go back to Ohio."

"You have to return with me," he said, tilting his head, assessing her as he spoke. "I need you."

She lifted her chin. "They need me more!"

"You are my wife," he reminded her.

"I am their daughter," she shot back.

The sharpness of her tone startled him. Yet, he knew better than to argue. He could tell by the determined look on her face. "*Ay*, Amanda, what am I to do with you?"

Her chest lifted as she took a deep breath. "I have to do this. You have to let me."

He shut his eyes and lifted his hand to his forehead, rubbing it for a minute. She heard him mumbling in Spanish, but she couldn't make out or understand the words. "Don't you see that I can't stay with you?" he finally said.

But he hadn't needed to say it. They both knew it was true. He had concerts and interviews, the New Year's Eve celebration at Times Square. People were counting on him. To cancel any of those engagements would be career suicide. Neither spoke as they stared at each other, trying to figure out the next step.

"I understand that, Alejandro," she whispered. "I have to do this, even if I have to do it alone."

He ran his hand through his hair, tugging at it in frustration. "*¡Ay, Dios, Amanda!* How long?"

"Until the farm is sold and my *daed* is better."

Alejandro shook his head. "You heard the doctor. He will be confined to a wheelchair for quite a while, Amanda. It could be months before he is well enough that your *mamm* can handle caring for him."

"She can't do it alone."

"Neither can you." He raised an eyebrow, calmly staring at her, despite the twitching of the muscle in his jaw. He was clenching his teeth, fighting his own emotions.

Silence.

Finally, he shook his head, but she could see that his resolve was breaking down. "Forget the concerts. I'll stay with you," he offered.

But Amanda simply smiled, a soft and understanding smile, as she shook her head. "*Nee,* Alejandro. You know that you can't do that. It will go quickly. You'll be busy; you need to work. I need to help here, to be here for my parents."

"The paparazzi will come back. You know that."

She shrugged. "I have nothing to fear from them anymore. You taught me, *ja?*"

"*¡Ay,* Princesa*!*" he said, frustrated and angry, reaching out to grab her arms and stare down at her. She hated seeing the pained look in his eyes, but it mirrored the pain in her heart. He took a deep breath and whispered, "Love over fame. I promised you that! I won't go back on my word, Amanda."

"You aren't. Besides, I want you to go," she replied, not unkindly. "Maybe I'm choosing love over fame, too."

Instantly, he glared at her as if her words stung him. "Whose love? The love of your family over me?"

She smiled and shook her head. "*Nee,* Alejandro. I'm choosing love. Just love. Shouldn't my sister be entitled to the same love that we have?" She leaned her head against his shoulder, wrapping her arms around him. After a long moment, she felt him pull her tight and return the embrace.

Elias stood behind Amanda as she helped with the evening milking. He seemed nervous, shuffling his feet as he cleared his throat, searching for words. Obviously, something was on his mind.

"Your mamm *and I," he began. Amanda stopped milking the cow and turned around to look at her father. He didn't meet her eyes but stared at the ground. "We think it's best if you and Anna go visiting Ohio for a spell. We have some relatives there. You both need to get away from this farm," he said.*

What her father was saying didn't make sense. "You are sending us away?"

Her father nodded. "Just for a short while. A month. Maybe longer. Just to get past . . ." He let the sentence trail off, and she knew what he couldn't say. Anna wasn't well. Ever since her intended, Menno Zook, married another young Amish woman, Anna had grown increasingly withdrawn and sad. They didn't want her home for the third anniversary of Aaron's death. She needed a change, to escape the memory of what had happened and how she had lost her beau. Amanda would accompany her sister, giving Elias and Lizzie time to plan for the future, a future that looked very different now without a son to take care of them or the farm.

"I don't want to go to Ohio," she said defiantly.

"But you will."

"I just turned twenty, Daed," she argued. "I'm an adult."

Her father leveled his gaze at her. "You live in my house. You live by my rules. You will take your sister to Ohio, Amanda. No further discussion." With that, he turned and walked away, not caring that the unspoken message that she picked up was that her parents wanted both daughters away, one to get better and the other to get out of their sight.

Amanda stood on the porch, watching as the car pulled out of the driveway. She felt a sob rise into her throat, but she forced herself to lift a hand and wave as the car turned to the left and drove up the hill. As the car disappeared, she covered her mouth with her hand, feeling the coolness of her wedding ring on her face. The tears began to fall as she turned to go into the *grossdaadihaus* and prepare for what would certainly be a tough couple of weeks. Perhaps even months.

He hadn't wanted to leave her. She had been persistent.

She hadn't wanted any extra help on the farm. He had been adamant.

After two days, he had no choice but to return to his life, only this time it was without his wife. He had fought his own emotion when the time came for him to leave. His reluctance to leave her alone to deal with the situation was countered only by the increasingly gaping hole that she felt in her heart when thinking of being apart from him.

She realized that she had done more than simply change over the past few months. She had grown into a friend, a woman, and a wife. Without Alejandro by her side, she wasn't certain how she would survive. Their last night together had been sorrowful. Amanda had clung to him, crying, for she didn't know when she might see him again. Certainly weeks; hopefully not longer. Even Alejandro had fought back tears, refusing to break down in front of her.

She heard the familiar ping on her cell phone. He had insisted that she keep the cell phone and had arranged for the utility company to come by later that week to hook up a line from the road to the house. Despite her protests, he had insisted.

"I will not be without a way to communicate with you, Amanda," he had told her firmly. "You need electricity to charge your phone. Your parents can ask to have it removed when you leave if it's so distasteful to them."

She picked up the phone and, through her tears, laughed when she saw the message from Alejandro.

I love you for what you are doing.
And I understand.
But I don't want to do this.
You are my heart and soul.
I'll be back for you as soon as I can.
Just remember . . .
I love you.
V

She caught another sob in her throat, trying to stop the flow of tears down her cheeks. Her heart hurt inside her chest, beating so hard that she felt weak. She reread his words, hearing his voice, his accent, in her mind. That made it even harder to know that she was left behind once again. Holding the cell phone to her chest, she lifted her eyes up to the ceiling, blinking rapidly in hopes that she might stop crying.

Then, as the sun began to set outside the window, she wiped at her eyes and looked back at the phone. She chewed on her lower lip for a minute before she finally tapped at the little keyboard:

<3
A

Setting down the phone on the counter, she took a deep breath and lit one of the kerosene lanterns that hung over the sink. Pausing for a moment, she listened to it hiss as light filled the room. She needed to go out to the dairy barn to finish the evening chores. In the morning, she was headed back to the hospital to check on her father's progress. She hoped that there were some more improvements in his condition and that he might be able to return to the farm soon. The first step to recovery, she thought.

Heading out the door, she reached for her mother's black shawl that was hanging from a peg. Wrapping it around her shoulders, she pushed at the screen door, finding a way to focus on what she had to do. One day at a time, she told herself. One day at a time . . .

Glossary

Pennsylvania Dutch

ach vell	an expression similar to *oh well*
Ausbund	Amish hymnal
bruder	brother
Daed, or her *daed*	Father, or her father
danke	thank you
dochder	daughter
Englische	non-Amish people
Englischer	a non-Amish person
ferhoodled	confused
g'may	church district
grossdaadihaus	small house attached to the main dwelling
gut	good
gut (guder) mariye	good morning
ja	yes
kapp	cap
kinner	children
Mamm, or her *mamm*	Mother, or her mother
nee, nein	no
Ordnung	unwritten rules of the *g'may*
rumschpringe	period of "fun" time for youths
wunderbar	wonderful
vell	well

Spanish

amigo	friend (m.)
ay, mi madre	an expression; literally *oh, my mother*
basta, papito	enough, little daddy
bienvenido	welcome
bueno	good
buenos días	a greeting; good day
cubano	Cuban
Dios *mío*	my God
dulce	sweet
escúchame	listen to me
gracias	thank you
linda	pretty
listo	ready
lo siento	I'm sorry
mamacita	little mama
mi amor	my love
mi gente	my people
nada	nothing
oye	hey
permiso	permission
por favor	please
por qué	why
qué	what
qué es eso	what is this
qué pasa	what's up
qué rica	how rich
Princesa	nickname; princess
sí	yes
tranquilo	be calm
vamos or *vámanos*	let's go

Plain Again

Book Three of the Plain Fame Series

Sarah Price

Chapter One

```
Thinking of you and missing you.
Daed doing better.
Enjoy your day and call later if you
can.
<3
A
```

The knock at the door surprised Amanda. She wasn't expecting anyone, especially since Mamm had left for the hospital already and the rest of the community had been avoiding the Beiler farm; now that the paparazzi had discovered that Viper's wife had returned to her plain roots, it had taken only three days for word to spread. And then, the privacy and peace that she had anticipated on her parents' farm quickly disappeared as the media descended again upon their farm in Lititz, Pennsylvania.

Amanda had no idea of how it had happened. Who could have possibly known? How had they learned about her *daed*'s condition?

How had they known that Amanda was there while Viper was on tour? But, by now, she knew that it was exactly what the media did for a living: discover things that others wished were kept secret. And the successful ones were quite good at it. They could ferret out information from even the most secretive members of Alejandro's entourage. Or, more likely, from the peripheral people who were involved in his life.

For the first few days after Alejandro had left her at the farm, Amanda had spent time with her *mamm* at Daed's bedside at the hospital. It was an unfamiliar and sterile environment with strange noises and smells. The nurses and doctors had seemed pleasant enough to Amanda and her *mamm*, but she knew that more than one person who worked at the hospital had done a double take when they realized who she was.

A few were brazen enough to outright question her. "Are you . . . ?" However, they never seemed to finish the question when they asked it.

As Alejandro had trained her, she merely smiled and greeted people who stared while remaining distant and reserved. After all, her entire attention was focused on Daed, making certain that he was properly tended to during his hospital stay.

On the second day, he had begun to awaken. He had blinked his eyes several times, trying to place where he was and what had happened. And then, his eyes found Amanda, sitting in the chair by the bedside. His eyes had sparkled, and he tried to greet her. But he wasn't able to speak, at least not very coherently yet. He had moments of clarity and a speech therapist was working with him every day. The doctors had seemed hopeful that he had not suffered brain damage and would fully recover. From his reactions, eye movements, and hand gestures, it appeared that the doctors were correct.

It was just a few days later when someone must have recognized her while visiting another patient at the hospital. A stolen photo posted on social media began the firestorm. And before Amanda knew it, she was greeted at the hospital with crowds of photographers, waiting for her arrival. For some reason, it had taken her by surprise that the paparazzi were there, eager for stolen photos of her and her *mamm*. But she wasn't taken by surprise when they returned to the farm and began to camp outside of the driveway, eager for more photos of Amanda when she would return in the evening. With telephoto lenses, Amanda knew all too well that anytime she stepped outside of the house, her picture was being snapped and sent over the airwaves to the media for distribution to the public.

This time, however, Amanda knew better. She knew how to handle the paparazzi. Alejandro had taught her well. During the day, she continued to go about her chores as usual. With the police once again positioned at the end of the driveway in order to hinder the photographers from trespassing, she had some degree of isolation. Yet she knew that, in the predawn hours, the photographers snapped her picture as she walked from the house to the barn, her head down and covered with a simple black knit handkerchief since the weather was turning cold. She was able to shut the barn doors before turning to the task at hand: the morning milking. When she turned out the cows, she knew that they were stealing her photograph from the road with their long telescopic lenses. This time, she didn't care. Her image would be sold to websites and gossip newspapers. There was nothing she could do about it, and truth be told, she really had no choice as she was determined to help her family.

"How can you get used to that?" her *mamm* had asked earlier, a look of disgust on her face, as she waited for the driver to pick her up for the twenty-minute drive to the hospital.

Amanda hadn't known how to explain it to her mother. Living it was the only way to understand it. So, rather than try, Amanda gave a weak smile and simply shrugged her shoulders. "Guess you just do, after a while."

"Is that what it was really like?" her *mamm* had asked, a curious look on her face. "Traveling with him?"

For a moment, Amanda had shut her eyes and a whirlwind of memories flashed through her mind: Philadelphia, Los Angeles, Las Vegas, Miami. After she had opened her eyes, she simply looked at her mother and smiled. "There were moments like that, I reckon," she replied. "But, for the most part, there's a lot of isolation from it. It becomes . . . white noise, I suppose."

Her mother had frowned, not familiar with that term. "White noise?"

"Background noise. Like the sound of a buggy driving down the hill. After a while, you just stop noticing it unless you are looking for it."

Now, however, there was someone knocking at the door. That was a noise that Amanda noticed, all right. No one came to visit the Beiler farm, not with the nosy photographers stationed outside of the farm, waiting for the million-dollar snapshot of Amanda Diaz, the Amish-born wife of Viper, the international sensation and superstar.

Cautiously, she peeked through the glass, surprised to see a man standing there. From the way he was dressed, she could tell he was a local man and most likely a farmer. While he certainly wasn't Amish, she thought he might be a Mennonite. Cracking the door open, she kept her foot at the bottom of the door and glanced over to make certain the police were still there. One of them was watching for her and waved his hand. Clearly, they had vetted the visitor.

"Yes?" she asked timidly.

"Mrs. Diaz?" the man responded, plucking his hat from his head and holding it in his hands. He was nervous and shuffled on his feet, avoiding direct eye contact.

It felt strange to have someone call her Mrs. Diaz. Among the Amish, such formalities were never used. While on the road with Alejandro, she had been known as Viper's wife or simply Amanda. No one ever referenced either of them by using his last name. In fact, most people always called him by his stage name. She often doubted that the greater part of his fans even knew his Christian name.

"Ja?" She made certain that her foot was positioned behind the door, just as a precaution.

The man glanced over his shoulder toward the barn as he said, "Your husband hired me to help with the farmwork."

"My husband hired you?"

The man nodded and glanced toward the barn. "With your father being in the hospital, he asked me to step in with the barn chores so you can tend to your *daed*."

Amanda frowned. *Daed?* That was a word used by the Amish. Yet, clearly, this man was not Amish. "What's your name?"

"Harvey," he responded. "Harvey Alderfer."

Alderfer? The last name was definitely Mennonite. Yet she wondered why Alejandro hadn't told her about hiring him. That worried her. Still, if the police had let him through, certainly it was safe enough to let him muck the dairy barn while she tried to sort this out with Alejandro. It would be just like him to do something so thoughtful, she realized with a warmth building inside her chest. Only Alejandro would think to hire help for the manual labor around the farm.

"Ja vell," she said, gesturing toward the large building that housed the cows. "You could get started with the mucking, I reckon, while I contact my husband to find out about what, exactly, he has arranged."

The man seemed satisfied by her answer and tipped his hat in her direction as he backed away from the door. She watched as the willowy stranger hurried down the porch stairs and wandered over toward the barn, his shoulders slightly hunched over and his hands in his pockets. Despite having lived in the area her entire life, she did not recognize the man, but she sure recognized his disposition: Mennonite.

Amanda made certain to lock the door after she shut it, and then, chewing on her lower lip, she hurried over to the place where she kept her cell phone. It was nearly eleven in the morning. She knew that Alejandro had a performance scheduled for last night and had to make an appearance at an after-party, but certainly by now he would be awake, she thought. Hesitantly, she pressed the button to dial his number. She disliked using the phone and, even more so, did not want to disturb him. She never knew whom he might be meeting with or what he was doing. But she certainly needed to find out about this man, this Harvey Alderfer, who had just shown up on her doorstep.

He answered on the third ring, his voice cheerful as he greeted her. "Princesa! You must have been reading my mind!"

"I was?" She said lightly, smiling as she clutched the phone to her ear and turned to look out the window. Her eyes scanned the empty fields, but her heart raced. "And what exactly was on your mind, Alejandro?"

She heard him move; a shuffling sound that was muffled. With a low voice, he replied, "You, *mi amor*. Always you. And if you knew about what, you'd blush."

She couldn't help herself and caught herself laughing. "I think I am blushing, even without knowing."

"I only have a few minutes, Princesa. I am headed to a lunch reception," he said, his voice thick with regret. "But I trust you are calling because the hired man showed up, *sí*?"

"Sí," she said back, her eyes sparkling just from the sound of his voice.

He laughed as he always did when she tried to speak Spanish to him. "I simply can't have my wife doing all of that farmwork now, can I?"

"I have done it for many years," she pointed out, still smiling to herself.

It had been almost a week, and she missed Alejandro more than anything in her life. Yet she knew that sacrifices had to be made. Life was greater than just her. And, at this time, her parents needed her at the farm. To not be there would risk her sister's upcoming marriage to her beau in Ohio. If Amanda had been selfish and continued traveling with Alejandro, Anna would have felt compelled to return home and help rather than marry her young gentleman friend from Ohio. Having already lost one prospect, Anna certainly could not risk losing another. At least, that was Amanda's perception of the situation and the main reason she had stayed behind on the family farm while Alejandro toured on the East Coast.

"Ah," he breathed, his voice deep and full of emotion. "But now you *are* my wife," he said solemnly. "And, despite the distance, I must continue to take care of you, *sí*?"

"Sí," she whispered back, feeling a growing sense of loss. She had not realized how much she had grown to depend on Alejandro, on his love and support. Now that he was gone, she knew that she had become far more attached to him than she had even imagined. Loving him was just one part of the equation: counting on him was another. "*Sí*, you will always take care of me, Alejandro."

She heard him catch his breath at her words and he swallowed, fighting his own emotion that continued to swell in his chest. "And your father, Amanda. How is he? Has he returned home from the hospital?"

"Next week," she said softly into the phone. "He'll be home next week." That's what the doctor had told her *mamm* just the day before. It was news that Mamm had been most excited to share with her *dochder* when she had returned home from the hospital last evening. Yet Amanda knew that coming home was a long way from being back to normal. She wasn't certain how things would work themselves out. It all depended on his recovery.

"We must talk, Princesa," Alejandro said, a sense of foreboding in his voice. "What to do with the farm in order to help your parents."

A sigh escaped her lips. She didn't need to hear the words to know exactly what Alejandro had meant. Her father certainly could no longer handle the farm, not alone. Without a son to take over, there was no one to inherit it. Not now anyway, with Amanda married to an Englische international superstar and her sister, Anna, getting married to a farmer in Ohio. Clearly, her parents' farm would have to be sold and her parents settled into a smaller home, one that her *daed* could handle. But that was definitely not something he nor his family were looking forward to, having lived on their farm for the greater part of their lives.

"Ja," she admitted. "I know. Decisions I don't want to make today, that's for sure and certain."

"Now, Princesa," he said, a noise in the background distracting him for just a second. She could hear voices and laughter. "I must say good-bye for now. I am needed to greet some people for this luncheon." She sensed the dread in his voice. She knew how taxing these events were on his energy level. Yet he had taught her how necessary they were for maintaining his image and fan base. "I shall contact you later, *sí*?"

"Sí," she said softly, wishing more than anything that she could be beside him. He had affirmed to her more than a dozen times how much her presence had soothed him, giving him the energy and motivation to face the crowds with a smiling face. She could sense that now this energy was forced as he faced endless streams of fans and reporters and sponsors, all of whom had no idea about the true essence of the man they knew as "Viper."

***

Outside, at the barn's entrance, she stood in the shadow of the doorway, her eyes adjusting to the darkness for just a brief moment. The pungent smell of the cows mixed with hay and manure accosted her nose. For some, it could have been a distasteful odor. But for Amanda, it was comforting, a smell that reminded her of her youth on the farm.

Growing up Amish had taught her a great deal about life and faith and family. Even though she loved her husband and wanted nothing more than to be beside him as he traveled the world and entertained his fans, she was secretly glad to be home with her parents, even for just a short while. Oh, she missed Alejandro . . . his teasing, his laughter, his attentiveness. But breathing in the strong scent of the barn made her realize that, indeed, there was no place like home.

As she walked down the hallway toward the dairy aisle, she could hear the scraping of a shovel against the concrete: the hired man was mucking the dairy. She made her way toward the noise, careful to step over loose manure. Her old black sneakers felt comfortable on her feet, but she realized that she was too aware of how clunky and unattractive they were. Pride and vanity, she thought and quickly chastised herself. Yet she was torn. Her new life with Alejandro conflicted so sharply with her old lifestyle on the farm. How had she changed so much in such a short period of time?

"Harvey?" she called out when she approached the tall man in order to avoid startling him. "How are you making out, then?"

Leaning against the shovel, he looked at her. "Just fine," he replied. "Been working farms for years. Nothing different here."

His tone was dry, his expression emotionless. The weathered look on his face told the story of years of laboring in the sun, toiling the soil and battling the elements. Amanda had seen that look before, among many of the Amish in her community. It dawned on her how much older the Amish, and in this case, the Mennonite farmers looked, both men and women. Unlike Alejandro's world where the youthful appearance of the face meant more than anything else, the Amish focused more on living well off the land rather than looking well in the world.

"You live nearby, *ja*?"

He nodded his head. "Just north of Ephrata," he said.

"Well, that's not too far, I reckon!" she replied. "How did my husband find you, if I may ask?"

"Not certain of that," Harvey admitted. He paused and glanced around at the barn. "Lots of work to do, Mrs. Diaz," he said. The use of her last name startled her. Most Amish and Mennonites did not call each other by their surnames. That was definitely an Englische method of addressing others. There was something different about this Harvey. As a Mennonite farmer, she wondered why he had called her by her last name.

"It's just Amanda," she said. "I'll make certain to have some coffee for you, then." With a slight smile, she turned and walked out of the dairy, pulling her black shawl tighter as she exited the barn and braved the cold to return to the house.

Inside, she looked around. Everything felt and looked smaller to her. And darker too, she realized, giving it some thought. It no longer felt like home, yet everything about it bespoke of her upbringing: the sofa in the kitchen where she had crocheted many a blanket, the kitchen counter where her *mamm* had taught her how to make bread and cheese, the table where they had enjoyed many a dinner and supper with her sister and younger brother. It had been a lively, happy kitchen until her brother had died. Then, the house had been shrouded in a cloak of sorrow and darkness. Until, she realized, Alejandro had arrived.

With a sigh, she fought the longing in her heart. She couldn't deny how much she missed Alejandro: his soft words, his attentiveness, his teasing, his love. Yet she knew that it was a big relief to both of her parents that she was there, helping to take care of the farm while her *mamm* took care of her *daed*. Just the other day, she had received a letter from Anna, a short note expressing her gratitude for Amanda's returning to the farm while she prepared for her wedding in just another week. She had promised that she would return home with her new husband as soon as they were married.

Married, Amanda thought. She would feel such relief when her sister was finally married to her beau, Jonas Wheeler. If the newly married couple traveled back to Pennsylvania, it would present the perfect opportunity for Amanda to rejoin Alejandro, at least until Anna and Jonas would return to Ohio.

And then what? That was the question that she kept asking herself.

Over and over again, she had made a mental list of options for her parents. Moving them to Pinecraft in Florida, a wonderful community of Amish where the weather was nice all year long; this was definitely one suggestion that she wanted to offer to her parents. The other was selling the farm and moving them to a smaller, more contemporary house on the outskirts of the church district. Many older Amish couples did that when they had no children to take over the farm. And young Amish couples were always in need of farms, so there would be no shortage of offers on their property.

Of course, there was always that last option, that spark of hope that was buried deep within her heart that, perhaps, she might be able to stay on the farm, stay with Alejandro. He had been so happy on the farm during the summer, and he knew how to manage the dairy. It wouldn't take much for him to be able to handle the farm chores, especially if he could afford hired help. Yet she knew that she couldn't ask him that. His leaving the Englische world had never been part of their arrangement. It would be most unfair to extend such a request. He had a life, a career—one that he loved—at least while she was by his side. No, she realized, her staying on the farm was not an option, indeed.

Amanda took a deep breath and buried her face into her hands, fighting the tears that threatened to spill from her eyes. If only Aaron had not died, she thought, but then realized that, had her brother lived, she never would have gone to Ohio last summer, and subsequently, she never would have met Alejandro. The thin thread of life that had spun itself from that one single event had changed everything, making her realize the interconnected nature of each moment in every individual's time spent living in this world.

That was the moment when the tears fell.

About the Author

The Preiss family emigrated from Europe in 1705, settling in Pennsylvania as part of the area's first wave of Mennonite families. Sarah Price has always respected and honored her ancestors through exploration and research about her family's Anabaptist history and their religion. For over twenty-five years, she has been actively involved in an Amish community in Pennsylvania. The author of over thirty novels, Sarah is finally doing what she always wanted to do: write about the religion and culture that she loves so dearly. For more information, visit her blog at www.sarahpriceauthor.com.